Kathleen,

Thank you for your support!
I wish you & your family all the
best!

Davidson L Price

**WHIPPOORWILL HOLLOW**

D1120398

# WHIPPOORWILL HOLLOW

## BY DAVIDSON LEE PRICE

*Whippoorwill Hollow*
© 2021 Davidson Lee Price

Published by J.D. Grayford Publishing

ISBN: 978-1-7368836-1-7

Cover design by Kapo Ng  |  Interior design by Liz Schrieter
Editing and book production by Reading List Editorial: readinglisteditorial.com

J.D.
Grayford
Publishing

*For David Wayne Price*

*Open wounds that never bled*
*and dry eyes where tears were once shed*
*as silent voices echo in my head*
*My stubborn memory will never forget*
*the end of day as my sun set*
*introducing the night when we met*
*The warm hearts that beat by my side*
*all turned cold the moment you arrived*
*as those you spared reluctantly survived*
*The fires with no flames as they burn*
*torture those of us awaiting our turn*
*for you to collect on the bounty you earn*
*You who I once feared I now admire*
*and your merciful reprieve is what I desire*
*to save me from damnation in my internal fire*

—*Merciful Death*
by Walter Lee

# PROLOGUE

The fading world pleases his eyes and soothes his mind. The fields and fences stand still as they pass by his view. The sun sinks slowly behind the rolling green hillside, while hay bales rest peacefully in the fields as their growing shadows merge into the oncoming night. The view is the only decent thing in his life, although he asks for nothing more. All he desires in these last few precious minutes of daylight is that peaceful world outside of his window. He ignores the words traded between the two men sitting in the front seat. The smoke exhaled from the men irritates his eyes and nose but fails to interrupt his focus on that window. On the contrary, the smoke deepens his focus and further calms his mind. He has grown accustomed to the smoke over the many rides he's taken with the man driving, but it usually fills the car during their return home, as darkness gives way to morning light and his wounds begin healing from the vicious fights of the night. He has no wounds this time, at least none that are fresh, only the lingering pain in his leg.

The man driving is the only family he has known since his earliest memories. Many others like the passenger have come and gone, but he is the only one the man has kept around through all the years. He seems to make the man happy, especially on these trips. Other men, friends of his family, have accompanied them on some of these trips, but never the stranger who accompanies them this evening. The stranger seems friendly to the driver, and the driver seems to trust the stranger. The passenger's trust in the stranger should mirror that of the driver, his family, but his cautious instincts sense the reflection of something sinister. The world outside his window has distracted him, but now that the sun has set over those hills, his full attention is on the stranger. The passenger sees the stranger clearly in the dark.

The fields, fences, and hay bales gave way to the trees just before night consumed the day. The dark trees stand tall along both sides of the dusty road as the car creeps slowly forward into the night. Unsettling glances from the stranger worry the passenger's once-calm mind. He looks to the driver for comfort, but the man never turns his head; he never even peeks into the rearview mirror as he normally does during these trips. His lone trusted friend pays him no mind at all. With his attention on the dark world beyond the lights, the driver turns the car around before parking on the side of the road. The engine continues to hum as the headlights go black, leaving the world outside the window in complete darkness other than the waxing moon in the sky; however, something much darker resides inside the car.

The stranger exhales one last breath of smoke before he exits the car. He opens the back door and pulls the big fella out by his restraints. Though wary of the stranger, and sensing an eerily familiar presence, the passenger puts up no fight and follows the man to the tree line. The stranger attempts to divert the big fella's attention away from him by throwing a stick, but he refuses to break his focus on the untrusted man.

He sees clearly now. Death is a cunning executioner who uses the distractions of life when coming for the living; however, nothing can distract the attention of someone who has lived most of his days in the company of death. He has witnessed death on many occasions. He himself has delivered death's cold message in brutal fashion when calling upon the beast. The familiar, empty reflection in the eyes of the stranger should alert the beast the passenger has called upon for every other threat he's faced in life. The beast always roars from within, charging the threat with his deadly arsenal and killer instinct, but not this time. Instead, the big fella woefully stares back at the driver's side window of the car. Through the driver's side window, his only family and best friend sits with his attention on the darkness before him. The window during the ride offered nothing more than a delightful illusion of this world; this window discloses the bitter reality.

Death is a cunning executioner who's found the perfect distraction. The stranger slowly swings his hand from around his back, but the big fella never looks away from his only trusted friend. He never calls upon the beast. Family betrayal is just too much for him to bear. The bright flash and explosion from death's device interrupt the darkness and silence of the night. Trauma and adrenaline supply the dog with more strength than the stranger can hold. The big red-nosed dog seizes the moment of freedom and leaps into the dark forest. Surprised and desperate, the stranger fires three more rounds into the night. Bullets chase the echoes of cracking twigs and crunching dead leaves, but none find their target.

The stranger listens and scans the darkness before him, but the army of trees stand strong in their formation as they provide cover and safety for the dog. The stranger takes a cautious step toward the dark forest, but stops short of breaching the tree line. He, too, senses a familiar presence lurking in the night. His eyes remain focused on the darkness surrounding the pines and hardwoods as he slowly backs away toward the car. Twigs crack and dead leaves crunch once again, but now they offer a grave warning to the hunter instead of revealing the location of the hunted. The stranger turns away from the trees and sprints to the car. He slides into the passenger seat, quickly shutting the door behind him. He trades a few angry words with the driver for a brief moment before the lights once again shine on the road. Gravel flies and dust fills the air as the red lights race away into the night, flickering on and off between the dark pines along the old road.

The dog cautiously approaches the roadside where the car was once parked. The bullet finally awoke the beast, and he was on the hunt for the stranger, but the beast was too late. He shakes the pouring blood from his head. The pain from his wound has yet to arrive; however, when the beast is gone, the pain is sure to come without mercy, as always. The dog slowly wanders into the family of trees that protected him earlier.

He follows an old deer path until the beast retreats into the shadows and his legs can no longer sustain his weight. He now feels the full painful force of his wound. The blood still oozes but has slowed from the hours after his family's betrayal. He staggers into a thicket just off the path, collapsing into the underbrush. His body fights off death as he sleeps through most of the night. The morning light gives him hope for life, but he has no destination, only this old trail. He stumbles and staggers along this path to nowhere until the sun once again gives way to the night. He is afraid, lost, and alone. He is hungry, but lacks the energy to chase prey. He is thirsty, but cannot find fresh water. The pain is insufferable. Still, he refuses to concede victory to death. He finds solace in the song from the dark brush. He stops every few yards to look up through the pain at the silhouettes in the quarter moon's distant glow, looking for the source of that soothing song. The bird pauses long enough for the dog to hear something different, something he desires more than song, the bubbling noise of a slow-flowing creek. Ahead in the dark, he can finally quench his relentless thirst, leaving only pain and hunger. Maybe the bird will again sing for him, soothing both.

## — CHAPTER ONE —
# SANDBAR

**E**very spring, about the time the dogwoods bloom, the Oconee River is chock-full of white bass as they make their spawning run. Years ago, before overfishing thinned them out a good bit, the white bass ran thick. They were quite a bit larger back then, some as big around as a supper plate; at least, that is how they looked to a young boy like Hudson. Every year as winter eased its cold grip on northern Georgia, Hudson Lee would anxiously await the white blooms of the dogwood trees. He'd stare out the window of the school bus every day, scanning the bare-naked trees for those little white flowers. He would ignore the chaos around him as he sat silently thinking about fishing on the Oconee.

Just before the end of the twentieth century, Grayford "Gray" Lee picks up his son from school. Hudson is ten years old and figures his father needs help on the farm, at least that is usually the reason he picks him up from school. Hudson thinks nothing further of it until they are down the highway a bit. That's when he sees them—the naked dogwoods of the morning wear white blooms by the afternoon. Hudson immediately looks at his father, who just smiles and says, "We'll hit 'em up Saturday. We'll brang Troy with us."

Saturday arrives with a blanket of gray clouds across the early-morning sky as the flat-bottomed boat skims up the river. Hudson sits up front looking out for debris in the water while Gray sits in the rear driving, also keeping an eye out for floating logs and other river trash. Cousin Troy Crenshaw, a year older than Hudson, sits in the middle enjoying a sausage biscuit while watching the water rip by the boat. Hudson stares off at the trees living along the red banks of the Oconee as they race to their favorite honey hole. The scenery pleases his eyes while the water splashing off the bow hypnotizes his mind. The turtles rest on top of fallen trees, patiently waiting for the sun to break through the clouds; meanwhile, snakes wiggle across the slow-flowing river as they come out of brumation. The trees along the bank sway ever so slightly even though there seems to be no breeze. The river is inviting and welcomes Gray and the boys for their first fishing trip of the year.

They pass by Sonny Perkins's campground, letting the boys know they are halfway to the sandbar. As the cool air blows by Hudson's cheeks, he drifts off into deep thoughts of the fishing adventures that await them up the river. He takes his eyes off the water's surface, looks back, and embraces the moment with Troy. As Hudson enjoys the moment with his cousin, he nearly misses the tree on a collision course with the boat. The clay of northern Georgia turns the river water brown, making it difficult to see floating debris, especially for Gray, who sits in the rear of the boat with his hand gripping the throttle. Troy points forward, causing Hudson to turn his head just in time to see it. Hudson quickly holds up a fist to let his father know to slow down, and then frantically waves his hand toward the left for his dad to veer in that direction. Gray reacts quickly, barely missing the tree, but is none too pleased. He keeps the boat slowly creeping forward while he takes a second to discuss the near miss with Hudson.

"Dammit, boy! Do I need to stick Troy up front?" Gray yells.

"No sir, I got it!" Hudson lowers his voice as he turns back toward the front. "We missed the dayum thang, didn't we?!"

"What's that, boy? I didn't catch what ya said there."

"He said we missed the dayum thang, Uncle Gray."

"Dammit, Troy!" Hudson scolds Troy for telling on him.

"Hey, boy, watch your dayum mouth!" Gray says as he points at Hudson. "Now turn around and watch for logs. That storm the utha day probly knocked all kinda shit loose, and I ain't got the money to fix'is mowtuh if we hit someth'n. And if we hit someth'n that knocks out my dayum mowtuh, you will paddle our asses back to the ramp. Ya got me, son?"

"Yes, sir!" Hudson replies, lowering his voice and head with it as he turns back forward.

Gray is fully aware of Hudson's passion for fishing and hates scolding his son, but the boy has to learn the importance of his responsibilities. He also knows Hudson's feelings will be just fine once they put a hook in the water. He throttles up again while Hudson keeps his focus on the river ahead; however, the promise of big white bass remains on his mind. Meanwhile, Troy makes sure all the rods and bait are ready to go, which is always the job of the guy in the middle, and he sure doesn't want Uncle Gray chewing his ass out also on this fine morning.

After a long, winding transit of dodging logs, limbs, and other river trash, they finally reach the sandbar. Gray cuts the motor, so they don't spook the fish, as they cruise into their usual mooring spot. Hudson quickly ties off the boat to a nearby tree. By the time he turns his attention back to the boat, Troy is already handing him his rod and reel.

"Let's go, cuz! They're pop'n the top!"

Sure enough, white bass are racing to the top of the water as they feed on small minnows. They knew this would be a good day to fish this spot, but they've underestimated just how good. Baited with curly tail grubs, the boys cast almost simultaneously. Immediately, Hudson's rod slams down, and his drag screams as a fish darts to the other side of the river.

"I got one! He's a biggin."

"Fish on!" Troy yells as his drag screams just as loudly.

Gray hasn't even pulled his gear out of the boat when the boys hook up with a couple of bass. He watches as the boys fight their fish, their eyes wide open with excitement and unbreakable concentration. Gray knows the boys will need help landing the mighty bass at the end of their lines, so he rolls up his pant legs, grabs the net, and walks out into the water in front of them. Troy manages to get his fish to the net first.

"How much you thank it weighs, Uncle Gray?"

"I dunno . . . Probly, one'nuh half . . . two pounds, I'd reckon."

"That's good eatin' right there!"

Hudson still fights on. The fish on the other side of his line is a good bit bigger. His drag begs for mercy. The six-pound test-line rating is truly tested. Gray and Troy watch on, both offering their advice— none of which Hudson has asked for nor listens to. Hudson is focused on his line, making sure he keeps out all slack. He lets his drag setting be, ignoring Troy's advice to tighten it and his father's advice to loosen it. Hudson walks out into the water next to his father, who anxiously holds the net, awaiting the massive fish that his son has hooked.

"I see it, Deddy!" Hudson yells out as the fish flashes his broad silver side near the top of the river's muddy surface before darting back off into the murky water, causing the drag to scream once again.

"Hold on to'm, son! Don't giv'm any dayum slack now!"

Gray is just as excited as Hudson about the fish. He continues to coach Hudson throughout the battle with the feisty bass. Hudson continues to ignore every word his father says. He continues to ignore Troy as well. He tells them to shut up a time or two so he can concentrate, but they continue yelling out random advice, anyhow. All traditional practices of fishermen, just like telling the story of how the big one got away—hopefully, not this time.

Finally, Hudson manages to get the fish close enough to the shore for his father to reach out with the net. Not yet ready to surrender, the fish darts up the river when Grayford pushes the net underneath it. While trying to net the big rascal, Grayford loses his footing and disappears into the brown water. Hudson's line makes a sudden turn downriver just before he sees his father's head pop back up. The water pushes Grayford right back into the sandbar about fifteen feet downriver. He quickly crawls onto the sandbar before getting his feet back up under him, while pulling the net up and out of the water. Hudson and Troy hold their breath for a moment as they watch the net rise from the muddy Oconee.

"Did ya get'm, Deddy?"

"Dayum . . . that water's some cold shit," Grayford announces, soaked from his unexpected swim. He catches his breath long enough to reply to Hudson's question. "Yeah . . . I got'm, but don't worry about me, heyull I'm fine."

Grayford pulls the net on up with a gargantuan white bass flopping around inside.

"Holy shit!" Troy blurts out.

Hudson runs over, pumping his right fist and then dropping his rod just before grabbing the net from his father. He drags the fish farther up onto the sandbar, letting out a victorious yell as he gazes upon the silver beast in pure astonishment. Holy shit is right—this is one of those supper-plate-sized rascals.

"How big, Deddy? How much ya thank he weighs?"

Gray walks up ringing the water out of his shirt, raising his eyebrows while looking down at the fish flopping in the net. "I'd say bout five . . . six pounds, I reckon. Biggest one I've ehva seen. Ya did good, son."

Grayford smiles at Hudson. The look in his son's eyes is an image that he wants to forever freeze in his mind. He admires his son's raw passion, with no worries in life and full of youthful exuberance. Life seems just right at this moment.

The day continues with ol' lady luck delivering a memorable morning in their favorite honey hole. The boys catch one bass after another and a few crappie here and there. They catch so many that they can barely lift their arms by the end of the feeding frenzy. Gray catches quite a few himself, but spends a good bit of his time freeing the boys' hooks when they snag one of the many logs and limbs in the river. He doesn't mind sacrificing his fishing time to help the boys, as that is part of his fatherly duties. He knows joyous moments such as these are far and few between, especially for adults. Gray understands that life's most exciting times, for most folks, are experienced in youth. He is selfless in his quest to maximize opportunities of happiness and excitement for the boys.

The fish stop biting just before noon, and the fellas head back to the pasture boat ramp with twelve good eating-size bass, seven crappie, and a trophy bass that will be talked about around campfires and in bait shops for years to come. They've released most of the morning's catch, probably around fifty or more, to help conserve the fish population in the river and lake. The fish will grow and be there for future battles at the sandbar.

It is truly among Hudson's happiest days. The world would be perfect if only he could stop the forward momentum of time and remain ten years old, fishing the Oconee with his father and cousin. However, time never stops, people grow older with each second that passes, and life persistently delivers one fateful challenge after another. Just like in a fight against a monster fish, momentum builds one way or the other. Life is full of fights and challenges, though not all of them as fun as Hudson's battle on the Oconee with that big bass. Many battles in life precede hard-earned victories and defeats. As most folks learn, life can be a merciless fighter who grows stronger each round while continuing to attack until an opponent fights no more. The only opponent undefeated against life is death. Life may win many rounds, but death always wins in the end. The question is how long does the fight last. Some fights go on longer than others. Some folks lose their fighting spirit earlier than others. Maybe life's brutality is too much to endure, and death's generous offer of mercy is too appealing. Such a tremendous quandary, and one that will soon present itself to Hudson.

# CHAPTER TWO

# HELEN AND HANK

Hudson surveys the blue skies just outside the airplane window as he recalls the monster bass he caught at the sandbar. The memory is the only happy thought to breach the despondency clouding his mind. The gray spirit within Hudson rarely welcomes life's good memories, but somehow the boy found the man in the fog of despair. He stands on the sandbar fighting that bass for as long as he can, trying to feel the boy's excitement once again. He never feels it, only sees it, like watching a silent movie. He watches the movie until the pilot interrupts his quiet view of the boy's fishing trip with the announcement of their final descent into Atlanta. After the announcement, Hudson searches for the boy once again, but fails to find him. He misses the boy.

Hudson has just finished up the final days of his four-year enlistment in the Marine Corps, which included two tours in Afghanistan. He's heading home a few days early, but he's shared the news with no one. He needs time alone. He is not ready to be around familiar people. He is not ready for happy reunions and welcome home parties. He needs no parade in his rain. So, rather than telling anyone of his early arrival, he'll spend a short spell in Helen visiting the Appalachian Mountains.

Throughout Hudson's youth, the Lee family took many trips to the German-influenced town nestled in the north Georgia mountains. He loved the beautiful green mountains, crisp air, and clear water. He loved standing in the melted-snow-fed river fishing for trout. He loved that he saw innocence, adventure, and beauty in the world back then. He wants to see the world once again through the eyes of the boy. He hopes the trip to Helen will call upon the boy. He hopes the boy will be waiting for him with peace in his heart to displace the man's turmoil.

Hudson rents a car in Atlanta and begins his journey north. On the way, he listens to dark blues-fueled music that reflects his pain, but does nothing to soothe it. He tries to revisit the sandbar on the drive up, but his mind stubbornly resides in a place half a world away, a place he reluctantly escaped. He's stuck in a place of mental fatigue and in an endless war that continues to snatch lives from young men and women. His thoughts navigate to the certain death that awaits every-one, though it seems to first take those most deserving to live. Maybe death delivers those people to a more serene place; a place Hudson desires but feels he does not deserve. He wonders if he will arrive at such a place if death strikes him down by his own hand. Deep down, though, he knows that to control his afterlife he cannot control his death. He knows departing this world by his own hand will not deliver him to the golden paradise. Heaven is reserved for folks like his good friend Hank Jackson.

Hank came from a poor family down in Alabama. He was named after Hank Aaron, his father's favorite baseball player. Hank's father served in the Marine Corps, which included a tour during Desert Storm. After his honorable discharge, Hank's father joined the Montgomery Police Department to serve his community as he did his country. He was not on the job long when he lost his life during a domestic dispute response. Fueled by a week-long methamphetamine binge, a woman who had stabbed her children to death after shooting their father in the head ambushed Hank's father at the front door. Death ripped a good man away from a good family. The tremendous responsibility of raising their three sons in this unforgiving world belonged solely to Hank's kind-hearted mother, who worked three jobs to keep food on the table and a roof over their heads. The only roof she could afford was located in a poverty-stricken part of West Montgomery.

Regardless of his mother's efforts to shelter her boys from bad influences and the fast-money temptations of their neighborhood, Hank watched his older brothers and several friends join gangs and die young. Though they made many more bad decisions than good, Hank spoke only of his brothers' talents and positive contributions to the world. He talked about the wonderful way they treated their mother. She was their rock, a woman who loved them more than anything. Before he died at the age of nineteen, Derrick, Hank's older brother, told him to learn from his mistakes, to be the one to make their mama proud: "Love her as she loves us . . . ain't no love good as Mama's love, lil bruh." That was the last thing Derrick told Hank before he died of stab wounds received in a fight with a member of his own gang. Derrick beat a man for trying to recruit Hank into the gang. The man's brother ran up from behind and stabbed Derrick in the neck. Hank's oldest brother, Anthony, watched over Hank during those hard times following their brother's death. However, Anthony died shortly after Derrick. He had turned his life around, helping guide the youth of their neighborhood away from gangs and toward education. He was hit head-on by a drunk driver who fell asleep at the wheel and crossed the median. Life can be unfair like that.

Hank made up his mind at an early age to do as Derrick told him and Anthony showed him. He dedicated most of his time to books and school. Hank was very intelligent, receiving several partial academic scholarship offers because of his high GPA and SAT score. He wanted to escape the poor neighborhood. He wanted to earn a degree from the University of Alabama, his father's favorite university. He wanted to find a good woman to raise a family and grow old with. He wanted to take good care of his mama. But first, he wanted to serve his country as his father did, so he enlisted in the Marine Corps. That is where his and Hudson's paths in life crossed.

Hudson admired Hank for his optimism in life. His entire twenty-one years on earth were full of struggle and heartache, but he always looked forward to visions of better places. Hank also loved to laugh and make other people laugh. No one was off limits when he told jokes, not even himself. As Hudson drives toward those north Georgia mountains, he tries to recall the good times and conversations he had with his friend. Only one sticks in his mind. The only one he wants to forget.

"Hudson, you hit?"

"Got some shit in my side . . . my head's fuckin' ringin.'" Hudson closed his eyes tightly in the moment and then tried to shake out the ringing.

"Shit, they messed up your pretty face, dawg! I can't move . . . Son, I can't move, man . . ." Hank smiled briefly, but the smile fled his face as he lay over his friend and mumbled two words.

Hudson shakes his head as he continues to drive. This time, he doesn't shake it to rid his head of the ringing, but to forget the memory. He rubs his left jaw through his beard. He can still feel the scar, but does not have to look at it anymore. Only when he removes his shirt does he see a painful reminder of that day. The long, jagged scar remains on his side. He wonders if he would feel the way he does if not for that day. He witnessed more death than just that day, but that day of death haunts him more than any other. He feels the world needed Hank more than it needed him—much more. Death took the wrong Marine.

After a journey that takes just as many mental twists and turns as the mountainous roads offer up, Hudson finally makes it to Helen. He finds a place to park out on the edge of town. Not eager to walk among the normal, he sits in the car for a while looking out at the quaint town full of old Bavarian-style shops. Through the window, the place is unfamiliar to the man. He needs the boy to arrive and be his guide. He watches the crowd of people grow by the minute and is in no hurry to walk with them, taking nearly an hour before talking himself into joining them. He convinces himself that a stroll among normal people will help him rendezvous with the boy and truly return home, maybe even become normal again. However, the more he walks, the more alone and lost he feels. All the people aimlessly bouncing around in different directions while lost in their own little worlds cause Hudson to have a panic attack. He was never one for big crowds, but now crowds anger him. He desires to fit in with them all but hates them at the same time. He hates the fact that they are oblivious to his torment, and the things that torment him derive from unimaginable sacrifices that protect their freedom to bounce around as they do. Their ignorance of war's mental ferocity is bliss, and it enrages him. He hates that he resents them for being normal. He made his choice and must face the consequences like a man; however, the horrific consequences are far more than he can bear. The war's mental aftermath weakens his spirit with every second that passes. He must escape this horde of normal people, so he races back to the car. He sits in the driver's seat sweating, dizzy, and feeling nauseous.

"I can't fuck'n do it, God . . . I can't live like this . . . Damn you!"

Hudson hangs his head by the vents pushing out cold air. He struggles to shake the anxiety. He turns up the air conditioner all the way, lifting his head so his face fully receives the cool breeze. He takes several deep breaths and then guzzles a bottle of water. Water is not what he really wants or needs. He needs something to take the edge off: opioids, liquor, Mary, or maybe all three to make him go numb. The drugs and alcohol will not free his mind of the torment, but they offer temporary relief of his senses. Numbness is all he desires.

Hudson drives to the rural area outside of town that is now covered up with campgrounds and vacation properties, replacing much of the endless green beauty he remembers from his youth. He drives around until he finds a private spot along the Chattahoochee where he can walk out into the river. Here he is isolated and safe from all the normal people. Maybe in serenity the boy will return. He rolls up his pant legs and walks right out into the middle of the cold, shallow river. He feels nothing. He doesn't even grimace as the cold water wraps around his legs and the river stones jab and stab into the bottoms of his feet. He stands alone in the river, surrounded by nature's peaceful gift. His eyes close. His skin and hair are touched only by the still air. His ears entertained only by the running water redirecting off stones. The world is finally at peace around him, but it continues to wage war within him.

Hudson is unable to escape his thoughts. The best he can ever do is briefly hide from them. Disappearing into the Chattahoochee is nothing more than a short respite from his mental agony. However, the river fails to deliver what he desired. Through the darkness of vision his face comes into view. Through the silence of air his voice is heard. He asks for help, but in that moment Hudson froze. He failed to save the friend who saved him. Hudson strains, but fails to open his eyes. His hands cuff his ears but fail to block the voice of a ghost. He begs for his friend's forgiveness, but his words are silent in the dead air. He only hears his own cries for help. Finally, Hudson forces open his tear-soaked eyes to escape the tragic memories. He finds himself alone no more. He is now surrounded by trout fishermen who are mouthing something to him, but sound has yet to return to his ears. A hand on his shoulder gains Hudson's attention, but the stranger's words fail to pierce the deafening silence. The boy stood him up in this river, leaving only the damaged man to interact with these strangers. Hudson snaps his head down at the hand on his shoulder, and then back to the stranger who dares lay this hand on him. His eyes turn red with boiling blood. The war drum pounds in his chest as fury invades his mind. He is not angry at the man; he is angry at the normal world the man represents. He is mad at himself for being here. He violently pushes the old fisherman, knocking him off his feet and into the cold water. Hudson readies himself for battle as the other three men close in on him; however, they stop short to help their friend up, out of the chilly water. They glare at Hudson but offer no further threat. Hudson slowly retreats a few steps to get distance between him and the men. Their glares evolve into bewilderment as they watch the angry young man respond with a scowl. Hudson turns toward the river's edge where he entered the water and pushes hard through the water toward the bank, slipping and falling on the slick stones below his feet along the way. He reaches the bank, soaked from his falls, and grabs his shoes before looking back to the river. The four men stand frozen, holding their fishing poles in the same spot where he stood a moment ago. They stare at him, but now with sympathy. Tears fall from Hudson's eyes as he realizes these four men were enjoying the very hobby he so deeply loves when they stopped to help a stranger. In return, the stranger thanked them with violence. Hudson knows he will never have their joy again, and they could never understand his torment. Or maybe the old men did serve and found a way home from war.

The old fisherman's silent words from earlier finally reach Hudson's ears, "It's OK, Marine, you're home now."

Hudson looks at the man he pushed into the water. The man raises his sleeve and points at the eagle, globe, and anchor on his forearm. Hudson looks down at his bare forearm, where he inked the same tattoo. He sobs with his head hung low. He wants the man to tell him how to return home, but he can't lift his head to face him—his shame is too heavy. Hudson turns around and chooses to walk away instead.

Hudson stops at a small diner a short distance down the road from Helen. He has to be away from all the people who are immersed in self-interest and hypnotized by all the new technology. He sits in a corner booth staring through the window while sipping on a cup of steaming-hot black coffee. As he waits for his food to cook, he struggles to keep his mind empty. All he sees through the window is his good friend. He is surrounded by normal conversations, but all he hears are Hank's last words, reverberating in his head to the point of insanity. The life given to Hank was filled with tragedy, yet his heart was always filled with joy. He had the greatest appreciation for life and deserved to return to a happier one than he left. Hudson sees death as more forgiving than life. Fate granted neither of them that which they desired most after their time of war.

The waitress slides Hudson's food in front of him, snapping him out of the painful past. He forces a smile on his face, and then he thanks the waitress.

"Can I get ya anythang else, young man?"

"No ma'am, this ought ta do it. Thank ya!"

"Wayull, enjoy. Let me top awf that cawffee for ya, hun."

Hudson watches as she pours the coffee. He looks up with a strained smile, giving her a nod of gratitude. He takes a few bites of his eggs and grits before drifting off in thought again. He tries to see his mama's face. He knows she will be the most excited to see him. He was always her baby boy. They had a wonderful relationship, and he always wanted to make his mama happy. His biggest regret is the pain and disappointment he will bring her. He thinks about the pain felt by Hank's mother. Though these thoughts should sadden him, he suppresses his feelings. An empty void grows in his heart out of necessity. He needs the emptiness to displace the pain. He cannot allow himself to think about the sadness of any mother—neither his nor Hank's. Thinking about grieving mothers will interfere with his ability to complete his mission, which is to kill the enemy. This time the enemy is his own mind, though. His mind is supposed to go into survival mode and forget the brutality by the enemy, the fatigue of the daily grind on foreign soil, the dead friends and lost souls; however, his mind refuses to let go.

Hudson sits there staring at his food when an old conversation with Hank interrupts his thoughts:

"Dude, my mama won't stop hound'n me about write'n her."

"Son, you best write yo mama. That woman endured a lot of pain to brang your dumb country ass into this world."

"No shit, Jacks! I do write'r, but I don't have somethin' to say every dayum day."

"You got no problem talk'n to me every day. Hell, be nice for ya to shut up every now and then."

"That's you, Hank—you won't shut the hell up."

"Oh, I know, son, but I write my mama . . . eeevery day, devil dawg. Ain't no love like Mama's love, so don't you go and break her heart!"

"Uh-huh, I guess."

"Ain't no guess'n to it, son . . ." Hank paused for a moment. "That was the last thang Derrick said to me. He told me it was up to me to make Mama proud . . . 'Ain't no love like Mama's love, so don't you break her heart like I did, bruh.'"

"You think your brother was a bad seed?"

"Nah, just a product of his surround'ns. Don't gimme wrong, D was into some heavy shit, but he also had a big heart. He would buy new playground shit with some of the dope money. Kinda his way of help'n the community, I guess."

"No offense, because my country ass grew up around cow shit and chicken houses, so I know noth'n of the streets, but I'd think gangs do more damage than playground shit does good. Am I wrong?"

"Nah, your country ass is right. D knew that shit, too. I think he partly stayed in the gang to keep me out of it. He died keeping me out of that life. My mama worked her ass off to keep me out of it. And guided me away from it and toward education. I owe all of 'em a good life."

"Is that why you're so dayum optimistic all the time?"

"I got one life to live for my brothers, and I got to do what I need to do so my mama lives the better life she deserves. So, yeah, I brang the sunshine when it rains. All tha dayum time. Gotta always be happy, son. Only way I wanna be in life."

"All right, I'm touched. I'll write Mama every dayum day . . . hell, maybe even twice a day. No love like Mama's, huh?!"

"Yup."

"Well, I don't know about you, but sometimes Mama's love sure did hurt, especially when she delivered that love with a belt. She would tell me she's whoop'n my ass cause she loves me."

"I'm sure you deserved that love'n, dawg."

"Oh, I did."

"Me too . . ." Hank chuckles. "That woman couldn't aim that belt for shit, either . . . hit everythang but my ass . . . with both ends of the belt, and that buckle is uh bitch."

Hudson remembers laughing at his friend's colorful descriptions of childhood memories, but his laughter died long ago. He feels hungry but can't stomach the food as he thinks about the life robbed from so many with the death of one. He feels nauseous and just wants to get home, go numb, and end the memories. He will have to see his family. They will have to see him. They will be thankful he made it back, only to be heartbroken again. Why bring that pain to his family? Why not end it here and now? He can drive off the mountain and make it look like an accident. He can save his family the embarrassment and pain. Why? Because this is not home, and his soul cannot be trapped here in these mountains. The pain will be the same for his family; death is death after all, as Hank's mother knows all too well. Home is where the body must rest and where the soul must reside. He may not get into Heaven's golden paradise, but for now, Whippoorwill Hollow is all he wants.

— CHAPTER THREE —

# MAXEYS

**P**ass by enough cow pastures, skinny pines, and red clay while heading west off Interstate 20 on State Route 77, and a traveler will stumble upon Maxeys, Georgia. Maxeys is a little speck on the map that would flash by in less than a second if it were not for the 35 miles per hour speed limit. Nearly abandoned, this middle-of-nowhere southern town consists of some empty roadside stores and an out-of-service railroad depot, and is surrounded by old houses, farms, forests, and green pastures enclosed by rusty barbed wire fences. Folks living in Maxeys have to drive about fifteen miles to Crawfordville or about the same distance to Greensboro for the closest grocery stores. For any extensive shopping, they would need to drive another fifteen to twenty miles to Athens. Maxeys is a place for folks who want to escape the crowds, noise, and traffic jams of the city to live in harmony with nature while rocking in their chairs listening to the critters perform a cappella.

On the outskirts of Maxeys, the Lee family owns about a hundred acres of rolling green pastures and patches of forest enclosed by some of that rusty barbed wire. Their property is surrounded by thousands of acres of fields, forests, and farms. This little slice of country paradise earned its name when Savannah Lee heard the eastern whippoor-will sing on the first night after her and Grayford bought the place. The nocturnal bird sings a pretty song that can be heard resounding through the forest most summer nights. Hank Williams heard sorrow in the whippoorwill's song; however, Savannah and the rest of the Lee family heard joy as the bird sang. The Lee family would sit around campfires on many Georgia summer nights enjoying each other's com-pany: talking, laughing, and listening to the whippoorwill perform just for them. Those nights by the fire, listening to that song, were some of Hudson's fondest childhood memories in this country haven, far from the city chaos.

Hudson is the youngest child of Savannah and Grayford Lee. To say Hudson is Savannah's favorite child is an understatement. Parents don't admit they have favorites, but they do, and Hudson is her favor-ite; although she loves all of her children equally. He has always been just like Savannah: strong willed, tough when necessary, someone who wears his emotions on his sleeve and who is, most of all, compas-sionate. Grayford and Savannah have two other children, a son and a daughter. Madelyn is the middle child. She is a feisty little thing stand-ing five feet five inches tall. In high school and college, she was a stand-out athlete, earning a scholarship from the University of Georgia for gymnastics. Ty, short for Tyrus after his great-grandfather, is the eldest. Ty is quick-witted and a bit on the wild side. He loves music, fishing, and smoking a little green herb. He is viewed as the black sheep of the family, but he is just fine with that. Ty can be found playing on stage at numerous bars in Athens on damn near any given night. He is a coun-try blues enthusiast and has assembled quite the band of characters. Hudson has always looked up to Ty. Growing up, he loved Ty's free spirit lifestyle, but also admired his loyalty to his friends and family, even those who openly disagree with his heathen ways.

Calling Maxeys a town is a bit misleading. The place has a small post office, but that is about it. Once upon a time, quite a few businesses were up and running, but most have closed since modern technology has come along. Still standing in a chain of buildings, along with the post office, are the antique and flower shop, a general store, and Bill's Tire Shop. The latter is no longer open for the business of selling tires, but it is still alive and well for the local fellas who need a place to escape their daily responsibilities, drink cheap beer and hard liquor, watch some ball games, and do a little gambling, all while telling dirty jokes. Somewhere around beer three or four, about the time the gentlemen break into the hard stuff, the conversations tend to evolve into political rants and gripes about the tax-happy government.

Grayford and Papa Lee are known to frequent Bill's underground watering hole. Harvey "Papa" Lee is Grayford's father. He is in his mid-eighties and can be rather ornery; not really something brought on by his old age or anything, but that's just the way he is. He ran a dairy farm for the better part of fifty years, until his wife, Olivia, passed away from brain cancer. Harvey was a lost soul in his youth, tearing up the countryside with a rough group of fellas until she came along early in their twenties and straightened him out. She was the reason he made it past the age of twenty-five. They were by each other's side every day once love took hold of them. Her death about broke his will to live, but somehow he just keeps going. He believes he is paying for his past sins by living long and broken. He sold the dairy farm and now passes time on the lake, tending his ever-shrinking garden, or at Bill's with the fellas.

Gray and Harvey join their longtime friends Pop Walters, Clive Elrod, and Bill at the old tire shop to watch Georgia's first game of the season just before Hudson is to return home. They smoked a Boston butt and cooked up a mess of baked beans for the opener against the Clemson Tigers. Bill has an old fridge in the back slam-full of beer and a cabinet filled with assorted liquor, not necessarily top-shelf stuff, though. The game between the Tigers and the Dawgs brings back an old rivalry, which is sure to be a good ole slobber-knocker, and the old gents are ready.

While waiting for kickoff, back-to-back campaign commercials interrupt the pregame show with negative rhetoric from the two politicians running for office. This comes on around beer three, just in time to get Gray all riled up.

"Cockroaches! Democrats, Republicans, Independents, Green, Libertarian, this party and that party . . . every dayum one of 'em. They're all crooked sons of bitches work'n for the damned lobbyists. Po man fights their wars, and rich man reaps the reward."

"Ain't that the dayum truth! They taxed me right out my business," Bill chimes in, referring to his old tire shop.

"Ah heyull, Bill, taxes didn't shut ya down . . ." Clive pauses to offer Bill a smirk before continuing, "shitty, cheap tires did."

"Dammit, Clive, you bought tires from me for many years, ya cheap ass. I could've sold betta tires if I didn't have the government hit'n me up for every extra dayum dolla I had."

"That's right! I sure did buy from you, which makes me quite the expert on your shitty tire quality, Bill."

"No one ever accused you of be'n an expert on anything, Elrod. Ah, to heyull with talk'n to you, ya mean ass. Pop, I'm surprised Uncle Sam hasn't taxed you off your farm. How's business these days?"

"Well, Bill, my peaches are ripe for tha pick'n, and my barbeque's fanguh lick'n, so bidness is good! But I gotta tell ya fellas . . . I got the feds take'n money outta my left pocket while the county is reach'n in my right pocket. Hell, with all these hands in my pockets, they could at least gimme a tug or two, how bout it?!"

"Wrap a twenty around yowuh peckuh, then they'll tug away on that sucka," Harvey offers up his sound advice on the matter.

"Sounds like you're quite the expert on gubment hand jobs, Harvey," replies Pop.

"Aw sheeyut . . . I don't want their greasy palms on my peckuh."

"See, this is what the hell I'm talk'n bout. While you two old farts talk about Uncle Sam hand jobs and you two argue about Bill's cheap, shitty tires, the politicians are up on the hill laugh'n their crooked asses off while count'n Pop's money and everybody else's dayum money. They divide us with race this, gender that," Gray preaches on, not ready to let up on politics, or Bill's tire quality for that matter.

"Oh, everybody wants to take a crack at my dayum tires. All you assholes had no problem pay'n rock-bottom prices for my tires, now did ya? I could've charged y'all a helluva lot mowuh, but I didn't. So kiss my old, country, hairy white ass," Bill so elegantly reminds the fellas while tossing his empty into the trash on his way to the cabinet for a hit off of the hard stuff. He usually hits the whiskey after the beer-three political conversations commence.

". . . pro this, pro that, religion, blame the good people for the bad and insane shoot'n up places . . ."

"Gray, what in the hell are you talk'n about?" asks Pop.

"The damned crooked-ass politicians that continue driv'n a wedge between the good folks of this country with an eight-pound hamma. As long as we argue about shit that does noth'n for our families and the hard work'n people of this country, then the government can continue dig'n in our pockets and rip'n away at the Constitution . . . without even offer'n up a greasy palm tug or two . . . Well, they will promise you a tug to get elected, but you ain't get'n that tug . . . I gare-on-tee-ya that shit."

Gray immediately turns to Bill, who's opening up the fridge, and shouts, "Bill, grab me another Natural Light from the second shelf, would ya?"

"Kiss my ass!" Bill yells, followed by a mumbling rant, "Call my tires shitty in my dayum stowuh!"

"Bill . . . now dammit . . . I'm sorry! Please brang me a cold one. Good God! Stop being so dadgum sensitive. I truly am sorry . . ." As Bill closes in on the table with Gray's beer, Grayford continues, "I'm sorry you sold shitty, cheap tires and lost your business!"

"Dammit, Gray . . . that's just shit-ass dirty!"

"I'm just mess'n with ya, Billy Boy. Hell, you had no chance. Folks used to be able to run a small business within their community. Taxes just eat 'em up anymowuh. Taxes that big businesses are exempt from . . . that's all Imma say."

"Well, at least you own this old build'n and the house out back Bill," Pop reassures Bill, who seems to be getting shots from everyone.

"Hell yeah I do! Assholes! Y'all sure don't mind hang'n out in my old tire shop when ya tired of your old ladies nag'n at ya. Watch'n football, play'n cards, drank'n beer . . . and ya wanna give me shit about my dayum tires?!"

"Aw, Bill, we love ya, buddy . . ." Gray pauses to pop the top. "Like Pop said, at least that ex old lady of yours left ya everything when she passed."

"This place and a few good memories is all that I have left from that crazy marriage. Dayum, I sure do miss her sometimes. She could be a real nag, but she sure could cook and gave a mean . . ."

"Oh shit, here comes the whiskey talk'n. Please spare us the nasty bedroom stories, Bill, would ya?" Clive immediately cuts off Bill before he can finish that thought.

"Oh, it didn't always happen in the bedroom, bubba. Quite a few times in this room, as a matter of fact . . . heyull, two or three times in that very chair, Elrod."

"Dammit, ya nasty sumbitch!"

The old fellas laugh for a few seconds as Clive switches out chairs after Bill's quick rejoinder. As the laughing dies down and the big smiles reduce to half grins, Clive looks over at Grayford to talk about something a little more meaningful, "Gray, when will Hudson be home? I'm sure Savannah is ready for her baby boy to be back from that god-awful war."

In an instant, the old fellas end their frivolous discourse. The remaining grins slowly disappear, and their old faces turn to stone in anticipation of Grayford's answer to Clive's question.

"Yeah, she sure is. We pick'm up from the airport on Thursdee. Clive, he just doesn't seem himself. Last time we talked . . ." Grayford pauses to collect himself before continuing, "He seemed to struggle to find the energy tuh talk. That boy always had the gift of gab and was full of life, but that war took someth'n from'm."

"He just needs to be home, Gray. It'll take'm some time, but he'll finally come back. Remember, it took Walt awhile to recovuh from Vietnam . . . God rest his soul." Clive holds up his beer to toast Walt before taking a sip.

Walter Lee was one of Grayford's younger brothers, a Marine veteran who served a tour in Vietnam. That traumatic tour left Walt deaf in his right ear and legally blind in his right eye, but the mental damage was his most painful injury. He returned to Georgia, but he never left those bloody jungles. After his return, Walt sat at the table with the devil and a fifth of Old Number 7 sour mash whiskey. He looked that devil in the eye and said, "Until the bottle's gone, we stay. When the last drop is drank, I'm goin tuh kill ya." Walt and the devil drank at that table for a long time and never did get to the bottom of that endless bottle, but he did kill that old devil just before losing his battle with cancer.

"Dayum, Walt wasn't right for a long time after he got back from Vietnam," Clive continues.

"Walt was crazy befowuh the war, Clive," Harvey says, pausing for a second, "and nevuh really was right til he made peace with God just before cansuh took'm. That boy was a pain in my ass befowuh he enlisted. I tell ya . . . jus as wild as he could be, jus like Ty."

"Just like you, Harvey. You're the craziest sumbitch I know. Before he passed, Pappy told me a little about y'all's operation back in the day," Clive responds.

"Yeah, don't get round like I did, though . . . and some thangs oughta stay buried. Anyhow, Hudson is too much like his mama."

"What in the hell does that mean, Deddy?"

"It means what the hell it sounds like, boy. That boy is tough but lets shit get to him, just like his mama. Don't get me wrong, Savannah is tougher than you lil sissies. She ain't afraid of shit and will tear ya a new asshole if you cross her family, especially her children."

"I know, she ripped into Gray's ass for let'n Hudson enlist into the Marine Corps. Didn't talk to ya for three damn weeks," Pop Walters points out.

"Yeah, that was bout the most peaceful three weeks of my life. Heyull, I didn't like his decision, either, but it's his life." Grayford pauses for a moment before changing the subject back to something more jovial. "Dammit, when are they gonna take the field? I'm gonna be too drunk to watch the dayum thang if they don't hurry up."

"Yeah . . . dammit, Bill, why did ya have to break out the whiskey so early?"

"Because you wouldn't shut the heyull up bout my tires, Clive."

"Damn if y'all ain't a bunch of nags. Pop, looks like it'll just be us after halftime, hoss," Harvey announces.

"Shit, Deddy, your old ass'll be knocked out by the end of the first quarter."

"That's no way to talk to your deddy, boy. I brought ya in and I'll take ya ass right out."

"Damn if I ain't heard that a hundred times, and I'm still here."

"Go grab me anothuh beeyuh, and I'll let ya stay here a lil longuh."

"Anybody else need anotha while I'm up?" Grayford asks while walking to the fridge. Regardless of age, a son is forever charged with fetching his father a beer when told, and best not shake the fresh one.

The game finally kicks off, and the old fellas continue poking fun at each other while drinking their favorite beverages and munching on boiled peanuts, or, as Pop Walters calls them, redneck oysters. At halftime, they feast on Pop's delicious barbeque while complaining about the horrid calls by the referees in the first half. Gray, however, has his mind on his son's return, even as the Dawgs pop pads with the Tigers. He remembers the days of watching Georgia games with Hudson, who was always there to watch them with his father. Nothing is harder for a father than to send his son off to war, but nothing is more honorable than a son who served his country. Gray never showed it much, but he wept for his son many days. When no one else was around, he shed quite a few tears while looking at Hudson's boot camp picture. He often prayed death would not call his son's name. Gray always made sure to hide his emotions around others, especially Savannah. He had to stay strong for Savannah, who often cried herself to sleep while looking at pictures of Hudson. No love is as powerful as a mother's love, and no worry is more crushing than a mother's worry. Hudson's four years in the Marines probably took ten years off Savannah's life, as well as Gray's. They are ready for their son to be home, safe from the war half a world away. They can only hope that war did not destroy their son's wonderful spirit.

# CHAPTER FOUR

# REUNION

Before Hudson headed off to the Marines, he had visions of returning home to buy a house and build a family. Of course, he planned for the future like most other teenagers—in five-minute increments—so he often turned to his father for advice about saving for a house. He also consulted with Harold and Ethel Pierce, an older couple he befriended and often helped, about house buying and other significant life goals. The old couple lived in a brick, ranch-style house on ten acres of land about halfway down the stretch of Highway 15 between Watkinsville and Whippoorwill Hollow. The land had a three-acre pond, fields, and forest, and was surrounded by farmland, perfect for hunting and fishing, which was the reason Hudson first approached the couple. Hudson was about fourteen, working for the farmer next door to Harold and Ethel, when he met them. They agreed to let the nice young man fish and hunt on their property, but Hudson would often stop by just to visit the old couple and take care of big projects around the house for no charge other than permission to hunt and fish. Neither member of the elderly couple got around that well, and poor Ethel had early onset dementia. Their only son died in a car wreck at the age of twenty-two, so they had no children of their own; Hudson also filled that void for them. When Harold's health took a turn for the worse, Hudson took over caring for Ethel as Alzheimer's disease chipped away at her memories until her life before never existed. Before she passed away, she would often call Hudson by her dead son's name. Hudson did not have the heart to correct her, because he could see the joy in her eyes, believing her son was there caring for her. After she passed, Harold's health went into rapid decline; his heart was too broken to continue fighting his ailments. Hudson wrote and called Harold often after leaving for the service, but one day Harold didn't pick up his phone. Day after day, Hudson called with no answer. He knew Harold was gone to be with Ethel again, but Hudson was saddened by the thought of his friend having no one there to say goodbye as they lowered his body deep into the Georgia clay. A letter from the lawyer confirmed the death of Harold. Hudson broke down sobbing as he learned Harold had left everything to him. Hudson thanked his friends every day in prayer for giving him and his future family such an unexpected blessing. Sadly, what Hudson once thought to be a blessing is now solitary confinement in the prison of despair while awaiting departure from this life, as it was for his dear friends, Harold and Ethel.

Hudson called his family the day before they were to pick him up in Atlanta to let them know he rented a car at the airport. He waited until late that night to call, so they would not pester him about coming over to the farm. Instead, they told him to come over the following day for a fish fry. Hudson knows that time will come, that time when he will have to reunite with his family and face the happiness of his return. He does not want to be annoyed by their happiness, but he is unable to feel any other way. Even when surrounded by many loved ones, he will be alone. He wants to remain alone. He wants to remain detached from all he knew and loved, all except that whippoorwill. He remembers happiness from another time but knows not the actual feeling of happiness anymore. He cannot envision himself ever returning to a normal life where happiness exists. His family can never know his struggle so long as he lives; therefore, he must conceal his despair.

Hudson sits on the recliner in his living room for an hour trying to muster up the motivation to go see his family. They are all there at the farm waiting for him. Grayford has fried up some catfish and hush-puppies while Savannah has prepared potato salad, slaw, and pecan pie—Hudson's favorite meal. He is supposed to be there by now. Eight hundred and sixty-two days have passed by since Hudson last saw his family. He missed them, and they missed him dearly. Yet, in the moment he is to return to them, he struggles to stomach the thought of seeing them. He sits in a chair staring at a .38 revolver and his truck keys lying side-by-side on the coffee table. The gun is the same one his great-grandfather used to end his life after growing tired of battling cancer. Hudson's disease is just as painful to the mind as cancer was to his great-grandpa Tyrus's body. His options are simple: drive over to visit his family and try to portray a normal, healthy mental state; or just end it all right now, so he is not forced to see the lives he will soon destroy. However, to die now means sacrificing the whippoor-will's song. Silence fills the room as Hudson empties thoughts from his head. As goes all thought, so does emotion. He detaches further from life as he stares intently at the gun and keys. His phone buzzes but fails to disrupt his focus on the choice lying before him. Grayford is calling, probably to find out when his loving son will join them at the family table. The annoying phone continues to buzz, interrupting the silence Hudson craves at this moment. He is tempted to smash it on the table, but the phone finally falls silent. In that instance of dead air, Hudson grabs the gun, empties all but one round, and then spins the cylinder. He provides death an opportunity to save him—right here, right now. He raises the barrel to his temple, pulls the trigger, but only a click fol-lows. He lays the gun on the table as though he did nothing more than finish a bowl of cereal. He reluctantly slides the keys from the table, slowly rises from his chair, and then walks out the door with his head hung low as though disappointed by life's little triumph.

Hudson finally completes his long journey back to the farm. Most folks are full of joyful anticipation of his return home, but one is con-sumed with dread. He fills his lungs with a few deep breaths of the thick, moist air to push down his rising nerves. He silently rehearses his role as the old Hudson, the young boy, but struggles to recall him. He must find a way to remember, to prevent any awkward exchanges, especially with Savannah, who has already stormed out of the door and charges toward him. She says nothing at first, just wraps her arms around her son. He can feel and hear her crying as she buries her face into his chest. She tightly grabs the back of his shirt with both hands. He is back, and she never wants him to leave again. She pulls away for a brief moment to talk—she tries to talk, but remains speechless. Relief fills her eyes and tears soak her cheeks.

Her shaky and broken voice utters the words she's waited years to say: "I have missed you so much. I was so afraid you would nehvuh come back home to us, my sweet boy. Thank God yowuh home!" She again loses control of her emotions and can only hug her son. After what seems a long, sorrowful eternity, she pulls away again and looks up at her son's face. "My goodness, baby, you really need to shave. Don't cuhvuh up that handsome face."

"I will, Mama." Hudson smiles at Savannah for a brief moment before continuing, "You are beautiful as always. Gotcha your hair did, didn't ya?"

"Oh sweetie, thank you! And I most certainly deeyud. I wanted to look my best fowuh my baby!"

"I missed ya, Mama . . . the prettiest smile in the world." Hudson offers his mama a wink and smile, which leads to another hug, one that about squeezes the breath right out of him.

"You can't ansuh your dayum phone? I'm starve'n! Smell'n all this fried fish and puppies for two dayum hours—wait'n on you. Here!" Grayford welcomes Hudson with a quick lecture, a firm handshake, and a cold beer.

"Sorry bout that, Deddy! I was drive'n. Looks like you could skip a meal or two anyhow." Hudson answers his father with that famous Lee sarcastic smirk.

Grayford looks down at his slight beer belly before replying, "Well, at least I can still see my peckuh. Get over here, son, and give your old man uh hug!"

"Grayford Lee!" Savannah scolds.

"Hell, Deddy, noth'n I wanna do more than hug ya after a good pecker reference."

"Welcome home, son! Dayum glad to have you back with us." Gray chokes back his emotions, but Hudson can see his father's eyes well up with tears.

"Glad to be back, Deddy." Hudson swallows hard as he pushes out the lie.

Everyone takes a turn welcoming Hudson home with kind words and hugs. Hudson seems to be the same ol' fella on the outside, but inside he struggles to stomach the act he must deliver for the people he loves the most. His stomach churns like one of them cotton candy machines at the state fair. He should want to live for them. Yet, nothing fills his heart. It remains dark and hollow, even after witnessing the falling tears from his mother's eyes. His heart must remain empty, because love makes him vulnerable to all those other emotions—the painful ones. The act appears to be working, as those who know Hudson best and love him most cannot see the despondent soul residing inside him. He must continue his Oscar-worthy performance to leave them with memories of the jubilant Hudson they've always known. They only know of the boy and must never meet the man. Nothing ever seemed to bring the boy down, except when the Dawgs lost a game or the big fish got away. However, the buoyant future the boy possessed slowly and miserably faded during the man's second tour, and died outright when life deserted his dear friend Hank. The man paid the ultimate sacrifice, but Hudson lives to feel its misery. Now, he must maintain emptiness, because remembering brings too much pain and darkness. Feeling nothing feels better.

While ingesting fried catfish and other Southern delights, the family talks about anything and everything, as is custom at a Southern table during supper. Hudson joins in here and there, but he mostly remains quiet, hoping no one asks about his time in Afghanistan or anything else. All is going well until Maddie, his older sister, mentions her husband's friend, who returned from the war last year. She talks about how he changed, became a recluse, even avoiding his wife and kids. Then, she drops the bomb, nearly blowing Hudson's cover. She says they found him dead two days ago. He had pulled over onto the side of the road near their home in Commerce, and then shot himself.

Immediately, Savannah looks at Hudson. "How are ya doin, Hudson?"

"Oh, Mama, I'm fine. I was fortunate enough not to see much action," Hudson lies to his mama. He has lied to her numerous times before, but mostly about trivial things like getting into the snacks or sneaking out with his high school buddies. This time, his lie carries much more weight. This time, his lie is life and death. He downplays his experience of fighting a seemingly endless war. He lies about his mental well-being. He has to lie, because his sister had to tell that damned story about her husband's friend.

"Well, I heard that soldiers are com'n back suffer'n mentally as much as, if not mowuh, than they are physic'ly. Hudson, if ya need help, son, you go get it, ya heeyuh me? Ya heeyuh ya mama?"

"Mama's right, brother. We know you are strong minded, but don't you hold that god-awful mess inside. We don't mean to put ya on the spot, but we love ya, bubba." Maddie offers her brother advice, but she is a stranger to the man she advises. The brother who left for war is not the same man who returned home; in fact, he did not return at all. As for her words of encouragement, ignorance prevents her from recognizing the mess within Hudson, and just how god-awful her advice is to him. She might as well waste her advice on her husband's dead friend.

Hudson enjoys none of this extremely uncomfortable conversation and needs it to end. "Y'all can stop worry'n. I am fine! I'm happy to be home. Plus, they did a full mental and physical eval on me before cut'n me loose." Hudson is telling the truth about the evaluations; however, his lie was just as effective with the counselors and doctors as it is right now with his family. Well, most of his family.

Troy and Hudson were inseparable throughout their childhood and teenage years. Troy knows the boy better than anyone, even more than Savannah. He knows the man should be more like the boy was, just a little bit more mature maybe. Troy can see his cousin's discomfort with the conversation, but also senses Hudson holding back the whole story. By his calculations, he'd say Hudson is giving about 1 percent of the story, enough to shut everyone up. He knows when his cousin is keeping secrets in the dark, because he knows them all, except for this one—the darkest of all his secrets. He figures he will bail out his cousin for now with hopes of him coming clean later. Troy offers Hudson an escape from Savannah and Maddie's direct approach with something a little more indirect.

"Hudson, when ya wanna hit up some largemouth, cuz? I know a spot full of bucket-mouth bass, dude. Caught a couple six pounders the utha day."

"Ya don't say?!" Hudson's reply shows interest, but does not offer an obligation to join him. More than anything, he is relieved to have a way out of the other conversation.

"Who caught this delicious fish y'all fried up?"

"Aw, some from Ricky, some from what Troy and I caught, and the crappie we had left over from early sprang. Ya oughta come on out with us, son. Ricky said he knows a spot," Grayford gladly answers.

"Shit, Ricky won't give up his secrets. That sumbitch sent us up to the railroad bridge last weekend. We didn't catch a damn thang. Meanwhile, he went up to the dam and filled the boat."

"He has a way of fill'n the boat when ya ain't with'm, don't he?!" Grayford sarcastically and rhetorically asks.

"Troy, listen heeyuh, you can tell yowuh little fish'n stories without all'at foul language, young man!" Savannah scolds Troy with a tone and look that silences the table.

"Sorry, Aunt Savannah!"

"You talk like'at again at my table, and you'll be doin all these dishes! Ya heeyuh me, young man?"

"Yes, ma'am," Troy replies respectfully, but with a slight smirk.

While they go on about Ricky's fish tales and other topics, Hudson fades into the background. He smiles and nods here and there to keep up his act; however, all he wants to do is finish eating, go back to his house, turn on the stereo, and drink whiskey until passing out. That moment seems so far away, and this act is exhausting, but he must continue pushing through this torturous supper with a normal demeanor, without disclosing his demons. He can't unlock those chains quite yet. He will be fine as long as his sister keeps her mouth shut. He shouldn't be upset with her, but her war tragedy story enraged him. Over and over, he tells himself to remain calm. He reminds himself that this moment will end as does everything in life, including life itself. The time will come when he will be free from this mentally exhausting reunion, but first he must tell his family that he loves them one last time.

After supper, Ty and Troy take Hudson for a ride around the farm on Gray's all-terrain golf cart. They drive him down to the other side of the creek on the backside of Whippoorwill Hollow. They have to get away from the house so Ty and Troy can enjoy some time with Mary as they catch up with Hudson. They offer a little to Hudson, but he passes. He needs a sharp mind to keep up his performance.

"Damn, son, good to see ya, cuz. Sorry your mama and Maddie got all up in your shit, dude. I'm serious about that honey hole, though. Looka here, Ty hung one that pulled the damn boat."

Hudson forces a grin to his face as he looks at Troy, and then looks at his brother Ty and asks, "Is that right?"

"I shit you not, son," Troy reassures Hudson.

"Yep . . . show nuff, lil brother . . . had ten-pound test line . . . sumbitch wrapped around a log or someth'n . . . snapped my line."

Hudson knows that Ms. Mary is taking hold of Ty's mind and tongue, because she tends to shrink his sentences down to the bare essentials. Ty continues offering sentence fragments with a permanent grin on his face. "Whatcha say, brother? Wanna hit 'em up? We'll load the boat right damn now!"

"Hell yeah! We'll get some snacks and Nattie Lights . . . Shit, son, no finer way to spend a glorious Georgia afternoon. Come on, watcha say, cuz?" Troy pipes back in.

Hudson looks at the two knuckleheads as he contemplates his response. All he wanted to do was come here, say hello, eat, and then go home, get drunk, and pass out. Getting roped into commitments is damn sure not on that list, so he kicks around the many excuses he could come up with to get out of this well-marketed fishing trip before settling on one: "As much as I'd love to go sit in the boat with you at the helm, Troy, I think I'd best stay here and visit with Mama and Deddy. You know Mama would be pissed off if I left, right?"

"Bucket. Mouth. Bass!" Troy yells as he exhales.

"I heard ya, Troy. You want me to go?" Hudson raises his voice with about as much fake excitement as he can muster.

"Hell yeah! Let's do it, son!"

"Awlright then, you go tell Mama."

"Hell with that, cuz. She already chewed my ass out today. Your mama would kick the shit outta me. Ty, you tell'r."

Ty cuts Troy a curious look as though he is contemplating what to say to Savannah, takes another hit off the rather loose joint Troy rolled, and then cuts his blood-red eyes back at Hudson. "Welp . . ." He pauses for a second to exhale. "I guess we can go tomorrow."

There in front of Hudson sit two fellas who have never backed down from a fight. They have won some and lost some, but never backed down; however, both are deathly afraid of the five-foot-six-inch feisty, short-fused firecracker who sits up at the house waiting for her baby boy to come talk to her. Neither of them will dare venture into the proverbial ring with her. Hudson knows that, which made it the perfect excuse.

On the way back to the house, Ty slips Hudson a few joints and a half ounce of Mary. "Welcome home, brother. Missed ya! I ain't gonna ask ya shit about what ya went through. Nor will I poke around in your business. I'm just damn glad ya made it back home to us. You are Uncle Sam's no longer, so enjoy what you earned . . ." He pauses for a second before continuing. "And this Earthly herb heals all, brother. Ya hear? Plenty where that came from, too."

"Thanks, Ty! Y'all still play'n?"

"You know it! Still rock'n the house. You oughta come out tuh see us sometime."

"Hell yeah, come on out, cuz. We come a long way since making noise in Chief's garage. Ty can actually sing now . . . his voice finally hit puberty."

"Aw, he's just mad cos I get all the ladies."

"Not all of 'em."

"Oh yeah, I forgot about that one. Did ya ever get that smell out of your sheets?"

"Kiss my ass . . . again with that?" Troy pauses for a second to pick up his beer that fell when Ty ran over a small log. "And no, I most certainly did not. I had to burn the sheets and throw out my damn mattress. Shit's not funny, dude."

Ty looks at Hudson and winks. "She partook a lil too much hooch and purged all over his bed."

"Dayum, Troy!"

"Yeah, apparently I have that effect on women."

"You give her some of that family shine?"

"Naw, man . . . Well, maybe just a skosh. Hell, she was fine until we toked the skunk. She lost her shit all over my bed. First she passed out, so I rolled over and fell asleep. I woke up to a nasty mess. Bad night, dude. Smelled like buld chitlins."

"That girl is probably scarred for life."

"Naw, I carried her to the bathroom. Told'r she heaved in there. I'm a gentleman, not an asshole, ya know?! I actually dated her for a while, but never had the heart to tell her what she did to my sheets."

"*Gentleman* is not quite how I would describe ya, but neither are you an asshole. So, you don't tell her, but then ya tell Ty?"

"Well, he asked about the smell. Tell'n ya, cuz, it was bad . . . I dunno what that poor girl ate, but mixed with a lil hooch it was like get'n sprayed by a skunk."

"Brother, cousin Troy's foul-smell'n secret is secure with me," Ty injects with a famous Lee shit-eat'n grin, as they say in the South.

"Hell no it ain't! You told the fellas five minutes after I told you! It was all I could do not to let that poor girl hear about that shit."

"Why did y'all go your separate ways? The sheets?"

"Naw, son. She was a good girl. I really did like'r. She ended up going into the Coast Guard after college. I still hear from her sometimes. She's a marine inspector or some shit like'at."

"Huh? So, what I'm hear'n is that she leaves you and makes something out of herself?" Hudson sarcastically asks, to his brother's amusement.

"Welp, I guess that is one way to look at it . . . ya smartass." Troy chuckles as he replies. Troy and Ty welcome back the ol' sarcastic Hudson, who has cleverly used their intoxicated minds to fool them into believing he is the same ol' boy who left years ago. Meanwhile, Hudson sits there forcing one grin after another to his face. He thinks about how these ridiculous stories would normally amuse him. Ty and Troy make it seem so easy to laugh. He would do anything to feel that exuberance once again. He would love to fully enjoy the hysterically filthy adventures of Ty and Troy. All he can muster, though, is a big, fake smile as he trades verbal jabs with his brother and cousin. His energy and motivation to keep up this act are wearing thin. He just wants to get back to his house, enjoy solitude, and get wasted like that poor girl. He wants to be as oblivious to the world as she was that night. Maybe, with no one there to take care of him, he will just choke on his own vomit.

After they return to the house, Hudson sits in the basement family room with his mama, dad, and sister. During their conversations,

Savannah mentions that she and Grayford are still heading to Topsail Island, North Carolina, for a week. Savannah and Gray planned their trip to the beach long before Hudson announced he was separating from the Marines. When he told them the approximate date of his return, his mother and father wanted to cancel their trip; however, Hudson insisted they go and enjoy the late-season trip to the beach. He likes the idea of having the farm to himself. No one there to interrupt the whippoorwill. When his mama brings up the trip again, Hudson initially worries that she'll ask him to feed her little dog, Macy, while they're gone. He wants no responsibility to interfere with his destiny. Fortunately, she plans to take her little Macy May with them. Hudson tells his mama that he will come by to check on the place while they are gone. He tells her how he missed the song of the whippoorwill. She tells him that the bird will fly farther south soon, but should still be here ready to sing to him. She has no clue that she just told her beloved son his bird will be singing while death escorts him from this life.

# CHAPTER FIVE

# WHIPPOORWILL

**D**ays before Hudson shipped off to bootcamp, Gray and Savannah held a covered-dish gathering for family and friends to wish him well on his travels. Some folks congratulated him as if he were heading off on an exciting adventure to explore the world, and maybe Hudson thought the same. Savannah, though, hated the high likelihood that her baby boy was going off to war in a time of global turmoil. She often grieved as though she already received the grim news and folded flag, but never let Hudson witness her sorrow. Gray was proud to see his son grow into a man and serve his country, but he, too, worried that he might be saying goodbye to his son for the final time. Gray and Savannah's emotional struggles mirrored that of all parents seeing their sons and daughters off to war. They did their best to hide those emotions, especially the night when they wished him well as everyone did—well, almost everyone.

Walter Lee sat outside all night, staring into a small fire burning in a stone pit. He could hear the distant voices coming and going wishing his nephew farewell. However, he made no attempt to join in the conversations, preferring silence and isolation as usual. He sat in the darkness on the edge of the fire's dim glow, sipping cheap beer while focusing his attention on the flames bouncing in the night. No one questioned why he was there if not to socialize; they had all become accustomed to his antisocial behavior. They wouldn't understand anyway, which is why he had yet to tell anyone how he lost most of his vision in his right eye and all his hearing in his right ear while fighting in the jungles and rice fields of Vietnam. He rarely talked much at all during that time of his life. He couldn't care less to talk to any of them that night, or any other night for that matter. He was not there for them. He was there for his nephew, who he knew was heading down a dangerous path. He knew all too well the internal war awaiting Hudson. He would provide Hudson with a glimpse of his future only if the young man asked for it. Until then, he would just keep the fire going, enjoy solitude, and leave celebratory farewells to the ignorant.

Hudson noticed his uncle a few times throughout that evening. He patiently waited for his uncle to talk to him, to answer his many questions. He knew Walt normally preferred to be left alone, but his patience finally ran out. The glow of the flames eerily reflected off Walt's glasses and face, which gave Hudson slight pause before approaching his uncle. He was not naive, he knew he would see the ugliest side of life, but wondered what caused his uncle to become such a recluse. Gray told Hudson stories of a wild and fun Walt during their childhood. That was before he went off to war, where something in those jungles permanently changed him. Hudson desperately wanted Walt's advice as he headed out to join the same Marine Corps his uncle served in so many years ago. He wanted to know the secrets Walt had never told anyone. He finally mustered up the nerve to go query his uncle for those experiences, approaching Walt from his left, so he could hear him.

"Uncle Walt?"

"Hudson," Walt replied, moving his head ever so slightly toward his nephew.

"You're pretty quiet as usual, Uncle Walt."

"Got noth'n to say . . . as usual, nephew."

"Well, I figured you'd be the one to give me some advice, as a Marine. You've been there, and I just . . . I'd like your advice on what to expect, Uncle Walt."

Walt looked at Hudson for a moment before turning back to the fire, and then answering in a low, deep growl, "What the fuck you want me to say, son? Want me to tell ya about honor or congratulate ya? Sounds like you got plenty of that bullshit fed to ya already."

"Well, shit, Uncle Walt, way to lift a man's spirit. Tell me how ya really feel," Hudson said, trying to lighten the mood in this dark and awkwardly unnerving moment.

"You think what you are about to do is a fuck'n joke?" Walt asked in that same low growl. Just as Hudson began stuttering a reply, Walt continued: "Lemme give ya some real advice, because they don't know shit, Hudson. You best remember the good, innocent life you've enjoyed up til now, because you'll never have that shit again. You will be the crazy, broken sumbitch sit'n alone staring into the fire, haunted by your unfortunate survival and the faces of the dy'n decades later . . . good dayum people dy'n . . . people that deserve to be here, while everybody else just goes on about their ignorant fuck'n lives like noth'n ever happened."

"Well, Uncle Walt, if not me, then who? Someone has to step up to fight terrorist assholes."

"Yeah . . . Why not your poor country ass, right?"

"Not doing it for the pay or cos I'm poor, Uncle Walt. It's my duty . . ."

"I don't doubt your patriotism, son. I doubt the motives of the devils sending your ass to hell."

"I don't concern myself with the motives of some—"

"Maybe you ought to." Walt cut off Hudson with a quick retort.

"What good will that do, Uncle Walt? Some leaders in this country will be corrupt, but I think most of them mean well and are patriotic. They are try'n to do the right thing," Hudson replied with the same sharp tongue as his uncle.

"Bullshit! Right thing by their own greed. Don't let inexperience and ignorance convince you otherwise. They are not leaders, they are representatives. They are supposed to represent you and every other fuck'n citizen of this country, but they don't. They're really only concerned more with their own job security, control, and pleasing the elite. And as far as their patriotism . . . well, that shit stops when it's time for their own to step up to that front line."

"I know y'all had no support from many folks back then, Uncle Walt, but shit has changed since then."

"Nah, same shit, different war . . . different way of spit'n in your face. Listen here, son, your family has neither money nor power. Those with money and power will send your poor country ass to the front line to ensure they keep both. You will see action soon enough. When you do, all that matters is your fellow Marines. Motherfuckers'll die for you, and you for them. They will be the ones who remember your ass, not the ones who sent ya."

Hudson sat quietly for a moment while he digested Walt's angry words. He thought Uncle Walt was just a bitter man who hated big brother and the powerful puppeteers who controlled the politicians. Hudson knew there was honor in serving his country and was put off by his Uncle Walt's bitter advice. However, he failed to realize that his uncle was as loyal to his country and what it stood for as any other. He did not understand that Uncle Walt became bitter when he, and all those who made tremendous sacrifices to retain freedom, were sent to foreign lands to fight other poor, loyal soldiers in the name of honor, only to return to this great country to find freedom dwindling from within. Upon their return home, Uncle Walt and his fellow Marines were met with vile greetings from those who had the right connections to avoid the battlefield. Walt's contempt was just as much with those people as with those who continued to divide this country so they could retain power.

Walt leaned forward toward his nephew as he delivered more dismal advice: "Hudson, along the way you may put down some truly evil people. Their deaths will give you some peace from what will come. You may also deliver death to some who are just like you, fight'n a war to defend their version of patriotism. The only folks sleeping peacefully will be the ignorant and the greedy sons of bitches sit'n safely up in their ivory towers, far away from the brutality of the war that they wage. The devil never dwells in Hell; he convinces other poor souls to go in his place." Walt sat back, and then once again faced the flames and smoke.

Hudson stood to walk over to his brother and cousin, disappointed by his conversation with Walt. A young man wanted to believe he was doing the right thing. Walt had the opportunity to provide such reassurance, but instead offered the truth of his experience.

"Hudson."

"Uncle Walt?"

"I'll save you a place by the fire in case you return." Walt's attention never strayed from the flames as he extended his invitation to his nephew. He could not bring himself to burn another dying face into his memory.

"I look forward to it, Uncle Walt." Hudson's reply told Walt that his nephew greatly undervalued his advice.

Hudson did indeed go off to war and return home, but he never left the battlefield. He now understands the painfully honest advice provided by Uncle Walt. Walt didn't warn him of the torment to scare or anger him, but to prepare him. Hudson now dwells in the same hell as his uncle did. Now, he knows why no one escapes Hell. Now, he knows that the flames of Hell depicted in many paintings and recounted in all those stories throughout human existence are not what they seem. The lake of fire does not really consume the body. The flames of Hell don't burn the body at all. Physical pain would provide relief from the true pain of Hell. For Hudson, there is only one way to remove the painful memories Hell burned into his every thought. Though his depression started before his friend's death, Hank's permanent residence in Hudson's mind has deepened his mental misery. The life lived in war will never release Hudson. The eighteen years of normal, happy life are no match for the one second that snatched the breath from his dear friend, a friend who would have made everything bearable. A friend who was his only chance to escape war. A friend who Hudson feels died because of him. Now, Hudson either lives a slow, painful death as did Walt by those campfires, or he extinguishes all light and ends the pain in an instant. Hudson had long made up his mind before his journey back to the farm. His world is too cold for any campfire to warm. The flames will only reflect the hell he lives, as they did for Walt; however, he does not possess the fortitude of his uncle.

On the backside of the farm sits a small fishing pond. Hudson sits down on the bank by the pond, resting his back against an old sweetgum tree. He listens as tree frogs fill the forest with constant noise while he waits for the whippoorwill's arrival with that familiar song. One last song to send him off from this wretched world. He tries to free his head of all thoughts and memories, but, once again, Hank stops by for a visit.

"You awlright, son?"

"Yeah. Just ready to get back home, I guess."

"You tired of me already?"

"Nah, I enjoy your colorful insight on life. I'd just rather enjoy your bullshit back home. I'm ready to do some fish'n, eat some buld peanuts, drank Natties, and watch the Dawgs."

"Watch 'em lose. Tide gonna roll over their ass. Saban got them boys undefeated. Bama is back, baby!"

"Yeah, yeah. They paid enough for his ass. He better win someth'n."

"Yeah, well, I will be there soon, dawg. Already submitted my application and everythang. I'm get'n student tickets, my brotha. You come'n with me when they play your puppies, right?"

"Dawgs, bitch! And hell yeah! Loser buys the beer. I'll keep it cheap for ya . . . Natties!"

"Best save yo money now, because I only drank the good shit."

That was the moment it zipped by them. A grenade landed just on the other side of Hank before Hudson could return a witty response. The explosion brings Hudson's attention back to the present. He was just talking to his Marine brother, his good friend, about college football. Now, he sits alone under a sweetgum tree with a bottle of whiskey, surrounded by darkness and critters of the night. A light breeze pushes through the trees, falling still afterward as though the world has just let out its last breath. Hudson closes his eyes and inhales through his nose, smelling the dying leaves of fall. The frogs and other nightly creatures silence their conversation as they, too, await the singing nightjar of summer to deliver his final concert before migrating further south. The absence of sound seems to go on forever, filling Hudson's ears with emptiness. Hudson stares into the pond's black water, quietly praying for that song. Just as he gives up hope and picks up the revolver, the whippoorwill breaks through the silence. Reverberating throughout the once muted forest are the repeating lyrics Hudson desperately desires this night. Upon hearing the first note, Hudson looks up to the treetops as he recalls the boy doing the same by those campfires so long ago. To the surface come his deepest emotions. The boy cries while the man remains made of stone. As the boy's tears stream down his cheeks, the man raises the pistol to his head, pulls back the hammer, and takes in another deep breath, smelling those dead leaves. The bird sings louder and louder, persistently begging the man to lay down his gun, to begin the rest of his life and not end his old life; however, the bird is too late. The man is too empty, has too much regret, and too much to forget. Death scares the boy, but the man welcomes the thought above all else. He will never return from war. He will never be normal. He will only wound the hearts of all who love him and whom he loves. Only dry eyes remain where tears were once shed. The severe mental affliction of the man deprives the boy of all hope. He continues looking to the treetops, not for the singing bird who performs from the brush, but to beg God for forgiveness. He prays his family will heal from the pain his death is sure to deliver. He prays for their forgiveness.

He apologizes to his friend. He apologizes to the boy. The song stops. Hank Williams was right: the whippoorwill's song is full of sorrow, and now he is too sad to sing.

"Forgive me, God!" Hudson begs aloud. His chest expands and collapses violently as he prepares for his departure from life. The silence returns after Hudson's short prayer. He shuts his eyes. Visions of the boy flood his thoughts before ebbing to black, ridding the mind of all distractions. He takes one last deep breath, relaxes his body, and presses the barrel of the gun into his temple. This time all cylinders are loaded in the .38. With his finger on the trigger, Hudson begins to squeeze the life from his body. "Is this how you felt, Hank? I failed you, brother."

— CHAPTER SIX —

# NIGHTMARE

North Topsail Beach in Pender County, North Carolina, is a less well-known stretch of white sandy shores than those found south of the Outer Banks and north of Wilmington. This barrier island provides refuge for folks looking to avoid the droves of tourists swarming endlessly up and down the more popular beaches. The glorious sand dunes stand tall, protecting the beach houses and coastal landscape from the fury of storms that use the ocean as a means of passage to attack the shore. When the storms are away, the beach awaits morning strolls with nearly pristine sand as the orange sun peeks over the Atlantic. Open windows invite in the uninterrupted rhythm of crashing waves that hypnotize the mind into stages of enlightenment while people sleep. North Topsail Beach in early fall offers visitors more beach space with fewer people for half the price of summer, which makes it the ideal vacation venue for a couple of middle-aged people on a tight budget looking to enjoy the tranquil side of life.

Savannah and Gray settled into their North Topsail Island condo before heading to a local seafood restaurant for brunch. Hudson had occupied most of the conversations so far during this trip. They both could tell something was troubling their son. They hoped that the

Hudson who had left for the Marines would eventually return after being home for a while. However, they have seen war stick with men for many years after returning home. Walt had struggled with the memories until the day he died. In his final year on this earth, he made an honest attempt to escape Vietnam. After years of declining trips to the memorial, Walt finally drove up to D.C. and read the names of those faces that had resided in his head for all of those years. He released all of his pent-up anger and sadness. He attended church a time or two to make peace with God. He finally made it home just before he passed away, freeing his spirit from all those malicious demons. Walt's slow turnaround took more than three decades, far longer than Gray and Savannah hope it will take Hudson.

After brunch, Savannah falls asleep on the couch while reading a book. Gray continues to read his book as she sleeps. Sleep has not come easy to Savannah for the past four years, so Gray figures she could use the sleep more than a late-morning walk on the beach. Gray lowers his book for a moment to look at the cloudless sky through the sliding glass door. His thoughts drift to past vacations with his wife and children. A young Hudson combed the undisturbed morning sand for shark teeth and shells. He remembers the pride and joy in Hudson's eyes when he found his first tooth. Hudson tied the tooth to a thin strap of leather and wore it as a necklace for years. Gray smiles as his eyes fill with tears. He silently prays to God that the boy will return home safely, because the man who visited the farm is still in harm's way. Gray saw the troubled man Hudson tried to hide; the same man his brother hid in plain sight for all those years.

Gray's fond memory is abruptly interrupted by Savannah's scream. She cries hysterically as she scrambles to rise from the couch. Startled by her screams, Gray slings his book to the floor as he jumps up from his chair. He runs over to Savannah, who has finally managed to get to her feet. She struggles to speak coherently as she screams about death. Gray desperately tries to understand what has her so upset.

"Sav, Savvy! Baby! What's the matter? Sugah . . . settle down and tell me what's the matter, hun!"

Gray gently puts his palms on her cheeks, rubbing away her tears with his thumbs. However, his calming demeanor is met with panic. Savannah tries to focus on Gray, but her heart nearly beats through her chest, and she begins hyperventilating. Her pale skin pours out beads of sweat. Her eyes are red and wide open. She seems to look through Gray, as though confined in a tragic place where her nightmare exists in reality. Gray hands her a bottle of water and attempts to hold her in his arms, but her frantic mind refuses his calming gestures. Savannah pushes Gray away from her, slings the water across the room, and then screams, "Hudson . . . Hudson's in trouble!"

"Savvy? Ya just had a bad dream, hun. Just a dream. Hudson's fine!" Gray uses a tissue from the box on the table next to the couch to wipe the sweat and tears from Savannah's face.

"No, Gray! No! My baby is in trouble . . . Death is comin' fohwuh him! Death is comin' fohwuh my baby boy!" Savannah hysterically yells as she pushes past Gray, running to the bedroom, where she throws clothes into her suitcase. Gray has never seen such terror in his wife's eyes. The look on her face scares the life out of him. He has never heard such fear in her voice. He continues his attempts to calm Savannah, but she only repeats that death is coming for Hudson. Gray knows no words possess the ability to temper Savannah's worry for her children. She never describes the details of her nightmare, and he knows not to ask. Whatever it was has convinced her that Hudson is in serious trouble. Though it was just a nightmare, Gray knows Savannah is right about Hudson. A mother's connection with her children is a force science cannot explain. Some call it intuition, but it is far more than intuition, far more than just a gut feeling. A mother feels her child's pain and sorrow as though it is her own. She can't describe the nightmare, because what Savannah saw is not as frightening as what she felt. She felt his desolation. She felt death's cold hand on his shoulder. She felt Hudson's satisfaction upon death's arrival.

Normally a cautious driver, Gray uses a heavy foot to shed as much time off the trip home as he can without ending up in a ditch. The traffic is light, and the troopers are not waiting on the side of the interstate now that summer is gone. Other than topping off the tank, they make no stops. Savannah quietly sits in the passenger seat steadily wiping tears from her eyes. She stares out the window at the scenery along the interstate, but notices nothing. Her mind is already home dealing with tragedy.

"He didn't pick up again, hun. I left'm anothuh message. I'm sure he's fine," Gray says as he tucks his phone back into his shirt pocket.

"Stop say'n that! You know he's not! I see feeyuh in yowuh eyes, too, Gray!" Savannah grows hysterical as panic consumes her again.

"You're right, Savannah, I know he's troubled. I just . . . We . . . we'll go straight to his house."

"Why won't he ansuh his dayum phone, Gray? I just know someth'n has happened. I can feel it. I can just feel it. God, please help'm . . . save our boy!" Heavy streams of tears flow from her eyes again as she passionately conveys her worries to Gray.

Gray continues his attempts to provide strength for Savannah, though fear for his son strangles the breath from him. He knows Savannah is too terrified to listen to him anyhow. She is convinced death is there to snatch the life from their son. Gray figures it is best not to say anything else. Instead, he reaches over and rubs her shoulder for a brief moment, and then gently grabs her hand. She immediately squeezes his hand with all her might, releasing a lot of the fear and panic that consumes her. Gray silently begs God to watch over their son. He fights back tears as the thought of Hudson's death consumes his mind. He must be strong for Savannah.

They drive straight to Hudson's house. His truck is not in the driveway, but the garage door is closed. They ring the doorbell and knock on the front and back doors. The lights are off, shades are drawn, and the inside is quiet. They try his phone again, but it goes straight to voicemail. They call anyone who may know Hudson's whereabouts, but no one has seen or talked to him since the reunion fish fry. They sit on his front porch for a bit, hoping he'll show. But after about an hour of waiting, Gray finally convinces Savannah to leave as the sun sets over northeast Georgia. They leave a note on Hudson's door, begging him to call when he comes home.

Neither of them spots Hudson's truck behind the trees as they speed by the first gate. Hudson purposely hid it in case his brother or sister happened to come out to the farm to check on the house. Back at their own house, Savannah and Gray don't waste time unpacking the car. They go inside and once again call Troy, Ty, Maddie, and anyone they can think of to see if they saw or talked to Hudson. Everyone says the same thing: his damn phone goes straight to voicemail.

Gray is on the phone with Ty, telling him about Savannah's dream, when he hears the unmistakable pop from the backside of the farm. He immediately looks at Savannah to see if she heard the same thing.

"That was a dayum gunshot, Savannah!"

"What in the hell did—" Ty starts to ask before Gray cut him off.

"I'll call ya back, son. Somebody's shoot'n guns pretty dayum close."

"Be careful now, Deddy."

Gray goes into the basement closet, grabs the twelve-gauge, some shells, and a flashlight, and heads to the front deck. He shines the flashlight across the pasture and back toward the pond area.

"You see anythang?" Savannah yells.

"Naw, I don't see a dadgum thang. I'm goin down to the pond to take a look."

"Grayford James Lee, don't you even thank about it! Yowuh not gonna do any such foolish thang by yowuhself! Call Ricky and have him come ova to go with ya."

Ricky, a family friend, lives about three miles away from the farm and can be there rather quickly, but Gray can't wait that long. The feeling in Gray's gut tells him this mysterious gunshot was the messenger of the news he and Savannah feared most. The thought of coming across some stranger spotlighting deer on his property comforts him. Even the thought of a crazy killer gives him peace. However, Gray knows a stranger did not shoot a gun down by the pond. He knows who pulled that trigger.

— CHAPTER SEVEN —

# STRANGER

**A**cry from the dark abruptly interrupts the silence. Hudson opens his eyes to blackness. Seized by confusion, he sits lifeless, awaiting another cry to fill the nothing in his ears. Mary and whiskey play in his mind during this period absent of sound. They were the source of the cry. Had to be—cried out from within his head. He shakes his head to snap from his trance and rid his thoughts of the distraction. He offers death no further delay. He squeezes his eyelids together once again only to see Hank flash before him yelling words he cannot hear. As Hudson strains to hear his friend, an even louder cry belts out. Reflexes force open his eyes again. He watches as Hank fades into the dark forest. He gazes across the black water as he contemplates the origin of the cries that overpowered his friend's words. He lowers his pistol and pushes forward to one knee, and then fumbles around for his flashlight. Once in his hand, he shines the light toward the other side of the pond, but whiskey and Mary distort his view. Blurry trees and dying leaves conceal who cries. Hudson slowly rises to his feet while keeping the light pointed across the pond. He walks to the corner of the dam, hoping the trees reveal the crying animal who interrupted his journey; however, the stubborn trees refuse to cooperate, so Hudson picks up the pace to a quick jog. Curiosity temporarily controls all thought. Death is absent for the moment. He turns the far corner of the dam to find two eyes reflecting back at the light in his hand. Hudson slows to a cautious walk. He lowers the light to where he can still see without blinding the eyes staring back at him. There, backed up to a young maple tree, is a big reddish-brown dog. His legs are wet and muddy from the soft banks of the pond. He holds his right paw up in the air while attempting to keep his eyes on Hudson and something else over by the pond—he is spooked by both. Pleading whimpers instantly shift to threatening growls as the dog retreats. Hudson stops in his tracks so he does not spook the dog, providing a pause in time to earn the dog's trust. With no leaves shattering or twigs snapping under his feet, Hudson is able to hear movement coming from the pond; something moving quickly toward the dog. He turns, bringing the light with him.

"Whoa . . . shit!" Hudson blurts out.

Hudson immediately recognizes the true threat to the dog. A copperhead slithers toward the big fella, ready to deliver its toxic gift. Hudson instinctively raises the .38, points it at the snake, and fires the round that was earlier meant for him. The snake twitches as though frightened before disappearing into the dead leaves covering the ground. Hudson turns back to the dog, who trembles from the snake and gunshot, but has muffled his growls for the moment.

"All right, big fella, I intend on help'n ya. I need you to trust me. Easy now . . . easy boy . . . easy." Hudson repeats the reassuring message with every short step he takes toward the terrified animal. The dog, still wary of the stranger, matches each of Hudson's steps with one in retreat. Mud and blood cover his reddish-brown fur from head to tail. Dried blood covers his enormous head, which bares nasty scars as Hudson closes in on him. He welcomes Hudson with a snarl, raising his top lip to reveal his weapons. Hudson halts again, repeating his calming message, hoping to gain the dog's trust. He knows the animal has no chance of survival if he does not help him. The head wound still produces fresh blood, and Hudson has no doubt the copperhead dug his venomous fangs into the dog's leg.

Hudson shines the light back on himself, so the dog can see him. The big fella can now see into the eyes of the stranger, and so suppresses the rising beast. The stranger appears to have good intentions in those eyes. The dog understands the grave nature of his situation and wants to trust the stranger, but stubborn memories recall the last stranger to enter his life. Just like when he followed the other stranger, he senses death around this stranger. No family is here to betray him this time, and he refuses the executioner's other distractions. He ignores the pain, fear, and desperation as he studies the stranger's every move. The beast will not remain absent this time, and the beast sees clearly. This stranger holds in his unlit hand the same weapon as the last stranger. From the deepest pit of his tortured soul charges his most vicious warrior, petrifying his enemy with his battle cries.

"Whoa now, hold the hell up, big boy!" Hudson shouts as he takes a step or two in retreat before continuing, "I ain't try'n to hurt you, dammit. I don't give a shit if you kill me—you will actually be doin me a favor. I'm just try'n to save your ass right now . . . we can both die here and now if ya want?"

The beast wants to attack, but the dog wants help. The beast is strong, but the dog is weak. He lunges at Hudson's arm only to fall directly to the ground. His muscular legs are weakened by his wounds, fatigue, and poisoned blood. Hudson backs away as the big fella struggles to stand again. He stops as he recognizes the dog's focus is on his right hand. He slowly and carefully makes the pistol safe, and then slides the gun into his back pocket. He shines the light on himself again, holds up his now-empty right hand as he pleads with the dog, "I intend to help ya, boy. I just want to help ya is all. See, I secured my weapon. My weapon is gone. Now, how about you put yours away? Let me help ya. You need help . . . that's all I'm try'n to do."

The beast reluctantly retreats as the dog fights for his life. He has no choice but to trust this stranger; although, he is in this dire situation because he followed the last stranger he met. This stranger is different, but just as dangerous. He senses that this stranger aims to cause harm, but not to him. The last stranger unfortunately leaves him no choice but to trust this stranger. He stows his weapons and silences his battle cry, gaining the stranger's trust. Hudson slowly reaches out his friendly hand toward the dog. With the little strength he has left, the rednose sniffs Hudson's hand; the same hand that intends to kill Hudson aims to save him. Without the strength of the beast, the weak dog collapses onto the ground. Hudson has witnessed life fade from many eyes and the dog offers the same desperate look. He can afford to waste no more time convincing the dog to trust him.

"All right, big guy! Either you bite me or not, but I need to get your big ass to the doctor if you're gonna have a chance to live!"

Hudson scoops up the dog and begins the long sprint to his truck. The dog looks up to the stranger and licks his face, causing Hudson to pull back his head. "Dammit! Quit that nasty shit, now." The dog nearly goes limp right after the kiss. The big fella is a heavy load, causing Hudson's arms and shoulders to burn. The steep hill causes his legs to swell, becoming tighter with every step. He didn't plan a return trip. He damn sure didn't intend to sprint up and down hills for nearly half a mile back to the truck with nearly eighty pounds in his arms and a gut full of Tennessee's finest. The shots of whiskey he threw back while waiting on the bird to sing boil and slosh in his gut. He pushes his physical limits; however, he is a Marine who is trained to ignore pain, overcome fatigue, and be fearless to accomplish any mission. His original mission remains, but he must save the dog right now. Maybe God will look more favorably on him for saving the dog, but that is not his reason to save this dog. Hudson's heart is too big to let this poor fella die a miserable, lonely death. He feels only he deserves such an ending.

Hudson finally reaches the truck. He purges the boiling whiskey from his stomach as his lungs fight to catch a good breath. His heart pounds through his chest. *No time for weakness,* he thinks. He gently lays the dog down on the passenger seat of his old F-150. He runs around the truck and hops up onto the driver's seat, gives the gas pedal a pump or two, and then starts her up. He opens his driver's door to get the rest of that whiskey out of his gut. As he spits out the taste of regurgitated Old Number 7 and reaches up to shut the door, he looks over toward the homeplace. Someone is there, shining a light in his direction.

"Shit! Who the hell is that?" Hudson ponders aloud.

Hudson has no time to worry about who's standing behind that light. He stomps the gas pedal, kicking up dust and rock as he tears out through the open gate onto the dirt road. He keeps the truck in the middle of the road to give himself room to slide and correct as he rips down the dusty path. He looks over at the nervous dog, who's fighting for his life.

"You're gonna be just fine. Lay back, big fella, and listen to Mississippi John Hurt do some pick'n. He'll ease your worry as he once did mine a long time ago."

On the way down Highway 15, Hudson thinks about the person shining that light. He wonders if his mama and father came back early. That light was damn sure bright enough to be the spotlight Gray keeps by the front door. Their return home angers him, as though they intentionally ruined his chosen departure from this world. He does not honestly believe they did such a thing intentionally, but his whiskey-soaked mind and the voice of Mary make the idea plausible. To his ignorance, whiskey and Mary are right this time—they indeed returned early with the intent to save their son. Then it hits him like a punch in his now-empty gut: *They heard the shot!* He will need to come up with a story to tell. Normally, carrying guns in the woods would require no explanation, quite the common practice out here in the country, but Maddie had to tell that damn suicide story. The worry he witnessed in the eyes of his mama will motivate the most intrusive line of questioning she has ever unleashed upon him. All because of that damn story. He has to be ready with one of his own just in case. He will be ready to lie again. His lies worked then, and they should work again. His whole life is a lie—living is a lie. When the time comes, death will finally reveal the truth.

# CHAPTER EIGHT

# NO NAME

D ark country highways tend to relieve a troubled mind. The dark blinds the mind of all but that little piece of the world lying just ahead in the lights. The eyes and thoughts only focus on right here, right now. Out of sight and out of mind is the rest of this big world, and every problem with it. He listens to his favorite bluesman pick and sing away while the engine hums and the wind whistles by his window, all the while keeping his mind as black and empty as the world beyond the lights. It feels good to feel nothing. However, good feelings are short-lived in a damaged mind. This is just life dangling that damn carrot.

Oconee Animal Care is the only twenty-four-hour veterinary emergency room within an hour's drive from Whippoorwill Hollow. Dr. Frank Howard and Hannah Henson are on the night shift when Hudson backs through the door, carrying the dog's limp body.

"Can I help you, sir?" Hannah asks Hudson as he turns, revealing the big dog in his arms.

Hudson's head snaps to attention as he turns around and tells the young lady what happened to the big dog in his arms. "This dog was bit by a copperhead about an hour ago." Hudson leans back a little bit to hold the dog's front half up just a little higher, and then continues, "Bit right here, just above his right paw."

"Do you know how many times?"

"As far as I can tell, it got'm just one time. I don't know . . . got'm good enough to give'm some bad shit. He also has a wound on his head. That's where the blood's come'n from."

"OK, well, let me notify Dr. Howard and get some information from ya, sir." Hannah picks up the phone to call the doctor, but he walks into the front room before she can dial a single digit.

"Hannah, could you . . . uh oh, what do we have here?" the doc asks Hannah as he looks at the dog in Hudson's arms.

"Well, mister, umm . . ." Hannah pauses for Hudson to provide his name.

"Hudson Lee."

"Mr. Lee's dog—what's his name, sir?" Hannah pauses once again.

"Not my dog. Don't know his name," Hudson immediately answers.

"OK, Mr. Lee, what can you tell me about the dog? What's the problem?" Dr. Howard jumps into the conversation and gets straight to the point of Hudson's visit.

"He was bit by a copperhead about an hour ago. One time, I believe."

"You sure it was a copperhead?"

"Yeah."

"Are you sure?"

"I am pretty damn sure it was a copperhead. Looka here—he also has a wound on his head."

"It is important that we know the species, Mr. Lee."

"Doc, it was a copperhead! I've seen 'em before."

"All right then. How'd he get that wound on his head?"

"I have no idea. He had it when he wandered up and got bit by that snake. Now I can see it, it looks like a small-caliber bullet wound."

"Dadgum, sure does. Now, tell me all the symptoms you've seen since the bite."

"Well, here's the puncture wounds. The leg seems to have swollen a bit; other than that, he shit and puked all over the passenger seat inside of my damn truck."

Dr. Howard takes a close look at the swelling and wound while continuing his questions. "What happened to the snake, Mr. Lee?"

"I shot it, but I don't think I killed it. Damn thang slithered off into the dark." Hudson answers while trying to calm the dog, who was waking up to more strangers and the bright lights of the hospital.

"You shot it, ya say? Were you taking a nightly stroll through the woods when you happened upon the dog and snake? Or where were ya when this happened?" Dr. Howard asks while looking at the dog's head.

"What does it matter what the hell I was doing, Doc?! The dog was bit by a copperhead. I brought his ass here to see if y'all can help'm. I'll fill out any paperwork y'all need, and then I'd prefer to be on my way."

"Well, hold on there, Mr. Lee! Treatment for the snake bite and venom will be rather costly. He is not your dog, as you said, and quite frankly he looks to belong to no one anymore, at least no one who wants him. As you pointed out, this wound on his head looks to be a gunshot wound—not too old, either, maybe a day or two. So, the bottom line here is, I can't use expensive antivenom on him and patch up his wound with no home or owner to go back to. He looks to have lived a hard life, so I'm sure there are other medical needs for this fella. Also, the type of dog he is and the injuries that I can see at first look—well, I'd be willing to bet he was a fight'n dog who was thrown out once he was all used up. These dogs don't make good family pets after being trained to fight . . ."

"Look, Doc, I know where you are going with this. If you think it is best to put the dog down, then go on and do it."

"Mr. Lee, I don't mean to interrupt, but that is horrible. Sounds like you just went through a lot to save this dog, only to say euthanize him? Makes no sense," Hannah says.

"Dammit, he is not my dog nor my responsibility! I am the last fuck'n person who should be responsible for'm."

"Mr. Lee, Hannah's right, and you didn't leave it alone because that is not who you are . . ."

"Not who I am? What? Doc, ya got no idea who the hell I am . . . I shoulda just let his ass be." Hudson takes a breath in frustration and then continues his thought: "Sometimes it is just time to die. Maybe this is his time."

"Mr. Lee, what I meant by that is that you obviously had it in your heart to save him. Someone who'd do such a kind act for a beat-up stray like this . . . well, just doesn't seem you'd do all this just to see him die anyhow."

"I did what most folks would do. I acted on impulse . . . a moment of sympathy is all."

"How about that sympathy now, Mr. Lee?" Hannah asks, trying to persuade Hudson to save the dog.

"Maybe sympathy is to put him out of his damn misery," Hudson replies after glaring at Hannah for a brief moment.

An awkward silence falls upon the room after Hudson's response. He glares at the dog. His glare turns into sympathy. He is full of anger, but none of it belongs to the dog. The sympathy he has for the mangled stray is a mystery to him. Hudson wanted to be put out of his misery, but he cannot project his desires onto the dog. The dog didn't just roll over and give up after being shot in the head and left to die. He continued to fight for survival. He must want to live. He must want life.

"Mr. Lee? I need to know what to do here, son," the doc says, breaking the awkward silence, "I don't want him to suffer any longer if—"

"How much to treat him? How much to find him a home?" Hudson cuts off the doc. He just wants to finish what he set out to do. He knows treating the dog and finding him a home will take time and lots of money. He doesn't care about the money, but the time is what will eat him up. The longer he breathes, the longer his mental agony continues.

"About twelve to fifteen hundred for costs. Maybe up past two grand depending on what we have to do for him. I can't give you an answer for locating a home, Mr. Lee. That will be up to you. What do you want to do?"

Hudson looks at the doctor while contemplating his options. He looks at the dog again. Maybe the remnants of that sour mash fermented whiskey cloud his mind with pity, or maybe his heart is just too big, but Hudson has but one option.

"Well . . ." Hudson throws up his hands in frustration. "Dammit ta hell . . . treat'm . . . Fix every fuck'n thang wrong with'm." Hudson continues under his breath, "Why the hell not save someth'n?!"

Hudson justifies his moment of pity with logic. He knows the odds of finding a home for the stray are much better if the dog is in good health, even if he is a trained fighter, maybe even a killer. His justification is a lie, though, just like the ones he told to his family. The truth is, Hudson hasn't got the heart to see death take this dog and, for the life of him, does not understand why. Sometimes, a big heart is a damn curse.

"You made the right choice, Mr. Lee," Hannah reassures Hudson with a smile that annoys the hell out of him.

"Just take the damn dog, please."

The doctor escorts Hudson back to the operating table. Hudson lays the dog on the table, and Dr. Howard immediately gives him a shot. The dog's eyes slowly close. Hudson watches in envy as the dog drifts off to that peaceful place, almost like the dog knows he'll be better off when he wakes up. Hudson wishes he could wake up in a better place, completely healed from his wounds. A wounded mind seems to never heal.

"Mr. Lee, I can take care of the medical issues, but you will need to take care of finding him a home."

Frank has a gut feeling that Hudson was not just on a stroll through the woods with a gun for protection. He can see something troubling in the young man's body language and attitude. He seems aggravated that saving the dog interrupted whatever he was up to. He doesn't know for certain that Hudson was out to harm anyone or himself, but something convinces him that Hudson needs to help this dog for his own sake. Frank doesn't question why this feeling gnaws at his gut, because he has wandered about this floating rock for a long time and learned to listen to that instinct of his long ago.

"Mr. Lee, why don't you come up with a name for the old fella? And make sure you leave a couple good numbers with Hannah. I'm not sure how long he will be here, but I imagine a week is a good estimate."

Hudson stands in silence for a second, staring down at the clipboard before answering, "Doc, I don't care what the hell ya call 'im. I'll find him that home and they can name'm."

"Humor me, Hudson—just write down a name."

Hudson looks up at the doc, annoyed by his persistence. "I dunno . . . shit . . ." He looks back down at the clipboard while mumbling, "What the hell does it matter?"

"I tell ya what, Mr. Lee, just think about a name and call us when you come up with someth'n. We'll list'm by your name for now. Hannah, will you please help Mr. Lee with the paperwork, and then join me back here."

"I sure will, Dr. Howard."

"Am I good to go after this shit's done? I need to go get a bite to eat," Hudson asks Hannah as he fills out the paperwork.

"Yes sir, Mr. Lee, you are good to go. Grab a late supper or early breakfast, and then you ought to go get some sleep. We'll give you daily updates. You really did make the right decision, Mr. Lee."

"Please, call me Hudson."

"OK. Have a good night, Hudson."

"Here ya go. For what it's worth, thank you for everything. You have a good night, too," Hudson says as he hands Hannah the clipboard.

Hannah looks up at Hudson and smiles as she responds, "Oh, you are most certainly welcome, Hudson! We will cawl you with those daily updates. Go on and get yourself a bite. Oh, and here is a couple of towels and cleaner . . . for the shit and puke."

After Hudson leaves, Hannah goes back to help Dr. Howard. He's already cleaned the wound and found that the snake bit the dog twice, so he begins the antivenom treatment. He looks up at Hannah as she prepares his instruments. "Hannah, did anything strike you odd with Mr. Lee?"

"He seemed awfully agitated."

"He sure did, didn't he? He also smelled of alcohol." Doc pauses while contemplating the situation before continuing, "Why do you think he was out in those woods in the middle of the night with a gun? Drank'n?"

"Well, my brother and cousins are always out at night with guns. They like to shoot armadillos, which are everywhere now."

"Hannah, do ya think Mr. Lee was hunt'n armadillos?" Doc asks with a hint of sarcasm.

"No, I don't think he was hunt'n armadillos, Frank. You just seem to be jump'n to a pretty big and terrible assumption about Mr. Lee, though," Hannah answers with just as much sarcasm as the doc.

"Did you notice how upset he got when I asked why he was out there with a gun?"

"Yes I did, but he—"

Frank knew what Hannah was about to say and interrupted her, "I'm not saying anything, Hannah. I'm just ask'n questions and think'n out loud, I guess. Hand me some dry bandages and tape, would ya please." Doc dresses the snake bite on the dog's leg before continuing his thought. "I've been around awhile, Hannah, long enough to know when a fella suffers from someth'n bad . . . hell, I don't know, maybe I'm wrong, but we ought to stay well engaged with young Mr. Lee to ensure he understands his responsibility to this dog. Maybe if he names him, well, he will have some sort of connection with the dog."

Frank stops for a second as Hannah hands him more bandages and tape. "Hannah, look here behind his ear. Looks like this dog was definitely shot recently. The wound is pretty fresh. Here, look here, bullet lodged on the top of his skull. Small caliber, just like Mr. Lee said, maybe a .22."

Sadness and shock take hold of Hannah as she looks at the bullet wound, "Oh my! It looks like it bounced off his thick skull. Who would do such an awful thang? Bless his heart!"

Hannah pauses as she surveys the dog's battered body. She sees more scars than she could count covering the dog's head. His body tells the same tragic story. Tears build in her eyes and roll down her cheeks as she thinks about the abuse he's suffered. She thinks about how cruelly he was treated by whoever owned him. She then thinks about the life he can have with the man who is willing to spend thousands of dollars to save a stray dog.

"I really hope Mr. Lee takes in this poor, damaged boy."

"Yeah, me too," Frank replies with the same sympathy as Hannah.

# CHAPTER NINE

# DIXIE DINER

Death was there to extinguish the flames of Hell engulfing Hudson, but life stoked his inferno with gasoline. He drives away from the animal hospital livid, disappointed, and dejected. He can only blame himself for intervening in death's attempt to spare them both from further pain. He can only blame himself for assuming responsibility for another life. He is in control of nothing, as guilt will not allow him to abandon his responsibility to the dog. He just wanted to drop it off, passing on any responsibility for the mangy stray, to be free to go. Death would have freed him, but now he must serve a longer sentence in the prison of life. To escape, he must break his promise to the doc, but his mind will not let go of that dog. That damned dog. The dog had obviously lived in Hell longer than Hudson, but, unlike Hudson, he seemed grateful for the opportunity to continue his life. Hudson justifies his own mental weakness by convincing himself that the dog simply knows no better. He does not know that death can bring him peace from this wretched life. Hudson wishes someone would put him out of his misery, as the dog's owner tried to do for the dog. His mind has managed to turn the devil into an angel of mercy. He tries desperately to persuade himself to break his promise, to let death take him and the dog. However, breaking the promise makes him sick to his stomach.

Hudson turns to his brother's homecoming gift again to deal with the nausea and mental struggle. Mary settles both.

On the way out of Watkinsville, before the road splits off to Highway 15, he finds the family-owned-and-run Dixie Diner. This fine-dining establishment is routinely visited by hunters, fishermen, church-goers, hellraisers, Dawg fans, and a plethora of others. The diner is owned by the Carter family, originally opened by Mary Beth and Thomas Carter. Tom tragically died a few years back, so now Mary Beth and their three daughters run the diner. Mary Beth's twin brothers, Joseph and Johnny Dalton, do the cooking. The twins can't get much of a job elsewhere on account of their mental challenges. Though they both have a severe learning disorder, they are amazing short-order cooks and love their job at the diner.

Mary not only idles Hudson's nausea and anger, she revs up his appetite. Hudson has not had much of an appetite for quite some time, so the thought of actually enjoying a bite to eat helps bed down that anger, at least for now while Mary accompanies him. Tonight, he is in the mood for breakfast food: scrambled eggs smothered in cheese, along with grits, sausage, and toast. He will fill his belly now, and then head home and fill the room with Floyd and his gut with whiskey until he passes out. He tosses back a couple Percocet before walking into the diner. By the time he gets home, he will damn sure feel nothing. By the third track of *Dark Side of the Moon*, he will remember nothing. The Marines taught him to adapt and overcome. Tonight he must do exactly that. Instead of death, he will just make a great mental escape from reality—from life.

Hudson strolls into the Dixie Diner fully under Mary's relaxing influence. He was furious at the world when he left the animal hospital, but now the world is a little more tolerable. Greeting him as he walks in is Katie Carter, the youngest of the three sisters. She is an absolutely stunning young woman with bright blue eyes and long straight blond hair that she puts up in a bun and holds in place with one of those little clips. She speaks with a delightful Southern drawl that reaches in and snatches the heart right out of most men. Hudson, though, is not most men, not at this point in his life. Love and lust must remain absent in his mind, regardless of the uncontrollable attraction building for this beautiful young woman.

Katie's blue eyes peek over toward Hudson, and with a soft Southern drawl she tells him, "I'll be right with ya, sir."

Hudson just nods before dropping his head toward the old tile floor. Shame and paranoia consume him. Mary sometimes convinces folks to worry about everything without explaining the reason. This time, Mary is not the culprit, though. Hudson was never shy toward women; however, he feels like less of a man at this point in his life. He wonders if it's because he was planning to kill himself. He wonders if she can see his shame or tell that he's not normal. He thinks, *There is a beautiful woman that some lucky, normal sumbitch will be able to spend the rest of his fuck'n life with, and I can't even look at her.* He despises that he is an outsider in his own mind, watching himself go through the motions of life. He should not even be here to feel this shame. He should be dead. Hudson thinks of Hank Jackson wanting to grow old with a good woman. He can hear Hank telling him, "If you don't talk to'er, then I will, son." His friend would inspire life if he were here, but he is not here, only Hudson is here. His stomach knots up again. He loses some of that appetite Mary provided him. He starts to turn toward the door, but before he can take a step the beautiful young lady quickly makes her way over to him.

"I'm sorry about that, sir! We're a lil busier than expected, and it's just me, Sissy, and Uncle Joe hold'n down the fort," Katie tells him.

Hudson snaps from his conversation with a ghost, presents a half-cocked smirk, a trait he inherited from his father, gives his head a little shake, and then replies, "Not a problem . . ." He pauses as he looks up at her without making eye contact. "As it turns out, I got all night." His eyes immediately fall back to that old tile floor.

"Well, dear, we are open until eleven, then you are on your own," Katie replies with a smile.

Hudson finally raises his head and locks eyes with the waitress. There is a slight moment of silence, but not one iota of awkwardness. He notices a strained smile from the beautiful waitress. She can't look directly at him. He thinks, *She can tell I am fucked up.*

"Would you like a bar seat or a booth, sir?" Katie says, interrupting the silence.

"Uh . . . booth please. Thank you!" No way Hudson wants a bar seat next to a bunch of strangers, inviting unwanted conversations.

Hudson follows behind the waitress with his gaze on the distant tile floor ahead. "Hudson," he says, offering his name.

Katie turns toward Hudson without looking directly at him. "OK, Hudson, here we are," she says smiling, "What can I get ya to drink?"

"Coffee and water please, ma'am."

"Katie . . . or Kate . . . Well, my friends and family always call me Katie, but it sounds so childish . . . in a good way I guess . . . anyway . . . Katie's fine." She looks up with a gentle smile, and this time allows her eyes to meet his eyes.

"OK, Katie . . . good to meet you!" Hudson again offers a smirk with his greeting, but this one is not forced. Silence lingers a little longer this time, as do the smiles.

"Likewise, Hudson! Be right back with your coffee and water," Katie says as she suddenly looks down and turns away from Hudson.

*What just happened?* Hudson thinks as he replays the interaction with Katie in his head. He sits there in the booth replaying every word and look they traded, mainly to make sure he didn't sound like an idiot, but also wondering if he correctly read something she said. She told him only friends and family call her Katie, and then she went on to tell him to call her Katie. Hudson allows his mind to travel down a road he knows has a dead end; however, something about the waitress races around in his head. Her beauty pleases his eyes, but something about her comforts his soul. He knows better than to envision a life with a woman, but he has no control over his mind right now. The painkillers have yet to kick in, but Mary sometimes causes folks to deeply contemplate certain thoughts. Something tells him that she may have her own demons eating away at her. She looked into his eyes for only a brief moment before shame pushed their attention down to the cold tile floor. At that moment, though, they wordlessly shared their painful stories with each other. Sometimes words cannot deliver the soul's message. He felt her sorrow and she felt his, but neither knew it at the time.

Hudson stares out the window into the parking lot, but he isn't looking at anything in particular. He is actually watching Katie's reflection in the window. He watches as they embrace each other; kiss each other; laugh, cry, and grow old with each other. He watches a life play out in the window that can never be. Hell doesn't allow such happiness. The reflection is only an illusion, serving only as a tease of what could have been. The window lies. His mind returns to reality as she approaches the booth.

"Here ya go," Katie says as she places coffee and water on the table. "And here is some creamer for your cawffee. Are you ready to order, Mr. Hudson?" Her eyes focus on her notepad. She, too, recognizes something unexplainable from this special customer. She does not dare allow herself to look directly at him. She does not dare allow herself to feel there is someone meant for her. She came to terms with her fate long ago.

"Sure. How about scrambled eggs with cheese, grits, sausage patties, and toast. Thanks!"

"Sure thang. Oh, you have a Marine Corps tattoo. When did you serve?" Katie stares at his forearm, still refusing to return to his eyes.

Hudson had changed out of his muddy and slightly bloody shirt into a plain white T-shirt prior to stepping out of his truck. The T-shirt exposes the Marine Corps tattoo on his forearm, one of a few on his arms. Hudson looks down at the tattoo for a brief moment before directing his eyes toward Katie. "The past four years. I just got home a few days ago."

His smile disappears and his eyes drift away from Katie as shame once again invades his mind. She may not know what he tried to do earlier and plans to finish later, but she might as well have been sitting right next to him by that pond. He can't hide the shame, the guilt, the pain, or any of the things eating him up inside. For a second he imagined having a normal life with a beautiful woman like Katie. No girl that beautiful and sweet will ever accept such a damaged soul into her life, nor should anyone as screwed up as him expect her to want anything to do with him. Uncle Walt warned him; he tried to prepare him for the struggle to come. Here it is. She deserves a good man, one who is mentally stable.

"I'm sure it does not make your sacrifices any easier, but thank you for your service, dear. My fiancé was in the Navy for a spell. He had a bit of trouble with the discipline required in the service, though. He didn't leave on good terms—they forced'm out. Anyway, thank you! I'll go put in your order for ya." Katie presents a genuine smile as she thanks Hudson, but her eyes remain on her notepad.

Hudson does not understand why her having a fiancé is hard to hear. Maybe because daydreaming about being normal with such a beautiful woman was the first halfway happy thought he'd had since recalling the monster bass he caught so many years ago on the Oconee. The dream had to end sometime during his visit to the Dixie Diner anyway. The search for good memories and thoughts of an impossible future is exhausting. He will walk out that door, find the damn dog a home, and reconvene his meeting with the charitable one.

Hudson keeps the conversation to a minimum for the rest of his meal. He eats, pays his bill, and tips Katie generously. He has no intention of saying anything else until she stops him as he approaches the door.

"Mr. Hudson, it was very nice to meet you. Please come back to see me—us—again," she says softly but sincerely.

"I'll try, Ms. Katie," Hudson replies with the same half-cocked smirk he presented when he first walked into the diner. Her remark confuses him, though. Did she feel what he felt? This night is full of confusion. She corrected herself to say *us*, but the soul desperately cried out for him to revisit her. Hudson does not realize that, though; he just figures she screwed up or was just being nice. He smiles at her before telling her to have a good night.

Katie smiles while forcing her eyes up to his. Once again, their eyes connect with a secret to tell. The moment seems like an eternity, but it's just a second at most—a much-needed pause in time. The power of a look can make speech impossible, a breath hard to catch, and a heart difficult to slow. This is one of those moments. A moment such as this makes no sense, as the mind fails to interrupt it with thought. Two strangers unknowingly sharing forever in a second. However, in a world where time is less gracious as it continues to advance, forever goes as quickly as it came. Katie abruptly breaks the connection. Her smile flees her pretty face while her skin instantly turns ghost white. Hudson recognizes the look in her eyes as he has seen fear take over many people before. He knows that look intimately. A voice booms from behind Hudson, filling the air with the ripe aroma of alcohol, "Katie! How about a booth, sweetheart!"

Sean Williamson, Katie's fiancé, barges into the diner with three other inebriated gentlemen. Hudson figures out pretty quickly who's just burst through the door demanding a booth. He thinks about something Katie said earlier, more precisely, the way she said it. She did not seem overly happy when she mentioned her fiancé. She damn sure does not seem happy or excited to see him and his friends walk through the door. None of it matters, though. This is none of his business. Hudson just nods at Katie and walks on past Sean and his friends.

Sean eyes Hudson as he passes him, and then turns to Katie, who looks as if she knows what's coming. "Who is your lil buddy, Katie?" he asks in that certain way to taunt Hudson.

Hudson stops immediately, and then turns his head toward Sean. Her fiancé's snide remark is an obvious attempt to belittle him. Hudson's diminishing sanity has left him with a hair trigger, and now his blood boils as fury consumes him. His anger is born not of embarrassment or disrespect, but of old mental wounds so easily opened. Katie can see anger in Hudson's face as he turns toward Sean. She knows Sean and his friends will beat the hell out of him in the middle of her family's diner, so she must act quickly to head off any trouble.

"He is just a customer, Sean. Y'all come on in, and keep it down please. We have a lot of customers here tonight."

*Just another customer?!* Hudson thinks. He wants to drive his fist through the man's face, but he understands the situation and why she said what she did. He tells himself not to go psycho, to just leave, smoke another joint, and calm the Marine. However, the beast within denies Hudson his peaceful decision. He stands in the doorway glaring at Sean.

"What the hell is that freak doin? He's still staring at ya, Sean," Rodney Gaines, Sean's cousin, says as he points to Hudson.

Sean turns to the man and throws his hands up in the air as he asks, "Can I help ya with someth'n, asshole?"

"Can you please leave before something happens? Please, this won't turn out good for anyone. He's just a drunk asshole. Please!" Katie begs of Hudson.

Hudson stares at Sean for a second more before moving his attention to Katie. He says nothing. His look has changed. The polite stranger from before now struggles to defuse the explosive rage within the warrior. Hudson knows he will fight until they kill him, and death is what he wants. This is the way to get what he wants, a warrior's departure from life. Katie again pleads for Hudson to leave. Hudson turns to Katie once more and raises his voice so her fiancé can hear: "An asshole like that does not deserve such a beautiful woman as you." He walks out the door, looking at Sean through the window as he slowly makes his way to his truck. Without a word, he begs Sean and his friends to join him in the parking lot. Katie watches Hudson as he walks to his truck, hoping he'll drive away before Sean goes after him.

"What the fuck is up with this dude?" Sean walks up to Katie, noticing her attention is on the stranger. He can't ignore what the man said to his fiancée, damn sure not in front of his friends. Rodney and the other two fellas follow close behind Sean.

"Noth'n, Sean, just please let it be!" Katie pleads with Sean as he heads toward the door.

Sean can't do that; he cannot let it be. The four men walk outside. Sean leads the pack with profane verbal attacks, but Hudson says nothing. He slams the driver's side door and stands in thought for a second or two. He just wanted to go home and go numb, but this is God answering his prayers. This is his fate, his reward for saving the dog. Hudson will not simply let them pummel him to death, as the Marine will not let that happen. No, this will be a glorious death on the battlefield. This will be a warrior's exit from life and his ascent up the stairway. He walks around the back of his truck and responds to the verbal attacks with silence. The lights from the diner cast shadows over his eyes, yet the empty stare pierces through. The four men fire off a series of threats, but only receive silent determination in return, giving them pause. They hold their ground as Hudson marches on in confidence, much more confidence than a man should have facing a threat who outnumbers him four to one. Even through the alcohol the men recognize the absence of fear in this man. Little do they know, in place of fear is relief.

Katie stands frozen inside, tasked with a difficult decision. If she calls the police, she will pay for it dearly later this night. If she chooses not to call the police, Sean and his friends will surely beat the life from Hudson. She can't help but notice how Hudson charges forward without a word. For a brief moment, she fantasizes that it will be this intriguing stranger who beats the life from Sean. She knows life is not that compassionate, though. She snaps from her fantasy and prepares to dial 911. She runs outside screaming at Sean, frantically trying to defuse the situation. She hesitantly announces that she called the police, who are on their way. Hudson finally stops marching toward the men. He stands about ten feet away from Sean as he looks toward Katie.

"You shouldn't have done that," he says.

Katie responds with silence, confused by his response. He looks disappointed. She is not the only one who recognizes his displeasure with her decision. Sean and his friends try to stand strong, but they see something truly disturbing in this man's gaze. Hudson looks back to Sean and says nothing more. He slowly walks back to his truck, secretly hoping the men take the opportunity to attack him. He knows better—as they saw disappointment in his eyes, he saw relief in theirs. He drives off slowly, expecting to see blue lights at any moment. They never come.

Sean grabs Katie's arm after Hudson's truck is out of sight. He pulls her close so his friends can't hear, and then whispers in her ear, "I don't like the way y'all looked at each other, Katie. You are my fuck'n fiancée and shouldn't be look'n at some other piece of shit like that. I catch you with anyone and I'll kill'm. That is because I love you . . . you know that, right?"

"I know, Sean . . ."

". . . and you should not have called the fuck'n police, Katie!"

"I didn't call them. I was just trying to stop y'all from doing someth'n stupid. This is our family's business, Sean!"

"No shit, Katie . . . Look, I apologize. I just didn't like the looks of that creep. You should really be careful who you get friendly with, Katie Belle. That nut job may show up tomorrow or the next day look'n for you . . . I'm just look'n out for you is all."

"Yes, I know, Sean, now y'all go inside and sit and don't cause any more trouble."

"Not until you give me a kiss . . . come on now, Katie Belle!"

Katie kisses Sean, trying not to grimace at the overwhelming fumes of alcohol escaping his mouth with every breath. She knows this is not the end of this conversation, just the end of the public portion. She dreads the moment Sean finally returns home later tonight, most likely early the next morning. He has yet to satisfy his cocaine addiction and thirst for alcohol. By the time he returns home, his transformation into the monster only she knows will be complete. She looks back through the glass door where she stood only moments ago with that hard decision. She imagines herself not intervening. She imagines the stranger beating Sean within an inch of his life. She imagines herself being stronger, even fearless, like that intriguing stranger.

As Katie fantasizes about beatings delivered in an alternate life, Hudson eases on down Highway 15 stewing over his interaction with Sean. He could tell that Sean spends a lot of time at the gym and even more time thinking highly of himself. He wanted that fight. He wanted to release his anger. He is angry that his struggle in life continues. He is angry because that asshole belittled him. He is angry that he will never have a chance at a normal life with a lady like Katie. He envies Sean, which enrages him most—he's envious that Sean has an opportunity to live a perfect life with a perfect woman. He was also angry at life's bias toward those who are most rotten, rewarding them with the best of everything. Sean was kicked out of the service for disciplinary reasons, yet he gets to live a normal life. Hudson served honorably, put his life on the line during battle, and he will never have a shot at that normal life. Hudson wanted that fight. He would have kept fighting all of them until death came for him. The fight was the perfect way out of it all.

# CHAPTER TEN

# HUNT'N HUDSON

The gunshot pierced the night air from the backside of Whippoorwill Hollow. Gray holds his shotgun in his left hand, while shining the light across the field. Savannah won't let him go down to the pond alone, so he waits for her to bring him his phone to call Ricky. He turns off the flashlight and grabs the spotlight from just inside the door, where he normally keeps it. The quarter moon glows in the black sky, providing just enough light to see the hilltop across the way. He does not disturb the peaceful glow of the moon with the spotlight right away. The glow is what brings him peace in this moment of woeful uncertainty. He is eager to call Ricky but terrified of what they will find. Frightening thoughts plague his mind until across the field and on top of the dark hilltop comes hope. Gray flips on the spotlight and shines it on the figure racing over the hill, but it's a bit too far for the spotlight to reach. Though he can't truly identify who it is, he knows, and he smiles. The figure disappears momentarily into the trees before lights illuminate the forest and swing around toward the dirt road.

"I'll be damned . . . That's Hudson's truck!" Gray shouts. He is confused, excited, and relieved.

"Are you showuh?" Savannah screams as she runs out the door to look for herself.

"I'm positive. At's his truck. I just know it."

"What in the heyull is he doin?"

"Hell if I know, but he sure is in a dayum hurry."

Savannah immediately grabs her phone and calls Hudson, but it goes straight to voicemail. She tries again and again, only to keep reaching his voicemail. She grows furious, sad, relieved, and worried all at the same time. She has many thoughts and emotions racing through her head right now, and she'll be damned if she lets him just ride off into the night. She will not rest until she knows her son is truly safe. She and Gray jump in their car and race down the dirt road after Hudson. Gray drives as fast as he can without sliding into the ditch. The dust has already settled from the truck racing away in the middle of the night. They fail to catch him before reaching the paved road. They continue to chase the truck down the old Church Road and Highway 15, until they reach Hudson's house. The note they left earlier is still stuck on the front door. They pound on the doors and peek into windows, but the shades are drawn and their knocks go unanswered. They sit on his steps once again and wait a couple hours before finally going back home.

Gray and Savannah drive back over to Hudson's house the next day. Again, all the shades are drawn and the truck is either gone or in the garage. The note is still stuck to the door.

"Well, I guess he never came home last night. Maybe he just wants some alone time, hun." Gray tries keeping Savannah calm.

"Alone time my ass . . . I don't like it. Someth'n is wrong, Gray . . . Dammit, I know it."

"Savvy, he is OK. We saw him drive off. He probably just wants peace and quiet."

"And he can have peace and quiet once I am damn well convinced my baby boy is fine. Until then, I'm not gonna let up, Grayford Lee." Savannah only calls her husband by his full name when she is upset.

Everyone in the family knows that when Savannah uses full names, well, they best walk softly and choose their words and actions wisely. Hudson recalls this important detail as he stands on the other side of the door listening to his parents.

Such a dark and miserable place is Hudson's mind. His mama is worried sick about him, and he can't even pull himself together enough to ease her concern. He can't just grant her temporary reprieve from her worry. He can't because he knows if he opens that door, she will not leave his house. She will move in and have Gray bring her clothes and hygiene products. No way will he open that door to take in his mama as a roommate. He will be like the many other soldiers placed on suicide watch, having to answer countless questions that deeply penetrate his private world. No damn way he'll open that door. He just wishes he didn't have to hear them discuss the state of his well-being. He just wants to be left the hell alone.

Finally, after sitting on his porch for three hours, Gray and Savannah jump into the car and drive off down the road. Hudson thinks about packing up some camping gear and heading to some remote area on the Oconee to escape all the uninvited guests who are sure to ring the doorbell on a daily basis. However, for days he chooses to remain home, sit in the dark, and numb his mind with pain pills and heavy doses of whiskey while ignoring doorbells and phone calls.

# CHAPTER ELEVEN

# THE ABUSED

High school offers a wide variety of experiences, anywhere from the pinnacle of life to memories that mentally, and sometimes physically, scar a person. For Katie, those years began with horrible decisions accompanied by disgusting rumors. Those first two years of high school created in her opposite but compatible traits: the brittle girl desperate for love, protected by the sharp-witted angry woman. Most people would come to believe that she was an unbreakable shrew, but, little did they know, deep inside she was already broken. The death of her father shattered her fragile security and self-worth. She desperately wanted to replace the void his death left in her life. She went with many boys in an effort to find that replacement. Her efforts only created her easy reputation. Many good guys desired the young attractive girl with bright blue eyes and long blond hair, but those dirty rumors prevented them from even trying to scale her high stone wall, until Sean came along. He was exactly who she needed at the time, a time of sad desperation. He not only scaled that wall; he tore it down as only he could do. He was popular among the black-sheep crowd and known by all as someone not to cross. He wasn't from the wrong side of the tracks or anything like that; his dad and uncle owned, and still own, a successful HVAC company. However, Sean was known to possess a hair-trigger temper with a quick iron fist to go along with it. Katie's love simmered his temper, and he silenced those dirty whispers floating through the school halls. She was in love with him. He was in love with her. Every thought they had was for each other during those early years. Back then, rarely did they spend time apart, and disagreements were far and few in between. When they did argue, anger was absent, compromise came quickly, and peace returned with no lingering emotional consequences. They were blind to each other's imperfections and faults. They were blinded by love. Then, as with most relationships, love eased its intoxicating grip. A couple of years after high school, their young love transformed from something beautiful to something ugly, vile, and inescapable.

Love is often accused of making people do strange things. Indeed, a person would not normally spend two hundred dollars on flowers, candy, and a card. Fiscal responsibility and logic argue against such foolishness. However, in this case, love is the influential culprit of such illogical actions and decisions. On the other hand, a man who believes his wife or significant other is unfaithful does not hit her out of love. Love is actually absent. In the place of love is an accumulation of darker influences. A sense of paranoia and possession mixed with chemical addictions were the most dominant reasons Sean's love evolved.

Love is also compared to many things in an attempt for people to define it; the highs and lows of love, for instance, are said to be like those of a powerful drug. Most drugs offer an intoxication that temporarily alters life into an exhilarating mental fantasy. Once the fantasy is over, though, anguish is all that remains. At that point, a person must make a critical decision: quit the drug and avoid its painful aftermath or embrace the drug to forever chase the fantasy. Katie chose the latter and, as a result, found the drug Sean pushed only offers the illusion of that fantasy. What it actually delivers is an all-consuming sadness, as mental and physical torture consume the majority of her private life.

In their twisted relationship, Katie chases love's highs while the lows control Sean. The transformation of their love changed him. The insecure narcissist buried deep inside gained control and never relinquished power. In the beginning, the constant affection and attention he received from Katie greatly satisfied his ego. He loved the way her love made him feel. As the relationship evolved and the novelty of their love subsided, his ego struggled to adjust. He tried to shower her with the same love and affection to feed his ego; however, the more he tried, the more desperate he became. He felt vulnerable and weak. The more vulnerable he felt, the less he trusted her. The less he trusted her, the more he had to control her. Obsession, insecurity, and narcissism are all that remain in the man who once fully satisfied Katie's desire for love. She clings to the hope that love will return, but feels the cause is lost. Katie saw a way out while Sean was in the Navy, but he sensed his control of her slipping away. He caught her trying to escape. He chose to sacrifice his honor and integrity with the Navy to return home and once again secure the shackles of his control over her.

Their relationship has tragically devolved further in the two years since Sean's dishonorable departure from the service. Formerly driven by love, it is now steered by his desires and periodic abuse, both of which are further fueled by his addiction to alcohol and cocaine. The inexorable control he has over her is suffocating. She is not the only one who is controlled by his paranoia and narcissism; Sean has front-row seats to his battle with both. He is frustrated that they are not what they once were. He blames her. She is routinely the target of his rage. After his demons surface and his fury is released upon her, he enters a time of guilt. He justifies his violent actions with explanations of love. Terrified and desperate, Katie always accepts his selfish apologies, which succeed only at silencing his guilt and starting the abusive cycle over. During this brief moment of the cycle, though, Katie again experiences love's fantastic high. Her fantasy period is short-lived and shrinks in time with each revolution of the cycle.

Sean's abuse is never witnessed by others, especially her family. He neglects her, abuses her mentally, abuses her physically, and then becomes apologetic just before he completely breaks her will. He has to let her maintain some hope to keep their secrets secret, but hope of love is not what keeps Katie silent. She never has discussed her torment with anyone, because she is ashamed of her weakness. The strong woman seen by family and friends is as much of an illusion as Sean's love. They are none the wiser. Sean never strikes her in the face, so she easily hides the bruises and scars. The most severe scars, however, are in her mind. She struggles to find the strength to face each day, to continue hiding her dirty secret, her pathetic weakness. She desperately digs deep in search for the strength to leave him, but his deadly threats persistently echo in her head. She often sits in a dark corner crying until her eyes are dry while her mind relentlessly searches for a way out. She knows he will kill her if she leaves; although, the thought of death relieves her, as it would end the psychological cycle of abuse. Of course, Sean would make her live in fear for years before actually killing her. The fear of living is why she does not leave him.

The night Sean and Hudson almost fight, Katie comes home after work, reflecting on the encounter between the stranger and Sean. She is confused by her intense attraction to Hudson. She ponders her inability to look into the eyes of the stranger but for a brief glimpse. She is able to fight her shame with everyone else. She can look any other customer in the eyes as she holds brief conversations with them, but not Hudson. Though she thought he was handsome, physical appearance did not induce the attraction. Looks actually had little to do with her stir of emotions over the stranger. Something unseen, dredged up from the depths of her soul, inspired her desire for this man. The feeling far outweighed the high school attraction to Sean, or anything she had ever felt for anyone. She can provide no answer for the way she felt toward someone she encountered so briefly. She stops searching for the reason and journeys to a place of tremendous happiness with the stranger. There in her thoughts he holds her and comforts her; he makes her feel safe. The girl within smiles, but the woman knows reality all too well. She closes her eyes to end the glimpse into that world, and then opens them up to reality. She is imprisoned by fear and wishes more than anything to be liberated by love. She barely talked to Hudson, but something intense and unexplainable consumed her in that brief exchange. Maybe it is just a silly attraction. Maybe she is just too desperate for love and security. She refuses to contemplate the reason any longer. The encounter and subsequent thoughts are but simple reminders of the life she will never have, and this life offers too much grief to continue.

The water is warm. The blade is cold. Silent is the darkness, and merciless is her torment. She has nothing left to give this life and can only end the empty life that remains. Courage to live is impossible, so she invites death to silence the victim within. She feels guilty for the pain she will soon deliver her family. She silences the guilt with alcohol and opioids. The potent mixture numbs her mind as well as her body. It numbs both well—too well. Her heavy eyelids fall, and her blue eyes roll back as the blade touches skin. Her closing eyelids squeeze out a final tear. The blade slides from her incapacitated hand, sinking to the bottom of the tub. Death is denied tonight, but it only falls back into the shadows to await the next invitation.

The banging on the bathroom door awakens Katie. Sean demands that she open the door. He is home, drunk, and demands she meets his needs. She lacks the strength to fight, so she asks that he wait in the bed for her, slurring every word she forces from her tongue. Katie rises from the tub and dries her body. She places the razor back in the drawer for another night. She walks into the bedroom, still naked, and slides into the bed. He rolls over onto her without a word. As he satisfies his sexual appetite, her mind, numbed from the alcohol and painkillers, escapes to another place. He never kisses her. He never holds her or embraces her. He only grips her throat without fully choking her. She fantasizes of him squeezing harder, so she could go to sleep and never awake. He finishes by releasing all over her. He never says a word as he rolls over and drifts into a drunken slumber. She slides out of bed and heads back to the bathroom. She showers to wash off his sexual contribution and then sits down crying uncontrollably as the water rains down on her. Life is hell. Her savior is death.

— CHAPTER TWELVE —
# NO HOME

Hudson loathes the mornings as the thought of residing in this world another day rots in his gut like last night's whiskey. He relies on Mary and pills to push through the day. He watches the seconds tick by on the clock, waiting for the night to comfort him again. Night is when the top comes off the bottle. He attempts to wash away his affliction with hours of unwavering dedication to his drink of choice. Alcohol may dull the mind, but those memories remain. The whiskey will never permanently remove the memories, but at least the pain recedes with every drop. Unfortunately, every bottle has a bottom, and the last drop is a sobering reminder of the dreadful pain that's sure to return by morning.

Every night, Hudson talks to a ghost. Every night, death talks to Hudson. He tries to talk to Hank, but his friend never answers. He begs for a sign that his friend's spirit is there, but it never comes. He watches the life disappear from his friend's eyes over and over. He is gone. A life wasted so a weak man can live. He apologizes to Hank. His Marine brother paid the ultimate price to give him the most precious gift. All Hudson can think about is destroying that gift. Alcohol eases the guilt and amplifies the suicidal thoughts. The gun on the table is his only focus. With one squeeze the emptiness, memories, and guilt will no longer exist, and the battle for normalcy will end. That moment when he has convinced himself to reach for the gun, he hears a much louder voice. The cry of that dog breaks his focus on the gun. The cry gnaws at him, repeating in his head until he retreats back into his chair. The life in the dog's eyes replaces the death in Hank's. The scars and wounds tell a story of a barbarous past lived by the dog. He has most likely only witnessed and experienced the most wretched side of life, yet he wishes to live on. Hudson wonders why he can no longer have the same appreciation for his own life—Hank's gift.

A week of this routine passes. Every morning presents the same struggle to hold down last night's bottle. When he is able to hold it down, Hudson eats the same breakfast: scrambled eggs, toast, a Bloody Mary, and a couple of pills to dull the agonizing pain in his head. Unfortunately, his addiction to alcohol and opioids further fuels his desolation. He spends his days looking at that damn clock—ticking away the day. He turns off his phone and tucks it away in a kitchen drawer. He has no desire to talk to anyone, nor does he want to see the names and numbers of those who are desperate to see him. He knows someone will eventually come by again to check on him, so his truck remains in the garage, the shades drawn, and house quiet until he is ready for his nightly ritual involving whiskey, hydrocodone, and music as dark as his damaged soul.

Hudson loves his family dearly, but makes every effort to avoid them. He cannot pretend to be normal, and he knows his family will eventually recognize his despondency. As he now knows, some already have sensed his struggle. Given the chance, they will discover the true depth of his agony and demand he seek professional help as if they understand. They will never understand, though, that every day alive is an arduous attempt to mask the incredible misery residing inside his head. In his mind, the only person who could understand and provide true relief is dead.

Since delivering the dog to Dr. Howard, Hudson has received a daily call from the animal hospital. Each call goes straight to voicemail as Hudson's phone has remained off and tucked away. After a few days, Hudson decides he best see if the Animal Hospital has called about the dog. The only other thing he desires other than the end of his misery is following through with his promise to the doctor and to silence the crying dog. Sure enough, between the many voicemails from his worried family, he has a message each day from Hannah. She always leaves the same message: "Hi, Mr. Lee! Hope all is well! Please call as soon as you can for an update on the dog you brought in. He is doing just fine and is in good spirits."

She adds the phone number at the end of each message, though she knows Hudson has their business card. Hudson listens to each message, unable to delete any of them. He finds solace knowing the dog is in good spirits. At least one of them from that night is in good spirits.

As Hudson deletes all the other messages without listening to them, the hospital calls. He freezes, staring at his phone while contemplating whether to ignore the call or get it over with. He goes with the latter. To free himself of his exhausting struggle without guilt, he must first settle the hospital bill and find a home for that damn dog. This time it is not Hannah, though, it is Dr. Howard.

"Hudson! It's Frank with the Watkinsville Animal Hospital. How are ya?"

"All right, I guess. You?"

"I'm good, real good. We've been try'n to contact ya."

"Been camp'n. Just got back."

"Ah, heck. Do some fish'n?"

"A little. What's the word on the dog?"

"Well, got some good news for ya. Ole boy is doing juuust fine and ready to go home."

"Is that right?"

"Yes, sir, sure is. You find'm a home yet?"

"Nope. Like I said, been camp'n."

"All right . . . well . . . we need someone to pick him up, Hudson. We just don't have the room for him to stay here—"

Hudson interrupts Dr. Howard as he is in no mood to hear a lecture. "Frank, I told ya I'd pick'm up and find'm a home. That's what I'll do. I'll be up that way in about an hour or so. Gotta finish up someth'n. That all right?"

"That'll be just fine, Hudson. See ya then."

Hudson hangs up with the doc, rubs his aching head, and gathers his thoughts. *All right, ya dumbass, you have to follow through with this bullshit,* Hudson thinks. He pours the Bloody Mary down the sink and opts for a quick smoke over painkillers before heading out. Ty often says that Mary is the one woman who always relieves headaches and never causes one. Hudson takes a few hits as he recalls his brother's amusing insight on women and weed, and then chases a couple of Excedrin with a big glass of water before heading to the hospital.

On the way to the hospital, Hudson mulls over possible homes for the dog. He knows finding someone to take in a monstrous male red-nose terrier will be nearly impossible. The dog has obviously been in a lot of fights and probably has as many scars on the inside as he does on the outside, something Hudson understands intimately. He wishes that bird would have been a few seconds earlier that night by the pond. His mental battle would be over had he not waited for that damned whip-poorwill. He and the dog both would have died, ending the turmoil within him and sparing him the trouble of finding a home for the dog.

Hudson pulls into the parking lot outside of the Animal Hospital. Mary and Excedrin have his head feeling about right. He sits in his truck out in the parking lot staring at the hospital, preparing himself for the gabfest to come. "Get in, get the dog, and get the hell out," he says to himself. He pulls his University of Georgia ball cap down a little lower and pushes his shades on a little tighter before sliding out of the truck and making the short walk over to the front door.

"Hello, Mr. Lee! Good to see ya!" Hannah cheerfully greets him as he walks through the door.

*And it begins,* Hudson thinks before replying, "How ya doin?! Is the doc in?"

"I'm just fine. How about you?"

Hudson hesitates for a second while he looks at the vibrant Hannah, then replies, "Good enough, I guess. How about the doc?"

"He's in. Hold on and I'll get'm for ya. Please have a seat if ya want to."

Hudson takes a seat away from the other folks in the waiting area. He has no desire for small talk with anyone, nor does he have the mental capacity at the moment to put together enough complete sentences to carry on a logical conversation.

A voice booms from the other side of the waiting area: "Hudson Lee! Come on back." The doc is standing there grinning from ear to ear as though his best friend has just stopped by to pay him a visit. Hudson hesitates for a moment as he considers bolting for the door to avoid Frank's apparent euphoric mood. But he doesn't run, instead he opts to get this shit over with. After all, he made a promise to find the dog a home, and Hudson is certainly a man of his word.

Hudson follows Dr. Howard to a little room down the hall. They walk in and sitting in the corner of the room is a cleaned-up terrier. He vigorously wags his nub of a tail, excited for no reason at all. The dog has a shaved spot on his big head that bears his healing gunshot wound. He has another on his leg where the snake bit him. The dog and Hudson stare at each other for a moment, trying to feel each other out. Hudson ends the stare down and looks at Dr. Howard.

"What are my walking instructions, Doc?"

"Well, he shouldn't need anything more than a healthy diet right now, Hudson. We gave'm the meds and shots he needed. But I gotta warn ya, Hudson, this ole boy has been through some bad stuff in his life. Real bad. He has more scars than fur. Tragic stuff, I tell ya. Ain't a doubt in my mind that he was a fight'n dog. His age and injuries made him worthless to the animals that used him for such a vulgar activity. They definitely tried put'n him down with a bullet, but were obviously unsuccessful. He is a tough rascal and musta been a helluva fighter to be as old as he is. Anyway, he is a damaged dog, trained to kill other dogs, Hudson. Going to be hard to find someone who will take him. He will instantly be euthanized at any shelter. I'll be honest with ya—gonna be hard to find someone brave and understanding enough to take him in."

Hudson stares at Dr. Howard, stupefied by the dismal news and limited options. His eyes slowly drop toward the floor as he kicks around some options in his head. "Well . . . dammit . . . all right . . . Welp, I didn't just pay all this money only to have him euthanized, I guess. I'll try to find'm a dayum place to live like I promised."

"This dog will need someone to love him, Hudson. Just finding 'a place to live' could be real bad . . . for him, other pets, children . . ."

Hudson throws up his hands and looks at Dr. Howard, obviously annoyed about the way the conversation has progressed. "I gotcha, Doc . . . dammit. I'll take'm and I'll find'm someone to 'love' him. What do I owe ya? Can I just pay and take his ass on outta here?"

Doc looks at Hudson for a brief moment as he contemplates what to say, and then tells him, "OK, Hudson. I know this seems to be a bad deal . . . a downright burden. I appreciate ya take'n the time to help the fella out. He needs someone to help him. You're probably the first person who ever actually helped him. All right, Hudson, go on out front and Hannah will settle the bill. I will get him ready and bring him out for ya."

"I don't mean to sound like an ass, Doc, but this is a damn burden. I'll keep my word, but shit . . . whatever, I appreciate your honesty, Doc! As shitty as it is."

"Well . . . you're welcome for my shitty honesty, Hudson!" Doc pauses for a moment as he smirks. "I hope ya find a good home for him. I really do."

Hudson settles the bill and heads home with the burden. A few days ago, he was responsible for only his life. That alone was more burden than he could handle. He knows of no one who will take in such a damaged animal. He feels resentful sympathy for the dog. Maybe he will get lucky and find a shelter. Life presents no such luck, though. The doc is right: those places will just put him down—a thought Hudson cannot stomach.

— CHAPTER THIRTEEN —

# WELCOME TO POP'S

Canned Heat's "On the Road Again" plays on the radio as the dog once again travels the scenic country roads full of the fields and fences. The lyrics of the mesmerizing song are a mystery to him, though they sure do fit his travels up to this point in his life. He never knew his mama and has no family or special friends, yet he does not travel this long stretch of lonesome highway all by himself. Maybe the dog is simple, but he asks for nothing more. He is just fine with his current situation and worries of no alternative world. Quite the opposite of the stranger sitting next to him, driving the truck with his elbow resting on the door, leaning slightly out the open window while cutting his eyes at him every now and again.

"Looks like you've been through some bad shit, my friend. You've been in quite a few fights."

The stranger speaks, breaking the dog's focus on the window. The dog looks over at Hudson, still wary of the stranger who rescued him. Hudson turns his attention back to the road while continuing his conversation with the dog.

"Yeah, I've been in a couple two three myself. Left me a bit fucked up as well." Hudson pauses before glancing back at the dog. "I guess we need to name ya at some point . . . or ya just have to wait until someone takes your ass in and names ya themselves." Hudson turns back to the road, grins, and then continues his one-sided conversation. "I guess you don't really give a rat's ass what anybody calls ya, huh?! Ya hungry?"

Hudson pulls into Pop Walters's barbeque joint, about halfway to his house from Watkinsville Animal Hospital. Owned by his father's friend, Pop Walters, this hole-in-the-wall restaurant seems to come out of nowhere down Highway 15. The friendship between the two families goes back quite a ways, back when Gray and Pop worked on a dairy farm together. Pop's son, Jacob "Griz" Walters, played high school football with Hudson; they were good friends. Jake was given that nickname for being as big as a damn grizzly bear and because of his bushy Grizzly Adams beard—only fella in high school who had a man beard. The Walter family's main income is from their peach farm. They charge folks to come out to the farm and pick their own peaches. Families love it, especially the kids. Along with peaches, they also sell barbeque. Peach season may be only three months long, but barbeque is year-round. Wesley "Pop" Walters has been long known around the area for his amazing barbeque and sauce. Recognizing a good business opportunity when he sees one, Pop began selling pulled pork sandwiches to the peach pickers. Sandwiches evolved into plates of barbeque pork and chicken, and now the peach farm BBQ joint is known all over the countryside.

Hudson clips a leash onto the dog's collar. He pretty much has to drag the dog out of the truck because those damned ole trust issues, but the dog's nose and stomach convince him that following the stranger just may be a pretty good idea. Hudson leads him over to the walk-up order window where he orders up some smoked chicken for the dog and a pulled pork plate for himself. Big Jake walks out of the smokehouse to greet his old friend.

"Ho-lee-sheyutt, how the hell are ya, son?"

"Good. How you been, Griz?" Hudson responds with far less enthusiasm as he shakes Jake's big paw.

"Been a dayum minute, son. When the heyull did ya get back?"

"About two weeks ago, I guess."

"Looks like ya got yourself a friend."

"Well, actually I saved him from a copperhead about a week ago. Down by Deddy's pond. I gotta find'm a home. You want'm?"

"Shit naw, son. I got a dog, and that big fella looks like he'd rather chew on my dog than play with'r."

Jake's sister hands Hudson his food, cutting short the boys' slightly awkward reunion conversation. "Here ya go, Hudson. Welcome back! Jake, we need more chicken, bubba."

"All right, sissy, I'll get on it. Well, welcome back, son. Let's get a beer sometime."

"Thanks, Griz . . . Well, I best get this boy some chicken." Hudson is not about to make any more promises to anyone. Finding this dog a home is about the only thing he cares to do. That promise is the only reason he is still here. About the only other thing he cares to do is eat the delicious pig on his plate, because Mary has been arousing his appetite since he left the house.

Hudson takes the food and walks the dog over to a picnic table just on the outskirts of the orchard, where the peach trees are nearly bare now. He pulls some chicken off the bone, reaches out toward the dog, and says, "Here ya go, boy. Some good chicken right here. Griz learned from the best."

The dog looks at the chicken and licks his lips. He sure enough wants that chicken in a bad way, but still struggles to trust the man handing him that wonderful-smelling smoked meat.

"Go on now, big fella, you're gonna wanna trust me on this one," Hudson says, trying to reassure the dog.

Finally, the dog cautiously slides over to the chicken. He sticks his nose up to it, gives it a whiff or two, and then eases it out of Hudson's hand with his mouth. The dog sucks that chicken down in a hurry, barely chewing it before sending it to his stomach. He immediately looks back up at Hudson with the expression of a child after trying ice cream for the first time.

"Good shit, ain't it?" Hudson asks with a half-cocked smile.

The dog eases back toward the table, licking his lips the whole way, bringing an even bigger smile to Hudson's face. Hudson pulls off all the chicken from the bone, puts it on a plate with some fries, and sets it on the ground along with a cup of water. The dog eases up on his mistrust of Hudson to devour the food and water—funny how a plate of good barbeque can change a fella's mind.

After finishing lunch, they slowly head back toward the truck, each weighed down by half a pound of smoked meat. As they walk to the truck, an SUV pulls up with a couple of Labs in the back. The dogs' heads hang out of the half-rolled-down window, taking turns barking at the big red dog accompanying Hudson. A young man and woman jump out, leash their dogs, and then head toward the restaurant. The Labs get a bit more excited once they are out of the car, leaping and barking at the ugly red stranger. The young couple pull on the dogs' leashes while pleading with them to calm down. The two dogs are well groomed and pretty. They don't have the battle scars of the dog with Hudson, but that does not stop them from barking and lunging at the big fella. The gentle giant, calm at first, begins a low, deep growl. The louder the Labs bark, the louder and more powerful the red stranger growls. Something savage begins to escape this once-timid dog. Before Hudson can tell the big fella to calm down, and with a thunderous roar, the beast introduces himself. He relentlessly drives toward the Labs, testing the strength of the leash and collar. Hudson's arm and shoulder feel like they are close to popping right out of the joint. The leash is now hooked up to a damn tank, ready for battle, full throttle ahead. The beast unleashes a furious series of barks and growls, lunging wildly at his pretty opponents.

Hudson grabs the leash with both hands, pulls, and yells, "Whoa, boy! Down, boy . . . Down, boy!"

The couple freezes, shocked and terrified at the sight of the ugly warrior who will most likely shred their beloved dogs within seconds. The beast continues his furious retort to the Labs' instigating barks, which have subsided. The couple pull their dogs close as Hudson wrestles the angry beast to his truck. He resists and fights Hudson every step of the way while giving those pretty Labs a piece of his mind.

"You need to control your damn dog!" The guy, who stands about six feet four or five inches tall, carrying about 250 pounds, shouts to Hudson as he puts his dogs back in his SUV.

Once the Labs are in the SUV and out of sight, Hudson finally manages to shove the big red beast into his truck. Hudson, who is barely six feet tall and only about 180 pounds, turns toward the guy and is none too pleased with the big fella's attitude.

"How bout you just worry about your own fuck'n dogs!"

"I know what you do with that kinda dog, you piece of shit."

"You don't know shit, asshole!"

"I know what people like you do with dogs like that."

A short fuse is all that delays the fury within Hudson. A normal person would try to defuse the situation. The big man is not threatening Hudson; he is simply ignorant to the circumstances, which is unfortunate. A normal person would tell the rescue story to the man, who will surely be more than understanding; however, normal is subjective. Just like the red beast in his truck who continues his vicious display of anger, Hudson has been rewired to know but one option during conflict. The big stranger's excessive confidence and attitude call out to the same beast within Hudson as the Labs did in the dog. The hidden madman is no longer contained inside. He controls Hudson now, and there is no leash holding him back. With his hot temper now boiling over, Hudson delivers an overhand right to the stranger's left eye. He put every ounce of his 180 pounds into the unexpected punch, knocking the guy onto the side of the SUV. The guy turns, lowers his head, and charges at Hudson in an attempt to tackle him. Hudson takes on the charge, guides the man's head into a guillotine choke hold. Hudson tightens the hold, shutting off the flow of blood to the man's brain. The big guy manages to get Hudson on the ground, but Hudson maintains the choke hold while wrapping his legs around the big man, locking his feet on the guy's back. Hudson squeezes tightly on the man's neck, continuing to stop the flow of blood to the man's head. The guy lets out a loud gurgling noise as he struggles to remain conscious. The big man, his brain now starving of oxygen, goes limp, but Hudson holds on. The man's lady friend screams at the top of her lungs, pleading with Hudson to let go.

"Let'm up, Hudson! Let up on'm, dammit!" Big Jake yells as he runs out of the smokehouse.

Jake is a giant at six feet seven inches tall, weighing in somewhere over three hundred pounds. This is not the first time he's had to pull Hudson out of a fight, but this time is different. This is not just some after-school dust-up. He can see Hudson has no intention of letting up on that choke hold. Jake grabs Hudson's right arm with his big paws and gives it a powerful yank. He sits on the ground with his legs straight, feet pushing on Hudson and the other guy's limp body as he pulls on Hudson's arm. He knows he has to let the blood pump back into the guy's head or else he will die. Hudson is unable to hold onto the choke hold as Jake pulls with every ounce of his three-hundred-plus-pound frame. Jake gets up to his feet, tosses Hudson away from the man, and quickly pulls the guy up off of the ground, sitting him up by the SUV. Hudson charges back over toward them. The lady screams for Hudson to stay away from her husband.

"Dammit, Hudson, keep the fuck back!" Jake yells at Hudson as he tries to wake up the other guy.

Jake jumps up and grabs Hudson in a bear hug to hold him back. The intense rage controlling Hudson refuses to stop the attack. He fights hard to escape Jake's bear hug, but the big fella's giant arms squeeze tighter the harder Hudson fights.

"Let me go, Jake! Imma fuck'm up!" Hudson yells as his big friend holds onto the wild man.

Jake wrestles Hudson over to his truck and shoves him in through the driver's side door, just as Hudson did the dog moments ago. The dog continues barking and Hudson continues yelling until Jake has had about enough of both.

"Get your ass outta here, Hudson. We will talk about this shit later. Just get the hell outta here! If you get out of this dayum truck, Imma knock you the fuck out, son. Now go on, git!"

His anger is in control, but common sense and respect for his friend wage a convincing argument. Hudson does not dare test Jake's might or sincerity. He knows he would have killed that man over a few dogs barking at each other. The thought of his mind going to such a dark place where he can incite death with so little provocation scares the hell out of Hudson. Jake would have been right to knock Hudson unconscious from the get-go, which means he would have had to explain his actions to Pop and Gray after awakening. Jake shoving Hudson into the truck saves him that embarrassment, for now, and he is grateful. Though he remains livid over his quarrel with the guy, Hudson knows it is best to leave before he delivers death to the wrong person.

Jake watches as Hudson drives away before turning back toward the dumbstruck couple. The guy is awake but struggles to catch a good breath and get his wits about him. While his lungs gasp, his wife takes the opportunity to speak her mind.

"Thank you for helping us!" she says. "Who was that maniac? I am calling the damn law on his ass and animal control on his damn dog!"

"No the hell you ain't, lady. I saw what went down. Your dogs started this whole mess—"

"Are you kidding me? That crazy asshole nearly killed my husband!"

"Who ran his dayum mouth to the wrong fella at the wrong time. Had your husband kept his mouth shut, that fella would've been on his way. Plain and simple." Jake then looks at the guy still sitting on the ground by the SUV. "Mister, ya may wanna choose who ya mouth off to more wisely in the future. You never know the state of a man's mind. Y'all are not gonna call the law on him, because he defended himself and because he is actually a good dude. He ain't watcha thank he is. He rescued that dog. He was just having a bad day. Take ya ass whoop'n, have a free plate of barbeque, and take a bag of peaches on the house, and then enjoy the rest of your day."

"A bad day does not . . . ," the lady starts to say.

"Thank you for pulling him off of me! We'll take you up on your offer. Name is Will." The guy interrupts his wife and introduces himself as he reaches out his hand to shake Jake's.

"I'm Jake. Welcome to Pop's Peach Farm and barbeque joint!" Jake replies with a big grin as he helps Will to his feet.

The lady doesn't agree, nor does she find any of this amusing, but she's polite enough. "Thanks again, Jake! I'm Linda, Will's wife . . . and nearly his damn widow. If your friend doesn't get help, he will kill the next guy. Something to think about, Jake."

As Jake makes good with the couple, Hudson and the dog head on down Highway 15. Silence fills the cab of the truck for the first few miles. After about ten minutes, when the boiling tempers have had time to simmer a bit, Hudson breaks the angry silence. "I guess we're both pretty fucked up." Their quick glance at each other says it all. Only they understand each other at this moment. Hudson knows nothing justifies such a violent reaction to a simple misunderstanding. His temper is the firecracker that detonates in the hand immediately after the fuse ignites. However, in the eyes of the dog, Hudson and his response seem perfectly normal. The dog slides over and lays his enormous head on Hudson's lap. This stranger seems loyal to him, more loyal than his previous family. He has no reason to focus on the world outside that window, as he is finally accompanied down this old lonesome highway. He is grateful for the stranger saving him. He is grateful to have a new friend. Hudson, on the other hand, does not share the same appreciation. He looks down, nods a little bit, and scratches the dog just behind his massive head, and then tells the dog, "We shoulda died by that pond, my friend."

# CHAPTER FOURTEEN

# ESCAPE

**K**atie is sitting quietly at the kitchen table staring out the window into the backyard when Sean walks in aiming to strike up a conversation with her. She stands at the edge of her sanity once again with the cries of fear and sadness coming from the darkness below her feet. She neither sees his presence nor hears his words. Her thoughts deafen her ears while only the view outside that window comforts her. Sean senses her distance. He senses her emptiness. He knows only that he was satisfied earlier that morning. No intimacy, romance, or affection existed between them, only her disgust and his lust. He senses her sadness. He knows the time has come to pull her from the edge. He will lose her if he does not pull her back, saving her from sadness and despair. His help, though, does not derive from guilt or sympathy, but from a sense of entitlement. He refuses to lose what is rightfully his. She is his. She will not take away what is his.

Sean calls out to Katie but fails to disrupt her focus on the world outside that little window. On the other side of that glass exists a world where she navigated the reciprocal heading of the one she traveled in this world. In that world, she did not continue on course into the storm; she turned around and abandoned her damaged relationship with Sean instead of sinking to the bottom with him. There, through that glass, the girl comes into focus. She smiles and waves for Katie to come join her. She speaks, but her words fail to reach Katie. The girl's voice cannot penetrate the ears congested with the noise of reality. Sean, frustrated by Katie's intense focus into that alternate life, moves in close and raises his voice to break her focus on that damned window. He pitches the same old promises that he has broken time and again.

"Look, Katie baby, I know I've been an ass and inconsiderate and that ain't right. You deserve better than that. I know you are unhappy, and I know why. You want me to be better to you. I want that, too. I want to be like we were in the beginning. I promise ya, from this day on, I'm goin to be a better man to ya. I'm done with the drank'n, smoke'n . . . all the drugs. I was just having fun, and I am ready to move on. I'm done with it all. You come first, baby."

His promise is saturated with desperation. Begging her angers him. He cannot let that anger take control. His desperate promise, however, is not really for her—it is for him. He doesn't care if he convinces her that he will finally make those changes, but aims to convince himself. He walks over to Katie, rubs her upper back, and then kisses the top of her head. Katie never budges. She continues watching the world through that little window. His empty promises fail to disturb her focus this morning. She has heard them far too often before. They have become meaningless, serving only as a reminder that her conscious world is a dark alternative to the one on the other side of that window. Finally, this time, empty promises fall on deaf ears. Unfortunately, the girl's words fall on the same deaf ears.

Anger continues building within Sean as the window appeals more to Katie. He moves over to stand directly in her line of sight, blocking her view of that damn window. Her concentration never breaks as she stares through him.

"Katie, baby, talk to me. How can I fix this? I love you and want to fix this," Sean pleads. He kneels beside her and holds her hand as he connects their eyes. "I'm a jerk, I know . . . I know I've promised to stop drink'n before. If I stop drink'n, I'd be a good man to you. You deserve a good man, and I know I can be that man. Imma sober up, baby. I mean it this time. I need you in my life. I can only sober up with you in my life."

Katie continues staring through his eyes to the window. The words that finally escape her tongue seem to come from someone else. She's never had the courage to admit her true thoughts to Sean. The girl outside the window has to be the one who finally admits the truth. Her softly spoken words deliver the harsh message: "I don't love you anymore."

Sean looks up and squints as he replies, "Do what? What did you say?"

This time Katie puts her face in her hands and yells the words, "I hate my life with you!"

Sean grabs her hand and leans in close to Katie. "You don't mean that, Katie. We are meant for each other. I love you and you love me. I know I've been an asshole, but you don't—"

"I hate you, Sean!" The words erupt from deep within her.

Shock momentarily silences Sean. His ego will not let him believe the words repeating in his head. He fights his frustration and growing anger to plead his case once again. "You don't mean—"

"I fucking hate you, Sean! I'd rather be dead than be with you." The dam has burst, and years of fear, anger, and sadness flood the room.

"Stop saying that bullshit!" Sean yells.

The room falls silent except for Katie's crying. She looks away from him as she weeps. Sean glares at her. He slings her hand out of his, throws his coffee cup across the room, and stands. He paces around the kitchen for a minute as he continues to digest her harsh confession. He blocks it out as though she never spoke the words. Deaf is the fool who hears only his desires. He calms himself before speaking again.

"I know you don't mean what you said."

"I do . . . I mean every fuck'n word of it!" Katie replies through the tears.

"Well, I'm not gonna just let you go and throw it all away because of a low point in our relationship. You'll see that I can change, and you'll be sorry for saying that shit!"

The pounding reminder of last night's good time mixes with the building anger within him. This explosive combination is what Katie has come to know whenever she tried to confess her feelings to Sean. Fear normally causes her to retreat, but this time she pushes forward. Katie looks up to Sean with tears rolling down her face. She forces herself to calm down enough to plead with the angry man.

"Please let me go, Sean . . . please, please, please . . . Just let me go! Please, Sean! We will both be happier . . . you're not . . ."

"Stop saying that fuck'n shit!" Sean yells, then pauses to calm himself, clenching his fists before continuing, "I do love you, Katie. I love you more than anything. I know you still love me. We are just goin through a bad spell. Just have a little faith in us—in me. I will quit drink'n. I will go to church. I will do whatever it takes to prove my love for you."

"I don't doubt you think you love me, Sean, but you can't be happy, you can't love me, or you wouldn't do the things you do."

"I know I love you . . . that's . . ." Sean stops to bed down his frustration again. "That's why I am will'n to give up all those things, Katie. I will walk away from my friends and bad habits for you! I will change for you."

"You did change, Sean," Katie says with a much calmer voice than moments ago.

He knows what she means by that comment. He is fully aware of the physical and mental abuse he has put her through; however, his view differs from hers. She caused his actions. He doesn't stare at the ground ashamed of his actions. He stares at the floor in frustration that she will not simply believe that he will change. At this moment, his sincerity is real. He is in the apologetic stage of his cycle. He is not apologetic because he feels guilt or shame but because he refuses to lose what is his. He feels they've both made their fair share of mistakes.

She should also apologize. He is angry that she won't admit her mistakes and apologize. She is his, and he will be damned if she will leave, taking what is his.

"Look, we both have done each other wrong, made our fair share of mistakes, and said things that . . ."

Katie lifts her head again and screams as she sobs, "Our share of mistakes?! Have I ever forced myself on you? Have I ever fractured your ribs? Have I ever put a fuck'n shotgun barrel into your chest?"

"I never raped you! You never said no . . . I was drunk, and I know that is no excuse for the times I hit ya . . ."

"You hit me not just because you were drunk, but because I rejected you, because you accused me of sleeping with every man I ever talked to."

"I am done with that lifestyle. I know I was a better man in the beginning, baby. I promise you that I will become that man again."

Sean kneels to get close to Katie. He begs her to give him a chance to change for her. He begs her over and over as Katie cries into her hands. The more he pleads, the harder she sobs. Silence momentarily interrupts the conversation. Katie lifts her head to look at Sean. A few tears roll down his cheeks as he softly pleads once again.

"Please, baby, just gimme this chance."

Katie continues to weep as she replies, "It's too late, Sean. I need space . . ."

"You're just gonna throw it all away, Katie? You are will'n to throw it all away?"

"I just need to be away from you."

"Yeah right! Uh-huh . . . ya met somebody, didn't you? I will fuck'n kill'm! I tell ya that."

"I didn't meet anyone, Sean—not now, not any other time you beat the hell outta me. I just need to be away from you. We are over!"

"I see you with anyone and I will fuck'n kill you too, Katie. You fuck'n hear me?"

"Then do it, Sean! Kill me, you coward! Shut your fuck'n mouth and do it already!" Katie screams the challenging words through all those years of pain.

Sean says nothing, just looks down at the floor for a brief moment before snapping his head back up. The look in his eyes instantly silences Katie. Her inability to breathe confuses her. She feels the pressure on her neck as he lifts her from the chair. He grips tightly with both hands as he holds her high in the air. She grabs his arms but does not possess the strength to remove his hands from around her neck. The chair she was sitting in a second ago flies across the room just before her back and head slam onto the floor. The man begging for another chance no longer resides behind the eyes staring into hers. Those eyes are just as empty as hers. She looks into his blank stare as her eyes glaze over. She smiles as her face loses color. She releases her grip and gently rests her arms on the floor. She will let him do what she failed to do in the tub. She welcomes the death he offers. This is her great escape.

# CHAPTER FIFTEEN

# REGRET

The morning brings an aching reminder of a forgotten evening. Hudson cracks open his crusty, bloodshot eyes to the bright, relentless rays of the morning sun and the dog giving his hands a few good morning kisses. He struggles to recall the events that preceded his drunken slumber outside on the back deck as he stares at the wide-open sliding glass door. He actually welcomes the void in memory, because there is no shame about what he cannot remember. What he does know and remember is that he would have taken that man's life yesterday had it not been for Jake. When he got home, he had to drown his anger. He had to extinguish that fire. It took the better part of a fifth of whiskey and a few doses of hydrocodone to do so; however, whiskey does not extinguish fire, it feeds it. He didn't slowly wet the fire with alcohol either; he doused it, and the flames raged. His knuckles are busted and bloody, so the dog tries to heal them by licking the wounds. His busted knuckles are not from the one punch he delivered to the face of the big man at Pop's. He has no idea what or who he hit, nor who or what hit him. His lip is a bit swollen. He can taste dried and slightly salty blood. He has a nasty cut and bruise under his left eye, and his swollen cheek narrows his vision. His ribs and back send messages of pain to his brain as he attempts to suck air into his lungs. His truck is parked by the deck with the driver's side door wide open. Nothing but an empty void exists from the time he came home, opened that bottle, and woke up on this deck.

"I don't suppose you know what the hell I did last night, do ya?" Hudson asks the dog, who has ceased his healing kisses and now looks confused at his strange new friend.

"All I know, it wasn't enough to kill my ass. Shit, here comes the whiskey . . ."

Hudson gets to his feet and lunges toward the railing. He doesn't quite make it before falling to the deck and purging the contents of his stomach onto the old boards. The dog sits a few feet from Hudson studying his new friend. Hudson seems odd, but friendly to the dog. The big fella has gained more trust of his new friend, not because he gave him that delicious smoked meat or saved him from sure death, but there is something else, something familiar to the dog. Hudson rolls over and sits up, resting his back against the railing, and takes in a deep, painful breath. He holds onto the railing while pulling himself up to his feet. Unlike a sober man, a drunk man can see the world spin, making it difficult to walk. Hudson takes a moment to time up the world's rotations before attempting his first step. As though he recognizes his strange friend's struggle, the dog walks over and stands next to Hudson, who takes the dog up on his offer to help, grabbing ahold of the collar as the dog leads him into the house and to the recliner. The dog lies on the floor adjacent to the recliner as he continues to study Hudson.

"Thanks for the tow, bud! I don't suppose you know what I did with my weed, do ya? Sure could use Nurse Mary right now—she sure knows how to tend to my wounds."

The big fella wags his nub a time or two, and then sits up, not because he has an answer to his strange new friend's question, but because he is fond of the fact Hudson likes to talk to him—gives him attention.

"I bet ya hungry, ain't ya. Lemme toke on this roach a time or two, and I then will get ya set up."

The dog vigorously wags his tail for a second before rising to all fours with his head slightly cocked to the side, indicating curiosity about his newfound friend's odd mood.

Looking through the smoke, Hudson continues to talk with a lung full. "What? Wanna know why I'm so fucked up?" Hudson pauses as he exhales. "I think you know. You've been there, big boy, just look at all those ugly scars. I'm just as scarred and ugly as you, slick. The real question is, why the hell do you seem to be so damned happy to keep on liv'n?" Hudson looks at the dog as if he expects an answer. "Who's really the screwed-up one here, my friend?" Hudson mumbles right before toking on the roach again.

Hudson's cell phone buzzes, diverting their attention away from the one-sided conversation. His dad is calling, probably to talk about what happened at Pop Walter's place. No way he can explain away his actions with a head full of last night's whiskey and Mary numbing the brain, providing no recollection of the details. Gray may also want to know about the night his son sped off down the dirt road, but no way can he have that conversation, either. He ignores that call. The voicemail notification dings, but there's not a chance in hell will he listen to it.

A week has gone by since bringing the dog home from the hospital and the fight at Pop's. Every night brings that same old ritual: blues from the speakers, whiskey in the glass, and nearly incoherent one-sided conversations with the dog. His ribs and face slowly heal, but his mind continues to suffer. During these dark days, Hudson makes no progress in his search for a place the dog can call home, nor has he tried to call anyone. He has yet to even think about naming the fella. He has pretty much done about everything he can to not let the dog grow on him. He fights every urge to take the dog for a walk, teach him tricks, or include him in anything that he does around the house beyond his drunken rambles. However, the big fella follows Hudson everywhere he goes. He sits and looks up at Hudson, hoping for a head rub or some more of that delicious smoked chicken. Hudson froze some beef bones with peanut butter stuffed into the hollows and gives the dog one every evening—it's no smoked chicken, but the big fella happily takes them. While the dog chews on the bone and licks on the frozen peanut butter, Hudson steadily pours whiskey down his throat as he ruminates on his decisions in life and attempts to wash away their agonizing consequences. Giving the dog a bone assures Hudson can go numb without the dog's lonely eyes staring at him. Sure enough, the dog chews and slobbers on those peanut butter bones for hours. He usually passes out with the hollow bone next to him while Hudson passes out in the recliner with an empty glass next to him.

Death comes knocking on the seventh night to solicit Hudson's life with promises of mercy. The whiskey, opioids, and persistent memories of Hank take their toll on his vulnerable mind as the week passes. Hudson chases oxycodone with the last of a fifth. He chugs it all down, trying his best to shut off his brain as Alice In Chains fills the room with "Angry Chair." Hudson stumbles to the back door and fumbles with the lock before sliding it open for the dog. He stops by the kitchen for another pint before stumbling back to the recliner. He has to wash away all the pain and dilute the memories. Whiskey washing fails to clean his mind of misery—it only drowns all hope for a better life. The daily grind, dead friend, and the boy he failed is all too much on him. He should have died, not Hank. Depression's argument that death is the only way out is too convincing to ignore any longer. The thing is, Hudson is not really trying to wash away the memories, only the thought of the pain he will deliver his family. In his mind, he has but one option to forever forget it all. His anguish is overwhelming whether drunk or sober. He suffers because he altered his destiny to save that damn dog. The dog's fate was not his to decide.

"I'm sorry I gave you hope. I'm sorry to abandon you before ful-fill'n my promise. I wish you the best. The back door is open whenever you're ready to leave," Hudson tells the dog, slurring every word, just before he polishes off the pint in just a few gulps, but death by alcohol is too slow. From underneath the chair, Hudson fumbles out the fully loaded .38 revolver. Six hollow-point bullets, one for each cylinder. He will not leave his demise up to chance as he did the last time he sat in this chair. He determines his fate. He cocks the hammer back and presses the barrel to his temple. No note this time. The earlier one remains stashed away in his dresser and will suffice once his family finds it. His eyelids are heavy from the whiskey and slowly lower. He puts his finger on the trigger to begin his long-awaited journey from this wretched life. No more memories, no more pain, no more anger will consume him. He incoherently mumbles gibberish as he continues to squeeze the trigger. This is it, the end of Hudson Lee: brother, son, Marine. Darkness surrounds him. The same darkness resides inside him. From the dark comes a small light. In the light, the boy holds a whippoorwill as he hangs his head. Hank steps into the light and puts his hand on the boy's shoulder. The boy looks up to Hank and smiles.

Hudson opens his eyes to remove the boy, the bird, and Hank. He opens his eyes as the dog's big head appears from the dark. The numbness delivered by the alcohol and oxycodone dulls the pain, but Hudson feels pressure on his forearm. The gun goes off but is no longer in his hand. The dog is in the chair with him: growling, snarling, and barking. He knew what Hudson had in his hand and has felt the pain it inflicts. The dog continues growling and barking, only a few inches from Hudson's face.

"What the fuck? This is not your life! This is not your death! Get the fuck off me!" Hudson roars as though an angry fiend within him is lashing out at the dog; however, Satan himself cannot intimidate the beast who dwells within the dog. He who normally delivers death when called upon now stands defiant against the cold one. He bares his arsenal of teeth as he responds to Hudson with a deep growl that would make even the most vicious of warriors tremble. Hudson does not tremble, though, because he welcomes death. He wants it. He begs for it.

"Go ahead, mothafucka! Do it! End me! Fuck'n kill me!" Hudson yells with tears streaming down his cheeks, pounding his chest and slurring each word. The dog stands his ground against the threat. Hudson tries to push him off, but the dog pushes back harder. Hudson attempts to stand, but the dog is too heavy for his weakened legs to lift. The dog growls again as Hudson reaches down, fishing around for the gun.

"I will kill us both, ya sonuva bitch . . . put us both out of our fuck'n misery!" Hudson shouts at the growling beast as he fails to find the gun. Hudson quickly succumbs to the heavy dose of whiskey he drank only a few minutes ago. His mind goes black as his head sinks into the back of the chair and his arm falls limp over the side. The beast within the dog recedes into the shadows. He means his troubled friend no harm, nor will he allow trouble to inflict harm on his friend. The gentle giant remains on Hudson's lap the rest of the night, standing guard against the executioner's relentless invasions.

Too much alcohol has a way of degrading time and memories. Hudson struggles to raise his heavy eyelids into his throbbing head. Everything hurts. The world spins again. He waits for the blurry room to come into focus before investigating the crushing weight on his legs. He finally regains enough sight to peek down without moving his aching head. Looking back up at him is that big head with those beady brown eyes. The dog opens his enormous mouth, rolling out his tongue as he yawns. While his tongue is out, he takes the opportunity to welcome Hudson back from the dead with a kiss on his cheek. Hudson tries to pull his face back to avoid the wet good morning kiss, but his head hurts too bad. The front of his head is a pounding reminder of last night's liquid overdose. The back of his head hurts for a whole other reason. He reaches his right hand around to the back of his head, immediately flinching at the slightest touch. He pulls his hand back around to find his fingertips coated in a mixture of dried and coagulated blood. He also notices the dental impressions on his forearm.

"I guess this has something to do with your big ass being on my lap?!" Hudson mumbles.

The dog looks up at Hudson, inching closer to his crazy friend as he shows him some attention. Hudson reaches out his left hand and scratches the dog up under his jaw. "Well, let me up, big fella. I need to clean up the mess on the back of my head."

The dog senses his friend is no longer in danger, so he hops down and sits next to the chair. Hudson stands up for all of a second before losing his balance and slamming into the coffee table. Along with losing time, too much whiskey has a way of complicating simple, everyday functions such as standing. Apparently, his legs are still drunk, or the bullet that ricocheted off the back of his head knocked his equilibrium out of whack, or both. Hudson pushes himself up off the floor. He manages to get his legs up under him for another attempt at standing. The second attempt ends up about the same as the first. Hudson takes one step forward before stumbling five or six steps to his right. Fortunately, the wall is there to catch him. Hudson leans against the wall for a few seconds hoping he can straighten out his balance while the world slows down a bit. Refusing to surrender to the rotating room, Hudson takes a step away from the wall. That step is followed by two steps back, three to his left, and then another four to his right before crashing down onto the floor. All the while, the dog watches in amusement as his clumsy friend bounces around the living room like one of those little rubber balls.

"You know, I can use a lil help . . . dammit . . . Imma puke . . . ," Hudson mumbles as he cups his left hand over his mouth.

Hudson tries to make a break for the bathroom as he pushes himself back up off the floor. Out of a three-point stance, he takes off with every ounce of energy he can muster. The first couple steps achieve good momentum. He is well on his way to the bathroom until he clips the couch and takes a nosedive into the wall next to the bathroom. He crawls into the bathroom where he is finally able to purge the remaining whiskey from his gut. Hudson keeps his head resting up on the seat as his arms drop down about midway on the toilet. The cool toilet seat feels pretty damn good on his aching head. His eyes struggle to focus, but they remain open to keep the world still. The dog waltzes into the bathroom to check on his crazy friend. He inches up to Hudson to give him a wet kiss on his arm.

"What the hell's up with all the dayum lick'n?! Knock that shit off! Let me be," Hudson mumbles, taking a breath between each sentence.

The pain prevents him from moving his throbbing head to look at the dog, so the big fella steps around to the other side of the toilet. Once there, he gives Hudson another kiss, but this time right in his nose.

"Dammit, asshole . . . ya slobbered in my nose—enough with that shit!" Hudson mumbles a little louder this time as he blows the dog slobber out his nose, and then immediately makes another deposit into the toilet.

"I musta died and went to hell."

After several minutes, Hudson finally gets his knees up under his chest. He makes another, much slower attempt to get to his feet. Finally, his legs once again prove capable of standing without tumbling. Hudson stands next to the toilet for a few minutes until he regains trust in his once-undependable legs. While his legs work to fully regain Hudson's trust, his eyes work to focus the blurry room. Hudson makes his way over to the medicine cabinet in search of something to dull the excruciating pain in his head and something else to patch up the wound on the back of his skull. He pours rubbing alcohol on his arm before wrapping a washcloth around the dog bite.

"Ahhh, dayum that burns! You bit me, asshole. I save your ass and you bite me?" Hudson asks the dog without turning to look at him as he wraps his arm.

After tending to his wounds, Hudson walks out of the bathroom and heads to the kitchen for a glass of water. The dog follows immediately behind him. They stop dead in their tracks as they look over at Hudson's favorite chair. There where his head rested last night is a bloodstain about the size of a softball with three or four streaks on the top where the blood ran as the chair was in the reclined position. Hudson stares for a moment as his eyes focus on the spot. He is still a bit confused about what exactly transpired, until he looks down at the floor. About three feet behind the chair against the back wall sits the handed-down .38 revolver. Though he can't remember every small detail, he realizes that the dog probably stopped him from shooting himself. Hudson takes a second to look down at the dog, who stands a short distance behind his unpredictable friend, before continuing to the kitchen.

"Of all the people who could've saved ya, you end up with this whack job." Hudson pauses before continuing, "Hungry? Here, you go out while I fix us someth'n. I ain't got much. We'll have to go shop'n later, I guess."

Hudson watches as the big fella walks out the door he left open all night. He watches the dog do his business and then take off after a critter into the woods. He walks over to the chair and stares at it for a moment before picking up the gun. He opens the cylinder and stares at the empty shell with the dented primer. Just above the floor behind the chair, a hole in the sheet rock confirms what he can't remember. He looks over as the dog walks through the open door. The dog needs someone unbroken who enjoys life as much as him, but there is little to no chance of finding such a person. Searching for that home seems futile.

Hudson walks the dog down to the tree line by his pond with the gun in his back pocket. The dog happily follows his crazy friend. He sits and looks up as Hudson pulls out the gun.

"I'm sorry, fella . . . I am sorry I'm this fucked up. But I made a promise and aim to keep it."

Hudson wraps the gun and box of ammunition in plastic, and then buries them. The dog deserves a good home. Hudson will find him that home, regardless of the tribulation he must endure while doing so.

— CHAPTER SIXTEEN —

# HIDEOUT

He denies her the departure she desires. He refuses to help her escape at the expense of his freedom. Sean stands over Katie's motionless body, shouting for her to wake up. He kneels beside her, and then lightly slaps her cheek. She remains still. He slaps her again, much harder this time, as he shouts louder for her to wake up. She remains still. He grabs the coffee pot off the hot plate and then pours hot coffee onto her belly, causing her to double up and cry out in pain.

"Are you crazy? You want me to kill you? What the hell is wrong with you? I'm not gonna kill ya. I don't know why you do this stupid shit. You need to get right!" Sean lectures Katie.

She ignored the apologetic man, hoping he would fall silent. She rejected the pleading man, hoping he would leave her. She challenged the raging man, hoping he would free her. They all failed her. Now, the apologetic man returns with a chip on his shoulder as he stares down at Katie crying on the floor. This is normally the stage of his abusive cycle when Sean shows sympathy for the woman he claims to love, but he fails to neutralize his anger with remorse. He blames his actions on her—she forced his hand by challenging his ego. He offers an apology for pouring hot coffee on her with the same conviction as a corrupt politician caught in a motel room with a prostitute and cocaine. He shuts his eyes and massages his aching head, frantically searching for the healing words to mend their relationship, but lingering alcohol and anger impede all thought. He fears she will run if he leaves the house to clear his head. She has never run before, nor has she said a word of their troubles to anyone, but this time feels different. He tells her that he will be back with an ointment for her burns, but reminds her that all other wounds heal through her silence. Normally, his threats are enough to control Katie, but this time he takes her keys with him to ensure she does not flee.

Katie has long fantasized about possessing the courage to escape Sean. She knows he will never free her of his control, whether in life or by death. She can no longer exist just to suit his needs and must take control of her own destiny. The opportunity to run is now, before he returns. For the past two years, she has planned and prepared for such a time. He may have taken those keys but knows nothing of the spare key she had made or the money from tips she has secretly saved in preparation to flee. She has no destination, though. The house belongs to Sean, and even if it were her house, he would not leave. She cannot stay with her family, because she will have to tell them about the private hell she's escaped. She does not want to have that discussion, nor does she want to risk their lives by involving them. She cannot live with any of her friends for the same reasons. She cannot go to work at the family diner as he will surely stake it out. She just drives and cries while contemplating her choices. Her heart pounds and her mind races as she turns fantasy into reality, though courage is not the reason; desperation motivates her.

Katie has traveled this part of Georgia all her life, but today this scenic highway with no destination in mind is unfamiliar to her. Most people would be terrified by such uncertainty; however, the more Katie drives, the more fear subsides. She knows, deep down, where this road will take her—where it ends. She drives more than forty miles before holing up in a cheap motel. The motel is the type of place where people don't ask questions about each other. They all have old skeletons they wish to keep deeply buried. They have no desire to share dirty secrets, which suits Katie just fine. No one here will interrupt her focus as she contemplates her limited options. She lies on the bed while staring at the locked door, afraid he will furiously burst through at any moment. Her fear of Sean is inescapable, except by way of death. Guilt for the grief her suicide will cause her family is just as inescapable, except by way of death. She destroys the suicide note she wrote before sliding into the tub last night. She wanted her suicide to reveal a heavy truth for Sean to carry, but the weight of guilt and regret will anchor her family in a flood of sorrow, drowning them all. Her death must be an unfortunate and less painful accident. Her secret must die with her to save her family, thus exonerating Sean of his atrocious deeds and concealing his monster within.

Katie pulls herself together long enough to call her mama. She lies to her. She asks for a week off, so she can attend a reunion with some friends. Over the next week, Katie spends her days walking trails at a national park a few miles down the road from her hideout. She hopes the beauty of nature will displace the ugliness of her life. When it fails to do so, she spends her nights lying in bed heavily sedated by a mixture of oxycodone and alcohol. For two days she begs God for a miracle. The girl makes her desperate plea as opioids no longer suppress the sadness of alcohol, enhancing it instead. By the third day, with no response from God, she convinces herself that she deserves no such miraculous gift, so the prayers diminish. Depression and thoughts of death fill the void left by the absence of prayer. Relief from this unforgiving life again whispers in her ears. Katie has yet to completely stop fighting for her life, but the excessive consumption of alcohol and heavy doses of oxycodone amplify the convincing whispers of death.

Hoping to silence the whispers, Katie finally listens to her mother's voicemails. She knows her family, especially her mother, will be worried about her if Sean has talked to them. He will tell Mary Beth his version of the truth, omitting the physical and mental abuse he perpetrated on her daughter. He will convince her family that she stormed off after a simple argument and tell them he has not seen her since. He will play the part of a concerned fiancé and use her family to find her. They will be none the wiser when they lead the wolf to the sheep. However, her mom's messages only ask that she call her.

Katie caves to guilt and reluctantly calls her mama. She keeps the conversation simple at first, fishing for information without saying much about herself. The conversation is simple for nearly a minute before Mary Beth tells her that Sean has stopped by the diner a few times, which is not unusual, but what he told her was disheartening.

"I asked how the reunion was goin, if you were have'n fun and all. And it kinda took by surprise, but he said you did not go to a 'dayum reunion.' He was a lil snarky, but not really at me. I asked'm what was the matter. He said y'all had an argument and you just wanted to get away for a lil while. Is that true, hunny?"

Katie contemplates her response. Sean did what she expected. He made her out to be a liar to her mama, something he knows her mother despises. She either continues to lie to her mama, avoiding looking like a liar, or she comes clean. Coming clean requires her to open up about other things, private things, to save face with her mama. She must decide quickly. As more time passes, it seems less and less likely that Mary Beth will believe her excuses.

"Well... we... we did have a fight, Mama. I just wanted to get away for a bit, so I tried to meet up with some friends. Instead, I decided to get out of town to hike and clear my head."

"Aw, Katie, that's all ya had to say, hunny. You don't ever have to lie to me. I have to tell ya, I am a little disappointed you felt that you had to lie to me."

"I'm sorry, Mama. I just didn't want to drag you into our fight. I wish he wouldn't have said anything to you."

"Well, he's just worried about you like we are, hunny. I hope you cleared your head."

"I did, Mama," Katie answers while holding back her emotions. He has everyone convinced that he is a concerned fiancé. He hides the monster very well.

"When are you come'n back, hun? We sure could use your help at the diner."

"I will head back tomorrow, so I'll be back at the diner the next morn'n."

"OK, hun. Drive carefully. I love you, and please don't ever lie to me again."

"OK, Mama. Love you, too!" Katie replies.

Katie is furious at Sean and herself. In her mama's eyes, Sean is a concerned fiancé and Katie is a liar. Those are the little games he likes to play. She regrets calling her mama in the first place, but guilt, drugs, alcohol, and those whispers have clouded her mind. Now, she must return to work, where Sean will surely visit every day to intimidate her. She did not run away only to return for more abuse and control. Anger and fear boil over, causing a panic attack. She throws back three painkillers, making it five in three hours, and chases them down with half a bottle of wine. She paces around the room waiting for the panic to subside. The alcohol acts quickly on her empty stomach. Not quick enough, though, so she guzzles the rest of the bottle, making it two bottles within two hours. She is defenseless when her body suddenly shuts down. The coffee table helps break her fall, but does nothing to interrupt her comatose state. Her mind is finally at peace.

# CHAPTER SEVENTEEN

# CATFISH

Hudson is two days dry since shedding his own blood. His mind clears with the absence of alcohol. His senses return with the absence of opioids. He does not practice complete sobriety, though, often enjoying Mary's company. He cannot completely leave himself vulnerable to the thoughts of a sober mind. She keeps life somewhat tolerable and helps to quiet the whispers. Ol' death is still there, like a troubled friend on a downward spiral with intentions of bringing Hudson down with him. However, the dog is also there as a reminder of Hudson's promise. He must find the dog a home before taking that trip with his troubled friend.

The light-gray sky and cool air outside perfectly reflect Hudson's spirit during these borrowed days. He stands on the back deck deep in thought, with Mary on his mind and a cup of coffee in his hand. The dog breaks from chasing critters to join his friend up on the deck. They stare off at the peaceful field where the grass continues the journey into fall dormancy. Silence fills their ears while the cool breeze gently brushes by them. Hudson takes a moment to enjoy the feeling before looking down at the dog.

"What the hell?! Whatcha say we go wet a hook?"

The dog looks up at Hudson with no clue of what his friend has said, but can tell it was something that should excite him. The dog swiftly wags his nub of a tail, scooting closer to Hudson and tapping his leg with his paw. Hudson scratches him up under his jaw, just like he likes it.

"Yeah . . . ya like that idea, do ya?! Let's load up the boat, then."

Many years have passed since Hudson fished the Oconee. He is not ready to approach his family to ask for a fishing report; he knows that will come with a lengthy and awkward conversation or, more likely, a lecture. To avoid any such encounter, he goes to the one person who will give him a good fishing report without intruding into his personal matters. They stop by Ricky's Bait 'N Tackle to grab some bait and snacks before heading to the boat ramp. Ricky has a little bell above the door to let him know when folks walk into the store, which jingles as Hudson and the dog enter. Ricky comes out from the back room, where he watches a little television when he's got nothing better to do, and, before even looking to see who's come through the door, he asks, "What can I do ya for?"

"Whatcha say, Ricky?"

"Well, I'll be. Hudson Lee! It has been a hot dayum minute now, ain't it?! What took ya so long to stop by, son?" Ricky asks as he shakes Hudson's hand.

"Been busy around the house."

"Uh-huh, is that right? Well, who's your handsome friend there?"

"He . . . well . . . he has no name. He was in a bad way when I found'm: had a busted leg, shot in the head, and bit by a copperhead down by Deddy's pond. Damn boy was backed up to a tree as that copperhead was going in to give'm another dose of the bad shit."

"Aw, heck. He's lucky ya found'm. I guess that's why ya tore ass out of there a while back."

"Yeah! Heard about that, did ya? You want him? He's a damn good dog," Hudson responds, trying to redirect the conversation.

"Naw, can't say I do, son. You know we got that lil wiener dawg. This ugly fella looks like he would use her as a dayum chew toy. But hey man, welcome home! Glad to see ya got back safe n sound."

"Good to be back, Ricky," Hudson replies with a bit of idle enthusiasm.

"I bet. Bet you saw some bad stuff over there, bud. You know ya mama's been worried sick. Yow deddy, too. Said they ain't heard shit from ya, son. You oughta call ya mama now."

Hudson looks at Ricky for a moment before again navigating the conversation in a different direction.

"Where the fish bite'n, Ricky?"

Ricky picks up on Hudson's attempt to avoid war and family talk, so he does not push the issue and, instead, happily switches to one of his favorite conversation topics. "Welp, the catfish are tear'n it up at the dam. Can't keep a dadgum hook in the water . . . I tell you whut!"

"Is that right?! What they hit'n on?"

"They tear'n up the shad. Now, whatcha gotta do is net some shad and throw 'em on ice. Be at the dam when they ain't pull'n, which they ain't been pull'n til around fohwer o'clock over the summuh. But they ain't been pull'n since thangs cooled down, and they probly ain't gonna pull tuhday . . . not supposed to get but sixty-five to seventy tuhday. Won't need all'at electricity if the folks in Atlanna aren't run'n the A/C. Anyhow, don't anchor and don't put any weight on your line. Motor up to the dam buoys, and then drift. Toss the line out as far as you can without weight. Hudson, we couldn't keep uh hook in the water two days ago. I mean we packed the live well full—couldn't even shut the lid. Mainly blues, but we did get a couple flatheads. Ya know, normally, flatheads like to lay'n wait for live bait."

"Awwl right, Ricky, I'll give it a go. Let me get a net and this shit right here and best give me a bucket of minnuhs just in case I can't net some shad." Hudson lays an assortment of snacks and some bottles of water up on the counter while Ricky goes to the tank for the minnows.

"Hey, Hudson, you should call ya deddy. I know it ain't my business, and I ain't try'n to get in your shit, dude, but he's worried about ya, son. He said ya damn near killed somebody at Pop Walters's farm," Ricky yells from over by the minnow tanks.

"Shit . . . ," Hudson mumbles before yelling back, "He did, did he? How pissed is he about that?"

"Just call'm. He's worried about ya, bud," Ricky says as he returns from the tanks.

Hudson looks down, grabs his stuff, and starts for the door, "Okie doke, I hear ya, Ricky. Thanks for the advice . . . about the fish. I'll see if I can't catch a few."

"Awlright then. Good luck out there, bud! Good to meet ya, big fella! You oughta name'm, son."

"So I've been told."

Hudson and the dog make it out to the Oconee Dam, where Ricky said the catfish were tearing up the shad. The dog is reluctant to get in the boat at first, but he sure is glad he did as they rip down the lake. He sits on the opposite side of Hudson with his mouth wide open, licking the drops of water out of the air as the boat bounces over the ripples on the lake. Hudson stops by an old drain-pipe where shad are known to run thick. He has no problem catching enough bait; the catfish, on the other hand, are not running as thick as Ricky made out. Of course, that's classic Ricky. He never gives anyone all his secrets, as no fisherman ever really does, and usually exaggerates his fish tales quite a bit, as most fishermen usually do; however, Ricky is a little better at it than most.

Hudson reaches into the Igloo and grabs a cold water to wet down the cotton in his mouth, compliments of Mary. Meanwhile, his big red temporary fishing buddy looks at Hudson for a second before deciding he has had enough of waiting for the fish to bite. He has had about enough of watching little fish popping the top of the water and swirling around, driving him crazy. Without any indications of his intentions, the big fella leaps off the boat, landing in the water with one big splash, startling Hudson and causing him to drop his bowl of greens.

"What the hell, dude?! You're gonna scare the fish . . . ," Hudson yells, then pauses as he picks up his bowl and its contents. "Which ain't hit'n on shit anyhow, but you made me drop my smoke, man," Hudson continues as he lowers his voice.

The dog has no idea what his crazy friend has said to him. What he does know is that lake water sure feels pretty damn good on all those healing wounds. He circles the boat a time or two, splashes around, and then lets off a few barks. Hudson sits back watching while eating a piece of jerky to quiet down his nagging belly, also compliments of Mary. Though his stomach makes noise, his mind does not. He thinks about nothing. He simply takes in the moment, watching the dog enjoy a good swim, even though it ruins any chance of catching a fish. He has gone a long while since taking in such a peaceful moment. He sits nearly immobile from Mary's intoxicating kisses, watching as the lake, dog, trees, dam, and everything else seem to fade into a Bob Ross picture. This is not a happy moment, nor is it sad. This moment is simply a welcomed nothing to his damaged mind.

Captivated by the charming scenery while mentally incapacitated by his drug of choice, Hudson completely loses focus on the fishing aspect of this day on the lake. He only notices that the pole to his left is doubled over into the water when the drag calls out for help. Even then, Mary delays his reaction as he witnesses something massive ripping out a ton of line in a hurry. Hudson finally breaks free from the mental clutch Mary had on him to grab the pole and set the hook.

"Fish on! It's a hawg!" Hudson belts out in pure excitement.

About the time Hudson settles in for a good fight, the dog decides he is done with his morning swim and ready to join his friend back up in the boat. He wants to see what all the excitement is about.

"Seriously, boy?!" Hudson yells, holding onto the pole in his left hand while grabbing the dog's collar with his right. He pulls the big, wet fella up into the boat, and then turns his full attention back to the battle with the hog on the other end of his line. The dog is soaked and needs to dry off, so he does exactly that. He dries himself in the same manner as all dogs, shaking the water off, soaking Hudson in the process.

"Dammit tuh heyull, boy! Oh shit, he's run'n with it!" Hudson yells.

The drag screams as the fish dives toward the bottom of the lake. Hudson holds onto the pole with his left hand, while reeling with his right. The dog watches and cheers on his buddy while turning circles and vigorously wagging his nub of a tail. He gives Hudson two or three more unwanted showers in between circles. Hudson cusses him every time, but is too focused on the fight to really care about the lake water showers, which are full of dog hair. Hudson fights the fish for about fifteen to twenty minutes before getting it up to the boat. The dog barks at the fish when he sees it. He has no idea what to make of the ugly, whiskered beast Hudson has just pulled from the depths of Lake Oconee.

"Hell yeah! Forty-five . . . fifty pounder! Wooooooo!" Hudson screams in excitement.

The dog barks and pants and barks and pants. Hudson nets the big fish and pulls it up into the boat. The dog relentlessly barks at the fish, jumping forward and backward as the mysterious creature twists and flops around, slapping his big tail against the boat. Meanwhile, Hudson pumps his fist, celebrating their victory. He knows exactly what they've just landed. He grabs the dog by the cheeks, rubbing them quickly before going back to his fist-pump celebrations. At least for a moment, glee displaces desolation; it even fills the nothing from earlier.

"Hot dayum . . . look at this hawg! Woooo!" Hudson yells as he continues his celebration.

A blast of cool air hits Hudson in the face. He closes his eyes, taking in the moment. His mind remains at ease from the smoke, but his heart pounds from the adrenaline rush. From his blank mind a name comes into focus. Normally it is a painful name to remember, but this time is different. This time the name felt right to remember. Maybe his friend can live on.

"Hank! How bout I call ya Hank? He was a good man. He is a good man . . . and a helluva a friend." Hudson offers the name to the dog, who is more focused on the catfish that is uglier than him.

When the dog finally looks up, Hudson gives him a good scratching up under his jaw, just like he likes it. He gives Hudson a couple licks, wags his nub, and then lies down by the fish. Hudson sits back in his seat. He finally thought of his friend and mentioned his name without having a panic attack. Maybe it is Mary that has his mind feeling peaceful in this moment, or maybe it is the thrill of catching the big flathead; either way he welcomes the calm response of his mind.

Hudson and Hank stop by Ricky's on the way home. He has to show off their prize catch and see how much the giant weighs. They walk into the bait shop to find Ricky and Big Jake telling stories, stopping them in mid-conversation.

"Whatcha say, Hudson? Whoop anyone's ass lately?" Jake says with a big smirk.

"About that . . . I'm sorry, dude . . . I . . ."

"Aw don't fret, son, I made things right with those folks and Pop. I tried call'n ya, and you just blew me off, son. Where ya been?"

"Just been . . . camp'n." Hudson nearly forgets about the excuse he planned to tell everyone. He looks over at Ricky as he recalls telling him he was at the house. Ricky's perplexed look indicates to Hudson that he's picked up on the difference in stories. Before Ricky can talk, Hudson quickly continued, "I tell ya what, Griz, I'll make it up to ya . . . I'll get you a case of beer."

"Hudson, I kept you out of jail and my dad's big foot out of your tiny ass. I'm afraid you're gonna have to get me three cases of the good shit . . . not that cheap shit you and your dad drank."

Hudson contemplates Jake's deal for a moment before responding, "OK, my enormous peacemaker, my tiny ass and I thank you. Hank thanks you, too. Three cases of good shit it is . . . from all three of us."

"Hank? You named him?" Ricky asks.

"I did. Just came to me on the lake."

"Why Hank?"

"Tribute to a friend." Hudson looks up with a slight grin as he answers Ricky's question.

"Ah, well that's awlright. Did ya do what I told ya, Hudson?" Ricky asks.

"I did."

"And?"

"Noth'n . . . not even uh dayum nibble!" Hudson responds, trying to hold back a bigger grin.

"Ah heck. I'm tell'n ya, Hudson, we tore 'em slap up the other day," Ricky responds, perplexed like before but for a different reason.

"Uh-huh, I hear ya, Ricky," Hudson responds with a touch of sarcasm.

"I'm tell'n ya whut, dude, it is the God's honest truth."

"Well, the least you could do is come help me fix my lights on the boat for sending us all the way up to the dam for noth'n. I was goin to stay into the even'n, but the lights wouldn't come on."

Ricky agrees and they all four head out to the boat. Hudson jumps up into the boat and starts toward the steering console to flip on the lights. Ricky and Jake head to the front of the boat and trailer to see if the running lights come on. As Ricky and Jake make their way toward the bow, they hear Hudson yell, "Maybe we did get one lil ole nibble."

They look at Hudson, who stands perched up there in the boat holding up the ugly monster like a victorious warrior on the battlefield, grinning from one ear to the other.

"Hot dayum, Hudson! I told you! I told you, son!" yells Ricky.

"Holy shit, son! What's that, about forty or fitty pounds?" Jake asks, just as excited as Ricky.

"I don't know. Where's your scales, Ricky?"

"Brang'm the hell on into the stower; let's weigh this hawg."

Hudson follows Jake and Ricky, holding the whiskered giant while strutting like a pimp. Beside Hudson, Hank trots like a show horse, as he, too, owns a piece of this trophy catch. They all run inside so quickly, they damn near rip that little bell right off the wall above the door. That moment before hooking up a big catch on the scales holds the same suspense and excitement for fishermen as the field goal for the win does for football fans.

"Fifty-two and a half, boys," Ricky announces after hooking the fish up on the scale.

"Damn, son! Let me get that belly meat, dude. That'll be the only decent eat'n off this big rascal." Jake's eyes disclose his stomach's excitement as he thinks of the tender white fillets from a flathead's belly.

"Not happn'n, big boy!"

"Hey dude, I kept ya outta jail and your tiny ass tiny."

"Three cases of the good shit is the deal. Flathead belly, my enormous friend, is a redneck delicacy . . . far more valuable than ten cases of the good shit. Anyhow, think I will just put'm in my pond."

"How about this: I'll catch a few tonight, and we'll have ourselves a fish fry real soon? I'll brang the fish and you brang the beer."

"Sounds good to me." Hudson, for the first time since agreeing to join Hank at a Georgia/Alabama game, makes a commitment without second thought—much quicker than the commitment to Hank.

"Me too. You wanna go to the dam, Jake?" Ricky can't pass up some good nighttime fishing.

"Let's do it."

"Well, good luck to the both of y'all. Hank and I need to get this hawg to the house and in the pond. See y'all later."

"You don't have tuh rush off, Hudson."

"Ricky, I know when it comes to fish'n, and after see'n this big cat, you will lock this place up the second I walk out that dayum door. Hell, y'all will probably beat me out the park'n lot."

"You right. Lemme help ya get this thang down so we can get goin."

Jake and Ricky help get the catfish off the scale while discussing their plan for the night. Afterward, Hudson and Hank hurry to the boat and put the big fish back in the live well. As they walk to the truck from the boat, Hudson looks down at Hank, who looks back up at him, "How about some Burnside on the way to the house?"

Hudson loads up Burnside's rendition of "Rollin' and Tumblin'" after they hop up into the truck. He turns up the volume a bit, rests his elbow on the door with the window down, while Hank pokes his big head out the passenger's side window with his tongue out, ready to whip in the wind and slobber down the side of the truck. Hudson pauses to soak up this moment free of anguish. He is not completely liberated from depression, and that damned ol' demon remains in there somewhere, but it sure does feel good to have one moment full of that boyhood joy. Maybe the boy will stay a while. Like his father always says, "No while to rush!"

# CHAPTER EIGHTEEN

# MAMA

Worrying about the well-being of their children is a lifelong burden for all devoted parents. Since the nightmare cut short their vacation, Gray and Savannah have occupied their time trying to track down Hudson and working around the farm. They do their best to provide fear no idle time in their minds while waiting for Hudson to return with his story. Though steadfast in their efforts to ward off the anxiety, trepidation of losing their son distresses their every thought. Their eyes droop from the lack of sleep. When able to nod off, a reoccurring nightmare of Hudson falling from a cliff, just beyond the reach of his extended hand, plagues Grayford. An exhausted Savannah lays sleepless every night. Anytime she starts to doze off, she sets her alarm for an hour later to offer her mind no time to dream—she cannot cope with the death who comes for her son. An ugly, lonely death seeks their son. Savannah ages years in just a few days. Gray is torn between anger and worry. Anger gnaws at him as he watches anxiety destroy Savannah. However, the god-awful worry about his son's mental well-being eats him up more than the gnawing anger. He knows his son very well, and, as they say in the South, that boy ain't right. Hudson has never been the best at calling home, but this time is different, at least it feels different. He ignores it at first, hoping all Hudson needs is time to adjust and acquaint himself with home again, but he can no longer allow himself to believe that.

Gray and Savannah have yet to receive a call from their son, but a phone call from Ricky helps bed down that nagging fear. He calls them after Hudson stops by the bait shop with that big ugly dog. Savannah and Gray bombard Ricky with questions about their son. Ricky puts forth his best attempt to settle their nerves, but for every answer he renders, they respond with at least two more questions. Ricky figures out pretty quickly that nothing he says will satisfy them. He becomes flustered as they overwhelm him with relentless queries. Fortunately for Ricky, that little bell above the door jingles a time or two, giving him a reason to let Gray and Savannah go. They are happy to hear Hudson is alive and well, but neither will be satisfied until they hear from their son directly. Only he can provide answers to their questions; however, for whatever reason, he seems to make every effort to avoid them. Whether he will answer their questions honestly is a whole other issue.

They are painting the front deck when they hear it. Many cars and trucks have kicked up gravel and dust on that old dirt road since they returned from the beach. Each time they race to the window hoping to see Hudson's old Ford, only to have disappointment fall upon them time and again. This time they casually turn to the sight of a red dust cloud trailing that long-awaited Ford. Time stands still on that front porch as it continues to tick for the Ford slowing up to turn down their driveway. Time creeps forward again as Hudson makes his way up to the house, boat in tow and a dog's massive head hanging out the passenger window. Gray looks over at an emotional Savannah with the intention of telling her to keep her emotions at bay; however, he knows that would only direct a bulk of her wrath his way. He worries that a vicious tongue-lashing may drive the boy away, but Hudson needs a dose of hard love and to see the pain he's caused his mama. Lord knows he needs to see how much he means to them.

Hudson pulls up next to the front deck with the driver's side facing his parents and the window down. "Hey, Mama! Deddy! How y'all doin? You oughta see what me and my new buddy here just caught up by the dam. Ole Ricky actually gave me some good—"

"Don't you hey Mama me, Hudson William Lee! You park'at dayum truck right now, young man!" Savannah cuts off Hudson midsentence while charging down the stairs to her son's truck.

"What's wrong, Mama?" Hudson asks, though he knows his ten-day hiatus has not gone unnoticed by Savannah, especially after speeding off the night of the whippoorwill and pretending he wasn't home when they came by.

"You don't ansuh yowuh dayum phone! You just disappeayuh after rip'n outta heeyuh in the middle of the night. We've been worried sick about you!"

"I went camp'n, Mama . . ."

"Camp'n my ass! Don't you dayuh give me that nonsense! You call yowuh mama before you go off and disappeayuh like'at! We know you were heeyuh last week. We heard that gunshot, and then you sped off down tha road like a dayum maniac. Go park yowuh truck and meet me at tha table. I won't say it again, young man!" Savannah yells, vigorously pointing her right index finger in all directions as she scolds Hudson. When that finger gets to going, it sends a threat far scarier than a loaded .44 magnum revolver; it's always a sure sign that the recipient of her tongue lashing has gone and crawled up her bad side.

Savannah storms off inside to await her son at the table in the basement. That table has hosted many scolding lectures in its day, most of them orchestrated by Savannah. Hudson knows he has quite the task ahead of him. He has to explain everything to his mama and father without letting out his true intentions. He attempted to convey many tall tales to his mama during his childhood, only to have her dig out the truth like a seasoned interrogator. All the kids were convinced their mama worked for the CIA, because she always seemed to know everything and detected lies better than any damn machine.

"Damn, Deddy, what'n tha hell's got her all riled up?"

"Just park'n come on in, son," Gray calmly answers.

"Well, shit, is she gonna gimme a whoop'n?" Hudson chuckles a bit, hoping to loosen up some of the tension.

"If you don't hurry up'n park'at dayum truck, she will," Gray replies sternly with a face of stone.

"Is it because—"

"Go park your fuck'n truck, son!" Gray can no longer contain his displeasure toward Hudson's frivolous attitude. His eyes and tone send an even harsher message than his words. Hudson now realizes he's misjudged his parents' concern for him and is terrified of the supper table interrogation awaiting him inside that quaint country home.

Hudson eases on down the driveway to give himself time to think about his story. The thought of stomping on the gas pedal and making a break for it crosses his mind, but he knows that will only delay the inevitable scolding, one-sided conversation. He knows he cannot avoid their questions indefinitely while finding that loving home for the ugly rascal next to him. Plus, running would only cause his parents further distress, and that guilt tears him up inside.

"Maybe you ought to hang out in the truck, Hank. I expect this shit to go sideways in a hurry—may get pretty ugly in there, my friend," Hudson tells a curious Hank. Hank senses the woman and man mean a lot to Hudson. He also senses he wants no part of whatever awaits his crazy friend. He licks his lips, lays his big butt in the seat, and enjoys the cool autumn breeze blowing in through the window as he bids farewell to Hudson.

Hudson slides out of the truck, shuts the door behind him, and takes a long time to make that short walk to the basement door. His heart pounds through his chest. His hands shake and his head spins. He hangs his head as if he's on the way to meet the executioner. His mama's wrath frightens the devil out of him. She can be, and usually is, relentless with her investigative queries. Hudson fears nothing, as he has already welcomed death into his life, but he is deathly afraid of this conversation. He takes a deep breath before creeping through the door.

"Mama, I—"

"Shut up and sit!" Savannah replies sternly before Hudson can finish his thought.

"Yes ma'am!" Hudson immediately replies with his newly adjusted attitude toward the situation.

Savannah grabs Hudson's hands. She looks directly into his eyes and asks, "Are you thinking about kill'n yaself?" She battles four years of worry, anger, and fear as the words leave her tongue.

Hudson struggles to maintain eye contact with his mama; he knows breaking eye contact is a sign of deceit. He also struggles to keep his emotions and guilt bedded down deep inside. Guilt would surely reveal the truth to his mama, and the truth cannot come out. His eyes well up, but he fights to keep the tears from falling. Falling tears tend to tell emotional secrets.

"Mama, what's wrong?"

"Don't you dayuh ansuh me with a question, and don't avoid my question. Are you thinking about kill'n yaself? Like that guy Maddie talked about?" Her anxiety is more urgent the second time she asks.

"No, Mama! Why are you asking me that?" Hudson replies without hesitation or further diversion; both would indicate to his mama that ending his life weighs heavy on his mind.

"Don't you lie to me, Hudson . . . not about this. You ansuh me truthfully!"

Her falling tears and the fear in her eyes nearly break Hudson, but he stands firm with his lie. "I am not thinking about taking my life, Mama. That is the truth."

"If you love me at all, you will tell me thuh truth. You swayuh on my life! You tell me thuh truth!" Savannah demands his honesty, but is terrified of the possibility her son hurts as bad as she believes.

"Mama, I am tell'n you the truth . . ." Hudson grabs her hand with both of his. "I love you with all my heart and soul, Mama. I will never swear on your life about anything, but I'm tell'n ya, Mama, I am not thinking about ending my life. I have been struggl'n to adjust since I've been home. I just needed to get away from everyone . . . clear my head, ya know. You and sis started in on me at the damn fish fry about this. I'm good, just gimme time and space to adjust. Please!"

Through the tears, Savannah remains focused on her son's face while she listens to his words. Years of worry clamp down on her tongue, rendering it speechless. All she can do right now is cry, delivering the hard truth to Hudson.

"Why didn't you call us before disappear'n for two dayum weeks, son?" Gray asks, taking advantage of the air in their conversation. He knows Savannah is about to break down, but he is not comfortable with Hudson's answers.

"I didn't really think about it, Deddy. Y'all were supposed to be in North Carolina for a week. I figured I'd check on the homeplace, and then go camp'n. I just wanted to reacquaint myself with good ole Georgia wilderness . . . clear my head'n all."

"We called and called and called. We were worried sick about you. You just come home from wohwuh. I heeyuh all these horrible, tragic stories of soljas commit'n suicide, and . . . we . . . we came home early because we ah worried about you, son!" Savannah confesses as she dries her eyes with a tissue. Her sadness drowns her eyes as she talks about the soldiers who have killed themselves and thinks about Hudson suffering from the same mental trauma.

"Mama . . ."

"And we hud a gunshot, and then you sped outta heeyuh . . ." She is unable to finish her thought. Her doleful heart hurts too much to talk. In the past, she could scold without sympathy, but not this time. She thinks about all those mothers who lost their children before their time by their own hands. The thought of those poor mothers and their suffering sons and daughters who came back mentally damaged is just too much for her. She cannot stomach the thought of her son suffering as they did and making the same permanent decision as them.

Hudson fights back his own tears as he watches his mama break down. He now witnesses the pain his death will deliver to his mama. He hasn't the thoughts or words to ease her sorrow. He should have never been here to witness her grief. His eyes are no longer blind to the future. He can no longer watch his mama's pain, so he looks up to talk to his father. However, Gray puts a finger up to his own lips, shakes his head no, and then points for Hudson to move over and console his mama. Hudson hesitates a moment to harden his heart. He then pulls his mama in and wraps his arms around her, holding onto the hug for a good minute before continuing the conversation just above a whisper.

"Mama, I came here to sit down by the pond and enjoy what I have missed for so long. You know I always loved to hear that whippoorwill sing. I'm happy to be home, but I did wanna just enjoy some alone time in the woods and on the river. Been awhile, ya know?"

"What about that shit the other night, son—gunshots and tear'n ass outta heeuh?" Gray asks, still wanting an explanation.

"Well, how bout y'all come on out to tha truck and I'll show y'all."

Savannah grabs a dry tissue and wipes the tears from her eyes, "Hudson, honey, ah you . . . have you thought about hurt'n yourself? Befowuh we leave this table, I need the truth . . . I need to believe you."

"Mama . . ." Hudson pauses to pull on the reins of his emotions before continuing, "I just wanted to have some time to myself. That's it. I felt a bit weird being back, and I just wanted to have a little time, ya know. I'm fine, Mama . . . I love ya, Mama, and don't plan on goin' anywhere."

"I love you, too, son, but that didn't ansuh my dayum question!" Savannah still struggles to believe her son.

"No, Mama, I'm not thinking about hurt'n myself . . . thought hasn't even crossed my mind."

Hudson feels a big knot in his chest when he answers his mama with such a tremendous lie. Not only is he still thinking about the end, he is angry for having to face days like today—to witness the agony of his death. Though his determination to end his life has subsided a bit, it's still there and his mama feels it. A thousand more questions trample through her mind, but she has no choice but to believe her son. The longer they sit at that table, though, the more likely his lie will reveal itself, so Hudson again shifts the conversation.

"Y'all just come on out to the truck. You'll see what the other night was about."

Savannah holds her son's arm as he escorts them to his truck. They see Hank's massive head at the driver's side window as he pokes his nose through the opening. He whimpers a little bit before getting excited about the thought of joining the pack who are making their way to the truck.

"What in thuh heyull is that ugly thang, Hudson?" Savannah asks, a bit frightened by the sight of the big dog.

"Well, Mama, I saved'm that night."

"He looks like one of those fight'n dogs. Is that what he is?"

"He was probably used as one . . . once upon a time, but not anymore. I do have to find him a home, though."

"Well, what the heyull happ'nd, son?" Gray asks.

"Well, Deddy, as I sat there by the pond listn'n to the whippoorwill, this big fella begins cry'n and yelp'n from the other side. I never even heard'm walk'n up. I got to the other side and found this fella bitten by a copperhead. Got'm right on the leg. Twice. I shot at the snake, and then convinced this guy to trust me. I took'm up to Watkinsville, to that twenty-four-hour animal hospital. Come to find out, he had a lotta other problems, including a gunshot to his head."

"Hudson, why did you have a gun in the middle of the night?" Savannah asks, still concerned about her son's intentions.

"In case I ran into—I don't know, Mama—a snake maybe." Hudson chuckles.

"Young man, I will snatch'at tongue right outta yowuh smaught-ass mouth. Don't you dayuh lie to me!"

Hudson's smile fades in a hurry as he does not doubt his mama's sincerity.

"Mama, we used to carry guns with us in the woods all the time grow'n up. I'm not think'n about kill'n myself. Please stop worry'n about that. Now, whaddya think about this big fella?"

Savannah curiously looks at the dog, struggling between fear and pity for the creature. "My goodness! How can people be so cruel to an animal?! Is he aggressive?"

"Well, Mama, I know y'all heard about what happened at Pop's . . ."

"Hell yeah, and we'll talk about that dayum shit later, too. Cost me some dayum catfish. Only way I could calm Pop down." Gray takes the opportunity to scold Hudson on that particular matter.

"Actually, speak'n of catfish, I have someth'n else to show ya in the boat, Deddy. Anyway, he has a tendency to get riled up around other dogs, I guess. That day, those people had two dogs who began bark'n at Hank first, so he gave'em a piece of his mind."

"Oh, Hudson, be careful with him. I'm sorry, son, but I'd rathuh ya not brang'm ovuh heeyuh if ya thank he'll attack Macy."

"Well, I'll just leave him in the truck or on a chain for now. I'll find'm a home at some point. I paid a lot of money to save'm, so I'd hate to take'm somewhere that will just put'm down, ya know."

"You're probably stuck with'm, son. Nobody wants a dayum vicious dog, except the assholes who made'm this way. Now, what about you fight'n that big fella?" Gray asks.

"Apparently, they didn't want'm anymore either, Deddy."

"Gray, do ya have to use all'at foul language?"

"Savvy, I don't thank God'll strike me down for call'n an asshole an asshole. Your mouth wasn't exactly a saint a bit ago, ya know. Now, what about that fight, Hudson?"

"The big dude threatened me and came at me."

"And?"

"And I knocked the hell out of'm."

"And?"

"Dammit, Jake told y'all the whole story, didn't he?"

"Yep."

"Then why in tha hell are ya ask'n me about it, Deddy? Yes, I choked'm out and Jake pulled me off'm." Hudson begins to get a little agitated. He really isn't mad at his parents, though, he's angry for reliving that moment—that moment of fury that upsets him again.

"OK, OK . . . ya can't lose it like'at, son. You're back home. You just need to walk away from shit like'at. Defend'n yourself is one thang, but Jake said ya woulda killed that man."

"All right . . . all right!" Hudson pauses for a moment to simmer his blood. "Yes, sir! I get ya. I'll keep my shit together next time."

"Don't lose your shit, son, that's all I ask. Now what's in the boat?" Gray changes the topic as he doesn't want to push his son too hard right now.

"If y'all don't stop with that nasty language . . . It's one thang to use it when someone is legitimately angry or upset, but to use it all the time is just downright filthy."

"Somebody make you supreme authority of foul language, Sav?"

"Kiss my hind end, Gray. See, I can say it without being filthy."

"Y'all mind if I show y'all this dadgum fish already? Good Lord!"

Hudson jumps up into the boat while telling the story of Hank jumping into the water and how the fish nearly ripped the rod out of the boat. He holds the massive flathead up for his parents to see. There it is, the smile on Hudson's face that Gray froze in his mind that day on the sandbar. That smile reassures him that his son may be a little better than they think. He may be telling the truth about his trip to the river. Still, it masks the torment that continues churning within his son.

Savannah walks back to the house to find her camera while Hudson and Gray stand by the boat drinking a couple ice-cold beers and talk about the fishing trip.

"Deddy, I'm sorry bout the fish I cost ya. I promise to pay ya back with a coola full of eat'n size next time I hit the lake."

"That'll be just fine. What's the plan for this big rascal?"

"I'm going to put'm in my pond. Should be big enough and plenty of brim for'm to eat on the rest of his days."

"Yeah, these big fellas just aren't good eat'n. I bet he was fun to catch, though."

"Shoulda seen it, Deddy. Not a bite all day until Hank jumps in. Next thang I know, damn rod tip is in the water and drag was scream'n. Fought'm for fifteen, twenty minutes or so."

Gray simply responds with a smile. The flathead may not replace the fish Gray gave Pop Walters, but listening to his son talk passionately about his prize catch is worth every bit he lost.

Meanwhile, Hank sits chained up to a nearby tree as they can't trust him around Macy, his mama's little miniature schnauzer. Hank has enough chain to sit with them, but he really wants to walk freely around the big yard or chase some of the critters playing nearby. As Savannah walks over to rejoin the fellas, she can't help but notice the wounds and scars on the big red dog. She feels bad for him, especially because of the things he obviously went through with his previous owners. She is a dog lover and would love to let him run around the farm, but can't risk this dog mauling her little Macy. Instead, to make him feel as part of the family, she gives Hank some leftover chicken and broth from the chicken 'n dumplings she made earlier. As he did with Pop's barbeque, Hank sucks it right on down without chewing. He loves a good chicken meal.

"He likes for ya to scratch him up under his big jaw, Mama," Hudson tells her.

Savannah scratches Hank under his jaw, just like he likes it. Hank pants a little bit before giving Savannah a few wet kisses on her hand. She does not see a vicious beast bred and trained to kill at this moment. She sees a dog deprived of love his entire life. He could've had such a wonderful life if he had a family instead of owners before meeting Hudson. She sees through his scars and intimidating appearance and into his gentle soul. However, about the time she starts to believe all he needs is enough love to run the devil out of him, her little Macy prances toward them. Old demons chase off his gentle soul. Hank instantly transforms into the vicious beast Savannah fears is inside him. He growls, snarls, barks, and nearly brings the small tree down as he relentlessly leaps at Macy.

"Hudson! Hudson!" Savannah yells frantically.

"Whoa, Hank! Whoa, boy!"

Savannah picks up Macy and runs to the house. Hank had been trained to fight using small dogs. Rage is not really what consumes him; embedded behavior from the devil himself is the reason for his vicious outburst. Hudson begs for Hank to silence the beast. He yells his new name over and over, but Hank has yet to learn his own name. Bark flies as the chain vigorously grates the tree every time Hank lunges and pulls. Hudson kneels in front of the big fella, begging him to calm down.

"It's OK, buddy. Calm . . . be calm. I'll take ya on to the house. Everythang is OK, Hank. It's OK." He offers Hank the same words as the fisherman offered him that day on the river near Helen. Finally, the gentle soul silences the beast. Hank whimpers as he offers Hudson a few apologetic glances.

"Son, that dog is too damaged. Can't have a dog like'at around other animals."

"I know, Deddy, which'll make it hard to find'm a damn home."

"Go ahead and get'm back into yuh truck. I'll check on yuh mama and Macy. Meet me back inside the house."

Hudson walks Hank to the truck and puts him in the cab. He scratches Hank on top of his head for a second to let the fella know he is not mad at him. However, Hudson refrains from scratching Hank under the jaw, because those scratches are saved for when he's good. After he shuts the door, Hudson heads over to the house. This is the second time he makes this short walk with a guilty mind.

"Mama, I'm sorry for Hank's outburst . . ."

"Son, that dog is too fah gone. He woulda ripped Macy to shreds had he got off that chain."

"I know, Mama."

"Nobody will take'm in like'at . . . and you can't just give'm to some-one know'n how he is."

"I know, Mama . . . I don't know what to do with'm. I'm kinda stuck with'm."

"You ought to think about put'n'm down son," Gray suggests.

"Can't do that, Deddy. I can't explain it, but that's just someth'n I cannot do."

"Well, he is your burden for the rest of his days, then."

"Certainly appears that way, Deddy. I guess I'll take'm home now. I'm sorry for not call'n y'all. Please don't worry about me, I'm fine. I love y'all. And sorry for scare'n the shit out of you, Macy!"

"Hudson Lee! Watch yowuh mouth, son. Now give yowuh mama a hug."

Hudson briefly smiles as he looks at Savannah, and then gives her that hug. Though his lips grin, his eyes stare off to the thousand thoughts racing behind them. His heart flutters and his eyes close as he thinks about the life he must live for now. Death only required one thought. He needs Mary to help talk him through all those thoughts, especially finding a home for Hank. Deep down inside, though, he knows there is but one home for the severely damaged fella. There is only one home damaged enough to accept him. However, he must con-tinue to think about searching for the impossible, because if he focuses on that one thought, if he has but this one goal in life, his mind seems to be more at peace. He squeezes his mama a little tighter as he tells her that he loves her. He shakes his father's callused hand as he tells him the same before walking out the door.

# CHAPTER NINETEEN

# THE WALK

I n his autobiography *Up From Slavery*, Booker T. Washington told of an encounter he had with a former slave. The man paid his master an annual fee to use his own body for work. He owed a few hundred dollars of this debt when all slaves were emancipated. Once his inalienable rights were recognized by executive order, he legally owed no man for the use of his own body. However, he traveled from Ohio to Virginia to pay his former master all he owed, plus interest. He gave his word and kept his promise, as that was the only way he felt absolutely free, regardless of the evil of his debt. Thomas Carter read this story to his youngest daughter after she failed to complete her chores as promised. He explained that she is only as good as her word and she will forever live with the guilt of her broken promises. He told her to appreciate all that she has, because many folks have paid much more for much less. Katie recalls this life lesson after awaking from her drug-induced coma and breaking the promise she made to her mama.

Katie will indeed live with this broken promise, though forever is but a day away. She lacks the strength to involve her family and disclose to them her private life. Her mama will intend no harm in her persistent quest for the secrets her daughter withholds, but she will mentally wear down Katie, nonetheless. Katie lacks the courage to face Sean. Her options are life with him—or death. No other options exist. Only death can abolish her fear. Her only hope for survival is if death calls his name, but death seems to never visit the wicked, at least not before they inject the world with evil. Life seems to hang on to people like him. Life seems to reward the wicked with longevity and prosperity. Life seems to demand more from the good and reward them only with impossible challenges and failure until they suffer permanent despair. She believes people like him are stronger than her. Her weakness is the reason she cannot face her family. Her weakness is the reason she cannot face him. Her weakness is the reason she can no longer face a life that prefers the strong. Tomorrow morning, she will see the world's beauty one final time. Tomorrow night, she will end the world's ugliness forever.

Katie does not sleep a wink the night before her final day. She sits on the floor leaning back against the bed with her eyes wide open. She looks at the clock not one time throughout the night. Time no longer holds any relevance in her life. She stares into the darkness through the window, searching for the woman who chose the better path. The woman never appears; only the sun comes for Katie. By the time the sun arrives, she has already cried her eyes dry, just like the night before she ran away from Sean. Katie rises to her feet as the sun peeks into the motel room window. She draws the shades, takes a shower, and slips into her final outfit. A pretty white sundress with colorful flowers that she loves so much she once told her friends to bury her in that dress if she dies while it still fits her. She pulls her hair back into a ponytail. She puts on just enough makeup to hide her despair and pain. She stands in front of the mirror. Her reflection presents a peek into a once-happy past. The little girl who loved playing dress up and putting on Mama's makeup smiles at her. She briefly smiles back at the girl. Guilt over killing the girl consumes the woman. Anger builds inside the woman for being so weak, for letting the girl down. Katie damns the woman as she shatters the mirror with an iron she found in the closet.

Katie drives to the park where she walked daily after escaping Sean. She parks her car in the nearly vacant lot across from the boat ramp. She hoped the park would be empty on this final day, but a truck sits next to the ramp with a boat and trailer hitched up to it. The truck looks familiar, but she can't place it. She can only hope the truck does not belong to a friend of Sean's. Even if it does, even if Sean's friend is here, telling him where she is will be moot by this evening. She scans the parking lot, but no one is anywhere to be seen. She parks on the opposite side of the lot, across from the boat ramp area and truck, to avoid any unwelcome encounters. She eases out of her car and ventures off into the woods, away from the beaten trail. She is greeted by the seclusion she desires. Clouds now hide the sun. The dark-gray overcast skies complement her downhearted disposition. Twigs and leaves lay quietly on the damp ground underneath her feet as the morning mist muffles the dead air. Nothing disturbs her solitude. She came for a peek at life's beauty, but receives nothing of the sort. The gray morning provides her relief. Life seems to have given up on her as she has given up on life. God has given up on her as she has given up on God.

The wet ground silences not only her footsteps but also those that sneak up from behind Katie. His heavy breathing gives him away as he approaches. Katie turns and stands frozen at the sight before her. Her lungs fail to breathe. Her mind fails to think. She can run, but he will catch her. She can call for help, but no one else is out here. She forces air into her lungs with a deep gasp. She forces her legs to move. She backs up, but he steps closer without even making a sound. He senses her fear. He remains silent as he again steps closer. Not looking where she steps, Katie backs into a tree as he continues his slow approach. An eternity seems to pass before a voice shouts through the silence.

"Hank! Get back here!"

"He's here . . . he . . . He's over here!" Katie stutters, but finally yells to the voice in the forest.

From around a thicket, a familiar face appears. Out of breath and holding a leash is Hudson, the stranger from the diner.

"Holy shit, I am truly sorry, miss . . ." Hudson pauses as he catches his breath. He looks back toward the direction from which he came and points as he continues. "A dayum squirrel went run'n across the path . . . I let'm off the leash for just a second. I'm sorry if he scared you, ma'am!"

"If! If he scared me?! I nearly ruined this dress . . ." Katie bends slightly forward trying to fully regain her breath "And I really like this dress. You should keep that big-ass dog on a leash."

Hudson has been so focused on securing Hank with the leash that he did not look up until he heard the familiar voice. He looks up and nearly falls as speechless as Katie when she first saw Hank.

"Uh . . . Kate . . . Katie, from the Dixie Diner. Right?" He knows very well who she is because she has visited his thoughts quite often since that night, more so since capping the bottle. Of all the places to run into her, at an old park in the middle of nowhere Greene County seems a bit strange. Disbelief by both causes a pause in the conversation. Neither can make sense of the improbable coincidence of this reunion.

"Yes . . . Hudson . . . I am Katie from the diner," Katie replies after catching her breath and bedding down her nerves.

"You remember my name," Hudson replies, pleasantly surprised.

"In the wonderful world of waiting on people, I have formed quite a talent at remember'n people and names." Katie does not want him to know that he has not just been a visitor in her thoughts but a permanent resident. She continues to settle her nerves from the sight of Hank while also dealing with the shock of running into Hudson in the middle of the forest.

"Why are you out here?" she asks him.

Hudson briefly looks back in the direction of the lake, points his thumb back toward the boat ramp, and replies, "I . . . We came to do a little fish'n."

"OK, then why in the hell are y'all out here scare'n the shit out of me in the middle of the woods?" she asks him in a Savannah-like stern voice.

"Well . . . first off, I am really sorry about that . . . I sincerely apologize! I didn't expect anyone to be out here. Nobody was in the park'n lot and my boat motor wouldn't start, so we decided to walk the trail a little bit."

"Yeah, but you are not on the trail, Hudson," Katie sarcastically points out.

"Like I said earlier, this big guy took off after a squirrel and—"

"The trail is way over there!" Katie exclaims as she points to the other side of the forest.

Hudson looks at Katie in silence for a brief moment. She is as skilled an interrogator as his mama, picking up on all those little irregularities and details that mark the trail of truth. He takes a deep breath before giving her the real story.

"OK, Katie, truth is—I'm stoned. Boat motor wouldn't start, that part is true, so I took Hank for a walk off the beaten path. We walked out this way, so I could . . . well, smoke up and enjoy quiet . . . silence. I let'm off the leash . . . I had no idea you were out here . . . Why are you out here?" Hudson contemplates that question for a moment before continuing. "Anyway, my attention wasn't necessarily where it shoulda been. Now, he was chase'n a squirrel—that part is also true. So . . . what the hell are you doing out here?" Mary and nerves scramble his mind as he comes clean about his activities in these woods.

"No, Hudson, your attention wasn't even close to where it shoulda been. So, let me make sure I understand how this all came to be: you were get'n high while your dog was scare'n the shit outta me?" Katie says while scolding him with her eyes.

"Uh . . . yep. That's the gist of it. By the way, that is a beautiful dress. I can see why you didn't wanna ruin it." Hudson offers Katie a little smirk to hopefully make amends with the beautiful young lady.

Katie briefly looks down at the dress, though she knows exactly what it looks like; she knows how beautiful it is, which is why it is her favorite. She looks back at Hudson with a slight smile. There it is again, that deep feeling she had from the first night they met. She cannot let herself believe this is anything but an inconvenient coincidence. She must end this unexpected meeting, a conflicted one that is both desired and unwanted.

"Well, Hudson, excuse me while I make my way back to my car and settle my nerves. Enjoy the rest of your day with your dog." She says the words, but does not actually desire to end the moment she shares with this familiar stranger, but this meeting is far too late—no reason she should hope for a fate different from the one that began the day.

"Ya know, Mary does a pretty good job help'n those nerves. I mean . . . that is if you partake?" Hudson blurts out without much thought, before she can walk away. The only thing on his mind is continuing this moment with Katie. She has been with him since that night at the diner, and a big part of him wants to know the reason. Asking a beautiful woman to partake is not a conventional approach to figuring out such a mystery, but nothing about them is conventional. The proverbial cat is out of the bag, so he figures he might as well offer her some of what has him wandering around in these woods.

Katie looks back at Hudson. "Is that your thing, Hudson? Offer'n drugs to women ya meet?"

"Nah . . ." Hudson smirks. "I really have no thing. I guess I . . . Been a while since I met anyone worth share'n anything with. I guess it was improper to ask you if you partake . . . I am—"

"Yeah, quite improper . . ." She returns his smirk with one of her own before blurting out, "But I'll take you up on your offer. What the hell, right?"

Life found it important enough to include the coincidental reunion in her life, so Katie, who hasn't smoked since high school, figures she might as well share a smoke and conversation with the intriguing stranger and his dog. Why the hell not is right. All she has to lose is already lost.

Hudson grins as he replies, "Awlright then. Here, have a seat on my jacket. We can't have that pretty dress get'n dirty, now can we?"

Hudson puts his jacket across a log for her to sit on, and then he sits next to her. They pass a joint back and forth a few times without a word spoken. It's a comfortable silence, with the exception of Katie coughing out smoke a time or two. They watch Hank hunt for critters through the rising smoke as he races from tree to tree. Mary moves quickly from their lungs to their minds, and once she has full influence of their minds, Hudson breaks the silence with a long-overdue apology.

"Hey, while I'm at this apology thang, I am truly sorry about my awkward behavior that night at the diner. That should have never . . . I just rescued this big guy after a snake bit'm, and your fiancé . . . what your fiancé said . . . well, I probably acted like a creep, and I am sorry for that! I shoulda never responded the way I did at your place of business."

His words seem to echo in her mind, or maybe they just echo throughout the forest. Her tolerance is low. Too many years have passed since those high school parties. Mary slowly repeats his words in Katie's head. She gives careful thought to his apology before blurting out, "Ex . . . he is my ex-fiancé, and you do not have to apologize about that night. He's an asshole." She chuckles as the words leave her mouth. Never have words felt so good. Her mockery reveals the bitterness toward Sean that Hudson suspected that night at the diner.

Hudson can tell Mary has begun entertaining Katie, which brings a smile to his face as he attempts to continue with what was supposed to be a serious apology. "Well, I still feel like shit for put'n you in a tough spot . . . at your place of business'n all."

"You did noth'n wrong, trust me . . . at my place of business . . . and all." Katie laughs as she pokes fun at Hudson's choice of words. The little green lady makes the simplest words humorous. The thing about Mary is, with some folks she only tells jokes, while with other folks she tends to lead them into deep, thoughtful conversations to the point they over-psychoanalyze themselves. Katie's grin quickly subsides as she involuntarily revisits that night at the diner. Her memory takes over—she can think of nothing else.

Before she can stop herself, she announces to Hudson, "That night got even crazier. Honestly, I wanted you to kick the shit out of'm, but I knew his friends woulda hurt you." Her grin returns at the thought of the alternate ending to that night—Hudson whipping Sean, that is, not the part about his friends hurting Hudson.

"I'm sorry to hear . . ."

"Don't be sorry about put'n that asshole in his place." Katie continues to smile as she once again enjoys Mary's humorous side.

"I mean, sorry to hear how things turned out. As for kick'n the shit out of'm, I'd been happy to oblige." Hudson's permanent grin grows as he cuts his bloodshot eyes toward Katie. That is when it hits him—how did this moment come to be? Onto Mary's couch he lays for his counseling session. He contemplates this coincidence as he takes in her beauty. How could such a damaged man end up sitting in the middle of the Oconee National Forest with the woman who has accompanied his every thought since meeting her? What are the chances? He questions whether he is dreaming. Maybe Hank still chases those critters while he daydreams with Mary on the log. But just then Katie's soft Southern voice eases into his ears.

"Well, unfortunately, those fools with him would've jumped on . . . out . . . at . . . in . . . in dammit . . . they woulda jumped in, and I didn't want that." They laugh for a brief moment as Katie stumbles through her words.

"Yeah, I figured they would. They look the type, ya know, chicken-shit'n all. Anyhow, I just wanted to apologize . . . and sorry things didn't work out for y'all . . ."

"Are you?" Katie smiles as she looks back at Hudson.

"Am I what?"

"Are ya really sorry things didn't work out for us?"

Hudson reciprocates a smile. "No, not really. Fuck'm."

"I didn't think so." The thought of kissing Hudson crosses her mind. One last fling before heading off into the sunset. She wonders how it would feel to make love to him. Her heart pounds at the thought. She wants him to take her. She wants to escape with him to the uncharted place she's never been. She wants to lose herself in that place. These thoughts must be Mary talking. Such a journey cannot happen.

Hudson saves her from this fantasy with a question she is ill prepared to answer. He again asks for the reason she is wandering these woods. She is obviously not dressed for hiking, but he leaves out that detail. She's known this question was coming, and he picked a pretty bad time to ask as she is currently on a romantic fantasy vacation. She wants no one inside her thoughts and definitely wants Hudson nowhere near her current mental trip. She owes him no explanation, but does not want to be rude to him, either. She wants to do what she does best, make light of the situation, but that damned Mary has a tight hold on her mind. She cannot let this woman tell Hudson her dirty secrets. She shakes her head to end her trip, smiles, and answers him. "Same as you, Hudson. Get . . . get'n stoned and enjoying this gloomy day . . . and try'n not to fall off this damn log. Been a while . . . I am . . . I'm good with that stuff by the way." She puts her hand up when he tries to pass her the joint.

Hudson knows he should have held back on that question and is not about to push the issue. He wants no part of anyone in his personal affairs, nor should he expect to visit her vault of secrets. He puts out the rest of the joint and offers her a grin before settling on a lighter, less intrusive conversation.

"Well, it's a good dayum thang ya ran into me and Hank; we happen to have some pretty good stuff."

She continues smiling as she looks at Hudson. "Not what I thought at first, but I guess so . . . but, yes . . . wow, it has been . . . I don't remember it being quite this intense." In an instant, she desires silence. She cannot have Mary helping her secrets escape over those high walls of hers. She revisits the conversations to this point, questioning whether some have already scaled those walls. Shame suddenly comes over Katie. She cannot lead this man down this dead-end road she travels. She cannot let him believe that this is the start of something. Just minutes ago, she wanted to escape with him, now she needs to escape from him. She should have never accepted his offer. Mary penetrates deep into her mind, unlocking visions and thoughts of her past. Her eyes zoom past the trees as her worlds beyond crash into each other. Her tongue remains silent for fear of sharing her ugly secrets and shameful desires.

Hudson senses silence is what she prefers. He will not disturb her thoughts. He knows Mary is a great tour guide into the depths of the mind as she helps folks depart reality to a much more amusing place. He does not interrupt her quiet joy ride. He eventually calls out to Hank, who has been running back and forth chasing squirrels up trees. He returns to silence while he scratches Hank up under his jaw, just like he likes it.

Minutes pass as though they are hours. Katie debates whether to stay or go. She questions her decision to take this trip. Her tolerance is low, and Mary firmly embraces her mind and body. Thoughts race around in her head, each one slowing down for a pit stop, allowing her to focus intently on each before they speed off again. After several minutes, all thought slows to the speed of a merry-go-round. Mary seems to have eased her grip just a little bit. Katie seizes the moment and decides to test her physical abilities. She slowly stands up as she tells the friendly stranger, "I need to head on back, Hudson. Would ya mind walk'n me back to my car? I am a pretty . . . That stuff . . . Damn, it has been a long time. I don't quite have my bearings . . . Ya know, I don't . . . Lots of spinning . . . Eyes are really . . . Can I trust you?"

Hudson grins as he deciphers her coded sentence fragments. "Sure thang! And yes, absolutely you can trust me! I guess I am a bit more used to this stuff. I probably shouldn't have offered this to ya." Hudson offers another grin for reassurance. He can tell the herb he scored from his brother has a pretty good hold on Katie, and though her struggles to speak are quite amusing, he knows he is responsible for her verbal challenges, and therefore his duty is to see her safely through this journey. "Hank and I will get ya back to your car safe and sound, Ms. Katie."

"Yep!" That is the only word she can muster up right now. She smiles and looks down at the dog. This bizarre meeting began with the big, ugly rascal scaring Katie to the point of nearly fouling her dress. Now, this dog is the most beautiful thing she has ever seen. Hank licks her hand and sits at her feet.

"He likes ya."

"Yep!"

They make their way to the beaten trail. They mostly walk in silence, until Katie finally regains a little more control over her thoughts and tongue. From that point, they walk and talk, steering conversations away from the darkness that plagues their minds. The awkwardness they felt around everyone else is absent. They feel normal, at least normal for them. Their conversations seem trivial, as go any conversations influenced by Mary. They manage to talk extensively about nothing, staying well away from their torment, mental struggles, or thoughts they had of each other. They simply enjoy each other's company. Though they feel comfortable with each other, they avoid eye contact for the most part. The tongue does not give away secrets like the eyes. They enjoy feeling normal for once in their adult lives. They are happy to hear a different voice as death lies dormant, at least for the moment.

Hudson takes Katie on a much longer route to the parking lot. She doesn't mind much. In fact, neither are in much of a hurry to find their way back as they are lost in conversation. To the disappointment of both, they eventually make it back to her car. By then, Mary has pretty much vacated their minds and invaded their empty stomachs, but neither works up the nerve to ask the other out for lunch. Katie would decline him and herself anyhow. Their morning journey is simply a good send-off and nothing else. Hudson does, however, work up the courage to hand her his cell phone number. Still not wanting to come across rudely toward the friendly stranger, Katie accepts his number, but offers him nothing. Her life would be different had he come along sooner. She would be on the other side of that window. No other worlds would be there to collide with that one.

"Thank you for walking me back to my car, Hank! Good name for a dog. Is he named after the singer?"

"Well, in a roundabout way, he is named after Hank Aaron . . . the baseball player." No way will Hudson explain the dog's name. No way will he open that door and risk those emotions peeking out. He smiles at Katie as he opens the door for her. Such a simple gesture, one that takes her by surprise.

"Make sure you tuck your dress under your legs. Ya don't wanna get that pretty thing caught in the door now, Ms. Katie . . ." Hudson pauses as he grins and watches her slide into the driver's seat before continuing, "I . . . we, uh . . . we enjoyed your company, Ms. Katie. We hope to see you again."

"Maybe y'all will," Katie replies with a smile just before shutting her door. She watches Hudson and Hank walk to their truck and then drive away. She sits alone in the middle of the old parking lot smoking the rest of the joint Hudson gave her as they walked. She enjoys the mental journey with Mary much more in solitude. No voices to disturb her peace. No ears to hear revelations by loose lips. Katie revisits her desires from earlier while gazing out the window at the muddy waters of the lake. Her body falls numb as the joint continues to burn between her fingers. She closes her eyes to push out the thought of what cannot be. In the darkness, she finds the girl crying. The friendly stranger and his dog sit with the girl, consoling her. They are too late. She drives out of the park at dusk and turns onto the old highway. She does not buckle her seatbelt. She speeds down the hill toward the bridge. She will plunge down into the rocks at more than 80 miles per hour, which is surely enough to end her complicated life while saving her family from the pain of suicide. A car accident will be easier for her mama to accept—so she tells herself.

# CHAPTER TWENTY

# BROTHER

Hudson's thoughts are only of Katie after leaving the park. He and Hank stop for a bite to eat but have to take the food to a picnic area on account of Hank. Hudson sits quietly during their meal and on the way to the house. He doesn't even strike up one of those one-sided conversations with Hank as he usually does during their time riding in the old Ford. Hank doesn't mind. He just lays there on the passenger's side with his head on the seat listening to Mississippi John Hurt pick away on that old six string. He seems to know his friend is deep in thought over their new friend, or maybe Hank is just simply exhausted from chasing gray squirrels all day. Either way, he lets his friend be alone with his thoughts.

Hudson has no idea why he picks up the phone to call his brother; maybe he needs someone to shoot him straight. Maybe Ty will talk some sense into him, saving him from the inevitable battle between his mind and heart. Hudson pauses for a brief second before tapping the dial button on his cell phone as he prepares to open up his personal life a little bit for the first time since Hank Jackson died. Ty, eager to hear from his little brother, picks up on the first ring.

"Hudson?"

"Whatcha say, Ty?"

"Well, I'll be damned, lil brother, I thought ya deleted my number. Hadn't heard from ya since the farm. Where the hell ya been?" Ty speaks as though he is on a date with Mary himself.

"Did a little camp'n. Other than that, just sit'n at the house. You?" Hudson already regrets making this call. He braces for the unexpected turns his stoned brother is sure to take while driving this conversation.

"Pick'n with the fellas. Hold on, let me get somewhere quiet . . ." Ty walks down to the bedroom at the end of the hall, away from the noise. "So, you been sit'n at the house. Well, lil brother, I rang your damn doorbell. You never answered. Please tell me you didn't just sit there listen'n to my dumb ass ring the fuck'n doorbell?"

"Nah . . . I was probably out camp'n when your dumb ass rang my fuck'n doorbell. Caught a big flathead while I was at the lake." Hudson yanks the steering wheel to navigate this conversation down a different topic.

"Yeah, so I heard. Also heard ya saved a big ugly dog . . . Looks like he went a few rounds with a grizzly bear."

"I did. Who told ya?"

"Ricky called me up . . . I dunno . . . day or two ago, I guess."

"Hey, since ya brought it up, you want a dog?"

"Heyull no, I don't wanna dayum dog. You're stuck with that rascal, jack. Ya better be careful, cos that big sumbitch sounds like he can rip ya apart. Dogs like'at turn on ya, brother. You don't know the shit he's been through or what will set'm off."

"Nah, he won't hurt me . . . Maybe he'll rip on you a lil bit or some other asshole, but not me. I won him over with some of Pop's barbeque."

"Is that right?! He does make a tasty plate of barbeque. Speak'n of Pop's, sounds like you and your ugly friend about killed a fella. And you know Mama and Deddy were try'n to hunt chu down, right?"

"Yeah, Mama already lit me up a bit. Not as bad as I thought she would . . . and that shit at Pop's is a story for another day."

"Yeah, and I also heard a little rumor that a dude with a Marine tattoo on his arm walked into a dive bar off Highway 15, just down from your place, one known to house some backwoods bikers. Said he wasn't leave'n til he fought every sumbitch in there. I heard he got one or two punches in before they put his ass down . . . hard. They woulda killed'm had he not served his country. They threw his ass in his truck. He was gone by the time the bar closed. Know anything about that?"

"Nah . . . can't say I do."

"Well then, a mystery remains, I guess. What the hell, son? Why did you ignore everyone, brother? Most importantly, why did ya ignore me?"

"I just took some time away from everything is all. Like I said, went camp'n." Hudson is about ready to give up on ever reaching the reason he called his brother in the first place. He now scrolls through the excuses to end this call, though he knows Ty will buy none of them.

"Yeah, whatever the hell that means. Square up with me, brother. I'm not gonna tell Mama or anyone. You went and got yourself a lil bit for the week didn't ya?" Ty changes course as he senses Hudson's frustration. He figured Savannah gave him enough grief.

"No, I did not. But let me ask you someth'n. Ya ever meet a girl and immediately connect with'r?"

"Whoa there, slick! Women you pay for are not rent to own, lil brother."

"Dammit . . . Ty! I'm serious! I'm not talk'n about one of your easy girls. I'm talk'n someth'n real. I am ask'n for serious advice. If ya can't give it to me, then I'll just be on my way."

"Hold up, son! I'm just give'n ya shit for not call'n me back. And don't be so harsh on easy girl; she gave me plenty of good nights."

"Is that right? Keep mess'n around with her easy ass, and she'll give you a lifelong reminder of one of those nights."

"Awl right then . . . lil brother, I will give you my utmost mature attention; though, quick disclaimer, I am three shots, four beers, and two bowls into the night. Now that we understand each other, did ya meet somebody?"

"I don't know, Ty . . . I think so . . . well . . . I . . ."

"Say what's on your mind, son. Keep it simple, so I can follow."

"I met a girl—twice now we ran into each other—who I can't get off my mind. We didn't really talk the first time, because I was at her work. A crazy twist of fate crossed our paths again today. I took Hank, the dog I saved, out to the old park off 278 to put the boat in and do a lil early morn'n fish'n. Damn motor wouldn't start, so we went for a walk. I can't walk'm around other dogs, so I took the opportunity to stretch our legs, ya know. He gets a little pissed off around other dogs. I didn't want to take a chance—"

"You mean like at Pop's and Mama's?!"

"Yeah, like that . . . dammit, why does everybody have to talk about my shit?" Hudson pauses for a moment, annoyed by everyone sharing his personal business with everyone else. "Anyway, I smoked a lil of what you gave me, which is kick-ass by the way, and Hank got to chase'n after a fuck'n squirrel. I chased after his ass, and there she was—in the middle of the woods as pretty as can be."

"On the trail?"

"Nah, off the trail, in the middle of the woods."

"Is that right? Kinda fuck'n weird, but go on . . . continue."

"Well, Hank ran up on'r first, scare'n the shit right out of'r. I apologized for that. Then, we talked a bit. She seemed stressed or someth'n, so I offered her a smoke. A half joint later, I walked her back to her car. We actually walked about an hour or two . . . hell, maybe three, talk'n the whole way. It felt right, brother. There is just something about'r. I can't get'r off my mind. I gave'r my phone number . . . just wrote it down and gave it to'r without really think'n about it."

"Well, that's what people normally do when they want to reconnect with someone. Chances of y'all run'n into each other in the middle of the woods again is pretty damn slim I'd say, so the phone number was a good call. Question is . . . How did she respond?"

"I can't remember. I was so nervous or confused or . . . still a little stoned, too."

"Confused? You are attracted to a pretty woman. What the hell are you confused about? Except the fact she's standing in the middle of the woods."

"I guess I can't really explain how I feel."

"Evidently."

"I'm tell'n ya, Ty, you know I've never felt like this about a girl before. Longest girlfriend I had was about seven months."

"Did she give you her number?"

"Well, no."

"All right, brother, before you start carv'n hearts and initials in trees and shit, that's not a good sign."

"Yeah, I know. I guess I'll wait."

"Ain't shit else you can do."

"Don't you think that is a pretty big-ass coincidence? Meet'n up with her in the middle of the woods at an old park? We were the only two people out there, Ty."

"Yeah, that is a pretty big-ass coincidence, but you know how I feel and I will just say that is all that was—a big-ass coincidence. It's not like some girl you met halfway across the world wound up in those woods with ya. This is a local girl who went for a walk in a local park."

"Yeah, I know, but women don't go out to that park to walk alone. You know that. And, she works in Watkinsville, so she's not that local. Not out there."

"She may live out there somewhere, ya never know. But you're right about a woman walk'n out there alone. That kinda stokes my curiosity. And say she was as pretty as can be? How was she dressed?"

"Why the hell does that matter? She had on a nice dress of some sort, hair up in a ponytail . . . I guess that is a bit odd. Why was she out there dressed up like that? Standing in the middle of the damn woods. I was too shocked and stoned before . . . That is pretty damn weird."

"You didn't ask her?"

"Actually I did, but she didn't say."

"Hmm . . . walk'n alone out in the middle of the woods at a park in the middle of nowhere, used mainly by fishermen, and dressed like she's goin to church is pretty damn weird if I do say so myself."

"So you think she's screwed up . . . damaged or someth'n?"

"Hey, that's just the way I think, which doesn't mean shit. I'm high as a kite, lil brother; don't start doubt'n this girl because of the dumb shit I say."

"Nah, you're probably hit'n on someth'n. I got this dog situation to figure out; last thing I need is a relationship with a crazy-ass woman."

"Son, it doesn't hurt to at least let shit play out. Don't walk away because of me. That's my official advice. Ya hear me?"

"I hear ya, brother."

"Now, I hate to change the subject, but when we goin fish'n? Boat, beers, bowls, and bass like before you shipped off?"

"Hey, hold on, Ty . . . got a call from an unavailable number. Never mind, they hung up. Let me call ya back in the morn'n, dude. I need to stow the boat'n shit."

"OK, brother. Listen, don't be heartbroken if she never calls ya. What happens, happens. Call me tomorrow, and we'll hook up the boat."

"What happens, happens?! Well, that clears shit right up. I'll give ya a call about fish'n . . . and hey . . . Ty . . ."

"Yes?"

Hudson takes a second to fight back the emotions that seemed to come out of nowhere, "Missed ya, man. Missed these types of talks . . . ya know. Love ya, brother!"

Ty smirks as he responds, "I'm glad you're back, lil brother. Love ya, too, ya sentimental prick. Talk to you tomorrow."

"Awl right. Tomorrow."

Hudson's mental struggles are far from over, although the whispers of death have subsided. Pursuing a future by handing the beautiful stranger his number was a big step. Confiding in his older brother about her was an even bigger step. He is afraid to allow himself to fall in love. He fears his lingering depression and melancholy will never evanesce or that she will see through his illusion of normalcy. A relationship requires access to places within the heart that are unknown by all others. To give her access to such a sacred place requires him to trust her with his vulnerable and fragile psyche. He believes she will be terrified of the demons trapped inside the tomb of his past. He can't keep them hidden forever, though, and the consequences of their escape terrifies him. His trust in fate begins fading as anxiety and fear rebuild the wall that Hank has started tearing down. Part of Hudson hopes she never calls, so he never has to worry about anyone meeting the tormented soul residing in those tombs with those old demons.

Hudson needs to clear his head of thoughts. He needs a good sleep, so he gives Mary a long kiss goodnight. The smoke fills the room as he watches Hank chew on one of those frozen peanut butter bones for a minute or two. Mazzy Star helps bed down his anxiety. Hope Sandoval's soothing voice fades as Mary numbs Hudson's mind and body. Before going completely blank, Hudson decides to let fate write tomorrow's story; it is not his burden to bear tonight.

# CHAPTER TWENTY-ONE

# CHOICE

**W**hile Hudson shares his private thoughts with his brother, Katie speeds down the highway at 85 miles per hour. She races down the hill with no seatbelt and tightly gripping the steering wheel with both hands. Mary is long gone from her mind, but Hudson remains. She yells for him to leave her be, to let her go. She tells the girl staring back at her in the rearview mirror that the man is far too late to save her. She turns her focus to her hands on the steering wheel, demanding they turn that damn wheel at the bridge. She then shifts her attention ahead into the lights where they shine on the road and bridge ahead. Just on the other side of the yellow cat's eyes reflecting back at her headlights is the point where she intends to plunge. She inhales deeply as she turns the speeding car toward the rocky embankment. The rocks seem to shine brightly in her headlights. She starts to close her eyes, so she does not witness the fall and crash. Before her eyelids shut, though, she sees a man and boy stand up on the other side of the guardrail with their fishing poles in hand. Her eyes open wide as panic sets in. Katie quickly veers the car back toward the middle of the road, causing the tires to skid and slide, nearly flipping the car in the middle of the old highway where it meets the bridge. She turns the wheel left and right a few times, finally gaining control of the car about midway on the bridge. She eases the car forward and pulls over at the turnaround just on the other side of the short bridge. She dials Hudson's number, but immediately hangs up. Katie cries loudly as she thinks about the people she nearly killed while attempting to end her own life.

A knock on her window startles Katie. The old gentleman and young boy stand outside. The old man says something, but his words are muffled by the window. He is here to scold her, so she believes. Katie dries her eyes with a tissue. She prepares for the man's harsh words concerning her reckless driving. She feels shameful and angry at the same time. She deserves what's coming to her, but is upset at yet another failed attempt to end her suffering. Katie cracks the window to apologize but is taken aback by the old man's genuine concern for her.

"You awlright, young lady?" he asks sincerely.

"I'm fine, mister," Katie says, still upset. His calm demeanor bewilders her.

"Wayull, ya came down the road purtee dayum fass, and yo teeyuhs say you ain't awlright. Somebody afta ya?" the old man asks her.

"No . . . I'm fine, mister."

"OK . . . wayull . . . I gotta ask ya to slow it down round heeyuh, young lady. A lotta folk fish out heeyuh on dis ole bridge."

"I . . . I'm sorry . . . I just . . . you won't have to worry about me come'n back around here."

Katie begins to roll up her window, but the young boy stops her as he steps out from the dark. He says nothing at first. He simply offers her a smile, and then hands her a piece of candy before speaking.

"When I'm sad, candy makes me happy. It's my lass piece, but you need it mow, ma'am."

Her sad voice cracks as she thanks the young boy. She looks up at the old man as he offers her one last piece of advice: "They is good in life, young lady. The good is worth all the bad."

She watches as the old man and young boy walk back to the other side of the bridge. They step over the railing onto the rocks from earlier.

Katie eases off down the dark highway, presenting a quick smile as she passes by them, still holding onto the candy.

Life seems to exist in a series of short stories. For some folks, those stories are separate from one another, existing as individual moments in time. The mind easily filters through recollections of each, removing unwanted details and adding more favorable ones to reach a desired narrative. These people—people like Sean—seem to easily move from one altered story to the next free of guilt. For others, though, all those stories are connected, each affecting the next. No mental filters and no added details, only accurate memories and consequences. Sometimes momentum shifts direction; other times it builds while maintaining course from one story to the next. Katie's misery was a little ripple in the water that became a rogue tidal wave. She was in the trough of that wave when Hudson came along. With the crest of anguish crashing over her, he offers but a life ring. The old man and boy gave her a second chance to grab onto that ring.

Katie begins her next story back in the quiet motel room where she feels the grip of fear and depression squeezing the air from her lungs and rational thought from her mind. She stares down at the piece of paper she holds in her hand. One call could reverse her momentum; it could also destroy more than just her life. Her phone lies next to her on the bed, but she is unable to move her hand to pick it up. Her mind refuses such a useless decision. She is a fool to believe this stranger can rescue her from Sean. She is too blinded by her past to see a future with Hudson. She thinks of her father, whose death left her insecure and led to her bad decisions in high school. Her bad decisions led to the dirty rumors, leaving her vulnerable. Her vulnerability led her to Sean. Sean led her to Hudson. No way one phone call will turn the tide of her misfortune. The wave is crashing.

Katie empties the bottle of opioids into her other hand. She grips them tightly, all the while staring at that damn phone number in her other hand. No one can provide her hope of love without the overwhelming fear consuming her mind. Even if she allows this stranger into her heart, Sean will never let her live on without him. He will keep his promise to end her life and that of anyone she meets, contrary to his promise to change his ways. Katie fears she will end Hudson's life while saving her own. For even considering that, she feels enormous guilt. She refuses to allow her desperation the opportunity to ruin a good man's life. Her mind is convinced that death remains the only solution, but something deep in her soul refuses to give death an easy victory in her internal debate. Her heart pumps so vigorously she can hear it in the silent room. Her lungs rapidly push air in and out as the thought of either choice terrifies her. She is tired of the fear. She is tired of the anger. She is tired of the weakness. She opens her hand and stares at the pills. She raises her head to look at her shattered reflection in the broken mirror. The mirror defines her psyche well. She cannot bring herself to involve Hudson in her mental struggles and increasingly volatile relationship with Sean. She shuts off her mind as she turns her open hand, dropping the paper to the floor. She tosses the pills in her mouth and chases them with nearly a half bottle of wine.

The wine numbs her body and mind within minutes. The pills will take a little longer to deliver their toxic contribution. The alcohol and opioids will not only be allies in their efforts to numb the body and mind, but will also silence the heart and soul once and for all. Katie lies back on the bed with the wine bottle in hand as she awaits death's arrival. She prepares a backup plan in case the pills don't work. The razor rests peacefully up on the side of the tub. Steam gracefully rises from the water. She waits for the tears to dry once again before submerging her body into the warm water.

Time seems to drag on as she waits, providing an excessive void between life and death. The void extends Katie's emotional battle. The drugs, alcohol, and fear continue protecting her mind from the heart and soul's last-ditch effort to navigate Katie away from the storm's treacherous seas and toward the light flickering in the distance. Katie can no longer continue lying in bed with such a ferocious mental battle weakening her focus. She turns to the edge of the bed, stands up, and slowly walks to the bathroom. She never takes off her dress as she sinks into the warm water. She finishes the wine. The bottle slides from her hand onto the hard floor, bouncing a few times, but never cracks before coming to rest next to the tub. She closes her eyes. Her head spins. She cannot allow herself to fall asleep as she did before—the pills may not work. She opens her eyes to grab the razor. She is startled to see the big dog she encountered earlier sitting in the bathroom doorway. She immediately closes her eyes, shakes her head, and looks to the doorway again. Hank is now next to the tub, standing over the razor growling. Katie just lies there in the water, nearly incapacitated from shock as she was earlier in the forest. She closes her eyes again and shouts, "Go away! Please God . . . Go away!" She gets her wish. Hank is gone when her eyes open again. Only the razor remains clear, though her vision is blurring.

# CHAPTER TWENTY-TWO

# GOOD FIRE

Hudson walks over the hilltop as the tall ryegrass gently sways in the breeze. His heart feels no pain. His mind suffers no anxiety. The light of joy fills the day. He easily recognizes where he walks but cannot recall his journey. The sunshine quickly gives way to darkness, but a peaceful mind remains. The whippoorwill sings a happy song, like the nights the boy had with his family by those fires. In the distant night burns a soft, warming light just like those fires. The bird stops his song long enough for Hudson to hear the echoes of laughter. He follows the light and laughter down the hill to the pond. Uncle Walt looks up at Hudson as he approaches from the darkness. The fire reflects in his eyes, but not like that night before Hudson shipped off for bootcamp.

"Whatcha say, nephew?"

Hudson stands quietly as shock temporarily seizes his tongue. Cancer and cirrhosis brought a painful end to his uncle's life and the mental struggles he shared with Hudson. Gray sent word to Hudson about Walt's demise, but yet here he sits by the fire he promised his nephew so long ago. Hudson finally regains control of his thoughts and tongue.

"Uncle Walt? I don't understand. Deddy said ya died . . . cancer and liver disease got ya."

"Never felt better, son." Walt offers Hudson a half-cocked smile. He has never seen his uncle smile before this moment. Hudson can't bring himself to completely shake the shock in order to return a smile. Instead, he sits in the empty chair next to his uncle.

"I . . . I've been pretty fucked up, Uncle Walt. I shoulda listened to ya, prepared myself for the hell to come."

"There is no preparation adequate enough for the awful aftermath of war, son. No easy way to deal with those demons."

"How did you go on so long deal'n with those demons, Uncle Walt?"

"I buried a lot of hurt, son. Tried to drank the devil out of me. I even wrote to get the thoughts out of my head."

"Well, I have some shit buried deep, and I've flooded my mind with whiskey. Shit made it worse. Did the writing help?"

"A little."

"What did you write?"

"Wrote about the torment in my head. I just wanted it gone from my mind. So, I penned the words to paper, then burned 'em. Only one I really remember is the last one—had to do with the hard truth the doctor gave me."

"You mind share'n it with me, Uncle Walt?"

"I don't mind if ya reckon it may hep ya?"

"Won't know if we don't try, I guess."

"Yeah, I guess. I knew I was in a bad way. I finally went to the doctor to see how bad. Well, the doctor told me:

If ya take another drank
Ol' death will call on your name
If you don't lay the smoke to rest
Won't be long til your last breath
If you don't give God your soul
Into the cold, hard ground you'll go
Well, to him I replied:

Old habits prove hard to break
when the devil whispers your fate
Black lung and a bad liver
Even'n sweats and the morn'n shiver
The struggle bears too much pain
I beg for ol' death to call on my name

That was the last one I wrote. I burned it, and then tried listen'n to God for a change."

"I need help, Uncle Walt. I, too, wish for death. My head's fucked up." Hudson chokes on his emotions as he confesses his pain to someone for the first time.

Walt looks over at Hudson, both eyes wide open and full of joy. He smiles at his nephew as he tells him, "I need to get another log for the fire. I like this fire. It's a good fire. It warms this cold world."

As Walt walks off into the dark for that log, the forest goes silent except for the crackle of the fire. The whippoorwill breaks the silence with a verse that lasts a solid minute before falling silent again. The crack of a twig catches Hudson's attention.

"Uncle Walt?"

"Nope, just us, son." Hank Jackson and the boy appear from the darkness. Hudson is too confused for a single word to escape his tongue. "No need to speak to us, brotha. She needs you, son!" Hank says as he and the boy step back into the dark forest.

# CHAPTER TWENTY-THREE

# AWAKEN

Relentless barking wakes Hudson from the deepest sleep he's enjoyed in quite some time. Hank has something on his mind that can't wait until morning. Hudson opens his heavy eyelids to the blurry sight of Hank standing next to the bed barking about a foot from his face. Hank licks Hudson's face a time or two, ensuring his friend is fully awake. Hudson mumbles a few choice words as he rolls out of bed, thinking an animal is prowling just outside the house. Hank has a tendency to get excited about such things.

"Awl right, boy, I'll let ya go outside and chase whatever the hell's out there, so I can get back to dayum sleep," Hudson mumbles as he rubs his eyes. He walks toward the bedroom door, but Hank does not follow. He remains standing by the nightstand, now whimpering instead of barking.

"Dammit, boy! You need to figure out what . . . ," Hudson starts to say when through the drowsy fog he sees his phone quietly light up the nightstand—no ringer and no buzzer to ensure his sleep is uninterrupted; of course, he failed to consider Hank while silencing everything else. Hank feels his crazy buddy needs to take this one. Again, an unavailable number is calling.

"Who in the heyull is calling at twelve dayum thirty in the morn'n?" Hudson mumbles before answering his phone.

"Hello?"

"Hudson . . . did I wake you?"

"Katie?"

"Yes . . . Katie."

"Your number said unavailable, so I didn't know who it was."

"I woke you, didn't I? I'm sorry. I will . . . Please go back to sleep. I'm so sorry . . ."

"No, no, no . . . I'm watch'n TV with Hank. I'm just surprised you called is all."

"Why's that?"

"I . . . I uh . . . Well, I'm glad ya did . . . Just didn't know if you would or not," Hudson answers with subtle joy in his tone.

"I know call'n this late is kinda rude, but I had a dream. I had a dream about your dog." A desperate sadness seems to accompany her acknowledgment of the late call. The girl fights through the woman's despair to seek out the boy.

"Ya did, did ya? What happened in your dream, Ms. Katie?" Hudson asks while offering a consoling smile that Katie can't see. He can hear sorrow in her voice. She is obviously intoxicated and not the same girl from the walk, but that doesn't worry Hudson at all. He is happy she called. He is happy to lend his ear to her sadness.

"He saved me," Katie softly answers.

"He saved you?! What did he save ya from?"

"Death."

"He did, did he?! How'd he do that?" Hudson eagerly asks. He doesn't understand why her one-word answer weighs so heavily on him, but it does. It reminds him of himself and his battles.

"He chased off a bad person who intended to kill me," Katie answers in that vague manner Hudson has used quite frequently himself.

Hudson looks over at Hank, who gazes back at him with curiosity as he replies, "Good thang he was there."

Hudson's thoughts drift back to the night by the pond. Her voice is as desperate and sad as his thoughts were in those woods that night. If not for Hank's cries, the empty silence of the dark forest after the whippoorwill's farewell song would have been all that filled his ears forever. That empty silence falls upon this conversation as he revisits a darker past and she travels a hopeful future. They listen to each other breathe as their minds race through the words needed to break the awkward silence.

"My dream is not the only reason I called, Hudson . . . I . . . I was wonder'n if you are busy tomorrow?" Katie nervously asks as though the girl speaks for the woman.

"Yes," Hudson replies without hesitation as he again offers a smile she cannot see.

"Oh . . . OK," Katie immediately replies with relief and disappointment, as the woman's desires conflict with the girl's.

"I'm hang'n out with you if you say yes." Hudson's smile grows a little bit bigger as he hopes his offer brings her a little satisfaction.

Air once again fills the conversation for a couple of seconds before Katie answers softly, "Yes. I would very much like that, but I would rather not go into Athens or any local town really," Katie says, a little less sorrow accompanying her words. The excitement of the girl is hard for the woman to contain.

"OK . . . I, uh, what would you like to do? Where ya wanna go, Ms. Katie?"

"I hear Charleston has good seafood," Katie suggests as she fights back the girl's emotions.

"Is that right?! I do like myself a mess of crab legs." Hudson's whimsical reply receives no reaction from Katie. He hears nothing, not even the breath leaving her lungs. He calls her name but hears nothing. He hears nothing because her hand covers her phone. She covers her phone so he cannot hear her cry. Her emotions erupt as this friendly stranger offers the promise of a happier future in life. She is afraid of the hope that he provides her, but she is grateful.

"Are you all right, Katie?" Hudson immediately feels bad for asking such an intrusive question. He would be furious had someone asked him that question. Had anyone else asked her that question, it would hold no value; however, Hudson asking that question further reinforces the girl's belief he and his dog can save the woman.

Before he can recall the question and apologize, Katie offers the best excuse her foggy mind could muster. "I am . . . I'm just a lil drunk on wine is all."

"I've been there . . . some nights more than others. I'm sorry for being nosey. I shouldn't have asked you that . . ."

"It's OK, Hudson. I hope it's not weird that I wanna go all the way to Charleston when we barely know each other." Katie tries to steer the conversation away from awkwardness, though his attempts to sympathize and help her avoid embarrassment are very much appreciated.

"Nah . . . feels bout right. Seafood in Charleston with you sounds like a perfect way to spend the day."

"I know it's a long way to drive for seafood. I just can't go . . ." Katie pauses to ensure secrets don't escape. Her mind scrambles for a reason other than the truth, but the drugs, alcohol, and emotions lie on her mind like a dense fog. Alcohol tends to hold back no secrets, so only silence fills the air until Hudson helps resolve her struggle.

"Well, if ya want good seafood, it's probably best to go to a place by the sea, Ms. Katie—that is all that matters." Hudson pounces on the opportunity to help ease her worry of running into whoever or whatever she wants to avoid. He has a pretty good idea who but respects her privacy and does not dare ask. He doesn't want to share his secrets, either. He hopes that her secrets will keep her from seeking out his. He remains afraid of this potential commitment to another, but there is something about this beautiful stranger that does not just bed down his fears but makes him feel normal.

"Yeah, I suppose you're right. Thank you, Hudson." Katie finds her smile again as that fog lifts and the light of clarity shines in the middle of this dark night.

"Thank you for what, Ms. Katie?"

"For answering your phone," Katie answers through the building emotions and tears. She fights to hold back both.

"Thank you for call'n!"

"It does feel right," Katie says as her voice trembles.

"It does, don't it?!" Hudson senses the secrets she holds back—the type of secrets that would cause most men to flee. He does not even slightly entertain self-preservation; instead, he only provides this beautiful but damaged stranger the compassion and reassurance she has deeply desired for so long.

"I guess we should go to sleep now."

"Yeah, I suppose we should. You want to meet me at my house in the morning?"

"Yes please!" The woman attempts to mask the girl's excitement and hope, but she, too, can't help but believe this wonderful stranger and his dog are special. Fate can only lead people to the crossroads in life; the direction taken is up to them. Before making the call, Katie sat in that tub until the water grew cold, never taking that razor into her hand. She purged much of the wine into the little wastebasket by the tub. In the contents were most of those pills—they failed to digest. She tried to concentrate on death, but Hudson stubbornly remained in her thoughts. He was all she saw after Hank disappeared, regardless of her determination to forget him and this world. The vision of Hank was probably a product of her alcohol-and-drug-influenced mind; however, it was her mind that was set on death while her soul begged for life. Maybe the soul won that round. What convinced her to eventually reach for the phone instead of the razor is a mystery to her, one she may never figure out.

Neither of them wants to end the phone call. They talk for another three hours before finally hanging up. During that long goodbye, Katie survives the pills that did enter her system. Hudson knows nothing of the pills, but feels there is more to her phone call than a dream and Charleston. He also gives her his address and she finally gives him her phone number. No longer is her number unavailable to this special stranger and his sweet, ugly dog. Neither understands why they feel so drawn to the other, nor do they question it. Only the girl and boy can answer the question they dare not ask.

# CHAPTER TWENTY-FOUR

# CHARLESTON

The once-green leaves of summer now die beautifully along this old road. Trees prepare to shed dead weight to survive the cold days ahead of them. Limbs will freeze during the long nights but hold strong awaiting the season of rebirth. What was once dead weight will bloom again, giving the trees new life. Katie wants to believe she, too, shed her dead weight with new life ahead of her; however, her rebirth is not as certain to her as the leaves on those trees. The dead weight of her past and the uncertainty of her future gives her pause. She drives by Hudson's house time and again, trying to convince herself to make that long trip down the short driveway. She wants to be strong like the limbs of trees in winter but is afraid she will be broken once again, killing all hope for new life. Most of all, though, she fears that her old life will kill her new life. She looks into the rearview mirror as she approaches his house for the fourth time. There in the mirror, in front of all those colorful trees, the smiling girl convinces her to let go of her dead leaves.

Katie creeps down the driveway, hoping Hudson did not watch her drive past his house all those times while she mustered the courage to make that turn. The sun fully breaches the hilltop behind his house, offering her comfort—such a warm welcome this new day. Hank and Hudson step out onto the porch as her car gradually comes to a stop. Before she can even put the car in park, Hank runs over and sits right outside of her car door. He looks up at her, patiently waiting for the door to open, but she hesitates at the sight of the intimidating rednose. Hudson steps out to the top of the steps on the front porch, scratches himself under his chin, and then points at Hank. She smiles, opens the door, and gives Hank a good scratch'n up under his jaw, just like he likes it. In return, Hank gives Katie a few of those big, wet kisses on the side of her cheek.

Hudson smiles as he watches Katie wipe off her cheek, "I think you just made a new friend, Ms. Katie."

Katie smiles back at Hudson. "Well, I only have room for one new friend, Mr. Hudson. Who will it be?"

"Well dayum! Hank, sorry fella, but I met her first. Come on over here, boy!" Hank ignores Hudson while he continues enjoying his jaw scratch'n. "Hank, now dammit, come on in the house and go to bed." Hank scoots behind Katie's legs, and then peeks his big head around to look at Hudson, not ready to concede to his crazy buddy.

"Well, Mr. Hudson, I do believe Hank has a different opinion about my choice of a new friend."

"He does, does he?! Then I should tell ya that he's not much for conversation."

"That'll be just fine; boys don't usually say the right thing anyhow."

"Nah, we sure don't. I am proof of that. Welp, just one other thing you ought to know before y'all high tail it to Charleston . . . ole Hank is allergic to seafood."

Katie looks at Hudson for a brief moment with a slight smile. "I highly doubt that."

"Awl right then, Ms. Katie, if ya wanna take him to Charleston, fill him up with seafood, and risk the inside of your car, be my guest," Hudson replies with a smirk.

Katie hesitates for a moment, then smiles back at Hudson before replying, "OK, Mr. Hudson, I guess you win. Sorry, Mr. Hank, but I just can't risk you turn'n the inside of my car into an outhouse."

Katie and Hudson have become proficient at hiding their troubled souls while acting normal around other people. This time is easier than any other; even through the nerves they make each other feel normal. Excitement and fear peck away at their minds about today's trip. Yesterday was an improbable reunion. They had no time to think about what they would say or do around each other. They leaned on Mary to make the weird coincidence seem normal. They leaned on Hank to keep air out of the conversations and provide a sense of security. However, Hank and Mary will not join them on their trip to Charleston. Their absence gives Hudson and Katie privacy and sobriety to get to know each other a little more, which scares the hell out of them.

Though curious where this road will lead them, they dare not intrude on each other's privacy during the drive to Charleston. Personal details are not offered nor sought. Getting to know each other is impossible without intrusive questions, but they know all they want to know for now. They hold plenty of fun conversations to entertain each other, but their moments of silence are more desirable to them both. Together in silence they find solace. They feel normal. They feel happy and secure. In those moments, words are irrelevant as they are not the true source of comfort and security for them. Unspoken secrets are more likely the source.

To think of the word *love* before the first real date actually takes place is ridiculous to consider. However, a voice in the back of their minds hints at such a lofty possibility. Another voice ridicules the thought, because love this early is nothing more than an illusion, a desperate plea for life to offer something organic and beautiful. The opposing voice argues that love must develop over time. Many couples felt what they thought was love at first sight, only to have love subside over time, turning the relationship into one of minimal tolerance between two people. Maybe love has nothing to do with the connection between Hudson and Katie. Some things are just too complicated for the mind to comprehend, and the voices will never settle the debate. Neither Katie nor Hudson knows about the darkness lurking within the other. They only feel the hope they bring each other—the promise of a life worth living. For now, hope, not love, is all they need to fend off the dark thoughts.

Charleston is the perfect place for them to share a day with each other. The town truly captures the spirit and charm of the south. The scenery is a pleasure to behold. Horses pulling carriages down cobblestone streets offer beautiful simplicity during times of complexity as they drive toward the battery by the water. Palmettos, old Southern mansions, and fountains in Battery Park reside on one side of the street with the morning sun glistering in the harbor on the other side. The atmosphere promotes passion, especially for a budding relationship. Charleston is not only charming; it is also home to some of the finest seafood restaurants in the world.

Katie and Hudson choose a restaurant in the middle of town, within walking distance from the mansions and Battery Park. Though the food is good, packing a little more flavor than anything they've had in recent years, the current company they keep is much more enjoyable. Smiles permanently reside on their faces as they chat away between comfortable moments of silence. The time they share this day helps ease those nerves that prevented their eyes from meeting yesterday. Today, eye contact comes more often and for longer stretches throughout their meal. Even the beauty of downtown Charleston fails to break their focus at times.

After lunch, they walk down to the park. They walk silently as they watch the surrounding world perform just for them. Many people occupy the park, more than the Helen horde, but this time Hudson only notices one. She stands next to him, now at the railing overlooking the harbor. His heart races as his hand drops to hers. He gently grabs her hand with his while looking over to see her reaction. The world slows in time as Katie stands frozen. She finally looks down at the water and closes her eyes. She gently squeezes her hand to his as she slowly turns her head to look at him. All her fears seem to recede like the harbor's ebbing tide. She smiles through the building emotions causing her eyes to tear up ever so slightly. Her heart races, as does his. Her smile is the long-awaited beauty he so desperately seeks in his ugly world. Hudson tries to think of the perfect words for this moment, but remembers what his father once told him: "Some moments are too perfect for words, son." He chooses silence, responding only with a smile.

Katie does not want to leave so soon after they arrive back at Hudson's house, but the longer she stays, the more she will struggle to leave at all. Hudson wants her to stay but does not want to look too aggressive or desperate. They both want to kiss, but neither works up the nerve. Even during a lull in the conversation, as Hudson strives to convince himself to go for the kiss, awkwardness does not fall upon them.

"Well, Ms. Katie, I enjoyed this fine day with you."

"As did I, Mr. Hudson." Katie smiles before looking at the ground, and then back up at Hudson.

"I would be grateful for another day with you."

"Well, maybe I should give Mr. Hank his turn," Katie replies as she looks at Hank, who has joined them next to her car. Troy was generous enough to come by and let the dog out a few times during the day; however, the big fella missed his crazy friend and his new, much better-looking friend.

"Are you sure there is not enough room for us both? I'd hate to hurt his feel'ns. He is physically as strong as any dog, but he can be quite sensitive," Hudson says, smiling.

"OK, Mr. Hank, I think I can make room for the both of you." Katie scratches Hank under his jaw again, just like he likes it.

"Would you care to escort us on another walk tomorrow? And then a ride up the river for a picnic spot? I know a perfect spot."

"Perfect spot, huh?"

"Yes ma'am, sure is."

"Well then, I can't pass that up. Been awhile since I enjoyed a good picnic."

The two trade smiles, but no kiss, not this day. Eyes offer a peek into the soul, but a kiss connects the souls, which may unlock their vaults. Both are simply happy to have found someone who makes this world seem right, not just tolerable, or in their case unbearable, until death. Both are afraid, though, of the potential outcome of whatever this relationship is or will be. Death seems to have fallen silent, so both feel there is no reason to rush anything. No kisses will be traded tonight, only smiles and goodbyes. Hudson and Hank stand in the driveway watching as Katie drives away. Hudson is no longer worried of the uncertainty that plagued him the previous night. His demon failed to convince his mind to ignore the possibility of living that life he saw in the diner window. Katie's demon suffered the same failure. Relief from her past tragedies continues as she drives back to the motel with a smile on her pretty face, joy in her mending heart, and only Hudson on her troubled mind. Their feet remain on the edge of life and death, but together they will determine their next step. Their two fates are now one.

# CHAPTER TWENTY-FIVE

# SORROWFUL RAGE

**S**ean performs as a brokenhearted man for his audience most every day. He often visits the Dixie Diner hoping to see Katie. The dwindling good within him sheds tears with her mama as they pray together for Katie's return. Mary Beth knows nothing of the conflict raging within Sean, nor is she aware of the pain inflicted on her daughter by the man who weeps with her. She not only shares in his sadness; she also tends to his mental wounds. Her ignorance confuses the wicked for the wounded. She knows nothing of the heavy casualties her daughter sustained in Sean's battle against addiction and selfish desires. The drugs he consumed to counter his demons were nothing more than chemical warfare that killed the innocent while empowering evil. When the daily act is over and the curtain lowered, Sean removes his mask and feeds his sorrowful rage.

Sean begins his nights with promises to himself that he will deny his addictions. He sits and stares at the door, waiting for Katie to walk through. Though the door remains closed, the bottle does not. He breaks promises to himself as easily as he does Katie. Once his heart cries tears of whiskey, his head incites fury of cocaine. The bulb burns and the angry fiend arrives hell-bent on waging war against the last bit of good remaining in his heart. The wicked spirit within is quick to remind him who to blame for his grief. It reminds him that just a few days ago he placed his heart in Katie's hands only to watch her toss it away like trash. His grief turns to rage. His knuckles bleed from the wall he hits. His whiskey glass shatters against the door Katie refuses to walk through. His eyes are red and his vision blurred by the tears. He damns Katie for causing him such conflict. She is to blame. She would only leave him for another man.

As the days pass, Sean increases the freebase he smokes and decreases the alcohol he drinks. He is tired of the sorrow. He is tired of blaming himself for her selfish decision to leave him for another man. He was ready to give up everything that satisfied him. He was ready to give up his friends. He was ready to do anything to save his relationship with her. Still, she left him. She left him broken. She left him to deal with his demon. He would have done anything for her had she not run off with another man. He remembers how she looked at the man from the diner the night before she ran away. He remembers the look in the man's eyes. He was not just some other customer. That man was far too angry and bold to be just some random customer. His anger is born out of desire for a woman. The woman this angry stranger desired is Katie—his Katie.

All that Sean seeks now is proper vengeance. He wants to sober up to devise his plan; however, grief, anger, and relentless thoughts of Katie with the guy from the diner are far too heavy for his heart to carry. Instead of cutting back, he increases his dosage. The cocaine persistently reminds him who to blame and what must be done, while the whiskey reminds him of the pain that Katie and her new man have caused him. He no longer wants the sadness from drinking. He only wants fury. He will not pay in pain for what they enjoy in happiness. He will find them, and, one way or another, he will kill what they have together.

# CHAPTER TWENTY-SIX

# SOMETHING IN THE AIR

**M**any years have passed since Hudson and Katie welcomed a day as much as they do this one. Normally, a lonely bed surrounded in darkness was too comforting to leave. Only during storms were those beds easy to depart as the dark-gray skies wept to the ground, exposing to the eyes their internal woe. Those dreary days made normal their sadness by sharing it with all. Despised by them were the bright, sunny days shining just for the happy people favored by life. Today, however, the sun shines for them and Hank.

Hudson feels he owes Hank a fun day after leaving him home yesterday. Hudson spent his day with their beautiful new friend while Hank spent his day with Troy—an unfair arrangement that did not go unnoticed by the big fella. Hudson knows he shortchanged Hank yesterday and is well aware that his furry buddy also took a shine to Katie. Hank makes no attempt to restrain his excitement as Katie creeps up the driveway. Just as he did the previous morning, he runs up to the driver's door before she can put the car in park. This time, Katie immediately opens her door and gives Hank a scratch'n under his jaw, just like he likes it. Hudson only briefly mentioned his perfect spot last night, but now, as Katie gives Hank some attention, he provides her a more thorough description of the sandbar that he was so fond of as a young boy. He describes how the out-of-place sandy bank seems to appear from nowhere, and how the river carefully eases around the bend. He seems to drift off to his paradise as he strolls through the little random spot in this big world. She feels the joy in his every word, offering nothing more than an envious smile as she can only pray to possess such passion for a special place. Hank also offers his undivided attention; he even breaks away from his jaw scratch'n. He may not understand the words his friend speaks, but he definitely senses the joy each one delivers.

Hank and Katie agree to accompany their friend to the sandbar. They must see for themselves the hidden retreat that he holds so dear in his heart. The zenith of Hudson's happiness resides at that sandbar, that is obvious, but exists in a time he can never retrieve but through the boy's memory. Maybe, given the right company, the sandbar will again provide jubilation. However, places that offer such opportunities are not easily accessible, and the sandbar is no different. They can physically arrive easy enough by boat, but access to the true spirit of the sandbar will require a much more daring journey for these broken souls. They will have to trust that pain and sadness are not all life offers. They will have to free the boy and girl who have long pleaded for their release from the dark mental prisons in which they are chained. The boy and girl can easily unlock the powers of the sandbar, but they can also open old wounds worse than before—wounds that never healed, and that they never thought to heal until now.

They decide to give the sun a little more time to warm the morning before riding up the Oconee. Hudson and Katie walk hand in hand down the tree line where the grass is lower as they make their way toward his pond. Hank bounces through the field's tall, dying grass, popping his head up every now and then to get his bearings. Fall has settled in a bit, cooling down that nasty summer heat and chasing off many of those pesky bugs with it. The wind swirls among the trees, plucking some of the colorful leaves from the limbs on the way through.

"So beautiful out here, Hudson. Very pretty with the changing leaves."

"One of my favorite spots. Definitely my favorite time of year." Hudson cracks a smile as he responds.

"Hank sure loves it."

"Yeah, he does. He needed something beautiful in his life."

"He is lucky to have found you."

"Maybe." Hudson grins briefly, but his eyes stray away from Katie as the night with the whippoorwill briefly sneaks into his mind. Hudson quietly looks up to the blue sky as he tries to forget that night.

"What's wrong, Hudson?" Katie asks, noticing the slight change in his mood.

"Oh . . . nothing, just reminded me of something is all." Hudson answers as though he is gradually returning from the darkness.

"What's that? If you don't mind me asking."

"No, no . . . it's OK." Of course, Hudson wants to just leave it at no. He wants her to believe he hides nothing from her. Questions like this are what he fears as they grow closer. He cannot divulge the details of that night, or the many days that followed, but he has to tell her something. Changing the subject indicates deception and continuing this conversation may uncover the truth. For the first time, a conversation with Katie makes him feel awkward.

"I just thought about why I named him Hank is all." The words blurt from his mouth without him thinking it through, but he had to say something. Anxiety sets in as he anticipates her next question. He knows she is just trying to get to know him a little better. He does not want her to know him, though. He only wants her to know who he can be, not who he is or was that night.

"Oh. So, why Hank? I thought you said he's named after the baseball player." Katie offers a smile as she can tell something weighs on Hudson's mind.

Hudson takes a second to remind himself that he can talk about his dear friend without becoming an emotional wreck. He takes a breath, and then lets the words flow. "I lost my best friend during our last tour. I was kneeling beside him as he passed away. I had the distinct honor to hear his last words . . ." Hudson pauses for a moment, looks at Katie who is clinging to his every word, and smiles. "That knucklehead . . . 'Roll Tide' . . . that is what he whispered to me. I think his brain was recalling the conversation we had moments before . . ." Hudson pauses again as he looks back out to the field and reflects on that moment. "Well . . . anyhow, his name is Hank Jackson. His father named him after Hank Aaron, the baseball player. Hank really had a great appreciation for life, even though he had it pretty tough grow'n up and spent his last months trounce'n through hell on Earth. This fella has the same appreciation after experiencing his own hardship. So, the name seems to fit."

"You said *is* his name. Did your friend not pass?"

Hudson looks at the ground for a moment before looking up at Katie. "He passed . . . at least from this life, but I get the feeling he is still here. I know it sounds crazy . . ." Hudson knows the direction of this conversation is coming dangerously close to the truth. It is stirring those emotions he wants to keep well locked away.

"Not crazy at all, Mr. Hudson. I am sorry you lost your dear friend." Katie offers Hudson a gentle smile with her condolences.

Hudson smiles to hide the building emotions, and then abruptly changes the topic. "Ya know, I got lucky to get this place for what I did. I guess I shouldn't say lucky, but I used to help the old couple take care of the place. I worked for the neighbor, met the old couple, and I grew fond of them . . . they grew fond of me, too, I guess. Ethel became very ill . . . old-timers . . ." Hudson pauses as he thinks of growing old with Katie, with someone who loves him and whom he loves, taking care of each other. "I helped take care of her. She passed, and Harold followed a couple years later, after I joined the service. They had no kids of their own—well, their only son died young—and they treated me as their own, so he left me the place when he passed away. Damnedest thang, though, not being able to thank your friends for such a wonderful and thoughtful gift. They were two of the sweetest people ever to bless this world."

"You have a good heart, Hudson. They saw that, too."

"I guess . . ." Hudson pauses, again uncomfortable with the mood of the conversation, before blurting out, "I would actually bring girl-friends over for them to meet and get their approval . . . shit . . . I'm not sure why just I told you that . . ." He knows the reason—he needed to change direction in the conversation, and it was the first thing to pop in his head.

"It's quite all right, Hudson. I suspected you have dated before." Katie smiles as she watches his face turn red. "Did you used to walk them down this same field?"

"Uh . . . a time or two. It was just as pretty then, and it set the mood . . . uh . . ."

"Look'n to get lucky, are ya?" Katie's smile grows as Hudson stumbles along, trying to recover.

"That's not what I was get'n at . . ."

"What were you get'n at then, Hudson? Did ya bring a lot of girls up here?" Katie smiles, on the brink of laughter.

"I'm just say'n that it was a beautiful spot to bring a date and meet people who were dear to me."

"Uh-huh, you seemed to ignore my other question, Mr. Lee." Katie looks over and smiles again at Hudson, who she had on the ropes for the moment.

"About get'n lucky?" Hudson finds his grin again as though the conversation has most certainly taken an even more awkward turn.

"Did ya get lucky on your walks?"

"Well, that is not a fair question, Ms. Katie."

"I'm just mess'n with ya," Katie says, still smirking.

"Are ya now?!"

Hudson smiles at Katie as he contemplates going in for a kiss. This seems like a perfect moment to finally take that huge step. His heart beats faster as he works up the courage to kiss her. Her heart beats faster as she anticipates the kiss. With their eyes locked and their pounding hearts full of excitement, Hudson finally makes his move—unfortunately, a second too late.

During Hudson's tour in the Marine Corps, a hog farmer set up shop on the other side of his place. Hudson hasn't thought about it since returning, he never cared to think about anything really, so he knew nothing of the hog farm. Maybe he knew nothing about the farm because the wind was never just right or he was always too far gone to ever smell the repugnant gift a hog farm offers the nose. Regardless of why he never knew, the fact remains that conditions are perfect this morning for him to find out at the worst possible moment. Today the wind blows just hard enough in just the right direction at just the right time to rudely interrupt that kiss with the foul fragrance of hog manure.

"Mmm . . . that is rather fresh." Katie laughs as she puts her hand over her mouth. "So this is your lucky spot, is it?"

Hudson smirks as he covers his nose and mouth with his hand. "Used to be in high school."

"Well, did ya get lucky?"

"I guess we'll see, won't we?" Hudson says while offering Katie a sarcastic grin.

"I will save you the suspense, Hudson; hog manure may work with the high school girls, but it won't get ya anywhere with me." Katie continues to smile as the smell lingers.

"I am truly sorry, Ms. Katie. I swear, this shit did not exist back then!"

Katie laughs before she replies, "Well, I am truly happy your girlfriends never had to endure this wretched smell while enjoying the beautiful landscape with you."

"I am truly sorry! They must really be stir'n deep in that shit!"

"It's OK, but maybe we come back and try again when the wind is blowing in the opposite direction."

They turn back toward the house and walk quickly, trying to escape the relentless stench of manure, which continues coming in waves, each stronger than the last. Hudson calls for Hank as they walk the quarter mile back to the house, but he is nowhere to be seen. He must not mind the foul odor as much as his friends.

"I'm really happy we met . . . that we ran into each other, so I could hear all about your girlfriends while enjoying the wonderful smell of manure." Katie continues to poke fun at Hudson while covering her mouth and nose.

"Yeah . . . again, sorry about the hog shit! Damn, that smell is pretty stout—I can actually taste it."

"Well, now I really want that kiss!"

Hudson winks at Katie and replies, "Well then, come on over—I thought hog shit would do the trick!"

"Hardly!"

They finally make it back to the house. Hudson is disappointed about the damn hog farmer ruining their moment. It was a perfect moment; the perfect time to kiss Katie until the rancid wind cut right in between them. Life has a way of ruining perfect moments, or maybe it just created a perfect memory—one they can look back at and laugh about when they take that future walk. Hudson feels pretty damn excited about what just disappointed him. He looks forward to many walks with Katie, but still feels something tugging on him, like it is pulling them apart.

They give the wind an opportunity to bed down while they pack a picnic for the sandbar. Once packed, they hitch the boat up to the truck and head to the pasture boat ramp. With the boat in the water, Hank settles in up forward so he can catch the splashing water in his mouth. Hank hardly makes much of a lookout and the air is still a bit brisk, so Hudson takes it slow up the muddy river. Katie sits in the middle admiring the passing scenery just like young Hudson did on the way to catch white bass. Hudson, as was the case when he was ten, is not the best lookout either, thanks to his drifting mind. This time his mind is not on fishing, though, it is on the beautiful woman sitting in front of him. Hudson knows he ought not to, but he ponders the secrets she holds. He questions why she is here with him. She is intelligent, funny, and beautiful, but he knows she hides something. He feels guilty for pondering her secrets as he wants no one questioning him. She briefly looks back at him, smiles, and then back to the riverside scenery. Her timing was perfect, like she knew his thoughts and wanted to lay to rest his fears. Little does he know, her fears are as intense and questions as plentiful. Her well-timed look may not answer any of their questions, but it sure eases their fears.

They finally arrive at the sandbar and beach the boat. Oddly, the years have not changed the sandbar much. Maybe it is a little smaller than Hudson remembers, though everything seems larger to a child. The sun shines brightly on the river's reddish-brown water. The breeze is cool and carries a much more refreshing natural scent than the hog farm breeze at Hudson's place. Hudson and Katie lay out a blanket and sit side by side, leaning back on their hands. Hank sprints into the river for a swim in the cool, slow-moving water.

"He really is a happy dog," Katie says as she watches Hank jump around in the shallow waters just off the sandbar.

"Ain't he?! Only time he gets riled up is when another dog comes around."

"Think he'll ever get past that?"

"Probably not, but ya never know. He has a loving heart the size of his gigantic head, but he has a dark place in his soul where some old demons reside. He gets pretty damn vicious around other dogs."

"That is so sad. If only he had you from the git-go, he'd be noth'n but full of love."

Hudson contemplates her words for a moment. She knows little about him. If he could be honest with her, he'd tell her that the dog would have been better off stumbling across someone else, someone who is not as unstable as himself. He recalls the liberating feeling of his honesty the night Uncle Walt came to him in his dream. For reasons unknown to him, he feels she, too, will understand the dolorous nature of his mind. Maybe one day he will be able to unload the weight he carries, but that day is nowhere in sight.

"Yeah, well . . . I guess things are the way they are meant to be."

"Yeah, I suppose you're right, Mr. Hudson."

"I apologize ahead of time if this sounds a bit cheesy—I know we haven't really known each other but a few days, but it seems longer."

"Not cheesy at all, Hudson. I actually feel the same way."

"Even though you know nothing about me or me you?"

"I think we know all we need to know for now," Katie replies with a gentle smile.

"How do ya know I didn't bring you out here to rob ya?"

"Well, if ya did, you are the dumbest SOB in the state of Georgia, because I am as broke as they come."

"Smart enough to get you out here on this blanket with me."

"I am actually here for Hank, thank ya very much."

"Is that right?"

"Yep."

"OK then . . . Hank! Get over here!" Hudson yells.

"Dammit, Hudson!" Katie laughs as she attempts to jump up. Without hesitation, Hank runs full speed, ready to deliver a rather wet and sandy hug. He stops just before he reaches Katie to dry himself off in that special way dogs dry themselves, the same way he did in the boat. Hudson covers up Katie to shield her from the river water dog shower.

"I'm sorry, Katie. I didn't think that all the way through," he says as he continues to shield her, putting himself in a rather intimate position with her.

"It's OK, Hudson. I think I can handle a little river water and sand. I'm a country kinda gal."

"Sorry, I'll move off . . . I am so sorry," Hudson says, realizing that he is lying on top of Katie.

Katie grabs his arms to keep him from moving away from her. She doesn't think about what she's doing, she just reacts. She wants to tell Hudson not to go anywhere, to stay with her, to hold her, but she says nothing. The girl begs the woman to not let go of the boy, but the woman quickly opens her hands. Without looking up, the woman apologizes to the man, but not to the girl.

"It's quite all right, Ms. Katie. I just didn't want you to get that river water and sand on ya. I was just try'n to be funny . . . big fat fail."

"No, no . . . it's quite all right." Katie pauses to give Hudson a quick smile. "You are doing just fine, Hudson. I just hope our lunch is not soaked."

"Nah, everything is in the plastic tub and cooler. However, the dayum blanket is soaked and sandy. I am really on a roll today, huh?!"

"You are doing much better than you think," Katie reassures Hudson with a smile.

Hudson grabs two buckets out of the boat for them to sit on while they enjoy their lunch. This may not be the picture-perfect day Hudson envisioned, but Katie seems to make the imperfect perfect. As for Katie, all those fears and doubts vacated her mind during Hudson's bumbling attempt at a perfect day. She actually enjoyed this day as much as the trip to Charleston. Where they are does not seem to matter, just who they are with.

# CHAPTER TWENTY-SEVEN

# MARY BETH

The sun has risen on Katie's dark world, though fear settles back in like a dense fog as she thinks, often, of returning home. Hudson lights her way, but the fog will never lift without fully revealing tragic secrets that were kept well hidden in the dark, a darkness that is soon to return when she goes home. The more Hudson shines that light, though, the more secrets he will find, whether in fog, darkness, or both. She prays his light does not extinguish when the hidden is revealed—she prays it burns brighter during her darkest hour.

Katie has not talked to her mama, or anyone other than Hudson and the old man at the bridge for that matter, since her promise to return—the promise she broke. She feels guilty for breaking her promise, but the worst of her anxiety stems from shame of the suicide she did not commit. The thought of her destructive intentions will be her burden every time she has to look a loved one in the eyes. Though Mary Beth had no clue of her daughter's plan, Katie will always see the pain in her mama's eyes, and shame will overwhelm her. She does not want to lie to her mama again, but she damn sure can't tell her everything, either. So long as she lives, she never wants her mama to know of her struggles to live. She stares down at her phone for an hour and a half before picking it up with a trembling hand to make the call she so horribly dreads.

Mary Beth picks up on the first ring and wastes no time voicing her concern. "Kathleen Marie Carter . . ." Mary Beth calms herself down before continuing. "Honey I have been worried sick about you. Are you awlright? Where are you?"

"Hey, Mama . . ."

"Please, Katie, hunny, answer my questions. I need to know you are OK." Mary Beth's voice trembles as she hopes for her daughter's safety.

"I'm good, Mama. I'm so sorry for being gone and not call'n you. I really needed time to think and . . ." Katie hesitates as she works up the nerves to continue. She needs to come clean about Sean without divulging too many details.

"And? What, hunny? What is wrong?" Mary Beth cries out as anger, fear, worry, and relief all have a hold on her mind.

"I had to run away from Sean, Mama. He's abused me for a long time. He has threatened to kill me many times."

"Oh my Katie, hunny, why didn't you tayull me? I woulda kept you safe, baby."

"I just didn't want to drag y'all into it, Mama. Sean is more danger-ous than you know. I am scared to go back."

"We can get a protective order, baby."

"No, Mama. That will just make it worse. He will surely come after me as soon as they serve him with it."

"Well, baby, tell me . . . how can I help you? You need money? What can Mama do to help you, baby?"

"Nothing, Mama. I don't need money. I want to come home. I can't let him dictate my life—I know that now."

"I don't want anything to happen to you. I just couldn't live with myself if you came back and something bad happened to you. Maybe you should wait until thangs cool down. I do want you to come home, but if Sean is as dangerous as you say, I think you should go stay with your cousin Julie in North Carolina for a while."

"I can't do that, Mama. I have to help with the diner. I . . ."

"The diner will be fine. We can hire somebody to replace you for a while. We can't replace your life, though, if someth'n bad happens, Katie!"

"I am come'n home, Mama—if I haven't been fired, that is."

"No . . . sweetheart, ya haven't been fired. Darn it, Katie, are ya gonna listen to anythang I say?"

"Yes, Mama, just not about this. I refuse to leave everyone I love because of Sean. I'd rather die here with y'all than live with a family I barely know in North Carolina."

"Katie, please don't talk like that."

"It's just the way I think, Mama."

"Well, why don't you just stay at my house for a while?"

Katie is hesitant to accept her mama's offer. She's already endangered Hudson's life without him knowing. Moving in with her mama will surely endanger her life, too. She also does not want her mama to know about Hudson. She hides many secrets from many people. She does not want to face any more challenges in life. She does not want to live in fear for herself or others. She feels helpless. Death was her way to gain control and truly escape it all. Still, she gave death no victory because of Hudson. He provides something death, or anyone else, could never give her. She can't let anyone, even her mama, take that away for any reason. She tells her mama that she will stay with her only long enough to find her own place. She wants to face her fears to test her strength. She wants her independence from everyone, but a partnership in life with Hudson. She wants to live on her own terms. In order for that to happen, she must use her newfound courage to face the consequences of the secrets soon to be discovered by all.

# — CHAPTER TWENTY-EIGHT —
# THE VISIT

Hudson again finds himself in a familiar place without any recollection of his journey. Fall continues to cool off that muggy
summer air while the absence of wind allows the pond water
to rest. Hudson sits in a chair on the bank and casts out his bait, disturbing the calm water. The haunting coos of the mourning dove fill
the air, reminding Hudson of his younger days, when he would cup
his hands together and blow into them to mimic their chilling song. A
blue cooler sits on one side of his feet, with Hank sitting on the other.
Hudson tosses a ball up the hill a little ways for Hank to chase. He
watches Hank sprint up the hill after the ball; however, the big fella
sprints past the ball and over the hill. His barks are the only sound
bouncing around the field as the doves have fallen silent once again.
*Squirrels must be out play'n,* Hudson thinks. Hudson turns back to the
pond as the barks fade. He concentrates on the end of his pole until he
feels the presence of someone standing behind him. He thinks Hank
has returned, but when he turns around the dog is not who stands
behind him.

"What's up, son?"

Hudson struggles with his thoughts and words. Shock consumes him as his eyes lie to him. No way the man standing next to him is actually here.

"Never thought you would see me again, did ya?"

"Can't be," Hudson says in disbelief.

"Can and is."

"I watched you die. I tried to save ya, but I watched you die."

"Nah, I'm still here with ya, dawg."

Hudson looks around at the field and then the pond. He notices all sound is absent. Only his friend's voice fills his ears. He's just cracked open his first beer, so Mary must be the culprit—she tends to play tricks on the mind from time to time.

"You died, Jacks. I saw you die, brother."

"Are you sure?"

"I watched you die . . . I'm sure. I've been fucked up bad over it."

"I know ya have. Are you sure that I am the one who died, Hudson?"

"What? Are ya fuck'n with me, Jacks? Shrapnel ripped you apart. You were look'n right at me as your life faded away . . . dead in my arms . . . I saw your life fade from your eyes, man."

Hank looks to the afternoon sky and smiles. He takes in a deep breath of the cool air and then looks back to Hudson, who remains confused. "What happened was nobody's fault. You are a good friend, son. You did all you could. Don't use me as an excuse to punish yourself anymore. Live your life free of guilt. You will need to let me go when the time comes. Ya feel me, dawg?"

"I can't let you go, Jacks. I don't want to . . . I shoulda been the one to go . . . death took the wrong man."

"God's plan, son. You left with free will . . . you make your own choices, but I'm ask'n ya, as your friend, lemme go when the time comes."

"Can you at least stay for a while? Have a beer with me? I fuck'n miss ya, man!"

"You got that cheap shit, don't ya?"

"I got that free shit. Do ya want one or not?" Hudson finally cracks a smile through the tears.

"Man, I make it all the way down here to talk to ya, and you offer me cheap-ass shit."

"Ya didn't tell me you were come'n, Jacks," Hudson replies, wiping away the last of his tears.

"Naw, guess I didn't . . . Awright, dawg, come on, gimme one . . ." Hank pauses for a moment as Hudson hands him a cold one right out of the cooler. "Didn't know I was comin . . . you woulda had the same cheap-ass beer if ya did know, son."

"Yeah, and it woulda still been free, so quit ya bitch'n."

The fellas drink a couple of those cold, cheap beers together as they cut up like their days in the Marines. Hudson tells his friend how badly he misses him. He tells him about the night with the whippoorwill. He tells him about Katie and the dog he named after him. Hank just smiles and listens as though he knows all about it.

"They are your life now, son. How bout you lemme go so y'all can live? I can't keep watch'n after ya," Hank tells his dear friend.

"All I can do is try, Jacks."

"Well, try without cloud'n your mind with drugs and alcohol, fool."

"Am I high right now?! Is that why I'm talk'n to you?!"

"Crazy-ass redneck . . . I gotta go, son . . ." Hank chuckles for a second before continuing, "Lemme go. Son, you will need to let me go to save'r." Before Hudson can ask his friend what he means, Hank hands him his empty can, and then walks back up the hill. He waves without turning back around. The loud bark from behind Hudson startles him as he returns a wave. He turns around to find nothing behind him. Again, another loud bark from behind him. The second bark wakes him up. He has nodded off while sitting in his chair by the pond. He wakes up to Hank barking and licking the top of his beer can. Hudson shakes his head for a second, and then gives Hank a good scratch'n up under his jaw, just like he likes it. "Ain't a dayum thang wrong with my choice of beer, is there, boy?!"

# CHAPTER TWENTY-NINE

# BLUES

Katie holds true to the promise she made her mama this time. She returns to Watkinsville and to the Dixie Diner; however, her sojourn with her mama only lasts two days. She uses most of what money she had left over for first and last month's rent on a little place just outside of Watkinsville. With most of her belongings remaining at Sean's, she has to use the rest of her savings on clothes and furniture. Her mama helps her as much as she can, as mamas do for their children; however, Mary Beth is none too happy about her daughter's decision to move into her own place. She begs Katie to reconsider living with her, just for a little while, until hot tempers cool. Katie convinces her mama that she will be fine, though she knows Sean's temper will never cool, or even simmer, as he fuels his fire with drugs and alcohol until his jealousy and fury finally boil over. She already feels guilty for risking Hudson's life, and has no desire to endanger another loved one, especially her mama. Mary Beth may have caved on letting her daughter get her own place, but did not compromise on when she will work. She only allows Katie to work day shift during the week so Katie can avoid Sean and so Mary Beth can keep an eye on her daughter as much as possible.

Fear chokes the air from Katie as she tries to go about her life as though all is right in the world. Only when she is with Hudson can she breathe freely. She visits Hudson and Hank every day after work, sampling the life she witnessed through that kitchen window many days ago. However, that sample is far too small to eradicate her fear, because she is sure Sean will shatter the window view when he learns of her return. Hudson is not completely ignorant to her fear, though her secret remains buried inside her; he senses she is broken and needs protection, just as she senses the same about Hudson. Both find peace with not knowing but sensing things about each other. Both are content keeping their skeletons hidden in their shallow graves. Withholding truth seems to be a potentially disastrous manner in which to begin their partnership in life, but unbeknownst to them their souls have already shared what words have not.

Katie and Hudson have yet to move the relationship beyond hand-holding and friendly partnership. They have yet to commit to anything as they let life play out. They worry about nothing when together; they simply enjoy their time with each other. He replaces her fear with courage, and she fills his emptiness with joy. Neither wants to ruin what they have, so they avoid talking about relationships just as they avoid divulging secrets. They also avoid meeting each other's parents, because meeting parents is pretty much an official step in dating, and neither wants anything official. They definitely don't want anyone shoveling up the loose dirt covering those old bones, which mothers are surely to do. They would prefer to avoid family altogether, at least for the time being, but Ty Lee can be pretty persistent when he has his mind set on something. He convinces Hudson to bring Katie to one of their gigs at a bar located just outside of Athens. Katie is hesitant at first, because she knows Sean runs the clubs of Athens; however, she is determined to face her fears, which is possible with Hudson by her side.

Hudson has always looked up to his older brother; though, he didn't follow in his footsteps because he knew their mama couldn't handle two wild sons. Ty is a gifted musician, but has no intent to take it anywhere beyond the Classic City. He always plays and runs with his regular crew: Troy, Curtis Campbell, Todd "TJ" Jenkins, Sonny Miles, and Jerry "Buddy" Johnson.

Curtis grew up down the road from the Lee family. He grew up singing old blues songs with his father on Saturday nights and gospel with his mama on Sunday mornings. Curtis is hell on a harmonica and has a deep, raspy voice that drives the ladies crazy. Curtis loves the ladies, and the ladies love him. However, this one-time philandering fella fell in love with a gorgeous college girl from Atlanta. She consumed his every thought. He wanted to do nothing but to be with her for the rest of his life. Then, she graduated from the University of Georgia and ripped out his heart before moving on. She sent an email thanking him for the fun times he gave her, but that their time together was done and to have a good life. It was a cold exit that left him badly brokenhearted. He found out what all those old blues folks really felt when they sang those songs.

TJ is on the bass and dobro. He says he's a cup of brown sugar and a teaspoon of spicy pepper, because his mama is black and his father was a smidge Mexican. His mama was a Navy chief before retiring. His father passed away from cancer when Todd was eight years old, leaving his mama a mess. Todd's mama drowned herself in gin trying to wash away the depression for about a year before finding her way in music. As the old chief learned, so did TJ. Music healed them both and brought them closer as a family. Ty met TJ in elementary school, becoming close friends over the years. Ty and Troy would often go over to TJ's house to jam with him and his mama. Playing with the old chief is how the fellas learned and fell in love with country blues. His mama joins them on stage sometimes, but not tonight.

Sonny is actually more bluegrass than anything, but he can play about anything with strings. He made his way down from Tennessee when he got into a little trouble up there running weed and pills. He keeps that past locked away pretty tightly, because there may be a warrant or two out for his arrest. Sonny doesn't ask for much, nor does he want much: music and Mary are all he desires.

Jerry "Buddy" Johnson is a simpleminded fella who has lived a hard and tragic life. His father ran out on him and his alcoholic mama shortly after he was born. He miraculously survived his first few years of life, which were filled with severe neglect and abuse. His mama once beat him nearly to death for "ruining her life," which left Buddy even more simpleminded than before. Regardless of how nasty she was to him, Buddy loved his mama dearly. He'd do just about anything to get a little love and attention from her, but he never received either. She died after years of alcohol and drug abuse, leaving ten-year-old Buddy in the hands of the foster care system, where he suffered more neglect and abuse. Ty believes Buddy was created slow so he would never have to understand just how bad his life was back then. Buddy has no musical talent, but happily helps carry instruments for the only family to ever provide what he desired from his mama.

Hudson and Katie walk through the door and up to the bar. They are both a little nervous about her meeting his family and need something to loosen them up a bit, and alcohol has a way of doing just that if done in a small dosage. Hudson turns toward the small corner stage and sees Ty and the boys setting up. He looks over at Katie, smiles, and asks, "Ready for this?"

"Absolutely!" Katie smiles back as she nervously answers.

Hudson raises his eyebrows as he replies, "Welp, prepare yourself, because this may be quite interest'n."

That smile of Katie's grows as Hudson gently places his hand on her upper back to guide her toward the stage. His hand eases her anxiety of meeting Ty and the fear of Sean walking through the door. Just like in Charleston, she is all that exists in his eyes. Hudson is mesmerized by her smile—a little too mesmerized. With his eyes on Katie and not where he's walking, Hudson clips a barstool with his foot and stumbles a bit. Hudson's near fall grabs his brother's attention as he tunes his guitar. Without hesitation, Ty's eyes cut up toward the couple walking his way. Hudson knows his little stumble will draw some sort of sharp remark from his older brother, one to which he'll have no clever response as he remains captivated by Katie's smile.

"Careful, lil brother. A smile that pretty can brang a man to his knees," Ty advises as his eyes move from Hudson to the peach walking with him.

"Ty, this is Katie; Katie, this is Ty." Hudson grins at Katie, relieved that is all Ty says.

"Katie, good to meet ya! You are more beautiful than my brother described," Ty says as he smiles and holds his guitar against his body with his left hand while reaching out with his right hand.

"It's a pleasure to meet you, Ty," Katie replies with a nervous smile as she shakes his hand.

Troy is behind Ty setting up his drum set. Noticing that no one is in a hurry to include him in this little introduction ceremony, he clears his throat with a little cough. Ty looks back at Troy, and then back to Katie. He points back toward Troy with his thumb as he introduces him.

"This degenerate here is our cousin Troy." Ty points over to his right. "And those fellas there complete our band of misfits: TJ, Sonny, and Curtis. Buddy is somewhere around here."

Katie looks around at them all while collectively greeting them.

"Ms. Katie, it sure is good to see someone class up this joint. Hudson, how did you find such a purtee girl like'is?"

"Right place at the right time, Curtis."

"Uh-huh, where was this right place you speak of?"

"Well, the first place we met was the Dixie Diner. Her family owns it."

"Oh shit, that's y'all's place? Man, I sho do love the way y'all slang hash."

"Thank you . . . Curtis! We pride ourselves in hash slang'n," Katie replies with a smirk.

"Good cook *and* beautiful. You best not let this one go, son."

Fortunately for Hudson, who feels a bit uncomfortable with the direction of the conversation, Buddy diverts everyone's attention as he struggles through the door holding Troy's kick drum and a small guitar amp. He bounces off the frame, banging the equipment against the door, to Troy's displeasure.

"Dammit, Buddy! Don't drop that dayum kick drum!"

Of course Buddy does just that. He trips as he looks up to guarantee Troy he won't drop the kick drum. The drum hits the floor and rolls a few feet until it bounces back off the wall. Buddy looks over at the drum, fearing the tongue lashing he's sure to receive. He scratches the side of his head, a little nervous habit of his, before telling Troy, "I sorry, Troy! I pick it up, Troy. You mad at Buddy?"

Troy has never been one to hold his tongue. He just bought the kick drum a week ago, so his blood ran a little hot as he watched the drum make the short journey to the floor and wall. The look on his face says he is about to unleash a verbal hell on his slow-witted friend, but Troy takes a second to ice down his blood before saying a word to Buddy.

"Dammit, Buddy . . ." Troy pauses as he takes off his hat with his left hand and aggressively scratches the top of his head, a habit he has to keep himself from completely losing his temper, and then puts his hat back on before continuing. "Hell no I'm not mad atcha, but ya gotta be careful with my shit, dude. I just bought this dayum thang."

"OK, Troy. Buddy won't drop it again."

"No Buddy won't, because Buddy ain't pick'n the dayum thang up again. Just go get the small amps or some other easier shit to carry . . . less expensive shit."

"OK, Troy. Sorry, Troy."

"Just get the shit, Buddy!"

Katie looks a bit disgusted by Troy's interaction with Buddy as she watches Troy carry the kick drum over to the rest of his set. She can tell Buddy is slow minded and thinks Troy is a bit brash with him, which she doesn't much care for. She thinks that they may have Buddy around just for their amusement. Little does she know, Ty and Troy took Buddy in to ensure he has a better life than the one in which he was raised.

Ty recognizes Katie's displeasure. He is back sitting down on his stool after greeting Katie and giving his brother a quick hug. He leans on his guitar, crossing his arms over the top as it rests on his lap, and commences to telling Katie the story of Troy and Buddy,

"Oh, Ms. Katie, don't you worry your pretty lil self about Troy mistreat'n poor ole Buddy. Let me tell ya someth'n about Troy and Buddy. Troy and I rolled out of a bar one night after playing a set. Now, that bar was not the fine establishment as the one we currently occupy, my dear. Oh hell naw. That bar was a real shithole." Ty pauses to wink at Gary Kinderman, the owner of the bar and the fired manager of said shithole, then proceeds with the story. "Well, outside of that shithole were four drunk assholes push'n round ole Buddy. Buddy pleaded with 'em to stop push'n'm . . . to stop hit'n on'm . . . but the more he pleaded, the more they hit'm. Purely for noth'n more than the pleasure of whoop'n on someone weaker than their drunk asses. Well, those assholes knocked Buddy to the ground and took turns on the ole boy . . . kick'n'm . . . punch'n'm . . . and one of those sick assholes started to urinate on'm. Now, before I could say or do a damn thang, Troy had already reached into his truck and grabbed an old ax handle he had up under the seat. Troy may not be the biggest fella, but he is a tough sumbitch. He also has a soft spot for folks like Buddy . . . ya know, folks who've been beat on and torn down all their life. See, Buddy's deddy ran out on'm, mama beat'm til alcohol and drugs ended her pathetic existence, and foster care was never good on the fella, though you would never know it by the way Buddy tells the story. Anyhow, with a purpose, Troy charged on those assholes. He broke one dude's ribs, another's knee, and fractured another's skull by the time I got over there. I did manage to take care of the other piece of shit, who was zipping up after urinate'n on Buddy, but I think he was happy that he didn't feel the wrath of Troy's ax handle. Which he would have had Troy not broke the damn thang across that third dude's knee. So, before your impression of Troy sours too much, just know that he cares deeply for that simpleminded fella. Now don't get me wrong, Troy has many faults, all worth your disgust, but not when it comes to our good ole Buddy." Ty then smiles and winks at Katie as he tells them to grab a table, enjoy some booze and blues, and dance a little if the spirit so hits them.

Katie stands in silence for a moment as she lets the story soak in. She smiles at Buddy while talking to Ty.

"Well, Ty, I'm glad y'all were there to help him, as I'm sure he is as well."

"Yeah, well, Ms. Katie, now we are stuck with the rascal. Someone has to watch out for'm . . . make sure he doesn't run out in traffic or some shit. Ain't that right, Buddy?!" Ty smiles and winks at Buddy.

"You right, Ty. They my bruddas, Ms. Katie."

"I am sure glad to meet ya, Buddy!" Katie replies with a smile.

"Glad . . . Glll . . . Glad to meet ya, too! You purtee, Ms. Katie! You sho purtee!"

"Thank you!"

"You welcome, Ms. Katie!"

"Buddy, when you're done hit'n on my lil brother's date, how bout help'n Troy with his drum set so we can get started." Ty smirks as he knows that will get a rise out of Troy, and it does.

"I don't need any dayum help!" Troy shouts.

"You sho, Troy? Buddy'll hep ya!"

"Buddy! I don't need your dayum help . . . you know what? Here's a ten. Go get us a few beers."

Katie admires that Troy and Ty offer Buddy the family bond he never had. She wonders where he would be without them. He would have lain behind the bar beaten and alone if Ty and Troy did not walk out of that bar and into his life. People don't have to be saints to do God's will—Ty and Troy are proof of that. Katie also appreciates that Ty recognized her displeasure with the way Troy talked to Buddy. She knows that in order to recognize such displeasure in others, and to take the time to address it, a person has to actually care for other folks. She is not accustomed to such altruism. After all, she just ended a horrific relationship with a narcissistic fiancé who surrounded himself with people who would not dare challenge him, and they followed his every move. She smiles at Hudson as they walk away.

"See, brother, I'm not gonna embarrass your lady friend. Ladies and gents . . . Hudson fuck'n Lee! Welcome home, brother. Thank you for your service, Marine!" Ty toasts his brother to the cheers of the patrons.

Hudson does not look back at his brother, only shakes his head as he walks with Katie to a table over by the wall to the side of the stage. A round of applause, hoots, and hollers roars from the room that seems to fill up in a hurry. The boys' music blends north Mississippi hills blues and underground country blues. They have a great appreciation for the blues derived from the severe hardships of poor black folks. They also have a deep appreciation for similar hardships experienced by poor white folks who would also gather to play and sing their troubles away. Tonight, all those poor folks gather in this country bar for some good ole blues. Music is, after all, the great uniter. Ty and the band begin the night with a R. L. Burnside tribute, a gritty rendition of "Poor Black Mattie," which gets folks up and moving. Hudson looks over and smiles at Katie. Maybe in another life they would have joined folks on the dance floor, but they are not there, at least not yet. Instead they just enjoy the music and grab a conversation when they can. They enjoy a night free of thought and anxiety. The blues has a way of making folks feel a little better about their hardships in life.

— CHAPTER THIRTY —

# NO SECRETS

S mall towns keep no secrets. They have too many eyes watching, too many lips whispering, and too many ears listening. Katie knows trouble is destined for her when she walks through the door of the diner as Rodney's black truck passes by. She stands frozen for a moment before falling backward into the glass, and then turns around and stumbles through the doorway. Sean's cousin was too far away and moving too quickly to see, but she felt his gaze—she might as well have waved her arms at him. Her heavy legs halt time. Her closed eyes darken the room. Her incapacitated lungs fail to fill with the thick air her dry mouth draws in. Her pounding heart is all she hears. Her secrets will soon come to light. Those fears buried in her shallow grave are rising from the dead. Her eyes spring open again as panic sets in. The world that spun so slowly just a second ago now spins out of control. Ringing in her ears are all the voices in the diner that now drown out her pounding heart. She races toward the bathroom, hoping to arrive before her legs fully surrender to panic and fear. She hears her mother's faint voice as she barges through the bathroom door. She falls back on the door, spinning the lock just before pushing off toward the stall. She falls to the floor as her legs fail her. She crawls for what seems like a mile before finally reaching the stall.

"Katie, what's the matter, hun?" Mary Beth hollers as she knocks on the door.

"Nothing! Let me be, Mama!" Katie pleads as she purges into the toilet.

The violent storm lying just beyond the horizon already blows in those old whispers of death. The fear is too much for Katie to handle. She begs Mary Beth to let her be, convincing her mama that something she ate didn't sit right in her stomach. Once she musters the strength to leave that bathroom and diner, she convinces Hudson the same thing when she calls to cancel their dinner date. She once again needs alone time with her thoughts. Mary Beth just wants to help her daughter through these difficult times, but Katie only wants space to keep her mama safe and out of her personal affairs. Hudson makes Katie feel safe, but she only offers him danger. He gives her everything, and she gives him nothing—so she tells herself. Nothing she ingested provoked her vile reaction. She lies to her mama and Hudson because fear and guilt resurfaced with tremendous vengeance the moment she saw that damned truck.

The following afternoon brings an end to any speculation of what Sean knows or doesn't know. Katie goes through the day without a peep. She tries convincing herself the storm is going to stay over that horizon, and that if it does blow through, Hudson will provide her a safe haven. She tries, but she knows there is no escaping the hurricane-force violence heading her way. However, she refuses to give up hope with Hudson for now, but is willing to cut ties with him for his safety if need be. She clocks out for the day, ready to head home to shower and change for her daily dinner date with Hudson. She looks forward to dinner and wants to make up for canceling the evening before. She looks forward to happiness instead of back at fear. However, fear is now before her. Excitement is gone. Happiness is gone. Only shock and fear remain. Sean sits in the driver's seat of his Jeep. He's backed into a parking spot next to her car. His door is open so she can't access her driver's side door. She squeezes her eyes shut to shake off the shock. As shock diminishes, her hands violently tremble, her heart pounds, and her lungs become paralyzed once again. She closes her eyes and forces the autumn air into her lungs. Hudson and Hank appear in her mind's eye and she marches toward her car. For her to embrace the future, she must confront the past.

Sean begins the dreaded conversation while still perched up in the driver's seat of his Jeep and speaking through the open door. "So, it is really over between us?! Is that how it is, Katie?"

"Sean, please move your door." Katie's voice trembles with each word.

Sean pushes his door open a little more, to the point he pins her car door closed. "There's someone else, ain't there? You fuck'n found someone else, didn't ya?"

"Sean, please, I'm ask'n you to please move your door."

"And I'm ask'n you if you were fuck'n around on me all this time, Katie? There is nothing lower than an engaged woman spread'n her legs for another man. It's just damn trashy, Katie." Sean's eyes squint as he almost snarls his words from his tongue.

"Sean . . ."

"It was him, wasn't it? The asshole from that night here at the diner? I will pay your little fuck buddy a visit. I don't give a shit that ya left me, but I'll be damned if ya fuck around on me and get away with it. All you are is white trash. You screwed everybody in high school until I made an honest girl out of ya. Well, I thought I did. Once a whore, always a fuck'n whore . . . aren't ya?!"

"Just leave me alone, Sean. Just live your life and leave me to mine. I am done with your threats. You want to kill me, then go right ahead, asshole! I was always good to you and true to you, but your ego and jealousy got the better of you. You are nothing but a bully—always been. Look at what you are doing. Blocking me from my car? Threatening me and anyone I may meet—"

"You screw around on me, and I'm the bad guy here? You are a real piece of work, Katie. I would have done anything for you. Ya know,

I took a lot of shit from my friends because I was date'n the school tramp. I stuck up for you, and this is how you repay me. It was only a matter of time before you got back to your old whore'n ways."

"You know I was true to you. You know why I left you, Sean. Now please move your damn door, so I can just go on with my life."

"I will move my door, but we'll see about your life." Sean closes his door and starts up his Jeep, "Katie . . . I will find that piece-of-shit fuck buddy. I guarantee he will be of no use to you after I do."

"Ya know what, Sean? How about you go to hell. I refuse to live my life scared of you anymore. I should have left you a long time ago. All the beatings I took from you . . . all the nasty things you called me . . . I am done with it all. Do what you will, but you don't scare me anymore, you piece of shit."

Damn, that felt good to say, even though she was terrified. The strength gained from Hudson roared as she stood her ground against Sean. She knows he will not simply disappear, but it felt wonderful to shut him up by calling out in public the abuse he has delivered in private. Mary Beth comes running out the door as Sean drives off. Katie dries her remaining tears. She tells her mama that all is fine, not to worry, and to go back inside. She quickly gets into her car and drives off, leaving Mary Beth standing in the parking lot. She wants to relish in her moment of triumph without interrogation, without interruption, and definitely without judgment.

Her glory is short-lived as her adrenaline settles, leaving Katie alone to face her fear and guilt. Her guilt is fueled by the trouble she just invited into Hudson's life. She knows those small town eyes will watch her every move. She cannot continue endangering Hudson's life. He deserves better. She convinces herself of these things. Insecurity storms back into her mind as she recalls the bad decisions she made in high school—regretful decisions Sean keeps fresh in her memories. She calls Hudson with the intention to cancel dinner plans, but cannot say the words when she hears his voice—not this time. His voice is all she needs to forget those old regrets. She feels safe with him, but only offers him trouble; however, she can't bring herself to rid Hudson of his ignorance. She can't reveal her problems. She drives straight to his house and suggests they eat at an out-of-town hole-in-the-wall type of place. Just so happens, Hudson knows the perfect spot. She prays Sean will not follow her, but she knows God controls no man, and only vengeance, anger, and addiction control Sean.

# CHAPTER THIRTY-ONE

# BBQ

**P**op Walter's is the hole-in-the-wall kind of place that offers the seclusion Katie and Hudson desire this fall afternoon, especially Katie. She sits quietly next to Hudson on the way to Pop's with her eyes on the future and her thoughts in the past. Sean aroused her fear and insecurity with his visit to the diner. With confidence she confronted both, but now her mind plays out the many bad consequences of her courageous stand in that parking lot. She just wants time alone with the man who is the opposite of Sean in every way. Hudson senses that her mind resides elsewhere, and her request for privacy tells him she is again avoiding someone. The barbeque joint shouldn't have many folks visiting this time of the week, but Hudson wants to make the stop as quick as possible, so he calls in their order ahead of time. He will pick up their Styrofoam containers full of smoked meat, cornbread, and collard greens while she waits in the truck with her thoughts. It was a good plan, until they pull into the parking lot. Standing around Ricky's boat, which is up on the trailer and hooked to his truck, are Clive, Troy, Bill, Ty, Buddy, Gray, Ricky, and Pop Walters. Hudson stops the truck just as they pull in and turns to Katie.

"I am truly sorry, Katie, but all those country folks standing by the boat are family and friends. In fact, that is my deddy. We can go somewhere else if ya like. This may get awkward."

"Um . . . don't worry about it. This was bound to happen. Plus, it would be pretty rude for us to turn around now," Katie replies, pushing back her anxiety and disappointment.

"Yeah, I guess."

Time alone with Hudson is all she wants. She is in no mood to mask her anxiety with glee, but she must and will in order to have her time with Hudson. She wants that time without him anywhere near her secrets. Turning around will surely stoke his curiosity. She can only hope to muster enough energy to keep this moment from becoming awkward. Fortunately for her, this bunch of country fellas have a way of making awkward feel about right.

Hudson senses Katie's hesitation, but will not push the issue. He parks the truck and they hop out. They walk side by side over toward the group of fellas who all stand quietly as they fixate on the beautiful lady walking by Hudson's side, her hand in his.

"Whatcha say, son?" Gray breaks the ice as he greets Hudson with a handshake.

"Aw, notta whole lot, Deddy. Fellas . . . this is Katie. Katie, this is my deddy Gray; that is Ricky, Mr. Clive Elrod, Mr. Bill Hagers, Pop Walters, and you already met Ty, Buddy, and Troy." Hudson points to each one of them as he announces their name. Katie presents her beautiful smile as they silently tip their ball caps to her.

"Ms. Katie, good to meetcha."

"Likewise, Mr. Lee."

"Gray be just fine, doll, no need to make me sound older than I am," Gray responds while offering Katie a flirtatious but innocent smirk.

"Okie dokie, Gray it is then. I'm happy to meet all you gentlemen."

Katie's blue eyes, pretty smile, and sweet Southern accent have the men rather tongue tied, with the exception of Ty, who sports a shit-eat'n grin as he watches the old fellas ogle the beautiful lady standing next to Hudson.

"Katie, my dear, your beauty has done the impossible . . . rendered these old-timers speechless."

Katie nervously smiles after Ty breaks the awkward silence; however, Ty's keen observation manages to loosen the knots tied with all those tongues, making the moment a bit more comfortable. They all take turns greeting Katie, starting with good ole Buddy.

"Hey, Ms. Katie. You sho purdee, Ms. Katie! Ty sho right bout dat."

"Hi, Buddy! And thank you, handsome man!"

"Better watch it, son. Buddy keeps sweet talk'n Ms. Katie, and she'll be show'n up with him. Ms. Katie, sure good to meet ya!"

"You too . . . Ricky?"

"The one and only."

"Thank God!" Clive butted in.

"All right now, Clive, ya ornr'ay bastard."

After the old gentlemen regain control of their tongues long enough to put them back in their mouths and greet Katie, Ricky decides to start a rather inappropriate conversation, one that offers plenty of awkwardness or, maybe for some, helps ease the awkwardness.

"Hey, y'all ain't gonna believe the article I read the otha day," Ricky blurts out, gaining everyone's attention. The fellas know Ricky is no scholar, and most of what he reads will surely be inappropriate in the presence of a lady; however, no one stops him.

"Hunt'n, fish'n, or dirty magazine?" asks Clive with pure derision.

"Naw . . . none of those."

"Then no, I don't believe you read a dayum thang," Clive responds without even as much as a smirk, just that grumpy-old-man look as he cuts his squinting eyes toward Ricky.

"Hey now . . . I'm tell'n ya, y'all gonna like'is. Found it on the Internet the other night. Hell Clive, this might even help you get a lil bit from your old lady, ya grumpy rascal."

"OK, Ricky, by all means, lay your wisdom upon us." Clive sarcastically submits to Ricky's enthusiasm about his damn article.

Meanwhile, Ty leans over with a smirk and whispers to Troy, "Ya know, this is one of those times when ya know ya ought tuh head this thang off, but I just have tuh see how this shit plays out."

"Yeah . . . I was thank'n the same shit," Troy replies with a smirk of his own.

Hudson, unlike his brother and his cousin, is not curious at all about Ricky's article. Actually, Hudson wants to head this thing off, because he knows Ricky talks about three things and Clive laid them out pretty accurately. Hudson knows this article is not about fishing or hunting, which leaves one inappropriate topic. Before Hudson can intervene, however, Ricky wastes no time revealing the intriguing contents of the article once he gets the green light from Clive.

"So, apparently, certain smells tend to turn on thuh ladies. Awl right now, Ms. Katie, maybe you can help validate this list, young lady."

"Yeah, Katie, how about give'n ole Ricky a sniff and let us know if fish bait and deer piss make the list," Gray jumps in with a smirk.

"Ms. Katie, I would not recommend doin that!" Bill suggests.

"Oh, I don't intend to," Katie replies with a gentle smile.

"Hey now, do y'all wanna hear the dayum list or not?"

"Oh, by all means, Ricky, please continue." Ty eggs on Ricky.

"So looka heeya, the smells that get the ladies' juices uh flow'n are these right here: lavender, cherries, cucumbers, and—get this shit— barbeque." Ricky counts off each scent with his fingers, really emphasizing the last one on his list.

"Barbeque? Ah, bullshit!" Troy immediately replies.

"I shit you not, Troy, that's what the Internet said. Evidently, ya give a girl a plate of barbeque and she will be ready to give you a go. I tell you whut."

"Now that gives a whole other mean'n tuh pulled pork, now dawn it?!" Ty can't resist jumping headfirst into this ridiculous conversation.

"And a good rub!" Troy adds.

"Now hold the hell on! Before you young bucks start slather'n yourselves up with barbeque sauce and hit'n the town, take it from someone who knows a thanga two about barbeque. Look here, I've served tons of barbeque to thousands of women, and ain't a one of 'em ripped off their under-draws afterward." Pop, being a bit more mature, jumps in to set the record straight.

"Well, hell no, not for you, old-timer, especially when you call 'em under-drawers." Troy pauses for a second. "Anyhow, the girls I'm chase'n wear panties, thongs, or nothin at all."

"Troy, it will take a whole lot more than a plate of barbeque for you to get lucky, young buck. From what I hear, you have a rather foul effect on the ladies." Pop dredges up some rather disgusting memories from Troy's near sexual encounters of the past.

"Dammit, Ty! Why the hell do keep tell'n everyone that shitty story?"

Ty only replies with a shit-eat'n grin as he is too entertained by the look on Hudson's face, obviously displeased with the nature of this conversation.

"Awl right now, watch yowuhr dayum manners. We have a lady present!" Gray intervenes while trying to bring a halt to the momentum of this dirty conversation so as to not offend Katie. However, Ricky, who possesses no filter, can't resist the opportunity to seek validation from the only lady in the group.

"Well, Ms. Katie, is the list accurate?" Ricky asks.

"Uh . . . hmm . . . I do love a good plate of barbeque; although, I will never look at pulled pork the same after this rather interesting conversation. However, sorry gentlemen, you will need to do a lil bit more for your ladies than barbeque to get lucky. Of course, some women are easier than others," Katie says with a smile.

"Ah, hell! She musta met your ex ole lady, Bill."

"Shit, Elrod, I didn't need barbeque to get her goin."

"Yeah, neither did anyone else."

"You do realize that you're speak'n ill of the dead, now don't ya, Elrod?"

"Not speak'n ill of 'r. She'd been the first to laugh at this stupid conversation. Hell, I liked the gal—she knew how to have a good time."

"Hell, a girl who loves a good roll in the sack after tear'n up a plate of ribs is my kinda woman!" Ricky announces, not wanting the conversation to get too far from the barbeque question at hand.

"Oh, there will definitely be some roll'n, Ricky!" Ty pokes.

"And that'll be just fine by me," Ricky replies with a big, goofy grin.

"OK, enough with this nonsense. Ms. Katie, how about we ditch'ese nasty talk'n fellas and go for a walk through the peach trees? It is way too beautiful this even'n to waste it listen'n to this mess." Gray has had about enough of the dirty talk and offers Katie a gentleman's way out.

"Sounds wonderful, Mr. Gray."

Gray holds out his arm for Katie. He slowly starts walking away with Hudson's beautiful date into the rows of nearly bare peach trees as the sun sets to the west.

"No thanks, Deddy . . . hell, I'm good here with these dumbasses," Hudson yells to his father. Hudson offers Katie an apologetic look—this is exactly the opposite of what she asked for.

"Well . . . good. Get yourself a beer and enjoy some more of Ricky's relationship advice. We'll try to be back before dark."

Katie looks back with a nervous smile, and then winks at Hudson. Something about these country fellas makes her feel the comfort she needs after her encounter with Sean. She feels safe. The awkward conversation topic didn't offend her at all; in fact, it was exactly the distraction she needed to calm her anxiety. She turns toward Gray as he talks to her about subjects much more appropriate than barbeque aphrodisiacs. She smiles at him as he talks. She thinks about that little kitchen window and the alternate world she saw. These folks here were on the other side of that glass. Though relief from the dismay of Sean's return is temporary, Katie is grateful for this sample of that world she saw outside the little window. Maybe a sample is enough to help her believe she can fully escape the affliction of what was inside.

Meanwhile, back at the boat, Ricky turns to Hudson. "Dayum, son, you really hit the jackpot with her, I tell you whut . . . smart, purty, and witty."

"Glad I got your approval, Ricky. Of all the possible conversations you had to choose from, you landed on barbeque and sex. Flow'n juices'n shit . . . What'n the hell's wrong with you?"

"Sorry, son! Guess I didn't thank it'd go in such a dirty direction."

"In what damn direction did you see this thang go'n, Ricky?"

"Didn't really thank about it . . ." Ricky pauses as he chuckles with the other fellas before continuing, "Look-uh-here, I helped ya out, son!"

"And just how in the hell did ya do that?"

"Well, now ya know that it'll take a lil more than a plate of barbeque to butter up Ms. Katie."

"I already had that one figured out, slick, but thanks!"

"Here, have a cold one on me . . . to make up for the barbeque thang'n all." Ricky reaches into the cooler, grabs a beer, and hands it to Hudson.

Hudson then turns his attention to the rest of the bunch. "And y'all actually entertained this stupid conversation? With a lady present! Did ya think any of this was appropriate when I introduced you to a lady? Is that where you are in life?"

"Well . . . ," Clive starts to reply.

"Rhetorical questions, Clive!" Hudson says. "Listen, next time y'all meet a lady, don't encourage Ricky's unfiltered stupidity!"

"Hey now, I'm offended."

"Ricky, you just talked about roll'n around in barbeque while having sex. I highly doubt anything I ever say will offend you."

"Dammit tuh hell, ya ornery rascal . . . just like your dayum mama. Sorry for the immaturity." Clive grins while delivering about the closest thing to an apology he's ever offered anyone.

"Damn glad to see ya, Hudson! Your mama and deddy were count'n down the days from the time you left. We're all happy ya made it back, son." Bill offers a little more serious sentiment to the conversation.

Bill, Ricky, Pop, and Clive all take turns shaking Hudson's hand and patting him on the back. They all pop a cold beer while standing over the boat, which provides Hudson an opportunity to offer a long-overdue apology.

"Hey, Pop . . . I want to apologize for what happened. I lost my cool and I shouldn't have, especially at your place of business. I'm sorry bout that!"

"Naw, ya shouldn't have, but that shit is water under the bridge, son. Now, ya can't brang'at dog back here. I can't have someth'n like'at attack'n somebody. You can understand where I'm come'n from, right?"

"Yes, sir, understood. Hank has a big heart on'm, but he went through a lot of shit in his life. He's a good dog, just not around other dogs."

"Hey, cuz, check out what me, Uncle Gray, Buddy, and Ricky caught this morn'n," Troy says as he opens up the live well, revealing about twenty catfish ranging from a pound to six pounds.

"Dayum, boys! This come out of your honey hole, Ricky?"

"Naw, show didn't, we didn't make it to the dam. We hit up the 278 bridge first thang this morn'n. Damn thangs hit from the time we threw down the anchor til about teeyun . . . and I mean they just shut it awf right at teeyun. We problee only caught two or three after that. Couldn't keep a hook in thuh dayum water for bout two hours'oh . . . I mean they tore. It. Up. Son . . . as soon as the dayum hook hit the water, I tell you whut." Ricky never hesitates to jump in on a good fishing conversation.

"Well, heyull. Think I'll go down there and hit it up sometime soon. Y'all going to Deddy's to skin 'em?"

"That's the plan. Depends on when Uncle Gray gets done with his stroll through the peach trees with your girlfriend. What you up to tonight, cuz?"

"I'm damn sure not skin'n fish, I can tell ya that. I'm have'n dinner with Katie."

"Looks like you came to the right place, brother." Ty looks over at Buddy with a smirk and wink.

"Yea, we did, until Ricky had to bring up that stupid ass article."

"Ya mmmight get lucky iiiif Ricky's Internet article is . . . is true, son," Buddy says as he laughs.

"Buddy, don't tell me you get'n in on this nasty talk?!"

"Naw, Buddy just make'n fun, Hu-Hu-Hudson."

"Uh-huh. Listen, Buddy, you want to impress a good woman, don't listen to Ricky. Awright?" Hudson recommends as he pats Buddy on the back.

"Yeah, you right. Ricky fulla shit bout fish'n, too." Buddy accurately describes Ricky's tendency to tell tall tales.

"Hot dayum, Ricky. Buddy bout got you figured out," Troy points out as he chuckles at the serious look on Buddy's face. Buddy is dead serious about Ol' Ricky's fishing fibs.

"Purdee much, don't he?!" Ricky replies with a chuckle.

"Going to Athens after this?" Ty asks Hudson.

"No, not tonight."

"Well, we are play'n at the fairgrounds this week. They have the music festival goin on."

"Awlright . . . well . . . I'll see if Katie is up to it sometime. She likes to stay out of town for the most part."

"Is there a problem with Athens?"

"Don't go diggin, Ty, now dammit," Hudson quickly responds with more solemnity.

"Awlright . . . awlright, come on out if y'all want to, lil brother. And hey, bout what we talked about the other night, which I don't recall much, but you did hit the jackpot, brother. Bout the only thang Ricky got right out of that bullshit conversation."

After Gray and Katie return from their stroll through the peach trees, she and Hudson take the food they ordered nearly an hour ago back to Hudson's house. As Katie apprised the fellas earlier, barbeque does not have the magical effect the article stated. Instead, Katie is more distant tonight, barely saying more than a few words. Hudson senses the heavy thoughts weighing on her mind, so he only interrupts her silence to ask if she wants more food or sweet tea, but she declines every time. She barely eats, leaving a good bit of pork to go along with the chicken Hudson bought for Hank, who will eat as soon as he is done chasing critters. Hudson is tempted to inquire about her thoughts, but knows they share what they want and ask for nothing more.

Katie takes off for home as soon as they finish supper. Her distant behavior and impassive goodbye deeply concern Hudson. He sits back in his recliner watching Hank devour the delicious smoked meat. Mary helps ease his mind as he contemplates his odd evening with Katie. She definitely hides something troubling, but he doubts it is as menacing as his demons. He knows it probably has something to do with her ex. He tries not to think about it much. He feels guilty for even pondering her secrets, because of the ones he hides from her. However, he feels she may want to pull the plug on their relationship, draining much of his newfound admiration for life. He will still have Hank, but Katie fills that void in his soul with something beautiful. He desperately needs that beauty in his life, and so does Hank. As he thinks about what she offers him, Hudson is suddenly overcome with guilt. He should be thinking not about what she offers him, but what he offers her. He falls deep into thought about that very question.

Hudson's phone lights up and buzzes, breaking his focus. Katie has sent him a text message, a rather long text message. He can't bring himself to read it right away. He is not prepared for the heartbreaking news it brings. He takes another smoke, gives Mary a little time to massage his mind, and then reads the text:

> *I'm sorry for being so quiet tonight. A lot on my mind. You are always on my mind, Mr. Hudson. You've uncomplicated my life while complicating it at the same time. I know that makes no sense really, but I don't know how else to say it. I enjoyed meeting everyone, especially your father. He is a good man. I see where you get it from. I know I don't share much about myself*

*with you, nor you with me. I can feel we both like it that way. I also feel that the things we don't share are somehow responsible for the deep connection I feel for you. I don't want to complicate your life, but I love being with you. I know this is a lot to take in, and I am rambling . . . wine sends my head in a thousand different directions. Ty invited us to the fairgrounds for more music. I didn't know what to say, so I said maybe Friday . . . I would like to go with you on Friday Mr. Hudson.*

Hudson reads the message a few times while scratching Hank under his jaw, just like he likes it. He looks at his big friend and tells him, "I love her, Hank. I have since the night I first met her. I was just too blind to see who entered my life that day . . . both of y'all."

Then, Hudson replies to Katie:

*I enjoyed our silence, Ms. Katie. Words are not always needed to enjoy time with someone. I, too, love our time together. I apologize for my brother putting you on the spot, but I would love to go to the fairgrounds with you Friday. I will leave you to your thousand thoughts. I am here whenever you need me. So is Hank.*

They trade a few more text messages before saying goodnight. Both want to say more than just goodnight, but they are afraid to hear those feelings aloud or, in this case, read them. Hank rests his head on the arm of the recliner and looks up as Hudson begins another one-sided conversation.

"We are stuck with each other, aren't we? I'm good with that. Hell, I guess I'm fond of you, too, Hank. I guess I should thank ya for save'n me. Well . . . thank you, boy! Thank you for comin to me when ya did!"

Hank listens to Hudson as he moves in a little closer and then lifts his big head to let Hudson know that he will take some more of those scratches under his jaw.

# CHAPTER THIRTY-TWO

# HERO

**A** deer faces fear with every drink taken from the water's edge to satisfy a relentless thirst. The deer either faces that fear and risk being devoured by a predator or suffer a long, painful death by dehydration. Hell of a choice to make. Meanwhile, the hungry crocodile patiently waits just beneath the surface of the murky water, covertly watching his wary prey suffer overwhelming thirst. He knows the deer will soon risk life for water. Hunger does not control him as thirst does his prey. Slowly he floats toward the bank without making as much as a ripple in the water. As he eases toward the shoreline, he closely observes his prey make a cautious approach to water's edge. The crocodile salivates as the deer eases into his ambush. The watchful deer is blinded by the need for water. All the deer can do is take a chance and hope the crocodile is not there, out of sight, and ready to kill.

Ever since she decided to give life another chance with Hudson, Katie has stood at the edge of that water. Her desire for love and security is overwhelming. Sean knows of her desperation for both. Just like any skillful predator, he knows her strongest desires will blind her. That they have. He has been there, waiting patiently in the murky water for that perfect moment of vulnerability. Just as the deer knows the crocodile is out there somewhere, Katie knows Sean will always be out there somewhere. However, just as the deer fails to see the danger that lurks within striking distance, Katie fails to see the same.

Musicians performing from one of three stages fill the fairgrounds with the rhythmic entertainment folks need to help escape the pressures of everyday life. Alcohol releases the tension and excuses trained minds from proper behavior. With all those people lost in music, Mary helps wrap their free minds around all of the lyrics filling their ears. Meanwhile, Lucy escorts others on a mental tour of an alternate side. Katie and Hudson need no drugs as they walk the grounds hand in hand, lost in each other. The pandemonium surrounding their private world does nothing to disturb them. The rest of the world quietly fades as their vision tunnels on who they desire most, leaving them vulnerable to the danger lurking just beyond their peripheral view. Hidden in the chaos they ignore is the raging man observing their every move. Fueled by alcohol and cocaine, flanked by his two closest confidants, Rodney and Jimmy, Sean watches his Katie hold another man's hand in hers. He bears witness to the looks and smiles they trade. Their happiness fuels his fury. She no longer believes he will fulfill his threatening promise. She is free of fear as she walks with this man. He thrives on her fear as it satisfies his urge to share his misery with her. Without her, he will never be happy, so he will ensure she will never be happy without him.

Unaware of the danger prowling in the shadows outside their world, Hudson and Katie stand near the stage where Ty and the fellas slow things down with another R. L. Burnside tribute. As Sonny picks on the six string and Curtis sings about going with a girl anywhere she goes, a song that struck his heart after the love of his life just up and left him, Hudson stands behind Katie with his arms around her shoulders and his hands locked together in front of her upper chest. She hooks her hand over Hudson's arms. Their bodies move as one, gently swaying as they lose themselves in the melody of a song with lyrics that perfectly describe Sean's refusal to let go of Katie. Sean watches Hudson hold

Katie. Just as he thought, she is with another man, the angry man from the diner. He watches as they close their eyes and move and breathe as one. Fury, alcohol, and cocaine free his mind of all consequential concerns. Rodney and Jimmy ignorantly believe they will only deliver a painful lesson to Hudson at some point soon. For Sean, a simple beating would fail to satisfy the wrong committed by Katie. The death of the man holding her is the only acceptable punishment.

"We'll get that sumbitch, Sean. When we don't have shit on us," Rodney reminds Sean as he recognizes the angry scowl on his cousin's face that always precedes a fight.

"I'm gonna kill'm. I'm gonna fuck'n kill'm!" Sean discloses his true intent to Jimmy and Rodney. They briefly glance at each other with concern in their eyes, but neither dares to say a word contrary to Sean's intent. Neither do they desire a night in the tank or life in prison, so they must keep Sean at bay, at least for tonight, to avoid either.

Katie and Hudson stay for the rest of Ty and the boys' set. After the last song ends, they join the band over by the stage to say goodbye. Before heading to the exit, Katie excuses herself to the ladies' room. Hudson stays put talking to his brother, so she knows where to find him. He watches as she walks away, still smiling and still in awe of his beautiful friend.

"Brother, I do believe that fine lady has a spell on you. I'm happy for ya. She's one of a kind."

"She is, Ty . . . One. Of. A. Kind," Hudson replies without diverting his attention from Katie.

"Son, that is the kinda woman who can sho nuff change a man," Curtis offers as he gives Hudson a little smirk.

Hudson looks at Curtis for a second before replying, "Curtis, you don't know how right you are."

"Oh no, I do. That look only happens once in a man's life, only some are fortunate enough to experience it. Only a select few experience it for life. I had that look . . . right up to the moment that woman tore out my heart."

"Aw, now Curtis, don't bring down the vibe with that depressing shit, man. The right one will come along—patience, brother . . . patience. Don't put that negative shit in Hudson's head," Sonny says as he zips up his guitar case.

"Sonny, I don't need your positive hippy shit."

"Welp, I'm gonna give it to ya anyhow. You know what you need? A hippy hug. Get over here, my sexy brown bear." Sonny wraps his skinny arms around Curtis while offering a teeth-baring shit-eat'n grin.

"Dammit Sonny, you smell like sweaty armpit," Curtis points out as he pushes a grinning Sonny away from him.

"Come on now, don't resist it . . . the wetter the hug, the better the hug."

"That's not even right, Sonny! I'm gonna have to take three damn showers to get this BO off me. All these fine ladies walk'n round here, and I got yo funk on me!"

"And you're welcome," Sonny replies, still grinning.

While the boys listen to Curtis and Sonny discuss hygiene and hugs while breaking down their equipment, Katie disappears into the crowd. The restroom is only a short distance away, but well out of sight of the stage area. She exits the ladies' room, still smiling while thinking of Hudson's arms wrapped around her. She can't seem to slow her heart as she thinks of him. She crosses her arms as though he still stands behind her, hugging her. Lost in thought she does not see him standing in front of her. She turns her head just in time to stop herself from running into him. Her eyes open wide. Her arms drop. Her heart stops and sinks before pounding faster than before, but for a much different reason. She can't form a single word. She can't move. His mere presence freezes her in fear.

"Having a good time, Katie Belle?" He pauses to let her answer, but continues before she does. "Oh, can't speak? Looked like you had plenty to say to your lil fuck buddy."

"Sean . . . I . . . Please do not start anything." Katie's voice trembles uncontrollably as she begs him.

"I thought we had something special, Katie. I guess not. I told you what would happen, didn't I?"

"Sean . . ."

"What? Sean what, Katie?" he yells, causing Rodney and Jimmy to scan the crowd.

"I told you. We can't be together. Why don't you leave me be?" Katie replies, voice still trembling.

"Leave you to be a whore, Katie? That's all, right? You just wanted to run off like a fuck'n whore."

"I'm not going to stand here and listen to this, Sean. Leave me alone!" Katie yells, trying to gain the attention of people passing by; however, they are all lost in their intoxicated worlds.

"Yeah, run off with him, ya fuck'n slut. That's all ya are and all you will ever be!"

Sean blocks Katie from walking off. He continues to belittle her while standing three inches from her. Fear grips her tongue. Drunk and stoned people continue walking by in the distance as Sean's friends conceal his abuse toward Katie. They are afraid of getting caught with drugs in their pockets, but they are more terrified of Sean's rage. They, too, underestimated his wrath. Katie has no idea how to escape this situation. She is afraid Hudson will walk up and all hell will break loose. She is just as afraid he won't walk up, allowing Sean to take her. All the while, Sean continues launching nasty insults at her while his friends shield Sean from view. Sean grabs her by the back of her neck and head, immediately bringing tears to her eyes.

"Katie, you're coming with us!" Sean says, breath ripe with alcohol.

"No, Sean! Let go of me!" Katie responds, unable to look him in the eyes.

"Sean . . . we can't just drag her out of here, dude," Rodney says.

"Katie, I better not ever see you with that motherfucker again!" Rage, alcohol, and cocaine demand he strangles her right here and now, but he knows his cousin is right. Now is not the time.

"Sean, you can't control me! Leave me alone and get outta my way! Just leave me alone!" Katie reaches deep inside for her courage, but Sean answers only with a tighter grip on the back of her neck. The moment seems to go on forever. Sean again reminds her of his promise, threatening to kill Hudson if he sees them together again. She fights back tears because she knows Sean grows stronger from her fear. She fights and fights, but her fear continues to build faster than courage. A way out of this situation seems impossible until she hears a familiar voice.

"Ms. Katie! You awwight, Ms. Katie?"

"She's fine, half-wit! Get the fuck outta here," Sean replies.

"You . . . you not nice. Puh . . . please take yo hand off Ms. Katie."

"Are you fuck'n kid'n me? Who is this retard, Katie?"

"Take yo hand off Ms. Katie . . . mmmmmotha fuh-fucka!"

"Buddy, I'm fine, Buddy. Please walk away . . . walk away, Buddy. Please!" Katie begs.

"Ms. Katie is is is not fine. You cry'n, Ms. Katie."

"Enough of this shit. You call me a motherfucker, retard?"

Sean takes his hand off of Katie, and then pushes Buddy hard to the ground. Sean pulls Buddy up by the shirt, and then throws him against the dark side of the restroom building. Katie yells at Sean to leave Buddy alone, but that only fuels his inferno. Sean charges on Buddy with the intent to break his jaw; however, as he closes in, Buddy hits Sean with a surprising left hook. Sean backs up a step or two. Shocked at first, then he laughs. Unfortunately, Buddy fails to realize the time to strike again is the moment Sean has that stupid, confused look on his face. Sean shakes off the shock, steps toward Buddy, and then delivers an uppercut to his gut. Buddy drops to the ground, holding his stomach and gasping. Sean pushes Buddy with the heel of his foot just as Rodney pulls him away.

"Sean . . . dude is a fuck'n retard and we got some shit on us. I'm not goin to jail because of this shit," Rodney says as he pulls his cousin away from Buddy.

Sean stands in silence for a moment, staring down Katie, who still refuses to make eye contact. "Fuck it. Remember what I said, Katie. You don't get to just whore around. I'll be see'n you again," Sean says as he turns and walks away with Rodney and Jimmy.

As they walk away, Katie helps Buddy to his feet. "Are you OK, dear? I am so sorry!"

"Buddy hept Ms. Katie."

"You sure did. You saved me." Katie wipes the blood off of Buddy's lip from where he hit the building.

"Just like'at time Troy and Ty save me."

"That's right, Buddy. Just like that. We better get back over there."

"I gotta pee. Dat's what I came to do when I saw ya. I think I peed a lil bit when he hit me, dough."

"OK, Buddy. I will wait here for ya, darl'n."

"You sho, Ms. Katie? You sho you be awwight while Buddy pees?"

"I will be fine, sweetheart. Go on and take care of your business," Katie replies with a gentle smile.

Katie cannot allow Buddy to tell the fellas exactly what happened. She has to think of something fast to tell Buddy in order to protect Hudson. She hates to do it, but she decides to trick Buddy into thinking they were just some drunken strangers who tried to attack her. She tells him that she did not know those guys, and the mean one was high on something. She says the guy introduced himself when she was walking back, and then became hostile when she declined his advances. She hates lying to Buddy and feels bad because she took advantage of his low intelligence, but it's to keep Hudson safe. Sure enough, Buddy believes her. He really doesn't know what to think of her story, he just keeps asking her if she's all right. He's simply happy he saved her. In his mind, he finally has a reason to be proud of himself.

Katie still has that familiar queasiness in her stomach from the encounter with Sean. He can detect her fear instantly and enjoys it immensely. His power over her unnerves her. She struggles to decide whether she should run away from Hudson to save him from the danger sure to come, or to run to him for love and protection. Sean is sure to hurt her either way, and sure to come after Hudson. Her fear tells her to run. Her growing love tells her to trust in Hudson. The age-old battle between love and hate wages war within her. Sean's hate breeds fear while Hudson's love breeds courage. She knows deep inside that the power of love can create an impregnable union that hatred will never divide, but she must have the courage to face the terrifying challenges before her.

When they walk up to Hudson and the other fellas, Buddy immediately tries telling the story. He has a hard time as he easily confuses himself. He confuses the details of Katie's story with what actually happened.

"What in the hell are you try'n to say, Buddy?" Hudson asks, confused but concerned.

"I tell ya, son, the guy tried hurt'n Ms Katie!"

"What guy? What is he talking about, Katie?"

"So, I came out of the bathroom and started walking back here. This drunk guy and his friends approached me. He introduced himself and started hit'n on me—flurt'n, not physically hit'n. Anyhow, I told him thanks, but no thanks. Apparently, he did not like being told no and got nasty and a little handsy with me. Fortunately, my hero here walked up and stood up for me."

"I did. I hit'm wit my fist like Troy tolt me to do."

"You hit'm, Buddy?"

"I sho did. He pushed me down. He throwed me on duh build'n, and I hit'm. He hit me back real hard, dough."

"Who the hell did what?" Troy yells after catching the back end of the conversation. "Somebody hit you, Buddy?"

"Yea, but I hit'm, too."

"I don't give a shit. Where is he? Is he still here? Show me who the heyull hit you." Troy is very protective of Buddy. His blood boils at the thought of someone laying their hands on him and is ready to put in work on the fella who hit his dear friend. However, Katie has to stop Troy before her secret is exposed.

"No, his friends pulled him away, and they all ran off. One of them said they have drugs, so I'm sure they got the hell outta here. But ole Buddy is a genuine hero tonight." Katie tries to bed down Troy's growing anger while holding back her own fears and emotions.

"You hit'm, Buddy? Get a good dayum shot on'm, didja?"

"I sho did. Wit a fist . . . like ya showed me, Troy. You proud of Buddy?"

"Hell yeah I am, Buddy! You a bona fide badass now. Gonna buy you a drank." Troy's blood still runs hot, but he simmers a bit to congratulate Buddy on his bravery.

"Hold the hell up. Are you OK, Katie? Did he hurt you?" Hudson is more concerned about Katie than he is about Buddy's ability to throw a fist.

"I am fine, Hudson. Don't worry, not the first time some jerk tried getting aggressive with me. I deal with drunks all the time at the diner, especially dur'n football season. You mind if we head on, though?" Katie grabs Hudson's hand and forces a smile to her face.

"Of course, Ms. Katie. Are you sure you are all right?"

"I am just fine."

"OK . . . welp . . . Fellas, y'all have a good one. Buddy, you are a hero tonight, my friend!" Hudson smiles and winks at Buddy as he compliments his bravery.

"Bye, Ms. Katie. Bye, Hudson."

"Bye, Buddy. Thank you for saving me! My hero!"

"You welcome, Ms. Katie!"

"Hold up, brother. Troy and I will walk y'all out, just in case."

"No need, brother. We'll be fine. Buddy gave'em more than they can handle. Ain't that right, Buddy?"

"Dats right, Huuudson."

"Awlright. You want tuh be alone with Ms. Katie. I gotcha. Hell, maybe one day I'll finda damn good woman and finally ditch these knuckleheads. Until then, think I'll join 'em for a lil drink or two. You lovebirds go on, fly off, 'n enjoy your night," Ty says with a smile as he turns back toward the stage.

Katie is not as confident about their walk back to the truck. Unlike earlier, as they walk this time her focus is on the crowd instead of Hudson. She never takes his hand into hers. She knows Sean is out there, just like the crocodile in the water, waiting to strike. To her relief, he never appears from the crowd. She says little while they walk and even less when they sit in the truck waiting for a few cars to move so Hudson can back out of the parking space. Hudson senses the change in Katie. She is cold again just like the night after running into everyone at Pop Walters's place. Her change confuses him, and, as he did that night, he feels the enigma that brought them together will also tear them apart. He struggles to trust the love building in his heart. Hudson looks over at Katie as she turns to look at him, but her eyes drop to the floorboard. Her eyes remain on her feet to hide her shame, to keep it from exposing itself to Hudson. She lied about what happened and tricked Buddy into lying for her. Her lie endangers Hudson, yet she keeps hidden the reason for her volatile mood. Hudson quietly stares at the steering wheel, coming to terms with their fate. Their thoughts are miles apart as they sit two feet from each other. Neither speaks a single word on the way to Hudson's.

"Thank you for a good evening, Hudson. I am sorry for . . . I'm just tired," Katie says as she opens the truck door after arriving back at Hudson's house.

"I had fun, Katie. You go home and rest. Talk to you later?" Hudson replies, still unsure what actually caused her change. He feels it has more to do with the incident at the fairground than fatigue from the night.

Hudson does not stand out on the front porch to watch her leave this time. He feels it may be the last and cannot handle the emptiness it offers. He is greeted by Hank as he walks through the door. He gives Hank a good scratch'n under his jaw, just like he likes it. Hank looks up with sympathy. He senses his friend's solemn mood. Hudson escorts Hank to the back door and lets him out to chase a few deer and stretch his legs. He watches Hank sprint off the deck and out into the darkness. Hudson stands in thought as he stares into the night. He figures Hank will be a while, so he might as well enjoy a good smoke. He is startled to see her reflection in the glass when he slides the door shut. He turns toward her but says nothing. Their eyes meet and there they remain. She drops her purse and slowly walks over to him. As she gets closer, he sees her red eyes and falling tears. The kiss is gentle, though they pull each other in tightly. Passionately, they take the long-awaited journey into the heart of the other free of the mistaken thoughts and shame from earlier.

They continue the breathtaking kiss all the way to the bedroom. Katie backs away for a moment, but never looks away from Hudson. He thinks she wants to slow the moment down, but the opposite holds true. She removes her sweater, slides off her shoes, and unbuttons the back of her dress. It falls to the floor, revealing her old scars, some by Sean and some self-inflicted. Her scars tell a tale of pain, abuse, and heartbreak. Hudson pauses in the moment to fully appreciate her beauty before him. He briefly ponders the scars, but doesn't show his thoughts. Katie slowly walks up to him and unbuttons his shirt. Hudson removes his shirt, revealing his battered body sculpted by his years in the Marine Corps and war. His tattoos and scars tell a tale of tragedy and destruction from his past. Katie looks at the long, jagged scar that starts on his right chest and runs down toward his left side. The scar is a reminder of the explosion that ripped the life from his good friend. She gently traces the scar with her finger before wrapping her arms around Hudson's waist and looking back into his eyes. Their breathing grows heavier as their lips meet again. She lightly scrapes her fingernails around his side to his stomach before unbuckling his belt. Hudson steps out of his pants as they fall to the floor. With his arms around Katie and her arms around him, he walks her over to the bed, continuing their intimate kiss. He gently lays her on the bed and lies next to her with one hand under her head, while he slowly and lightly draws the fingers of his other hand up her cheek. Their eyes never stray. They never say a word.

Some people believe there is only one person in this world meant for them as their life partner. They believe that person is their soulmate. Maybe that is true; however, those two people must meet at the right time. Life has to shape people before they fit together in such a perfect way. Katie and Hudson may have lusted for each other if they met as teenagers, but the connection between them now is far more than lust. The years of neglect and abuse have left Katie starving for attention, the kind of attention that makes her feel like she is not only the best girl in the world, but the only girl in the world in the eyes of her man. War tore down Hudson to an empty shell going through the motions of life without hope of normalcy. Only the truly powerful and gentle love of a woman can reach deep enough into his soul to rid his heart of the relentless pain and regret that remain. Life has shaped their union into something beautiful by way of the ugliest means imaginable.

Hudson and Katie make love until the early hours of the morning. They never let go of each other, not even in their sleep. When the sun delivers its rays through the window to welcome in the morning, Hudson realizes he never let go of Katie, not even to let Hank back into the house. He rushes to the back door and there stands Hank, looking through the glass with his tongue hanging out of his mouth while panting. Hank's look tells Hudson that he is not mad at him for leaving him outside. Instead, he looks happy for Hudson and Katie, who now stands behind Hudson with her arms around his waist and her hands locked together in front of his stomach. Hudson opens the door for Hank, who gladly walks in and sits next to them. He gives Hank a good scratch'n under his jaw, just like he likes it. The three of them travel their own rugged road, severely damaged along the way, to rendezvous in this wonderfully unforgettable moment as life planned.

# CHAPTER THIRTY-THREE

# FISH'N

Some stories are so magnificent they are told generation after generation. As time passes, some parts are forgotten while others are greatly embellished. Variations of stories depend on the author and the times. Greek mythology has produced some real doozies, such as the tales of Helen. She seems to pick up some of the most fantastic story lines along her journey from lips to ears and print to eyes. A daughter of a god who unintentionally started a war over a love affair, who brought sure death to the son of a king, who was at the heart of Troy's fall from greatness—that was quite the affair. Though she didn't deliver the Trojan horse, her love affair is said by some storytellers to be the reason it wound up inside those great walls of Troy. Poor ol' Paris knew what he was getting himself into, unlike Hudson. The guilt of his ignorance weighs heavily on Katie. She does not want to bring the same demise to Hudson as Helen did to Paris and Troy. She contemplates when and what she will share with Hudson for his own safety, but throughout their weekend together she cannot bring herself to uncover her skeletons to him just yet. She wants him to decide for himself whether she is worth the risk he faces, but she's waited so long for a love like this and does not want it to end. The love that holds back her secret will also convince her to disclose her secret—just not yet.

Mid-fall usually provides the last days of fishing before giving way to hunting season and winter. The morning after the music festival, the one that brought an early conclusion to their slumber after making love through most of the night, Hudson receives an invitation to join his father, Ricky, and Troy for a little fishing on Lake Oconee. A day on the lake is a perfect escape from the peril of her past, so when Hudson asks about joining the fellas, Katie gladly accepts the offer, though she is not much of a fisherman. She also finds comfort around Hudson's family, at least those she has met so far. They don't know what she hides, but she feels that they would not judge her even if they did know.

Katie, Hudson, and Hank meet up with Gray and the other fellas at the boat ramp over by the Highway 278 bridge—that same place ole fate intervened during Katie's last walk. Hudson backs the boat down to the edge of the ramp, which takes a few attempts because of his lack of sleep from the night before. Once Hudson finally backs the boat to the top of the ramp, Katie moves food from the truck to the boat while Hudson and Hank go down to the dock to chat with the fellas for a little prefishing storytelling as is tradition. Hank walks over to Troy, takes a seat next to him, and looks up.

"He wants you to scratch'm up under his jaw."

"Is that right?" Troy gives Hank a good scratch'n up under his jaw, just like he likes it. "That musta been why he kept stare'n me down when I let'm out your house . . . you know, when y'all took off to Charleston."

"I guess I shoulda told ya bout that."

"He looks like he had to heal up from some bad shit, dude."

"He did. Healed up just fine, too. As a matter of fact, he was out chase'n deer all night."

"You look'n a lot happier these days, son. Kinda makes me wonder what you were chase'n all night," Grayford says while giving Troy a wink.

"I know where ya head'n with this conversation, old man. I fell asleep right after I let'm out. I just forgot that he was out there until this morn'n."

"Uh-huh . . . you look like you got a lotta sleep last night," Grayford replies, still smirking.

"Y'all musta ate some barbeque last night," Ricky jumps in, still hung up on the article he read.

"Don't start with that mess now, Ricky, dammit. How bout we just do some dayum fish'n and shut the hell up bout my night! Ain't nobody's damn business."

"Ms. Katie, you show look jovial this morn'n. You musta got more sleep than Hudson did last night," Gray says to Katie as she walks toward the fellas.

"I got all the sleep I needed, Mr. Gray," Katie replies without ever breaking her friendly smile.

"Y'all have some good barbeque last night, Ms. Katie?" Ricky sarcastically asks while sporting an even bigger smirk than Gray.

"Best barbeque I've ever had, Ricky!" Katie replies with a smirk of her own.

"Well, I'll be damned. The article was right." Ricky laughs a little bit. "Hell, I like her!"

"Awl right . . . dammit . . . not to change the subject or anything, not that our sleeping habits make for an exhilarating conversation or are anyone's dayum business, but where we goin? The tracks or two seventy eight?"

"Hudson, Imma tell you what, dude, get ready to catch some hawgs. Gonna teach you someth'n today. We'll run over to the pipe, throw the net, and then head over tuh two sebentee eight. That dadgum bridge is covered up with fish, but ya gotta use fresh bait."

"Sounds good, Ricky, let's get to it. And not another dayum word about barbeque!"

"I'm gonna go with y'all and let the dog go with Ricky and Troy," Gray proposes.

"You gonna behave, old man?"

"I'm an angel, son."

"Uh-huh, I don't know about that . . . Welp, all right, y'all good if Hank goes with y'all?"

"Fine by us, cuz."

"Now, hold the hell on. He ain't gonna make a bunch of noise now is he? I don't want him screw'n up my fish'n." Ricky blurts out his concern about Hank.

Hudson cuts Ricky a smile, because he knows Hank tends to get rather excited in the boat and around the water. "Ah hell, Ricky, he'll probably sleep the whole time. Remember the luck he brought me, don't ya?"

"I guess, but this sumbitch starts get'n antsy, he's take'n his ass right back over to y'all, I tell you whut."

"Fair enough, Ricky."

Hudson, Katie, and Gray ride out and anchor just off the bridge. The sun squeezes through a few clouds, and the fall air is just right for a light jacket. Somehow Gray knows not to meddle, but is curious about his son's adorable lady friend. He senses the attraction between her and his son seems a little more intimate than just a few days ago. Gray doesn't need to ask, he can see the old Hudson finally coming home, and seeing his son happy again is all he needs.

"Ms. Katie, when ya goin to come out to the farm and go on a four-wheeluh ride wid me?"

Katie hesitates a bit and nervously looks at Hudson before answering, "I am ready anytime you are, Mr. Gray."

"How bout tomorruh? We'll fry up a few fish and beer puppies."

"Tomorrow . . ." Katie is unsure of how to answer and looks to Hudson for help.

"Uh . . . I don't know about tomorrow, Deddy."

"Oh, I musta misunderstood the mean'n of anytime I'm ready?!"

"Well, honestly, Deddy, I know Mama will ask too many dayum questions and embarrass us."

"Don't worry about your mama, son. I'll make sure she behaves."

"Shit, Deddy, everybody knows Mama will do what Mama damn well wants."

"Trust me, son, she'll be glad to meet Katie and see how happy y'all are together."

"Well, we'll see. I'll let ya know later tonight."

Gray knows Hudson didn't want to put Katie on the spot, so he doesn't press the issue. He figures his son and Katie will come over when they are ready. So, he sits back admiring his son's happiness while nibbling on his sausage biscuit. All three enjoy the comfortable silence in the conversation as they take in the scenery. That moment ends abruptly, though, when Ricky comes motoring up from behind them. He is sure enough unhappy with Hank.

"Dammit, son, you gotta take'is dog!" Ricky yells out as Troy laughs hysterically.

"Why? What happen, Ricky?" Hudson, who is already sporting a sarcastic smirk, knows what has Ricky all spun up.

"The sumbitch hauled off into the dayum water. Splash'n everywhere. Make'n all kinda racket. When he finally settled his big ass down and started swim'n, I hung a big hawg. That's when this sumbitch just had ta crawl his ass back up in the boat . . . shook dayum water all over me. I dropped my pole. Fish drug it off into the dayum lake . . ."

"Well shit, Ricky, that's how he fishes. He's probably pissed you lost the fish after all his hard work," Hudson laughs as he yells over to Ricky.

Troy beds down his laughter just enough to yell out, "Ricky fell in the lake goin after his pole. You shoulda seen his ass tryna get back in the boat . . . damn near flipped us . . . took'm four tries . . . looked like a fat duck tryna take off outta water . . . legs just uh kick'n."

"Take the dog, son! He ain't get'n his ass back in my boat dammit tuh hell." Ricky rudely interrupts Troy's hysterical recollection of events.

"Awlright, awlright. Hank! Come on, boy!" Hudson yells out as they all continue laughing at Ricky's expense. Hank jumps in and swims over to Hudson's boat, makes two laps around the boat before

Katie hangs into a good one. As she fights the fish, Hank swims up to the boat. Hudson helps the big fella into the boat while Gray helps Katie with her fish. As expected, Hank showers them all with a little cold lake water, which they don't mind as much as Ricky. After about ten minutes, Gray nets the big cat for Katie, about a fifteen-pound Arkansas Blue.

"Looks like he knows what he's doin, Ricky. You sure y'all don't want'm widja? He might teach you someth'n," Hudson yells out while smiling ear to ear.

"To hell with'm, son! That lake is some cold shit this morn'n. Freeze'n my nuts off." Ricky had no grin. Unlike Hank, he was seriously unhappy with his morning swim.

"Ya know, Mr. Gray, a fish fry sounds like a good time. What do ya think, Mr. Hudson?"

"Sounds good to me, Ms. Katie," Hudson responds with a smile before looking over at Ricky and Troy and yelling out, "Had your chance, Ricky, and ya blew it."

Ricky simply responds with a finger . . . a chubby, wet finger.

"I guess he didn't appreciate his dip in the lake, Deddy."

"Well, fuck'm if he can't take a joke!" Gray so elegantly responds with a smirk.

# — CHAPTER THIRTY-FOUR —
# MEET'N SAVANNAH

**M**eeting parents is something they would prefer to defer to a time much further down the line, but rarely does life cooperate with people's plans. The meeting at Pop's was a perfect example of undesired surprises afforded by life, but that meeting turned out just fine. Katie has met most of his family, but Hudson has yet to meet anyone in hers. He would like to meet them, but Katie's just not ready for the complication that meeting will introduce. Mary Beth will not be too keen on Katie's relationship with another fella so soon after the end of her daughter's engagement to Sean. Then there is Savannah, who is sure enough red hot that she has not met the young lady in her dear son's life. In Savannah's book, mamas should be the first family member to meet girlfriends of their sons. Maybe Mama would have been first if all were normal; however, Savannah's knack at burying her nose in her son's business, quite frankly, scares the hell out of Hudson. There is no way to predict the extent of prying his mama will do during her interrogation of Katie given her tremendous concern for Hudson's mental health. Hudson wishes he'd had time to warn Katie about his mother's interrogation skills before she spontaneously RSVPed to the fish fry. However, she did agree to the fish fry and four-wheeler ride, so now they just need to prepare for meeting Savannah.

Hudson does what he can to prepare Katie for his mama. Katie is no doubt nervous, but it's Hudson who dreads this meeting most. Before heading over, he calls his father to ask that he talk to his mama. He asks Gray to make sure she doesn't come out guns blazing with the questions. Gray promises that he will do what he can, but he knows Savannah will not listen to a damn thing he has to say.

Savannah and Gray are standing on the front deck when they drive up. Savannah stares intently at Hudson's truck as they make their way down the driveway. She's trying to get a good look at Katie. Normally, Gray would shy away from telling Savannah what to do or how to act, because it would do no good anyhow, but this time he wants to ensure she does not complicate things for their son.

"Savvy, don't you embarrass the boy. And don't pass judgment befowuh ya even talk to the girl."

"I'm not embarrass'n or judge'n anyone, Gray. I just don't know why I am the last dayum one to meet this girl. I'm his mama. I shoulda been the first."

"Uh-huh, you start in on that mess and this will be the only time you meet'r."

"Don't lekcha me, Gray. I don't need nowuh want yowuh advice. I just want Hudson to be happy. I don't want someone break'n his already fragile haught."

"All the more reason not to embarrass'm by put'n his girlfriend through the wringer."

"Gray, dammit, shut the hell up, would ya?!"

"Savannah, it is not an interview . . . remember that."

"And who the heyull said anythang about an interview?"

"She is a good girl, and they really like each other. I'm just say'n don't ruin it."

"Grayford Lee, you best shut yowuh dayum mouth. You act like I am some insensitive witch. I will get to know the young lady as I dayum well please."

"Well shit, Ms. Sensuhtivity, go on and meet'r. Just don't . . ." Gray pauses, because he knows he best choose his words wisely.

"Just don't what?" Savannah quickly pounces on his hesitation.

"Just don't make this uncomfortable."

"How bout you kiss my ass, Gray. Uncomfortable?! I've nevuh done such a thang!"

"Hell naw, not you. Nevuh . . ."

Savannah does not stick around to hear Gray finish his sentence. She walks down the steps and cautiously approaches the truck. She closely observes Hudson and Katie to see how they interact while letting that intuition do its thing. Katie is in the middle of the bench seat, sitting close to Hudson to help bed down her nerves. She is dressed conservatively in jeans, a sweatshirt, and with no makeup. She does not pretend to be someone she is not by dressing up in her Sunday's best. She worries her decision will make a bad first impression with the woman slowly approaching the truck, but is a bit relieved now that she sees Savannah dressed nearly the same. Hudson holds the door for her as she climbs out. She starts to grab his hand, but feels his mother would think she is possessive of him or a bit clingy; although, the reason she wants to grab his hand is because she is extremely nervous to meet the woman who now stands right in front of them.

"Hudson, give Mama a hug!" Savannah and Hudson hug each other for a brief moment before Hudson introduces Katie.

"Mama, this is Katie. Katie, this is my mama, Savannah."

"Great to meet you, Mrs. Lee."

"Hunny, you can drop the Mrs. and call me Savannah. Now give me a hug."

Katie and Savannah hug each other for about a second before Savannah pulls back and continues, "I am glad, so glad to finally meet you. I do believe I shoulda met you earleeyuh, but that is neethuh heeyuh nohwuh thayuh," Savannah says as she cuts Hudson a look of disappointment, because she's last to meet Katie.

"Katie, you wanna ride on the foh-wheeluh?" Gray asks as he walks toward the truck, hoping to give Katie a way out of what is surely to come.

"She is going inside with me, Gray. You can flirt layda," Savannah interrupts before Katie can answer. The ladies walk inside, leaving Hudson and Gray standing by the truck. They watch the women walk away toward the house, Savannah's arm hooked around Katie's.

"Wanna a beer, son?"

"Nattie?"

"Well, hell yeah. I only carry the good shit. If ya wanted someth'n else, then ya oughta brought it."

"A Nattie'll do just fine, Deddy. You reckon Mama's gonna behave?"

"Welp . . . depends on what ya mean by *behave*."

"Is she gonna keep her nose where belongs or not, Deddy?"

"Yowuh mama has the nose of a bloodhound, son. Once it locks in on a scent, that nose will zig zag all over the place until it nails down the source, and ain't a thang anybody can do about it."

"What the hell does that mean, Deddy? I'm goin in there to make sure she's not sniff'n around."

"Whoa, slow down there, hot rod. Katie'll be just fine. Believe it or not, yowuh mama knows her limits."

"Hell no she don't! You just said she's a bloodhound locked in on a scent. Does she think Katie's hiding someth'n? She just met'r for God's sake."

"Katie's not really the scent she's locked in on."

"Would ya cut the redneck riddles, Deddy, and just tell me what the hell ya mean."

"She's worried about ya, son. Yowuh mama just wants to convey her concern and love for ya. I told her how happy you two are togethuh, so trust that yowuh mama is not goin to ruin anythang."

"I'll give'r one chance. I better not find'r bloodhound nose all up in Katie's personal business."

"Fair enough. How bout grab'n a couple out the fridge while I get the fryer goin?!"

Hudson and Gray sit out by the fryer drinking Gray's favorite beverage while frying fish and hush puppies. Hudson listens to his dad ramble on about things the family has been up to and a variety of other trivial topics. Gray may be in Hudson's ears, but Katie is in his thoughts. He worries that his mother is inside that house grilling her for information, trying to unlock that vault of secrets. He can't imagine the extent of verbal prying and prodding Katie suffers through while he's throwing back Natties with his father. He stares off at the house with a busy mind, pondering different excuses to bail out Katie. Meanwhile, it does not take Gray long to figure out his son is not listening to a damn thing he is saying.

"Dayum, boy! At girl has really gotta aholta you. Hell, I might as well just sit out here by my dayum self," Gray says with a smirk.

"Nah, Deddy . . . well, she is wonderful, but I'm listen'n to ya."

"No the hell you ain't. Shit, I stopped talk'n ten minutes ago."

"I'm just concerned with what Mama is ask'n . . . that's all."

"I'm sure Katie can handle yowuh mama just fine, son."

"I'm not sure if anybody can handle Mama, but Katie did hold her own during that barbeque bullshit."

"Didn't she, though?! How about hand'n me that other basket of puppies, would ya?"

While Hudson and Gray go on about their frying, drinking, and talking, Savannah is indeed inside firing off questions. Katie's nerves settle a bit after the hug, but she is uncomfortable with some of the questions. However, just like Hudson, she has mastered the act of normalcy while hiding her crazy.

"So, what do ya do for a livin, Katie?"

"I help with the family business. We run the Dixie Diner over in Watkinsville."

"I'll be! I thought you looked familyuh. My friends and I go in thayuh to eat sometimes, befowuh we go off intuh town. Y'all make such a delicious sausage gravy and biscuits dish. That is my favorite."

"Thank you! That is my mama's recipe. I don't cook much at the diner. I wait tables and handle accounting. Although, my granny taught me how to cook a mess of collards, cornbread, and pinto beans."

"Ah yes, the key to any Southern man's haught—country cook'n. How did you and Hudson meet?"

"Well, he came into the diner one night. That was the first night we met. We didn't really start get'n to know each other until a little later when we ran into each other at a park. His dog had run up on me."

"Oh, that dog. I worry about that dog hurt'n Hudson or someone else or anotha animal. He should really considuh put'n that dog down. I hate to say it, because I love dogs, but that one is trouble."

"Actually, Hank is pretty gentle with people. Him and Hudson are adorable together."

"Yeah, I reckon. So, are y'all serious?" Savannah has a way to lead the conversation in one direction, and then surprise someone with a sneak attack. She knows most people don't think quickly on their feet and the sneak attack tends to expose the truth.

Caught off guard by the question, Katie indeed stumbles a bit. "Uh, well . . . we care for each other deeply, Savannah."

Savannah looks at Katie for a very long and uncomfortable second before responding, "Hudson has a big but tenduh haught, hunny. He has been through a lot. He is my precious baby boy, but he wasn't quite the same when he came back from the Marines. Please, please don't hurt him."

Another awkward second passes before Katie responds, "Savannah, nothing I say will offer you relief from your worries about Hudson's heart. But please understand this, every bit of my heart is in his hands, as much as his is in mine."

Savannah sits quietly for another few seconds, carefully absorbing Katie's words. She finally interrupts the air in the conversation with a little advice. "Hunny, I've been travel'n God's green Uth for many yeeyuhs. I have seen a lot. I have met many people who were at different places in theyuh journey—many of those places I've been to myself. I can tell something troubles you. Call it muthuh's intuition. Now, I don't ask what it is, because that is not my place, nohwuh would ya tell me anyhow. Howeva, thayuh will come a time when you will need to tell Hudson. Thayuh will also come a time when he will tell you what he has yet to shayuh with anyone. I will always worry about my baby boy, but, as his mama, I know he needs a good woman. He needs you, Katie. And I can tell that you need him just as much. Take kayuh of'm, and he will nevuh let anything trouble you again."

Katie listens intently to Savannah's advice. She absorbs every word, taking each one to heart. She wonders how in the world Savannah could sense her troubles with so few words traded in this short period of time. She does not ponder on this mystery for long. She looks at Savannah, smiles, and then asks, "Savannah, how would you like to have that biscuit and gravy recipe?"

Savannah smiles and chuckles as she gently grasps Katie's hands. "I would like that very much, deeyuh, if it's awlright with yowuh mama. Tell'r it goes no furtha than me."

"I sure will, Savannah," Katie replies with a smile, not only from the offer of the recipe, but from relief that she's offered the truth of her feelings toward Hudson without exposing any secrets.

Meanwhile, as Gray and Hudson continue frying fish and balls of cornbread, Papa Lee pulls up in his old Dodge truck. The old man has a knack of sniffing out a good fish fry and cheap beer. In no hurry to do anything anymore since retiring from dairy farming, he slowly opens the door and slides out of the truck.

"Whatcha say, Deddy?" Gray is the first to greet his old man.

"Aw, not a whole helluva lot. I hadda run up tuh Greensberuh to get some gas and ull for the chainsaw."

"Chainsaw! What the hell ya up to with the chainsaw?"

"Aw, that ole sweetgum finally gave way. Almost fell on my dayum barn."

"You need hep with it?"

"Well heyull yeah, that's why I stopped by."

"Well shit, here I am think'n ya stopped by cos ya like our compnee."

"You sure thank uhlotta yoself, dawn cha?!" Papa pauses for a second as he looks over at Hudson. He walks over to Hudson, puts his hand out. "Hudson, good to see ya again, son!"

Hudson shakes his grandfather's hand as he responds, "You too, Papa! You wanna beer?"

"It show is nice to know someone gives enough of a sheeyut bout an old man to offer'm a beer. Heyull yeah, I'll have one or two widja."

"Well yeah, of course he's generous, he's offer'n up my dayum beer," Gray sarcastically points out.

Hudson hands his grandfather a cold one as he tells him, "Papa, let me know when you wanna take care of that old tree, and I'll help ya."

"Thank ya, son. I can use all the hep I can get."

"Heyull, Deddy, enough hep and you want have tuh do shit."

"That's tha plan," Papa replies just before taking the first sip of his Nattie Light.

Katie and Savannah walk out of the house and toward the fellas, still chit-chatting about recipes. Papa has his back to them, but notices Hudson's attention immediately looks past him with a concerned but happy look on his face. Papa turns to look at what or who took away Hudson's attention from him and his tree.

"Hudson, I'm gonna guess she's here wid you?"

"She sure is, Papa. That's Katie."

"Hot dayum, boy. You show you can handle a woman that good look'n?"

"We'll find out, Papa."

"Yeah. I reckon so."

"Katie, this is my grandfather, Harvey Lee, aka Papa Lee." Hudson introduces the two as the ladies approach.

"Good to meet you, Mr. Lee!"

"You too, Ms. Katie. How bout givin me a hug and tell'n me about yaself a lil bit." Papa gives Katie a quick hug before escorting her by the arm over to the covered swing by the fire pit.

"Good to see you, too, Papa!" Savannah fires off after receiving no greeting from Harvey. "You dayum Lees lose y'all's minds around a purty young woman."

"Now, don't go and get jealous, dear."

"Ha. Ha. Ha. Kiss my ass, Gray."

"Anytime, sugah."

"Well, that's my cue to go use the bathroom."

"OK, hunny. Hey, Hudson! How about grab'n the coleslaw out the downstayuhs fridge and brang'n it when ya come back?"

"Will do, Mama."

Savannah turns back to talk to Gray while her attention is on Papa entertaining Katie. "I like'uh, Gray. I really like'uh."

Gray looks back at Katie, and then turns back to the fryer before responding, "I knew you would, Sav. I just hope you didn't say any-thang tuh embarrass the boy."

"What the heyull could I say; he doesn't tell us a thang. I just hope he opens up to huh and huh to him."

"Dammit, Sav, you didn't go dig'n in her affairs, did ya?"

"No, Gray. I did not. I can, howeva, tell when something troubles anotha woman. I just know they both hold secrets. I don't need to ask anyone anythang to know that."

"Yeah, I guess. Let's get ready tuh eat."

The five of them sit around the picnic table, say grace, and enjoy one of Hudson's favorite meals. The nervousness shared by Katie and Hudson has long subsided by the time they sit to eat. Papa has to sit by Katie, but she doesn't mind as he reminds her of her late grandfather. Papa reminds Hudson three or four times that he is a lucky man to have found a woman as beautiful and smart as Katie. Hudson smiles each time, responding simply with, "I sure am."

As Hudson and Katie get back into the truck to leave that evening, the disappearing sun brings about the whippoorwill. The bird should have already started migrating southwest to Mexico, but not this one. The bird is like a ghost in the brush somewhere, but its song echoes loudly throughout the woods.

"Oh my, a whippoorwill. Unusual for this time of year. I've always loved their song!" Katie says, pausing a brief moment to enjoy the song before climbing into the truck.

Hudson pauses as well, while looking up to the treetops recalling that night by the pond. "It is quite a song."

## — CHAPTER THIRTY-FIVE —
# STORM

The battering storm within her psyche has finally lifted. Her eyes reflect the light that now fills her every thought. Joy was absent from her heart for years, maybe she never had it, because she remembers no other time in her adult life when she fully felt the buoyant spirit of the girl. She smiles every second of the drive home from Hudson's. She turns down the radio, so her thoughts are only of him. He makes her feel good about herself. She likes feeling good about herself. He helps her forget the fear and troubles of old. Death whispered promises of relief from the mental battles, from the abuse, but life now presents her the tremendous reward for those who push forward and fight. With Hudson by her side, she has the strength to march forward, pushing through all adversaries and overcoming all adversity in life. She quietly thanks God for Hudson. He did listen to her pleas for a miracle.

Katie walks into her house still smiling. She is tired but will not be able to fall asleep quickly as her mind races thinking about Hudson and their future together. She still has that guilt nagging her to divulge her secret to him. She will not concern herself with that right now; instead, she will watch a little television, eat a slice of triple chocolate cake, her favorite, and wash it down with a glass of cold milk. She turns on the television and pulls up the guide.

"What we watch'n tonight, Katie?" a familiar voice eerily pierces the dark hallway behind Katie.

Katie turns on a light to see Sean standing at the entrance of the hallway. The sight of him sucks the air from the room. She stares at her past life coming to invade the new. She wants to run toward the door, but fear, shock, and disbelief paralyze her legs. She has often witnessed the rage in his eyes subside until the little bit of good within him felt remorse for his abuse. There was still something in him, fighting to genuinely love and care for her. That man is not anywhere in the eyes scowling back at her tonight.

"What are you doing in my house, Sean?"

Sean grins. It is a bad grin, one of evil intent. When that bad grin is gone, he replies, "No reason to yell, Katie. I just wanted to check out your new house in your new life. The life without me. Right? Oh, you will need to replace the window in your spare room. See, ya didn't leave me a key to the front door."

"Get out!" Katie yells so loud that her voice cracks.

"Nah . . . think I'll stay. We have some catch'n up to do, Katie Belle," Sean calmly responds. He stands by the hallway, satisfied by her fear.

"I have nothing to say to you, Sean. You need to leave!" Katie pleads. Her voice quivers. Her body shakes. The room spins as her skin turns pale. Katie wrestles her cell phone from her pocket. She struggles to unlock her phone as fear grips her fingers as tightly as her tongue. She re-enters the code again and again. She fails each time. Sean quickly closes in on her and rips the phone from her desperate grip. She feels pressure on her neck, just like the morning she ran. Her airway closes and eyes bulge as she looks into his eyes. Nothing is in those eyes.

"You gonna call the fuck'n law on me, Katie?" Sean screams in her ear with his cheek pressing against hers.

Katie cannot reply as his grip tightens, squeezing her vocal cords and shutting off the blood supply to her head. She grabs his wrist and tries ripping his hand from her throat as darkness drapes her vision. Sean slams her phone on the floor, shattering the screen, and then throws her against the wall while keeping his grip on her throat. He pulls her back toward him, and then slams her back against the wall. He repeats this display of power three more times, shoving her against the wall harder and harder each time. A hole remains in the sheetrock where her head hits the wall.

"You fuck'n whore! I love you and would do anything for you!" Sean screams, this time nose to nose with her, his eyes glaring into hers.

Darkness is all she sees. Before, she wanted death by his hands to relieve her of the fear. Not this time. This time death is absent from her thoughts, as is Hudson's love. Love is of no use to her other than providing a will to live, only the beast that dwells within can help her fight the maniac. For whatever reason, she thinks of Hank. She has never witnessed the beast within him, yet there it is in her thoughts, just like the night by the tub. Her eyes are blood red when they open. He thinks nothing of it as he is in complete control of her life. He disregards her hands on his shoulders as he focuses only on the life he chokes out of her. He only realizes the threat when she drives her knee between his legs, using her grip on his shoulders as leverage. She drives the knee again and again, until he releases her throat and stumbles back. Katie attempts to run for the door but, deprived of oxygen, she falls back against the wall. She struggles to breathe, and her throat feels crushed. Barely a whisper comes out when she tries to scream for help. She stumbles along the wall toward the door. All she can think about is getting outside and over to a neighbor's house for help. As she picks up momentum, Sean lunges at her, grabbing her arm and pulling her to him. Katie swings around and claws at his face and eyes, trying to blind him. She again pushes Sean away and makes another attempt for the door. She screams another whispering plea for help. She feels a tight grip around her torso as she reaches for the doorknob. Sean grabs her in a bear hug from behind, takes two steps, and then slings her across the room into the breakfast bar countertop. Katie screams in pain as her ribs crack against the bar. She attempts to stay upright on her feet, but the room briefly goes black before she crashes to the floor. Sean had punched the back of her head as she stumbled from the breakfast bar. He straddles Katie, wraps both hands around her neck, lifts her upper body up off the floor, and then drags her by the neck to her bedroom. She opens her eyes, and then drives her fist into his face again and again. Sean head butts her, and then slams her down on the floor, while never releasing his grip on her throat. Though she barely hangs onto consciousness, Katie alternates left and right hooks to his head, desperately fighting to live this time. Sean slams her down on the hardwood floor over and over until blood runs from the back of her head. Just before she loses consciousness, he releases his grip, lets her gasp for air, and then grabs her neck again. He drags her to the bedroom and releases his grip as she lies on the floor gasping for air. Katie rolls over and tries to crawl toward the door. He waits for her to get to her hands and knees before kicking her ribcage, knocking the air from her lungs. She gasps for air before trying to crawl again.

"You wanna be a whore, I will fuck you like a whore!" Sean threatens her before driving another kick into her ribs. He kicks her two more times until she finally rolls over onto her back. He walks over in front of her, grabs her by the hair, and raises her head up about a foot from the floor.

"I would have done anything for you, but you just had to go and fuck someone else. You cheat'n. Fuck'n. Whore. I told you that if you ever fucked around on me, I would beat your fuck'n ass. I am a man of my word."

Sean rears back and punches Katie, driving his fist into her cheek. He punches her three more times. She tastes the blood from her swollen lip, but her face seems to go numb after the first punch. Sean releases her hair. She no longer falls to the floor when he drives his heel into her stomach with such force she curls up upon impact, though she barely hangs on to consciousness. He rolls her over onto her back. Blood and tears roll off the sides of her face as she looks to the ceiling. He kneels beside her, pushes her head back with his left hand so she looks into his eyes, and unbuttons her pants with his right. He stands up, straddles her, reaches down, and then rips off her pants and underwear. Katie lies beaten and half naked on the floor, staring at the ceiling again. Her mind is blank. All she hears is the devil whispering, "I can do whatever I want to you, any fuck'n time I want. You remember that. I'm not gonna kill you tonight. I'm not gonna fuck you, either. You been spread'n those filthy legs just like in high school. You're not gonna tell a soul what happened here tonight. Tell anyone, and I will kill you and your little fuck buddy. I don't care anymore. You took everything from me, and I will take everything from you. Next time I see you with him, I will kill you both. And ya know, I will just have to put your family down, too, even your dim-witted uncles. Don't go to the hospital, and you best call out of work until you heal."

Sean stands up and looks at Katie. He stares down on her with pure satisfaction after executing his vengeance. Whatever love he had for her has long departed his heart. In his mind she wronged him. She took what was his. He no longer feels guilt after beating her; he feels satisfied. He heats the bulb so the fiend can enjoy his diabolical deed. He admires her gasps for air, bloody face, and tears. He stands over her briefly after feeding his chemical addiction. He disappears into the shadows, away from Katie's blurred vision. She hears the back door open and shut, but she is too broken to move. She lies on her back in the middle of the room, bleeding and crying for most of the night. She eventually struggles through the pain to pull herself up into a sitting position. She manages to put on a pair of shorts and lay a blanket across her lap. She holds her fractured ribs and rests her back against the bed as the sun ushers in a new day, a day she wishes would have never come to be. She wishes Sean would have ended her life, but that was not his intent. He only served her a reminder that love is no match for his rage and envy. He reminded her that life will only be with him and no other. Once again, death entices her with an easy escape. Her death will save Hudson's life, as Sean is sure to bring Hudson the death he spared her. She must end the relationship with Hudson. The thought of ending their relationship severely sickens her. She cries uncontrollably through the pain in her ribs. This time her eyes don't dry.

# CHAPTER THIRTY-SIX

# CHECKUP

The night is crisp by the pond. The whippoorwill should be long gone by now, yet it sings from the dark. The small fire burns as Walt, Hank Jackson, the boy, and a girl stand over a freshly dug hole in the ground by the sweetgum. Hudson calls out to each of the fellas, but none answer. He has never seen the girl before, but feels he knows her well. He walks toward the group and the hole in the ground. The bird falls silent. All but the girl focus on the ground. She looks to Hudson with deep sadness as she says, "Can't be saved." She turns back to the makeshift grave without another word. Hudson walks up to the grave to look inside, but as he approaches the hole in the ground, agonizing cries from the dark woods extinguish the light of the flames. All goes black. All goes silent.

The morning light shines onto his bed as Hudson rises in confusion. Hank lies up on the bed with him, but does not give him his morning kiss on the hand. Hudson scratches the big fella under his jaw, just like he likes it, but Hank lays his head back down on the bed. Hank's eyes focus forward, looking at nothing in particular. Hudson stares off in the same manner. The memories of his wonderful weekend with Katie clash with the bizarre dream he suddenly awoke from. He cannot shake the girl's sadness, even as he tries to focus on the woman's happiness. He contemplates who it was in that grave. Normally, Mary invokes such odd dreams, but he slept with a sober mind the night before—he wanted nothing to interfere with his newfound appreciation of life. He shakes the dream from his thoughts and escorts Hank to the back door.

"What's wrong, big fella? Ya don't seem yourself. Go make your rounds and take care of your business . . . got an appointment for ya this morn'n," Hudson says as he watches Hank slowly walk past him. Hank normally sprints after critters in the morning, but not this time—he just stands in the backyard, gazing off to nowhere. While Hudson stands on the back porch watching Hank, he calls Katie to say good morning. Her phone goes directly to voicemail. He figures she is working, so he leaves her a short message. He calls his dad afterward and arranges a fishing trip for later, after him and Hank are done at the hospital. Troy is at the farm helping Gray fix a four-wheeler and jumps at the opportunity to go fishing with Gray and Hudson, just like the old days.

Hudson and Hank head to the animal hospital after a quick bite to eat. On the way, Hank remains disconnected—off chasing thoughts in some other place. Normally, he sits up and humors his friend, who likes talking to him as he watches the countryside pass by his window. Today he pays neither any mind.

"What's eat'n at ya, boy? You miss our new friend or someth'n? Me too. Maybe we can get her to come over after we get home from fish'n this even'n." Hank doesn't even raise his head, just cuts his eyes up toward Hudson as he talks.

"Awl right, I can take a damn hint. I'll let ya be with your thoughts big fella. We'll be at the doc's momentarily anyhow."

"How y'all doing, Hudson?" the doc says as he enters the small room where Hudson and Hank are waiting.

"Good, Doc. You?"

"Can't complain, I am still on the right side of the dirt."

"Hey, Doc, how long will this take? We have a fish'n trip this afternoon."

"Aw, not too long. I just want to see how the big fella is doin. Looks like he's eat'n good."

"Yeah, he likes Pop Walter's barbeque."

"Heck, who doesn't?! Has he been running around just fine?"

"Yeah."

"You got the samples I asked for?"

"Here ya go."

"He looks to be in good shape, Hudson. Let me take a little blood here. Hold'm down would ya?"

Hudson helps hold down Hank as Frank pokes the big fella with the needle. "I guess he's used to pain," Hudson says as he lets go of Hank, who paid the big needle no mind at all.

"Yeah, I spect so. Well, Hudson, I don't wanna hold y'all up too long. He seems to be just fine. We'll run some lab work on this stuff. How's he been acting?"

"Well, he's been good up until this morn'n. Seems a lil out of sorts."

"Hmm, is that right?! Did he eat this morn'n?"

"Yeah, he never skips a meal, but didn't inhale it like normal and didn't eat nearly as much. He doesn't seem sick, just lethargic is all."

"He seems fine to me. I'll be more certain once the labs come back. I tell ya what, Hudson, keep a good eye on him and don't hesitate to bring him in if need be . . . ya know, if he doesn't return to his normal self."

"Thanks, Doc! I appreciate everything ya did for Hank."

"Heck, Hudson, if not for you, he'd be dead."

Hudson remains silent for a moment, looking at Hank before responding, "Yeah, seems that way. Awlright, Doc, we're gonna hit up Pop's before head'n to the ramp. Have yourself a good day!"

"You as well, Hudson! Hank! Y'all enjoy the day on the water. Good luck out there!"

Hudson and Hank head down Highway 15 after checking out with Hannah. They grab a few plates from Pop's to take fishing with them; of course, Hank has to stay in the truck. On the way out to meet Gray and Troy at the ramp, Hudson tries calling Katie again. Just as before, her phone goes straight to voicemail. Again, he figures she's working; however, he notices her car is not at the Dixie Diner as he passes by while heading out of Watkinsville. He does not leave a message or stop by the diner, because he thought that would seem clingy. He figures she will call or text soon enough. Sometimes folks just want a little time to themselves, so he lets her be.

"You'd be dead, he said, Hank. Shit, I owe you a lot more than you owe me, my friend," Hudson admits to Hank, who still refuses to join the day.

# CHAPTER THIRTY-SEVEN

# BAIT SHOP

"Ricky, where the hell they bite'n today? We're head'n down to the pasture to put in," Gray asks as he walks into the bait shop—after that little bell quits ringing.

"Ah, is that right?! Now, I had some luck bout midway between the dock and sandbar . . . big ole pine tree fell along the bank. You'll see it on the left as ya head toward the sandbar. Tie up on that pine n cast some cut bait out toward the otha side of the river. We caught about nine, ten good'ns last week in that hole on some cut bait, I tell you whut."

"All right, we'll give it a go. I'll take some of these Eagle hooks and those half-ounce bullet weights right theyuh."

"All together, that's nine seventy eight, Gray."

"Shit, Ricky! For some hooks n weights?"

"Yes, sir, and the worms."

"Dayum! Fish'n get'n expensive. I need to just dig up my own worms."

"Now hold on, Gray, you can't find these on your farm. These here are some big ol' night crawlers—I mean sure nuff fat sumbitches right here. And you know fish are like the ladies—they love the big worms."

"Well, I might not have the biggest worm, but I've been purdee lucky with what I got."

"Shit, Uncle Gray, you caught the same fish for years."

"Damn young bucks . . . they think we were not young once. I was in the Navy when I was younger than you, boy—did a lot of fish'n, good dayum fish'n, over in Japan."

"Does Aunt Savannah know about your Japan fish'n trips?"

"Hell no—some fish'n stories don't need to leave the bait shop, and that was before I hooked her anyhow. Now go on and get whatcha gonna get. I'll be out at the truck put'n these high dolla fat worms on ice . . ." Gray pauses for a moment as he checks out the expensive worms before looking at Ricky and continuing. "Damn, Ricky, these are as big as a small snake. I'm just try'n to catch some bait with 'em. Hell, one worm will catch all the bait we need."

"Well then, they are well worth the investment. That's why they are so expensive—the bigger the worm, the more fish you catch."

"Hell, I always have to use the whole worm, be a nice change to only need part of it to do the trick. I'll let ya know how we do. Troy, see ya at the truck."

"Be right there, Uncle Gray . . . get'n some beer."

The bell jingles as Gray walks out of the bait shop to a crisp but sunny fall afternoon, perfect for fishing. Life is good today. Hudson has finally returned home safely and will soon join them for another trip up the river—been awhile. He is so lost in thought; he doesn't pay any mind to the Bronco pulling up in front of his truck. Gray continues about his business, putting the overpriced worms in the cooler and tackle in the boat, as four men step out of the old Bronco and head his way. He finally looks up at the men, who continue walking toward him, and just figures they intend to ask about fishing; however, that is not their intention at all. Sean has been following Hudson since that night at the fairgrounds. He rented different cars so Katie would not spot his Jeep. He recognized Gray from the boat ramp on the Saturday morning after the fairgrounds. He assumes Katie has shared her secrets with him, especially after his run-in with Hudson at the diner. Sean intends to send a message to Hudson, a message that he will hurt everyone he loves if he continues seeing Katie. Moreover, he wants to send the same message to Katie. He wants to make sure she believes the sincerity of his promise. His knuckles are still a little swollen from the beating he gave Katie, and his face displays the remnants of the few punches and scratches from her. Only he knows the origins of his wounds. As they approach him, Gray greets the gentlemen, as he is ignorant to their intentions.

"Afternoon, boys!"

"Hey, is your son date'n a girl name Katie Carter?" Sean asks while ignoring Gray's greeting, getting straight to the reason he is there.

Gray stops what he's doing and turns toward the four men walking his way as they gain his full attention and asks, "Do I know you?"

"Doesn't matter if ya know me, just answer the question," Sean sharply replies.

"I take it you have an issue with someone date'n Katie?" Gray sarcastically asks.

"Yeah, she's my fuck'n fiancée is my issue."

"Is that right?! Well, maybe someone oughta tell her that," Gray continues to smirk.

"Best watch your smartass mouth and tell your son to stay away from other men's women! You hear me, fucker?" Sean raises his voice and points his finger in Gray's face.

Gray looks past the man's finger to his eyes. He looks at the bruises and scratches on his face. He knows men don't normally scratch across another man's face during a fight, and these marks are definitely from a fight.

"Or what, you goin to hurt us like you hurt that girl? Where did you get those scratches? You hurt that sweet girl?"

Sean looks at Gray for a moment, then over at the fellas standing behind him. Only Sean knows the extent of his fury. He stands in silence, stewing on Gray's smart tone in his questions, which Sean dares not answer.

"What's wrong, boy, ya can't think of an excuse? They know what you do to that girl, or they too chicken shit to question you? Why don't you just leave'at girl alone. If she wanted to be with ya, she would be. Big tough guy—hit'n on a woman. You and your friends just climb on back into your . . ."

Sean stops Gray in the middle of his sentence with a surprise right hook to the cheek, knocking him to the ground. Sean kneels over Gray and delivers an overhand right to his eye. Sean's punches surprise his friends as much as they did Gray. They thought he only intended to tell the man that his son is messing with an engaged woman. They underestimated the rage within Sean, same as Rodney and Jimmy did at the fairgrounds. No logic behind his actions, just rage and that chemical warfare. Sean rears his fist back to deliver another punch to Gray's face, but stops his swing as he hears glass shattering behind him. Troy has snuck up behind Sean's friends from around the back of the bait shop and busted one in the back of the head with a beer bottle.

"Hit 'em again, and I'll fuck'n kill ya," Troy yells as he pulls out another beer bottle from the pack.

As the other two fellas start to move toward Troy, Ricky comes out of the bait shop with a shotgun in hand.

"I suggest you boys get the hell outta here before I put some buckshot in your fuck'n asses. And if I kill one of ya, I'm gonna have to kill all of ya."

Sean looks back down at Gray and tells him, "You tell your boy to stay away from Katie or I'm gonna kill'm . . . Got me?"

Before Gray can say a word, Troy tells Ricky to keep the shotgun pointed at Sean's friends. Troy walks up to Sean, looks the man in his eyes, and then sends a message of his own: "If you come after my family, if you ever threaten my family again, I will sink your ass to the bottom of the Oconee. I promise you a hard, painful journey to your final rest'n place . . . You fuck'n got me?"

As Sean stands up and concentrates on Troy, Gray drives his heel into the side of Sean's knee, instantly dropping him to the other knee. With pretty good quickness for an older fella, Gray smacks Sean on the side of the head with the back of his hand.

"How's that knee feel, asshole? You come after my boy, and I will end your pathetic existence. Leave'at girl alone. Don't know ya, but you don't seem worthy of'r. Move the hell on with your life and leave'r the hell alone. Now, it's in y'all's best interest to get the hell on outta here . . . go on now, git." Gray belittles them like mangy mutts, but fully understands the threat this man poses to his son.

Sean stumbles to his feet. He glares at Gray for a moment before limping over to his friends. They lay the unconscious fella Troy hit with that bottle in the back seat of the Bronco. He'll need a stitch or two to patch up the gash on the back of his head, but it's doubtful he will ever see a doctor. Once they drive off out of view, Gray and Troy walk over to Ricky, who now rests his shotgun on his shoulder.

"You awl right, Gray?"

"I'm fine, Ricky. Either of y'all know anything about that piece of shit?"

"Just that he's a piece of shit. You reckon he'll go after Hudson?" Ricky says.

"I'm sure of it. Hudson is crazy about Katie," Troy answers as he looks over at Gray. He knows his cousin well, and he knows the intent of guys like Sean just as well.

"He's been mistreat'n'at girl—probably been beat'n on'r. Savvy said she felt Katie had some troubles and now we know," Gray says.

"You know Hudson is gonna go after'm for jump'n on you, Uncle Gray."

"No he ain't, because we won't say a dayum word to'm about it."

"Well, we have to tell'm about that asshole threat'n'm, Uncle Gray. If we don't, then he's gonna jump Hudson and maybe kill'm."

"Yeah, I know. I'll talk to'm, but don't either of you tell'm about what just happened! This shit stays right here."

"All right, Uncle Gray. I don't agree, but all right."

"I don't give a damn if you agree, Troy. Let me handle this with Hudson. He's my son! I don't know where his mind is and don't want'm to end up in prison for kill'n that piece of shit."

"I said I won't tell'm!" Troy looks down at his beer while attempting to cool his blood. After a brief moment, and realizing he is now a beer short of a six pack, he looks up at Ricky.

"Hey, Ricky, you think I can get another Bud Light to replace the one I broke over that sumbitch's head?"

"Sure thang Troy. A dolla fifty."

"You shit'n me?"

"Hell nah. I have to make my money back on it, Troy. This is a business."

"I can't believe you are hit'n me up for a dollar fifty for a beer. Wasn't like I wasted it."

"Hot dayum, heeyuh, Ricky, two dollas." Gray throws a couple of wadded-up dollar bills at Ricky.

"All right, Troy, now you can have that Bud Light. And hey, how bout clean'n up all this glass? I can't have all my customers get'n flat tires or cut'n their feet. My keeyuds are always up here run'n around with no shoes on."

"Then tell 'em to wear fuck'n shoes, Ricky. I ain't clean'n this shit up."

"Troy, I'll run in for your dayum beer. Clean this shit up so some keeyud doesn't slice off a toe. Ricky, I'm gonna need a little ice for my eye—sumbitch got me purdee good," Gray says as he storms into the bait shop.

"Fine, I'll do it. Damn kids need to wear shoes out here anyhow . . . run'n round barefoot . . . at least put some damn flip flops on 'em." Troy continues venting about cleaning up the glass while Gray and Ricky head into the bait shop.

After tending to Gray's eye and Troy's busted beer bottle, the two men head on to the river. Gray continues stressing the importance of silence to Troy—that Hudson knowing about the incident will achieve no good. They discuss what should be said, but never really agree on the way ahead. All Troy knows is to keep his mouth shut, which he is not good at doing when he feels strongly about something.

"What in the hell took y'all so long?" Hudson yells as his father and Troy slide out of Gray's truck. Him and Hank have been sitting and waiting for them on the tailgate when they pull up.

"Ah, Troy busted a beer bottle at Ricky's. Glass went everywhere. Ricky made a big stink about the glass and his barefoot keeyuds," Gray replies.

"What the hell happened to your face? Looks like you got in a fight."

"Yeah, I did, with those damn stairs on the front porch. The first one gave way and down I went. Fortunately, my face was there tuh break my fawl."

"Dammit, old man! I'm gonna help you fix those steps; hell the whole porch for that matter. Can't have you get'n any uglier."

"Help me?! Hell, I was think'n you would do it all yaself."

"Buy the stuff and I will. Can we go do some fish'n now? I want to be back at the house early this even'n."

"Yeah, your dog is gonna sit up front with you, though. And when his big ass jumps out and climbs back in, he will do so up front with you," Gray says.

"Fine by me, he knows how to fish better than any of us anyhow."

"Why do you need to be home early, son?" Troy asks. He has been silent, wrestling with his instincts about the threat to Hudson. He can't help himself, and Gray knows it. Gray cuts his squinting eyes toward Troy to remind him that he best keep his mouth shut about the bait shop incident.

"I'm wait'n on Katie to call. Sorry, gents, I'd rather spend my even'n look'n at her pretty face than your ugly mugs . . ." Hudson pauses for a moment as he notices the look Gray is giving his cousin. "Is there something y'all need to tell me?"

"Nope. Let's pack up the boat n go," Gray immediately answers his son, providing Troy no opportunity to admit the truth.

They load up the boat, launch, and head up the Oconee to look for Ricky's pine tree. They never find it, but are able to make a decent trip out of it. Hank remains off his game all afternoon. He just does not seem himself—never even takes his dip to stir up the fish. He isn't the only one out of sorts; Gray is just as quiet, as is Troy. The cut above Gray's eye keeps opening up, and his cheek has quite the knot on it, which seems to keep growing taller and darker. Troy comes close to letting the cat out of the bag a few times, but Gray's dirty looks snatch that cat by the tail to keep it bagged. However, Hudson notices the rising knot on his father's cheek. As the knot grows, so does Hudson's suspicion about Gray's front porch story.

"Hell of a tumble, Deddy."

"What?" Gray responds, seemingly startled.

"I said, that was a hell of a tumble . . . down the stairs."

"Oh, shit, yeah. I'm surprised I didn't break my foot. Sumbitch went right through that rotten board. I shoulda fixed it months ago. Yowuh mama has been after me about it."

"How about I come over right after we leave here?" Hudson offers, doubting his father's story.

"Nah, just come over tomorrow. I gotta head to Watkinsville this even'n," Gray replies, quick on his feet. He needs time to mull over the threat to his son and what to do about it.

"What's in Watkinsville, Deddy?"

"Pick'n up someth'n for yowuh mama . . . What the hell is with all the dayum questions?" Gray asks as though he is annoyed, but he is more concerned as he knows his son does not believe his story.

"Deddy, I've been in enough fights to know what someone's face looks like after get'n punched."

"Who the heyull do you think I've been fighting? I fell down the dayum stairs like I said befowuh. Someth'n going on that I don't know about?"

"Nope. I'll mind my own business."

"Good, damn . . . a man can't fall down the stairs without a thousand questions. Sound like yowuh dayum mama."

"Uh-huh. Well, I'll be there to help when ya need me. Just call me when you're ready." Hudson doesn't believe his father, but won't push the issue any further out of respect. He knows how it feels to hide something and not want folks looking for it.

"Will do. Y'all about ready? They ain't hit'n on shit anymore," Gray says as he looks over at Troy, who sits quietly as Hudson and Gray go back and forth about the fall. The restraint is no small task for Troy; it eats at him as they pull up lines and head back to the ramp. They nose up to the pasture dock, so Hudson and Hank can jump out. While Hudson goes to get the truck, Troy motors back out to the middle of the river. He idles the engine so Grayford can hear what he has to say.

"Uncle Gray, I'm gonna ride back with Hudson. Now, I know you don't want me to tell'm what went down at Ricky's. I can't let that slide, Uncle Gray—"

"Dammit, Troy! I said no. Hudson is just get'n back to himself. He obviously saw some ugly shit over there. He fought like hell to get back here alive. Last thang he needs is to get back home just to fight again."

"You know this asshole won't quit, Uncle Gray. You know Hudson has two options: leave Katie alone or handle the ex. Have ya seen the way Hudson looks at Katie? And there ain't but one way to handle a sumbitch like her ex. Someone with the stones to walk up to you like he did . . . he ain't bout to leave it be . . . You know that."

Troy's right and Gray knows it. Hudson is ate up with love for Katie. He sees the same look Katie has for Hudson, and they need each other to heal old wounds. He also knows situations like this one breed tragedy. He doesn't want Hudson surviving war only to come home and die at the hands of a jealous man or serve time for ending that man's life with his own vengeful hands.

"Dammit, Troy! Any way you slice it, this doesn't bode well for Hudson."

"No sir! Not with the way he feels for her."

Grayford lightly massages his forehead before turning toward Troy, pointing at him, and then telling him, "Don't you say shit to'm, Troy. I will let'm know when the time is right."

"Don't wait too long, Uncle Gray. I know ya try'n to protect Hudson, but that sack of shit is ballsy enough to come up to you, he will go after Hudson. Right now, Hudson has no idea this asshole is even after'm. Can't let your son get blindsided by this maniac."

"I know! Troy . . . I know . . . dammit tuh hell, I know."

"I'll watch after'm as much as I can until he knows. I'll be there with'm. I'll die for my family, Uncle Gray. I'll go to jail, I don't give a shit . . ."

"I know, Troy, yowuh damn good people. I tell'm: he will go after'm and will probably end up in jail or maybe hurt bad or dead. I don't tell'm: he could be blindsided and wind up dead. I tell ya what I'm gonna do, I'm gonna tell'm that he just warned us. I'll tell'm when he comes over to help with the steps tomorrow. I want him to believe there was no fight, just a simple tumble down the steps. That way, he knows her ex is making threats, so his guard's up, but no need to retaliate."

"Steps ain't busted and you obviously got punched, Uncle Gray."

"Not yet they ain't. Listen, Troy, I need ya to be with me on this. Ya hear me? We don't know what demons lay dormant in Hudson. He loves'at girl, and Lord knows what he will do for her."

Troy looks at his uncle for a long second. Gray is trying to protect his son, but Troy feels this is wrong. Ignorance and an abundance of testosterone flood his young mind. Sean driving his fist into the side of his uncle's head and threatening his family just doesn't sit right at all with Troy. Gray's idea may buy time, but that's about it. Troy finally and reluctantly agrees to Gray's idea, though silence and lies will eat him up.

Troy puts the engine in gear as Hudson backs the trailer down the ramp and into the water. They get the boat loaded up on the trailer, and then Hudson pulls forward up onto flat ground. Hudson and Troy lock the engine in the up position and strap down the boat. Meanwhile,

Grayford grabs three beers from the cooler. The three of them gather around the boat to shoot the breeze and have a beer as they always do after fishing.

"Thanks, Uncle Gray!"

"Thanks, Deddy!"

Grayford pops the top, looks up at Troy. "You still mess'n round with that lil gal from Gainesville, Troy?"

"Every now and then. When the urge hits me, I guess."

"Yowuh a young man, that urge should be knock'n the hell outa ya every dayum day."

Troy chuckles before replying, "Who says she's the only one I get the urge for?"

"Sheeyut, boy! You best watch where you stick'at thang. Of course, I can't say anything. When I was in the Navy—"

Hudson quickly interrupts Grayford. "Get ready, Troy, here comes the nasty Navy stories. Sorry, old man! Please, by all means, continue."

Stone-faced Grayford looks at them while they chuckle a bit. "You boys go on n laugh it up. Enjoy it while you can. Get to my age and it don't work like it used to. You can pull a rope all you want but ya damn sure can't push one."

Hudson laughs for a little bit, finishes his beer, and then looks up at Gray. "Well, on that note Imma head on. Enjoyed it as always, Deddy. See you soon for those steps. Come on, Hank! Troy, you ride'n with us?"

"Yeah, man. We'll talk to ya later, Uncle Gray."

"Awlright, boys. I'll call ya tomorrow bout them steps, son. Y'all drive careful now." Gray looks at Troy as Hudson and Hank walk on. "Troy, watch after'm . . . dammit . . . watch after'm!"

"I got'm, Uncle Gray."

# CHAPTER THIRTY-EIGHT

# STEPS

**A** father will do anything to protect his family. Gray despised the lie he was forced to tell Hudson, falling through the steps and all, but he knows his son battles many of those same demons as that dog he saved. Hudson is stuck somewhere between the explosively violent world of war and the peaceful security of home. Katie is the key to his full return home. However, with her comes the risk of him returning to the battle ground. The troubles that accompany her are not of her doing, but must be addressed. Gray has no idea what Sean has done to Katie, but he can see the good in her and the love she has for his son and his son for her. If it takes a lie and a few broken steps to give them their best opportunity for a wonderful future together, then so be it.

After Gray stows the boat and parks the truck, he wastes no time starting in on those steps. He has to make it look like a board or two gave way, which should be no problem since there is a rotten spot or two, but not enough to call for replacing the steps. He had no intentions of replacing any of these old steps until he had to tell that damned lie. Now he has to make truth from the lie, so Gray takes an eight-pound hammer to the oldest-looking step and the handrail post, which gets the attention of Savannah.

"Gray! What on Uth are you doin out heeyuh?" Savannah yells as she storms out of the front door onto the deck.

Gray stops and looks up at his wife as he simply replies, "I'm bust'n up the steps. The hell does it look like I'm doin?"

"And just why in the heyull are ya doin that?"

"To replace the dayum things. Now let me be."

"What happened to yowuh face?" Savannah asks as she walks closer to Gray.

"I fell down the steps this morn'n, which is why I'm fix'n 'em . . . nosey," Gray replies as he pauses his demolition of the steps with his heavy hammer.

"Grayford Lee, you did no such thang! No fall caused those cuts'n bruises! What happened to yowuh face? And don't you lie to me!"

"Would you just let it go dammit. I fell. What difference does it make?"

"Were you drunk? Did you have an accident?"

"If I did, will you shut the hell up about it?"

"If it's the truth I will."

Before Gray can respond, he hears a vehicle ripping down the dirt road. Hudson's Ford sure enough comes speeding up the driveway, coming to a quick stop by the front steps where his father stands with that big hammer and his mama stands wondering why her son is driving so fast down the dirt road.

"You can just knock that shit off, Deddy!" Hudson shouts as he jumps out of his truck. Troy decides to stay in the truck with Hank for good reason. Hudson continues, "I know what happened. No need to keep bust'n up them damn steps."

"Hudson Lee, you watch yowuh mouth, young man!"

"Not now, Mama!" Hudson says with a sharp tone.

"Who in the heyull do you thank you ah come'n up heeyuh, talk'n to yowuh parents with that disrespectful tone?" Savannah scolds Hudson.

"Did Deddy tell ya that Katie's ex assaulted him? At Ricky's?"

Savannah stands silent for a few seconds before turning to Gray. "Is that what happened to yowuh face?"

Gray looks up to the sky and takes a deep breath. He turns his attention to the truck, looking around Hudson, and yells, "Big mouth! I will deal with yowuh ass layda, Troy."

"Don't be mad at Troy, he's just try'n to protect us."

"No, he's just try'n to get back at those boys, son. Don't be stupid about this. We put a few bruises on them as well. Shit is done and over with."

"What about Katie, Deddy? What do ya think this piece of shit did to Katie when they were together? That is what she was run'n from and for good dayum reason. I bet that's why she ain't answer'n her phone either. She's worried he will come after me or all of us . . . just as he damn well did! And you kept that shit from me?"

"I know, son. I just don't want you goin and doin someth'n that'll get ya put in jail or hurt."

"Yowuh deddy is right, son . . ."

"Mama, please don't you start in on me right now. I'm taking Troy home, and then head'n over to her house. The only thing I am worried about is protecting Katie. I'm sorry for this . . . for my life blow'n back on y'all and everything, but I'm not gonna do anything stupid. I'm just gonna protect'r."

Gray walks over to the passenger side of the truck where Troy sits. "You opened yowuh big mouth, so you best be there for'm. Keep'm outta fuck'n jail and make sure he doesn't get hurt, Troy. Ya heeyuh me son?"

"Yes, sir! I hear ya . . . loud and clear!" Troy intends on doing just that, regardless of what happens to him. "Me and this big fella right here will be there for'm."

"Damn right you will be! We'll be talk'n about that big fuck'n mouth of yowuhs, too!"

"Deddy, Troy just did what was right. I needed to know. Now, I'm gonna make sure he doesn't come for Katie. I gotta protect'r."

"Dammit to heyull . . . you be careful, son! Don't you go after that piece of shit on account of me. What happened at the bait shop is done. Done!"

"Yes, sir! I ain't gonna mess with'm over that. You say it's done, then it's done. I gotta go, Deddy."

"OK, son, be careful."

Watching that Ford drive away is just like watching Hudson leave for boot camp all over again. The battleground was half a world away back then, and Hudson was sure to find himself there. Unbeknownst to them, he found the heart of war over there and has battled more than terrorists and enemy forces ever since. After escaping the mental war waged within him, he found a little peace. However, true peace will only come through battle—been that way since the get-go. The cycle of peace and war will continue as long as people exist—sad but true. They can only watch as Hudson drives off to the battlefield that is now just down the road. Gray drops the hammer and then wraps his arms around Savannah as she weeps.

# CHAPTER THIRTY-NINE

# REVELATION

A northern cardinal is so aggressive when protecting his mate that he will attack his own reflection in windows. A man's reflection can cause the same outburst. Sean attacked Katie instead of the man looking back at him, because he values himself above all else. Hudson, on the other hand, will destroy the man in the window to save Katie, just like that cardinal.

After dropping off Troy, who was reluctant to leave his side, Hudson and Hank drive straight over to Katie's house. Hudson witnessed the destructive mental ramifications of abuse that first night at the Dixie Diner. He did not realize it at the time—his mental battles and ignorance prevented him from doing so. He thought she was simply unhappy with her relationship and afraid to end it. Hudson has seen many people extend broken partnerships to avoid loneliness or for some other innocuous reason. He has also seen partners show deep affection for each other and work through all challenges as they journey through life together. But never has he beheld the wretched aftermath of the abuse Katie has suffered for years. She could not look at him but for a brief moment that night, and when she did offer a peek into her eyes, he saw the girl's cry for help turn to fear when Sean walked into the diner. Even now, as he races to her house and recalls her fear from that night, he has yet to see the full extent of her mental and physical wounds.

A sick feeling comes over Hudson as they pull into her driveway and see her car. He feels bad for coming over unannounced. He feels worse for not trying harder to make sure she is doing well after not hearing back from her all day, though. She always sends a good morning text, but not today. Until now, her troubles have been a mystery to him. He's never pushed for information and she's never offered any. He does not want to scare her off, but instead intends to reassure her that he will protect her.

Hudson rings the doorbell four times with no answer. Hank senses someone inside and lets out a few barks. Hudson knows she is in there. He is worried that she is too afraid to talk to him; she is afraid of what Sean will do. He has to relieve her of that fear, but that means he has to give away his knowledge of her secret, at least the little bit that he knows of it.

"Katie? Is that you in there?" Hudson remembers what it was like listening to people ring the doorbell while he just wanted to be left alone. Maybe that is all she wants, but he has to talk to her about what happened at the bait shop.

"I'm sorry I came by without call'n you. I don't understand what's goin on right now. I don't know why you have ignored me today, but I will guess it has something to do with your ex. He attacked my deddy. He would've probably hurt'm bad, him and his friends, had it not been for Ricky and Troy. I'm sure he's not . . ."

Katie cracks open the door, but hides behind it. She's only opened the door so he can hear her apology and the heartbreaking news he's dreaded since their first date. She pleads with Hudson to leave. She tells him that she is not worth the trouble—she is not worth the danger she poses to him and his family. Hudson listens as she tells him to save himself and his family, to let go of her. He briefly considers releasing his own secret, so she can understand why his safety is of no concern at all to him. There's that cardinal willing to attack himself to protect his love.

"You don't have to fear'm. I will do anything to protect you."

Katie cries without a word spoken. He decides to crack open his vault just a little bit.

"I am not try'n to pressure you into anything. I . . . I love you, Katie. I know we haven't known each other all that long. But the truth is, I felt something words can't describe the moment I saw you. I believe you felt the same way. I was in a bad way that night . . . for a while. You brought something beautiful to this world. I will never let Sean do anything to take you away from this world. He'd have to kill me before he hurt you."

Katie remains hidden, weeping silently, as she contemplates opening the door or slamming it shut. She cannot bring herself to risk more lives than her own. She fears the chain of events that will unfold if she opens that door. However, if she shuts the door, Hudson will never appreciate the peril he and his family face. To save Hudson and his family, she will show him and end the relationship.

The door opens wider and Katie steps out to the light of day. Lacerations and severe contusions mask her beautiful face. Tears sting those fresh wounds as they fall from her swollen eyes. Her left eye is nearly swollen shut. Shame causes her to stare at the ground. She attempts to deliver her heartbreaking decision but fails to contain her agony long enough to do so. Hudson stands speechless, overcome with sympathy, sorrow, and guilt as tears well in his eyes. He gently guides her head to his shoulder and wraps his arms around her head and waist. She buckles and cries out in pain when his arm touches her ribs. He lifts up her shirt enough to see the wrapping around her midsection, and then eases her shirt back down. She never looks up. She says nothing. She cries hysterically on his shoulder.

"My God, Katie. This was him? He did this to you?" Hudson asks with a broken voice.

Katie only cries harder. The pain nearly causes her legs to give. Trauma and despair from the years of emotional and physical abuse pour out. Thoughts race through her mind. Hidden behind the door she possessed the confidence to end their relationship. Now, in his arms, she flounders, unable to speak the words necessary to save Hudson. She cannot allow the comfort of his shoulder to dissuade her from doing the right thing by him. Her anguish subsides a little after a long cry on his shoulder, calming her enough, but not enough to say the heartbreaking words she intended to. What escapes instead is the truth from the girl inside.

"Yes, it was him! Oh God! He was inside when I came home . . . he beat me, Hudson . . . worse than ever he beat me. He said he will kill us."

Hudson listens to her reveal the truth of her pain and fear. He cries with her. Her pain is his. She cries for several more minutes as Hudson holds her as tightly as he can without causing her pain. Once her tears slow, she invites him inside to talk. She reveals her ugly past with Sean with one gut-wrenching story after another. Hudson says nothing as he listens to her. She never looks over at him as she confesses to the awful abuse perpetrated on her by Sean. Hudson never looks away from her, though. He listens to every word, hanging on every detail. She tells him that she aimed to kill herself that day they found her wandering those woods, because death was the only way to escape Sean's evil cycle of abuse. After sharing her tragic secret, she falls silent. Hudson gently places his palm on her cheek to turn her head toward him. He softly asks that she look at him. She finally musters the courage to overcome the shame and guilt to look into Hudson's eyes.

"You are beautiful inside and out. Nothing he can do will ever take that away from you. He tried to tear you down. He tried to break your spirit. He tried to beat the beautiful soul out of you. He will soon find out just how bad he failed. Nothing . . . no one, will ever hurt you again."

Katie wishes more than anything to believe Hudson can deliver on his promise without harm falling upon their families, but she knows

Sean has submitted to all that is evil within him. The sight of her battered body fails to convince Hudson of the danger they all face. Now that she has finally shared her tale of torment and cried her eyes dry, her mind is clear and emotions under control. She asks Hudson to leave and never return. She tells him they met too late. She confided in Hudson a secret only she and her abuser know, and now she asks Hudson to forget it all. She thanks him for the time they had and then tells him that she wishes to never see him again. Hudson makes a tearful plea that she does not deny her love for him and his for her. She says nothing in response. She lacks the fortitude to face the heart she breaks, as hers, too, is broken. The floor holds her focus as she replies to his pleas by opening the door. She never looks up as Hudson and Hank walk out that door and out of her life.

# CHAPTER FORTY

# RETRIBUTION

Hudson recalls his talk with Uncle Walt by the campfire before bootcamp. He recalls what he said about the devil convincing others to dwell in Hell. Walt referred to the totalitarian regimes who want complete power to control the masses and are willing to sacrifice anyone but themselves to gain that which they desire. Sean covets the same control over Katie and is willing to hurt anyone but himself to have it. That devil comes in many shapes and sizes, but the wicked intent is always the same. Hudson understands this just as well as his uncle did. Sean will not leave Katie be; he will continue to deliver misery to the woman Hudson loves. Katie asked Hudson to forget her, her terrible secret, and what Sean did to her. Hudson will not forget, though, nor will he forget that which demands retribution.

The vengeance Hudson seeks causes a man to ignore all fear and logic that normally give him pause—time to think about the best course of action. He will respond in kind to the violent message Sean relayed through the beating he gave Katie. Personal safety and legal consequences are of no concern as he recalls her tears and wounds. Judge and jury cannot award a sentence harsh enough to make right the evil Sean enacted on Katie. Only Hudson can exact such punishment. Only his fist will rightfully tear flesh from the bones he intends to break. He recruits Troy to help in his search for Sean, but Troy will do more than just help find the man, he will be by his cousin's side as he delivers his harsh message.

While Hudson and Troy hunt down Sean, Katie suffers the woeful consequence of her decision. Her options were Sean's promise of violence or Hudson's promise of protection. Katie has never witnessed the fierce warrior within Hudson. She only knows his love. On the other hand, she has routinely experienced the wrath of the evil monster within Sean. She believes nothing could exist in a gentle soul like Hudson to match the brutality of Sean and his demons. She sacrificed love and happiness to shield Hudson, his family, and her family from Sean's deadly obsession with her. She will never tell her mother what happened to her. She will never tell her about Hudson. She just wants to leave and never return. She will leave in the morning and, just as before, intends to never return.

Troy takes only a day to find Sean. Hudson receives the call as him and Hank are climbing up into the truck to go cruise the roads of Athens in search of Sean.

"Hey, Troy. What's up?"

"Hey, son. I found'm. His old man and uncle run a HVAC business. He works with them."

"What's the name of the business?"

"Williamson Brothers. You remember Jon Grady from school?"

"Yeah, what about'm?"

"He's been working for 'em about two years now. He can't stand the guy. Says he had a feel'n he was hurt'n that girl. Said he acts like the love'n fiancé around everybody else, but one night at a company party Jon saw how he treats'r when no one's around. He said it was pretty ugly between 'em. He actually interrupted the fight when it looked like he was gonna hit'r, and he sure as shit would have if Jon hadn't been there. Said he grabbed her pretty hard. Sean told Jon to mind his own fuck'n business."

"Troy, I know that piece of shit is a piece of shit. I need to know where to find'm."

"That's why I'm call'n, cuz. I know where he is. Listen to me, son, you know I got your back and ready to crack skulls with ya, but Jon said Sean's deddy has money and is quick to help his son outta trouble."

"Maybe you ought to stay out of it then, Troy. You know what I have to do. You know there is only one way to protect Katie."

"Son, no fuck'n way I stay out. I'm just say'n we don't know how many guys are with'm and cause'n trouble on a jobsite doesn't look good, dude."

"Where's the site?"

"Hudson, maybe we ought not do this on the jobsite."

"Where, Troy? I don't give a fuck about how this looks!" The beast within Hudson rages.

"Awl right . . . fuck it . . . we'll do it there then. About half a mile past the Hull Pantry store on the left. The house sits back off Hull Road a little ways. I will meet ya at the Pantry."

Hudson and Hank ride quietly, passing by the same dying leaves Katie saw the morning before Charleston. Unlike her, they offer no attention to the colorful leaves as they go to remove the leaf that refused to fall from her tree. They concentrate on the road before them, with their thoughts miles ahead. This ride reminds Hank of all those from his past, except when the stranger made an attempt on his life. He has an instinct for the violence that awaits them. He prepares his mind for battle, as his friend is doing quietly beside him. All their battles before now were on behalf of others, by the orders of others—all go back to that ol' devil Uncle Walt described. This time they are going of their own accord. They are going to right the world.

Hull is a small town just outside Athens, about an hour's drive from Hudson's house. Hudson and Hank make it in forty minutes. Troy is already there waiting for them. Hudson quickly parks and steps out of his truck.

"Where's the house, Troy?" Hudson shouts to Troy as he approaches his truck.

"I'll show you once Ty gets here. I called him . . . Look, dude, he thinks this is a bad idea. He actually cussed me out for tell'n ya."

"Troy, I ain't wait'n. I'll pull into every fuck'n driveway until I find it."

Hudson is unwilling to waste a second of time. His mind is made and Troy knows it. Hudson returns to his truck, where Hank eagerly awaits. Troy quickly pulls his truck in front of Hudson's, but not to stop him. He waves at Hudson to follow him. No way he will let his cousin go hunting for the man without him by his side. Hudson follows Troy down a long driveway to a house sitting alone in a small field, surrounded by trees. About five or six guys, including Sean, are sitting on tailgates eating lunch when the two trucks pull up and park about thirty yards away, behind some other work trucks.

"Who the hell are these guys, Sean?" Jimmy asks, not really thinking much of it—maybe just some other contractors.

"Hell if I . . ." Sean stops midsentence as he recognizes Hudson's truck. "Ah shit, this is that asshole Katie's been cheat'n with. Get my back, boys."

Hudson slides out of the truck with Hank on the leash. He hands the leash to Troy, telling him to only unleash him if the other men jump him. Hudson walks quickly, with a purpose, toward the truck where Sean is rising up off the tailgate. He knows why Hudson is there. He is nervous, but confident with the number of friends by his side.

"What the hell are you doin' here? This is a damn jobsite, asshole. Our place of business. You got a problem, then we can handle this elsewhere!" Sean shouts to Hudson.

Just as he did at the diner, Hudson replies with silence. His scowl sends a far louder message than can his words. No one can talk him down. Nothing can stop him. His intent is to send a hard lesson to the animal who brutally attacked the woman he deeply loves.

Sean's friends look over at Hudson, ready to pounce on the man they see marching toward them. Sean fires off threats to help restore his rapidly dwindling confidence. Sean's work crew fires off obscenities at Hudson with more conviction than does Sean. They are unaware of the man's motivation. They are unaware of his resolve. They can see his intent is violent, so they start to circle around the angry stranger. They fail to complete their flank, though, as Troy and Hank appear from around the truck to Hudson's side. They freeze at the sight of the massive dog, whose hair rises down his spine as the men try circling around his family. The rising hair reveals all of his vulgar scars, like stripes earned from past battles. His vicious snorting growl nearly defeats the enemy before the first blow is even thrown.

Sean uses the dog as a distraction to lunge at Hudson, throwing a straight right. Nothing distracts Hudson, though. His training and reflexes are too good. His focus is unbreakable. He takes a slight step to the left, dodging the punch while delivering a shot to Sean's ribs with a left, followed by an overhand right with all his momentum and weight, making direct impact with Sean's nose. Fury and a broken heart deliver an iron fist that knocks Sean onto the truck bed with blood splatter across his face. Dazed by the powerful blow, Sean tries to kick Hudson to keep him away, but only makes contact with air as Hudson sidesteps once again. Hudson grabs Sean's leg near the ankle, takes one step back, and pulls the man right off the truck. Sean hangs in the air for a short second before gravity pulls him down. His breath escapes his lungs when his back crashes onto the hard, red clay. Hudson drives his heel into Sean's rib cage to make sure all the air is completely out of his lungs. He quickly straddles Sean's torso, pulls his head up by the hair, and then drives punch after jaw-breaking punch into Sean's face, just as Sean did Katie.

Jimmy heads toward Hudson while yelling at Troy to stop this thing before Hudson kills him.

"Your boy should learn not to hit women and old men. My boy is simply teach'n a valuable yet painful fuck'n lesson, slick," Troy yells back while struggling to contain the tank on the end of the leash.

Ty comes to a sliding stop in his truck after speeding down the driveway. He sprints over to the fight, yelling Troy's name.

"Don't let'm kill'm, Troy!"

"Fuck this!" Jimmy yells as he starts charging toward Hudson. Ty runs up and heads off Jimmy with a left hook, knocking him off balance. Two of Sean's friends jump Ty from behind. One of the other crewmen tackles Hudson off of Sean. Jimmy stands back up, grabs a hammer out of the truck bed, and then charges toward Hudson.

Hank only knew violence and rage before meeting Hudson, before becoming part of Hudson's family. He exhibited a little ferocity at Pop's and the farm, but even Hudson has yet to witness the level of savagery Hank can reach. It just takes the right environment; the right threat to flip that violent switch. When flipped, the loving dog is no more. The beast is here now and wants off that chain. He knows what he is here to do. He saw Katie. He felt her sorrow as tears poured down her swollen cheeks. He felt Hudson's sorrow when they walked out her door. His heart is broken, too, just like his friend, who is now fighting the other man with another charging toward him, wielding a weapon. His time is now. Hank rips the leash from Troy's hand as Troy swings a right hook at one of the men jumping on Ty. No hesitation exists from the moment he is freed to the time he lunges at the man who aims to hurt his friend. He leaps about four feet in the air at his target. The former pit warrior digs his teeth into Jimmy's flesh, latching down onto his arm. His powerful jaws clamp down like a bear trap. Violently he twists and shakes his muscular neck, immediately breaking the man's arm. The hammer falls to the ground, and so does Jimmy. He screams to the point that his voice cracks. It is a horrific scream, one that causes everyone to stop fighting, everyone except Hank. He seems to grow more violent the louder his opponent screams. His eyes roll back as his teeth sink deeper into the man's arm. He snarls, yanks, twists, and pulls Jimmy by the arm from one side to the other.

"Get'm off me! Get him off me! God . . . dammit . . . Get'm!" Jimmy yells and begs. Hank twists the man's shoulder so viciously it pops right out of the socket. They all hear the sound. His lower arm flops around as Hank rips his head side to side. The beast eyes the man's neck, setting him up for the kill. He intends to end the threat once and for all.

Ty runs over and grabs the leash, pulling with all his might. "Let go, Hank . . . Hank, let go, boy!" he shouts and pulls to no avail. Hank is not the one in battle. It's the beast, who has no name and knows but one end to battle.

Hudson pushes aside the man who tackled him. He gets to his feet and then runs over to Hank. He grabs the leash close to Hank's neck. "Come on, boy! Release! Release him! Release, Hank, release!"

The internal battle within the dog wages on as much as the fight with those men. Hudson continues to shout for the dog to release. Over and over he yells for Hank. Finally, Hank comes back. The beast retreats into the shadows. Hank lets go and licks some of the blood from his face. Hudson pulls Hank with all his might to get him away from Jimmy, who continues to scream in pain.

"You're a real badass with that fuck'n dog in your hand!" Rodney blurts out from the other side of the truck.

Hudson hands Ty the leash and steps over Sean, who remains unconscious on the ground, and points his bloody finger at Rodney as he finally responds to the men. "Were you there when this piece of shit hit my father? Were you there when he beat the shit outta Katie? Did you see what this fuck'n coward did tuh her?" Hudson bellows.

Rodney faces an opponent armed with tremendous fury, driven by love, and afraid of nothing. His demons are unchained and on a warpath, like the beast that attacked Jimmy. Even loudmouthed Rodney knows this is not a man to cross—not now.

"Answer me, mothafucka! Did you see what he did to'r?" Hudson shouts.

Rodney remains silent.

"Hudson! We gotta go!" Ty shouts, but Hudson ignores his brother's command as he waits for Rodney to answer.

Troy waits a brief moment before walking up to Hudson, and then whispering in his ear, "People are calling the law, Hudson. Listen to Ty, and let's get the fuck goin. Shit is done . . . message delivered."

Hudson continues glaring intently at Rodney for a few more seconds. He scans around at the other folks who have come out of the house. The electricians working at the jobsite are on the phone with Madison County Sheriff's dispatch. Hudson wants to beat the life from Sean, but he knows killing the man will destroy his family and Katie. He hopes this beating is enough to drive Sean away from Katie. Hank's relentless snarls and barks abruptly snap Hudson from his thoughts. He marches over to Ty and grabs the leash from him.

"Let's go, Hank. I gotta get you outta here. Gotta calm ya down, my friend." Hudson turns to the men who are now kneeling to help Sean and makes clear that any man who threatens Katie or comes near her will pay with his life. They respond with silence. They are angry, but anger is no match for madness. They turn their attention back to Sean, who remains unconscious, and Jimmy.

"Ty, you or Troy take Hank with y'all. Get him outta here. I'll wait for the police to get here. They're gonna come for me anyway. I don't want them to get Hank, brother. They'll put him down. Get him outta here," Hudson asks his brother and cousin as they hurry to their trucks.

"Get in your truck and lock the door until they get here. You armed?" Ty replies, uncomfortable with leaving his brother alone with the men they just fought while he waits to be detained by the sheriff's deputies.

"No, didn't want to lose my shit and kill someone today."

"Fuck, Hudson! Well, that was the right thang to do. Dammit, brother!"

"We ain't leave'n you, Hudson! No fuck'n way!" Troy shouts.

"Troy!" Hudson shouts back at his cousin before continuing with a calmer demeanor. "Get outta here, dammit. Get Hank outta here! They will arrest me, but they will put him down. I can't let that happen."

"Hudson, staying here is stupid. That asshole will not press charges, because he attacked two people, one of whom will press charges against him for sure to protect you. We gotta leave now before the police get here. They gotta come from the otha side of the county . . . unless they already have a cruiser over here somewhere," Ty pleads with his brother.

"Shit . . . all right . . . Troy, you gotta take Hank, though!" Hudson demands of his cousin.

"I got'm. Come on, Hank!"

"Get in your fuck'n trucks and go, dammit!" Ty once again shouts as he starts his truck.

They race away from the jobsite, splitting up at the highway. Hudson rides alone. His anger and adrenaline subside and logic eases back into his head. Before the fight, his anger dictated his actions, rather than logic. Involving the police after Sean's attack on Katie would have been the much wiser option, though it was not what she wanted. Nor did she want Hudson to attack Sean. She wanted Hudson to leave and save himself, to save everyone. No man can look at a woman beaten the way she was and not do something about it, especially when the man deeply loves the woman. His broken heart and fury called for retribution, but now Hudson comes to realize what Katie knew all along: Sean will violently respond after first weakening his victim. He will ensure Hudson and Hank cannot protect her. He will press charges and ensure the dog is put down.

Hudson calls Katie, but she does not answer. He is unaware that she blocked his number and deleted it from her phone. He has to tell her he did not do as she asked. He has to warn her of the mess he made. He drives straight to her house and bangs on her door. He fears her reaction before she opens it. She yells through the door, telling him to leave.

"I couldn't do noth'n Katie. We found'm," Hudson yells.

"Oh, Hudson, what did you do?"

"I fucked up, Katie. They are gonna come for Hank. They are gonna come for me. I tried to protect you, and I fucked up."

"What did you do, Hudson?" Katie yells.

"I beat him pretty bad. Hank hurt his friend pretty bad. I fucked up."

Katie opens the door before Hudson finishes talking. She looks at him for a brief moment. She can see the regret in his eyes, but she is upset that he did not listen to her.

"Why, Hudson? Why?" Katie shouts, crying.

"I'm sorry, so sorry, Katie! I just wanted to protect you. I still just want to protect you from'm. I'm sure he will press charges. Is there somewhere safe you can go until—"

"Oh, Hudson. This is bad, Hudson. I was trying to protect you and your family. If you would have done what I asked and stayed away, everyone would be safe. You promised you would do nothing, Hudson. Why did you have to go and do this?" Katie yells.

"Look at what he did to you, Katie! Look at what he has done for a long time—"

"I know what he did! I lived it! I wanted to end it, but you came along. I just want it to end, and you fucked it up."

"I'm sorry. I am sorry I broke my promise, but I love you, and there was no fuck'n way he was not goin to pay for what he did. I told you that I'll protect you, and I aim to do it. You won't hear from me again, but I will make sure you never have to hear from that piece of shit either."

"Hudson, please know that I love you more than I can ever say, but you need to just leave and forget about me. That is the only way to protect anyone without causing any more troubles for you and your family."

"There is only one way to end this problem for everyone. This world needs you, not him. If good people do nothin, there'll be nothin good left. I will always love you, Katie."

"Hudson! Don't you dare! Please! Hudson!" Katie shouts, but Hudson does not acknowledge her plea as he walks away. His mind is made.

# CHAPTER FORTY-ONE

# SAVING HUDSON

For years, Katie has prayed for freedom from Sean, but refuses to allow a good man to throw away his life to give her that peace. She confided in Hudson to make him understand why she had to end their time together—to save the man she loves from the man who abused her. Now, she must come out from hiding, not to run away as she planned, but to bring to light her dark secret for all to see in order to save Hudson from himself. She drives directly to the farm to tell the only two people who can convince Hudson not to kill Sean. Only Gray is home, working on the steps he busted.

"Gray! You have to help'm!" Katie shouts out of her window as she comes to a stop by the steps.

"Katie, what's wrong?" Gray asks as he walks toward her car.

"Hudson is going to kill the man who attacked you."

The severity of Katie's injuries renders Gray speechless momentarily. He is not the only one to recognize the results of Sean's rage; Katie immediately feels guilty for the cuts and bruises on Gray's face.

"My dear girl. That animal did this to you?"

"Yes, Mr. Gray! I will tell you everything, but we have to stop Hudson."

Gray rides with Katie to Hudson's house. Katie lets Gray drive, because she knows her emotions will pour out as she tells her story. She tells Gray the disturbing details of Sean's abuse and how it led her to Hudson. Gray immediately recalls the scratches on Sean's face that day at the bait shop. He feels extraordinary guilt as he thinks of Katie fighting for her life and him doing nothing to check on her—he was too focused on Hudson at the time. Gray does not call Hudson, because he knows his son will ignore him and leave the house before they arrive. He gently grabs Katie's hand as she struggles to share her vulgar story.

They pull into Hudson's driveway just as he is leaving. Gray blocks the driveway with Katie's car and immediately jumps out, shouting at his son.

"Hudson, get the fuck out of that truck!" Gray yells and points his index finger.

Hudson tries to drive around his father, but Gray runs over and stands in front of the old Ford. Hudson rolls down his window to shout back at his father.

"Get out of my fuck'n way, Deddy!"

"Don't you dare talk to me like'at, boy! Now, you go on and get out, son. Get the hell outta that dayum truck!"

Hudson slings open his door, jumps out, and runs up on his father shouting while pointing at Katie. "Look at'r! Look what the fuck'n coward did to'r! She will never fear'm again, Deddy. Please, move or I will have to move ya."

"You threat'n me, son? Your anger has your mind twisted. There is another way—a much better and legal way to handle this. You fucked up by beating that asshole and sick'n your dog on his friend. Can't undo that."

"Look at what he did to'r! Deddy, he bout killed'r." Hudson sobs as he shouts at his father.

Gray steps to his son and hugs him tightly. He waits until Hudson's emotions bed down a bit before calmly continuing his plea. "Son, you beat'm up, and I understand why. I wish you would have simmered down and thought it through, but what is done is done. Listen, this is not the battlefield—you're home now and can't go around kill'n people, regardless of how shitty of a person they are. We love ya, son. That poor girl loves you more than anything. We are gonna make this right. Gonna do it the right way. Just do as I say, son."

Katie slowly gets out of the car and walks over to Gray and Hudson. Gray steps back from his son, who continues to weep. Katie begs Hudson to listen to his father, and then hugs him as tightly as she can. She apologizes to Hudson for telling him to leave and forget her. She says she will never leave his side again nor will she ask him to leave hers. She will stay with him tonight. They will accompany Gray in the morning to press charges against Sean and get a protective order for Katie.

— CHAPTER FORTY-TWO —

# MESS

Savannah was none too pleased when Gray told her about Hudson going after the man who attacked Katie. She called and lectured him for the better part of an hour. She told him that he ought to have called the law on the man, not have taken the law in his own hands. Though a mother is capable of most anything, undoing the mistakes of her children is a miracle she cannot perform. All Savannah can do now is support her son and Katie during this uncertain and trying time. All she can do is hope Gray's plan will keep Hudson free and Katie safe.

The next morning has given way to afternoon when the Greene County Sheriff's cruiser pulls into the driveway accompanied by a Madison County cruiser. Savannah steps out onto the front porch, watching the cruisers creep down her driveway. Such a god-awful feeling overcomes her knowing the deputies are here to haul away her son, so he can stand and be judged. He beat that man badly. He let his dog nearly pull the arm off of another man. No judge will allow such vigilantism and will indeed make an example of her son and his dog.

"Ma'am. How are ya today?" the Greene County deputy greets Savannah as they approach the front deck where she stands waiting.

"Depends on yowuh intentions, deputy."

"Well, ma'am, I have a warrant out for Hudson Lee. That's your son, right?"

"He is my son, but he ain't heeyuh. What's the warrant fowuh?"

"Uh-huh, I see. Oconee and Madison deputies went to his house this morn'n, Mrs. Lee, and no one came to the door."

"Then I guess he wasn't home, deputy. Now, how bout tell'n me what the warrant's fowuh?"

"He attacked a man at his jobsite and fled the scene. Put'm in the hospital. Broke his jaw and maybe a couple ribs. Busted him up pretty dayum bad. His dog put another man in the hospital. Damn near lost his arm. We have to take'm both in."

"That the animal who beat a woman and attacked my husband?"

"I don't know anythang about that, ma'am. I am just carry'n out this warrant."

"Well, deputy, just so you are awayuh, the man lying in that hospital viciously attacked a young woman. He also attacked my husband."

"Well, ma'am, nuth'n was filed concern'n either of those instances. I suggest doin what's right here and tell'n us the location of your son and his dog."

Before Savannah answers the deputy, the sound of gravel crunching and a rooster tail of red dust following Gray's truck interrupt the conversation. Gray does not take as long as the deputies did making his way down the driveway. He drives with a purpose.

"Is that your husband, ma'am?" the Greene County deputy asks Savannah while watching Gray pull up.

"Sure is."

The conversation pauses again as they all wait for the truck to park. "Deputies, what brangs y'all out this way?" Gray asks sharply as he steps out of the truck.

"Mr. Lee, I believe you know, sir. We are try'n to find your son and his dog. He didn't answer the door when the Oconee deputies went to his house."

"Well, that's because he was with me. Him and Katie—Kathleen Carter. We went to file charges against Sean Williamson for beating the young lady sit'n in my passenger seat and for attacking me at the bait shop."

"That's fine, sir, but we still need to take Hudson in. We also need to have animal control take away his dog for the attack on the utha fella, who I believe didn't attack anyone. He damn sure didn't put any-one in the hospital where those two fellas lay as we speak."

"Hold on there, officer. That dog jumped on that fella because he was charging at Hudson with a hamma."

"Either way, I gotta take him in, sir. We'll collect statements from everyone. The courts will sort it all out. Your son should have stayed put instead of run'n. And y'all oughta had called law enforcement after being attacked instead of your boy take'n the law in his own hands."

"Deputy, you know dayum well if he stayed put, someone would've been killed. He left the situation to prevent furtha violence. He turned himself in. He's ova in Oconee County right now. You want'm, that is where you will find'm. Meanwhile, how bout y'all take a look at the reason those pieces of shit lay up in that dayum hospital. Ms. Katie, will you please step out here with us?"

"Sir, I understand, but we still have to get him to Madison County. I also need to know where that dog is."

Gray walks over and helps Katie out of the truck, paying no mind at all to the deputy's demand for the location of Hank. As they turn toward the others, Savannah is stunned by the severity of Katie's inju-ries. For the first time she sees the battered remains of Sean's fury. Savannah cups her hands over her mouth as tears well in her eyes.

"Oh my! You sweet child. What did he do to you?" Savannah hur-ries over to put her arm around Katie's shoulders.

Gray walks up to the deputies once Savannah has Katie. "Gentlemen, just because someone is not lay'n up in the fuck'n hospi-tal doesn't mean they were not hurt bad. That maniac my son busted up threatened to kill her if she went to the hospital or police. Now, the courts may sort this out, but you men take a look at this young lady's face. You look deep inside yourselves as men. The animal who does this to a woman deserves more than what he got—so does anyone who calls him a friend. I don't know where the dog is, but he is a damn hero in my eyes."

"Nor would ya tell us if you did know, right, Mr. Lee?!" the Madison County deputy asks before looking over at Katie. "I'm sorry for what happened to you, miss. You did the right thing filing a report. The court will do the right thing to ensure he is punished for what he did to you. Now, Mr. Lee, hero or not, we have to find the dog and get him to a shelter. I need you to tell me where the dog is if you know."

"I don't know. Now, if y'all don't mind, we need to tend to this young lady."

"Mr. Lee . . . here's my card. I expect a phone call if ya happen upon that dog. Don't get yourself in trouble here. Thank you for your time!"

Gray scowls at the deputy as he takes the card. He knows the men are just doing their job, but he does not need a man half his age lecturing him about breaking any damn rules. He watches as the deputies head on down the dirt road. He walks inside where Savannah and Katie are sitting on the couch.

"Where's Hank?" Savannah asks Gray.

"Over at Troy's for now. Once we hear about bail, I will go get Hudson."

"They ah not gonna let Hank live aftuh attacking someone like that, not with his histree, Gray."

"Yeah, I know."

"It's my fault. I should have never . . . " Katie starts to apologize.

"Hunny, don't you dayuh put the blame on yowuhself." Savannah tries to reassure Katie.

"I knew what he would do, and still . . . I am so sorry for get'n y'all mixed up in all of this. I am so sorry!" Punished by guilt, Katie cries and apologizes over and over.

Savannah pulls Katie's head to her shoulder and sheds tears with the young lady. She feels her sorrow.

"My sweet girl. The Lowud works in mysterious ways. Hudson's whole life prepayud him to help you. Yowuh's prepayud you to help Hudson. You didn't bring anyone into anything. Fate did. God's plan did."

"He will never leave us alone," Katie says as she continues to weep on Savannah's shoulder.

"Hunny, that man is going to jail fowuh a long time. He should nevuh see the light of day again fowuh what he did to you," Savannah replies as she holds and consoles Katie.

Katie offers Savannah a slight smile, but she knows this world will never punish Sean. He is a skillful liar who will use his father's connections, money, and lawyers to walk freely as a good man remains caged behind blocks and bars. He will deny beating her and claim self-defense against Gray and Hudson. Gray hit Sean while Ricky was pointing a shotgun at him. Hudson and Hank attacked Sean and Jimmy in the eyes of the law. Such an unbalanced system that tilts the scale hard toward the wicked. Even with Savannah's reassuring words, Katie believes she's dragged a good family deep into her mess. She truly believes she made the wrong choice at the bridge and in that motel room. Now, this good family has to clean up her mess.

"Katie, hunny, does yowuh mama know?" Savannah asks as she rubs Katie's back.

Katie shakes her head no, and then replies, "I didn't want her to see. It would upset her too much."

"I think you oughta tell'r, sugah. As a motha, I'm sorry, but if it wuh me, I'd be very upset if I wuh not told."

"Savvy, that decision is Katie's. She knows her mama best. Don't pressure her," Gray intervenes.

"No, Mr. Lee, she's right. If y'all don't mind, I would like to call her to come and get me. It's time for her to see . . . to know. I appreciate everything y'all have done and all your kind words. I'm sorry to involve y'all in this mess. I best go stay with Mama for now."

"We understand, hunny. Go call yowuh mama. Just know we ah heeyuh for you. Please don't give up on you and Hudson. I know my boy. I know he loves you deeyuhly. I can tell you love him the same." Savannah gives Katie a quick and gentle hug before she calls her mama. Katie nods in response, but she continues to feel extraordinary guilt for involving Hudson and his family in her nightmare. She doesn't really want to involve her family either. She just wants to escape it all, taking her troubles with her.

# CHAPTER FORTY-THREE

# GOOD GOODBYE

After a short stint in a Madison County holding cell, Hudson is released to Gray late in the afternoon, a few days after turning himself in to Oconee. The charges against Hudson are dropped. In return, Gray drops his charges as well. However, it's Katie's dropped charges that actually convince Sean and Jimmy to drop their charges. She does so against the advice of all her loved ones and the prosecutor. Instead, all she asks for and receives is a protective order. The order is temporary. She will have to go face Sean in court for the permanent order.

Hudson walks out of the sheriff's office and climbs into his father's truck. He says nothing. Gray looks over at his son for a brief moment before pulling out of the parking spot. Neither says a word until they're halfway home. Gray thinks Hudson just wants silence, but Hudson is just trying to collect his words to break the news to his father.

Unfortunately, the hunt for Hank continues. His attack on Jimmy demands punishment. When an animal attacks a human in such a violent manner, regardless of his motivation to do so, he must be put into a shelter, and then euthanized. Such little value is placed on the lives of dogs. Authorities will be at Hudson's house every day, if necessary, looking for Hank. That is the promise the sheriff made. He also promised to visit everyone Hudson knows until he has that vicious animal in a shelter and put down.

"Dogs like that have no business around people. You would've faced murder or manslaughter charges, young man, had that dog killed that man. When someone attacks another person, you call the damn authorities, you don't sic a killing machine on him." The sheriff lectured Hudson for a good half hour before turning him over to Gray. Hudson refuses to turn Hank over to animal control. He knows of only one way to protect Hank and Katie.

"Deddy, I'm gonna put my place up for sale. Katie and I are going to leave the state. We are taking Hank with us. Let 'em visit every damn person I know, but they will never find Hank. I can't let that happen. I am the reason he was there to begin with. I also need to get Katie out of here before that piece of shit defies the order. That damn order will just piss'm off more. He will come for his vengeance. I just need you to understand that this is the only way, Deddy. I can't let 'em put Hank down and will not let that coward kill Katie."

Gray doesn't want to lose his son again, and he knows Savannah will be crushed. However, he knows this is Hudson's life, his pursuit of happiness, and will support him anyway necessary. "I will covuh for you the best I can, son. One day this oughta blow over, and it'd be nice if y'all made yowuh way back."

"Maybe one day, Deddy, but right now I need to get Katie and Hank the hell outta here."

"You got any money to get you by until yowuh house sells?"

"Yeah, a little."

"Well, Jerry Floyd's been after me about the ten acres on the utha side of the homeplace. I will let'm have it. You can have that money to get ya started."

"Not necessary, Deddy. That's family land. Keep it."

"A burden is what it is. Dayum taxes have shot up so high with all the rich folks move'n to tha lake—drivin up taxes but not land value.

Damn politicians use any reason to steal our hard-earned money and property. I'd rather just sell it and be done with it."

"Up to you, Deddy. Don't sell it on account of me. I have enough saved up to get by for a while. Plus, I get some money from the VA for . . . for a few other things." Hudson nearly lets his secret escape. He's told his family that he saw no action while deployed. He's never told them about the shrapnel that killed his friend and ripped into his side and face. He hasn't shaved his beard to reveal that scar.

"Awlright, we'll see, I guess. Offer is there if ya need it."

"Thank you, Deddy. For everything."

"You will need to leave soon, son. I hate it, but ya will. We love ya and will miss ya. At least this time . . ." Gray pauses to choke back emotions. "At least this time you will be in a better place than befowuh."

"We'll visit when we can, Deddy."

Gray replies with a silent nod. He is too choked up to speak, but refuses to let Hudson see his tears and sorrow.

"My truck still at your house?"

"Yep."

"I'll go straight from the farm to Troy's. I have to pick up Hank. I'm sure they will check his house at some point pretty soon. Unfortunately, that damn sheriff and Sean's uncle go back a ways. He is determined to find Hank. I gotta get'm outta here tonight."

"Before you rush off, you give yowuh mama a proper goodbye, son."

"I will, Deddy. Katie is meet'n me at my house. She will let me know if anyone comes by before I get there with Hank."

"Dog means a lot to ya, don't he?!"

"More than I can explain right now," Hudson responds under his breath as he turns to look out the window at the passing fields, fences, and dying leaves.

Savannah is heartbroken to see her son leave again. However, she knows Hudson has to follow his heart; he has to protect the dog and Katie the best he knows how. She can see the love her son has for both. All a mother can ask for is that her children are safe and loved. Since

Hank and Katie have come into his life, she no longer has that gnawing feeling that her son is ill. She does not feel a lonely death calling his name anymore. She agrees that leaving the state is the right decision for now. She cries on his shoulder for a good five minutes before saying goodbye. All that comforts her is that this goodbye sends her son away from harm this time. It is a good goodbye.

# CHAPTER FORTY-FOUR

# BAD GOODBYE

Endless country roads pave the way through many of this old world's natural blessings, but only these dusty roads of northeast Georgia are home to the heart. Time slows down when driving these heavenly highways to provide the soul ample time to appreciate simplicity. All worries of life seem to wash away down the muddy waters gently flowing underneath the old bridges out here. However, the same roads that bring home the sons and daughters of this land also lead them away. Leaving it the first time was much harder on the soul than expected. Coming home to die was essential to never leaving again. Now, leaving is essential to living. While looking for the mercy of death, Hudson has found the gifts of life. He has to do that which is necessary to protect those who have brought love back to his heart.

Hudson drives directly to Troy's house to pick up Hank after leaving Whippoorwill Hollow. He thanks his cousin for always standing by him regardless of the situation or the consequences. He says goodbye to Troy in a way that says he may never return. Troy wants badly to convince Hudson to stay, but he can't bring himself to do such a selfish thing. He knows he owns a big part of Hudson leaving, and now he must simply accept the repercussions of their decision. After his quick goodbye, Hudson races to his house, where Katie awaits them both. He pulls his truck around to the back, out of sight from the road, and parks next to Katie's car. They have little time to pack and head out, but Hudson takes a second to reflect on life's twisted path while Hank uses the bathroom. Hank once again is not himself, almost like he, too, is sad to leave his new home.

"What's wrong, boy? Ready to see Katie? Me too, but I need you to wait in the truck for now. We are gonna pack up real quick and roll out. Got to get ya outta here. Too many people seek'n retribution for the wrongs of our demons. Maybe we can return one day, but we gotta go for now."

Hank looks up at Hudson, stubbornly refusing to jump up into the truck. "I know you'd rather run around, chase'n critters, but we can't risk you get'n caught up playing with the squirrels bud. Go on now, get in the truck!" Hudson pleads. Hank replies with a slight whimper while continuing to stand in protest. Hudson has no choice but to pick up the big fella and wrestle him up into the truck. Hank immediately goes limp like a whiny child pitching a fit, but Hudson manages to shove the hundred-pound dog into the truck and shut the door before he can leap out. Hudson cracks the window a bit, and then quickly slams the door before scolding the boy for his damn stubbornness. Hank barks a couple of times, and then follows up with a few whimpers.

"Oh, you will be just fine, ya big cry baby. We will be out in less than fifteen, twenty minutes," Hudson promises Hank. The big fella again replies with barks and whimpers. Hudson turns away from the truck and walks toward the house. The back-porch light goes black as he grabs a hold of the hand rail. At that moment, Hank's barks and whimpers are silenced and replaced by the battle cry of the beast. Hudson looks back at the truck, to Hank tearing at the driver's side window, viciously growling and snorting. Hudson witnesses the flash of that grenade propelling by en route to take yet another precious life. He turns back to the porch and leaps up the stairs. The door slides open as he clears the top step. There ol' death steps out to greet Hudson with a shotgun barrel pointed at his head.

"Get the fuck inside, asshole!" Sean struggles to push the words through his broken jaw.

Sean has stalked Katie ever since he learned of her return. He drove by Pop's as they stood around Ricky's boat. He rented a car after that day so Katie would not spot him. He followed her to her new home. He broke in when she was not there to learn the layout of her house. He followed them to the fairgrounds, where he called in backup. He followed them to Hudson's from the fairgrounds and saw Katie go into the house after sitting in her car for a few minutes. He burned the bulb all night to stay awake, but this time he chose meth over freebase cocaine. He watched as the dog remained outside all night, and then tailed them to the boat ramp the following morning. After watching them ride off across the lake with Gray, Sean spent the rest of that morning learning the layout of Hudson's house, preparing for this night.

This countryside is full of old wells, most unknown and unvisited. Jimmy knows the perfect place to dump all three bodies deep into one of those long-abandoned holes in the Georgia clay. They will kill the dog, drive Hudson's truck into the deep water at the quarry, and then kill Katie and Hudson at the empty well. They will clean any potential sign of trouble from the floors and walls of Hudson's house. It will look like the three of them simply disappeared. Sean assumes the only reason charges were dropped is because Hudson and Katie intended to run away with each other. The suitcase Katie has packed proves his assumption is correct. He will be damned if Katie runs off with another man to live happily ever after. Sean thought of nothing but a proper reckoning during his brief stay in the hospital. He dropped his charges and had to convince Jimmy to drop his charges to create this opportunity. Jimmy took little convincing; he is too eager to please Sean and wants his opportunity to avenge the beating they both received. Sean promises Jimmy the dog, but Hudson and Katie belong to him.

Hudson steps inside the darkened house, eagerly looking for Katie. There she sits, tied to a kitchen chair with her mouth taped shut. Hudson can barely see her as his eyes continue adjusting to the dark house. He can't see the tears flow, but he can hear her muffled cries. The ambient light from the moon now glows a little more, and Hudson finally has complete night vision. He can see that Sean has opened up her healing wounds and added a few fresh ones. Blood drips from a gash across her forehead. Before Hudson can say a word, Sean strikes him on the back of the head with the butt of the shotgun. Hudson drops to a knee, refusing to fall completely to the floor. Sean drives the barrel into the back of Hudson's bloody head, demanding he lie on his stomach. Hudson knows he cannot comply. He cannot get into a defenseless position. He presses his head back into the barrel. He can tell Sean has a tight grip and is in a wide stance to brace for the recoil. He is ready to kill. Hudson contemplates the odds of him successfully making a move to disarm Sean. He feels the barrel press harder into the back of his head as Sean orders him to the floor once again. Before Hudson can respond or comply, Jimmy walks over to Katie and shoves his pistol onto the side of her head.

"Do what the fuck he says or watch her die!" Jimmy shouts. He is furious that his arm will never be useful again. His eyes are wide open with insanity and the invincibility of methamphetamines, his drug of choice. Hudson has no choice but to comply with their demand. He reluctantly puts his hands onto the floor and walks them forward until his chest reaches the tile.

"Get that fuck'n gun away from her head, and go shut that dog the fuck up, then get back in here quick, so we can tie his ass up and get 'em to the hole. Do the shit in the dark," Sean tells Jimmy right before he drives his heel into Hudson's ribs. He kicks Hudson twice on the side of his head, and then drives his heel into the back of his head. The world fades as little white dots flash before his eyes. All Hudson hears are Katie's muffled screams. Blood pools underneath his head as he fights to stay conscious.

Hudson, just as Hank did the night he was shot, sees clearly in the dark. He has witnessed death up close and personal. A sick feeling in his gut returns as he watches the blurry image of Jimmy walking out the door with his pistol in hand. There goes Death to take his friend. He can't save him. His only thought is to save Katie. He silently begs God for strength. He begs for Him to right his head. He cannot let them bind him. His only chance to take control of the situation is while Jimmy brings an end to his friend—the friend who saved him from the same death he will soon face. He will use death's distraction to eliminate Sean. Hudson fights the rage, sadness, and remorse consuming him to focus on a plan. Hank tried to warn him, but he didn't listen, and now Hank is going to die. He can't let Hank's death be for nothing. They were brought into Katie's life to save her. Hank Jackson told him so in his dream. When he hears the shot, he will shove Katie's chair over behind the wall. Shoving Katie will build momentum and reduce the number of steps he has to take to reach Sean. She will be covered by the wall and away from gunfire. Though Sean served briefly in the Navy, Hudson assumes he has never been trained for combat. Sean has a shotgun, probably loaded with buckshot, but Hudson hopes he rushes his first shot and misses. Hudson just needs an opportunity to get his hands on the shotgun to wrestle it away from Sean. Hudson accepts death but must live long enough to kill both threats to Katie.

Hudson can hear Hank barking, snarling, and growling. He lived such a violent life and is about to meet a violent end. Such a horrific life for something so full of love. He is losing his best friend Hank all over again. Silence again precedes death's anticipated arrival. Only this time, there will be no familiar song to fill the air.

Hudson looks at Katie. Though his vision is blurry, and the room is barely lit by the glow of the moon, he admires her beautiful soul through her blue eyes one last time. "Love you, Katie," Hudson mumbles as he tries to hold his head up off the floor.

Katie sees that Hudson's intent is to sacrifice his life for her. Tears flow down her cheeks. She's waited so long, gone through so much to find a love this true. There is no other Hudson; he is the only one. She wants life no more if he is gone. Two gunshots crack through the dead air, interrupting Katie's thoughts. Tears continue flowing as she thinks of Hank's final moments. Another shot rings out. Then, nothing. Hank is quiet.

Sean does not break his concentration until the third shot, providing Hudson his opportunity to strike. Hudson gets his hands and feet underneath him in one quick motion. He darts forward, pushing Katie's chair as hard as he can, making sure she is fully covered by the wall. He uses his momentum from the push to run toward Sean. The blurry room still spins from the head trauma Sean inflicted. His injuries slow his charge, giving the enemy longer to react. Sean turns and, as expected, fires his first shot slightly off target, but it is enough to send one shot into Hudson's shoulder and another into the side of his rib cage. The force of the shots turns Hudson sideways, causing him to fall on his back. Sean chambers another round and shoves the barrel into Hudson's face.

"You sorry piece of shit. I hope that whore was worth it. Now you, the whore bitch, and your fuck'n dog are dead! Won't have to worry about you fuck'n other people's women, now will we?!" Sean screams through his wired jaw, wide eyes full of anger and the same drug as Jimmy.

Jimmy had walked out the door toward the truck. There in the cab was the dog that nearly tore off his arm, growling and foaming while continuing to rip at the window.

"Time to put you the fuck down," Jimmy shouted at Hank.

He walked up to the driver's side window where a furious Hank met him, relentlessly tearing at the glass with his paws while baring his large canines. Jimmy raised the pistol. There's death, staring down Hank through the man's eyes just like the stranger the night before he met his new friend—his new family who truly introduced him to love and loyalty. Hank knew this man meant to kill him, just like death's stranger, but this time he would not allow the beast to sit idly by while this stranger delivers death's cold message. Jimmy raised the pistol up to eye level, taking aim at the big fella. Hank jumped back, digging his hind paws deep into the truck seat. Just before Jimmy pulled the trigger, Hank leaped toward the window with every ounce of power in his body. He will charge on death like the warrior he is. Though he's felt the power of this beast, Jimmy has underestimated Hank's agility and determination. The first bullet burst through the window, missing its target as Hank leaped just before Jimmy pulled that trigger. Hank exploded through the compromised glass and locked on his target. His canine arsenal sunk into the man's flesh, but this time on his throat. His powerful jaw silenced the man's screams. Jimmy desperately fired another shot. This bullet found its target, but failed to deter the beast. Without flinching, without so much as a whimper, Hank held fast his crushing grip on the man's throat, twisting and turning his body just like the day at the jobsite. Another round went off as Hank knocked the pistol from Jimmy's hand with his big body. Blood from the man and the dog pooled in the driveway next to the truck. Both lay still after the struggle.

Sean would have seen the commotion outside when he heard the extra shots if not for Hudson's charge. He would have definitely heard the snarling if it were not for the shotgun blast and adrenaline. However, the situation inside is back under his full control. His hearing is keen once again. He hears boards on the back porch creak. The growl sends chills down his spine. He turns his head to see Hank limping into the doorway. Blood drips down his back leg. Blood from Jimmy paints his face. Death may have not yet claimed the beast, but neither does life exist in his eyes. The beast is the deliverer of death. Much of his life was spent ripping the lives from others. He was made this way by using his loving, faithful heart. His only curse was being too loyal and full of love. However, this moment is when he amends for those past sins. The beast no longer resides in him. The beast is not who stands in the doorway. Hank, the loyal and loving friend with the heart of an angel, is here to pay the ultimate sacrifice for his family, so they can be free and heal.

Hank charges as Sean turns the gun from Hudson's chest. Hudson grabs the barrel just as it clears his body, causing Sean to fire into the floor. Hank leaps, latching onto Sean's right arm. The two of them roll around on the floor. Hank puts in work on Sean's arm, just as he did on the dead fella lying in the driveway. He is focused with a tenacious grip on the arm in his mouth. He is focused on making his death move to the man's throat. He is too focused, so he doesn't see it coming. Sean unsheathes his hunting knife from his opposite hip. With all his might he buries the entire eight-inch blade into Hank's side just behind the front shoulder. Hank immediately releases his grip. He stumbles into the wall and falls over. The knife remains buried in his side. Hank's lungs struggle for air. His blood surrounds him.

Sean gets to his feet and walks over to the dog. He leans over to pull the knife from Hank. He aims to rip the knife through the dog's throat to ensure he bleeds out. As he leans down, a familiar sound fills the silent room. The round racking from the magazine as it tosses the empty shell from the ejection port is unmistakable for anyone who has ever heard it. Sean turns to find Hudson pressing the shotgun against his left shoulder. He fights the pain to steady the gun. Sean starts to talk, but Hudson has no time to think about what he is doing or to hold a conversation with someone who intends to murder them. The love of his life is bound in the other room, and his best friend is bleeding out. Every pellet of the double-ought buckshot slams into Sean's chest, knocking him back against the wall. Sean's lifeless body drops to the floor.

Hudson runs into the kitchen. He cuts the duct tape with a kitchen knife. Katie rips off the tape from her mouth, and then wraps her arms around Hudson.

"We have no time. Hank's hurt. He's hurt bad, Katie. We gotta get'm help!"

Adrenaline numbs Hudson of the pain from his own injuries. He grabs up Hank on their way out the door, struggling to carry him. Katie jumps in the truck and slides to the middle of the cab. Hudson puts Hank down on the passenger's side seat, resting his head on Katie's lap. She cries as she pets his head, telling him everything will be ok. Hank lies still, but he hears her reassuring words. His lungs continue to gasp for air while blood gurgles in his throat. He blinks, his gaze unfocused. Katie holds a rag around the knife and over his wound with her right hand, while giving him a scratch up under his jaw, just like he likes it.

# CHAPTER FORTY-FIVE

# BY HIS SIDE

In an instant, death can break even the hardest of hearts. Loved ones are but one phone call away from life's most devastating news. One fateful moment that forever pains those left behind. The grieving are told to celebrate life and not mourn death. Foolish are those words to the shattered hearts deafened by grief. The death of one is the end of life for another. Other reasons to live will keep a scarred heart beating, but that mended heart will toughen like leather to resist the pain of losing those other reasons. Hudson's heart of leather rips open as his best friend lies lifeless in his arms as he barrels through the door. Hannah is at the desk just like the first night he walked through those doors. She instantly sees the blood covering Hank, Hudson, and Katie.

"Where's Frank? He's dying, Hannah. Goddammit, he's dying! Where's Frank?" Hudson shouts.

"Oh my Lord... Hudson. What happened?" Hannah asks frantically.

"What's all the noise?" Frank asks as he comes through the double doors leading to the patient rooms. "What happened, Hudson?" He lays his eyes on a bloody Hudson holding a lifeless Hank.

"He's been stabbed, Doc. Help'm. Please, Frank! Help'm!" Hudson shouts and begs.

"Bring 'em on back! How in the heck did he get stabbed, Hudson?"

"Just save'm, Frank! Please . . . God . . . save'm."

They make their way back to the operating table. Hudson gently lays Hank down. At that moment, Frank can see that Hank is not the only one hurt. Hudson had wrapped an old towel he had in his truck around his arm. Blood leaks through the hole on the side of his shirt, dripping to the floor.

"Were you stabbed also, Hudson?"

"No, I was shot."

"Well, what in the hell are ya doin here, son? Young lady, get him to the dayum hospital . . . right now!" Frank shouts.

"I'm not going, Doc. I ain't leave'n him!" Hudson shouts back.

"Son, if you don't get to the dayum hospital, you will bleed out. You don't know how bad you're hurt. Let—"

"I will not leave Hank! He'd never leave me. Save'm again, Frank . . . Save'm again . . . please!"

"I'm goin to do everythang I can, Hudson. Ms. Hannah, will you please call for a dadgum ambulance." Frank never takes his eyes off of Hank while controlling the situation.

"I'm not fuck'n leave'n, Frank!"

"I didn't say you have to dammit, but we need to get those wounds taken care of, Hudson. We will get some EMTs in here to render some care to you while I tend to Hank."

Hudson kneels next to Hank, holding his paw. He looks into Hank's eyes as Frank sedates the big fella. Hank is in serious pain, but he remains still as he gazes back at Hudson. The death stare Hank had back at the house is gone. Love is all Hudson sees in Hank's eyes now, and love is what Hank sees in Hudson. As chaos surrounds him, Hank is at peace. He found a good family—he found someone worth loving. He had no more room for those ol' demons with all the love in his heart.

The drugs are able to take away the pain, but nothing Frank does will save Hank. Deep inside, Hudson knows Hank's fate, but he resists the thought. He thinks about Hank surviving that first night. He thinks about the torture he'd been through all his life, and how he survived all those times.

"Doc is gonna fix you right up, Hank. Hang in there, buddy . . . hang in there . . . please hang in there." Hudson continues to hold Hank's paw while talking to him. He shifts his attention up beyond the sky to beg for His healing touch. "Save him, almighty God . . . save Hank . . . guide Doc's hands and give Hank strength."

This is Hank's fate, though. He did his deed—he saved their troubled souls.

Frank does all he can to remove the knife and save Hank. The knife is wedged in at an angle, and it's punctured a lung and liver. Too much blood has drained from Hank. Frank knows these are the last seconds of Hank's life. He looks at Katie and shakes his head to indicate Hank is not going to make it. Tears stream down her face as she wraps her arms around Hudson.

Hudson looks into Hank's eyes as they struggle to stay open. "You saved us, bud. You saved me more times than I can count in the short time we've known each other. I hope I gave you what you gave me, reason to love and to trust . . ." Hudson pauses as his emotions get the best of him. "You didn't just save my life, you saved my soul."

Hudson watches as Hank's life fades from his eyes. All of the emotions the man buried in war come to surface as he cries over his deceased friend. Katie squeezes her arms a little tighter before kissing Hudson on the side of his head, providing him the comfort he needs at this moment.

Frank walks around the table and places his hand on Hudson's shoulder. "I'm sorry, Hudson. I truly am sorry. Did all I could . . . his injuries were just too deep."

Hudson continues holding Hank's paw in his hands as he bows his head and lets out all those built-up emotions. He tries to look up at Hank a couple of times, but immediately drops his head back down. The sight of his beloved friend's lifeless body is too painful to behold. All he can think about was the torture Hank lived through, survived, and overcame only to die after finding a family to love him as much as he loved them. Hudson calms himself, settles the emotions, and looks up at his friend. "I don't know what I did to deserve you, but I am grateful. We will be together again when it is time."

"Hudson, son, I am truly sorry for your loss, but we have to get you to the hospital before we have to bury you, too. The ambulance is here now," Frank says with stern compassion.

"I'm not ready to leave'm, Frank. His paw is still warm."

The EMTs race into the front door. Hannah escorts them back to the operating table where Hank's body rests. They immediately run over to Hudson, who's still kneeling beside Hank.

"Sir, mind if we look at your wound?"

"Go ahead," Hudson responds without looking away from Hank.

The EMT cuts away Hudson's shirt to see the wounds to his left shoulder and rib cage. Hudson has been bleeding the entire time. His skin is pale. He is dizzy, but still can't muster the emotional strength to leave his friend.

"Sir, if we don't get you to the hospital right now, you will bleed out."

"I can't leave'm," Hudson says softly while continuing to look through tearful eyes into his friend's lifeless eyes.

The other EMT nudges Frank and whispers, "Can you remove the dog please, sir, so we can get him out of here?"

"Nobody's gonna fuck'n touch'm!" Hudson belts out.

"Please, Hudson! Please let them take you to the hospital. I'm beg'n you! We can't lose you, too. Your mama and daddy are head'n to the hospital," Katie pleads.

"Hudson . . . sir . . . let the doctor take your friend. We need you to go with us in the ambulance."

Hudson tries to defy them again, but his head leans into Katie's shoulder as he struggles to maintain consciousness. Katie holds Hudson around his shoulders to keep him from falling. One EMT grabs his upper body while the other grabs his feet. They lift him up on the gurney and rush him to the ambulance with Katie following.

# CHAPTER FORTY-SIX

# HEART OF WHIPPOORWILL HOLLOW

From the silent forest of darkness, Hank drifted upon a troubled soul. Had Hank not stumbled upon that pond and been bit by that snake, the despondent stranger would have vacated this life into an even darker afterlife and their beloved friend would have completed that final walk as she intended, and then met the same fate as Hudson. The moment replays in Hudson's mind as he constructs a small wooden box. He ponders the reason he was saved by this wonderful angel. Though he is grateful, he does not understand what he did in life to deserve such a gift. He knows, to do justice for his friend's selfless act, he has to share his dark secret with his family and friends. Hudson finally shaves off his beard and invites his family to join him by the pond on the farm. The pond is where they met, and it will be his friend's final resting place.

Hudson and Katie arrive at the pond about three hours before everyone else. Hudson has had his friend cremated to give him time to heal from his injuries and plan a proper service. He places the .38 revolver in the box he built, and then covers it with Hank's ashes before sealing the box shut. Hudson and Katie dig a deep hole by the sweetgum tree that he rested against that special night. Hudson has said little since the death of his friend and remains quiet as they dig. He is quiet so he can collect his thoughts and muster the strength to divulge his private struggle to his family. He has not even shared with Katie the reason he chose this spot, why he put that gun in the box, or anything about the scar on his jaw, nor does she ask—she will wait until he is ready to share. Once they finish digging that hole, they sit silently on Hudson's tailgate and patiently wait for everyone to arrive.

Hudson hugs and greets everyone as they arrive. Once surrounded by his loved ones, Hudson eases the small wooden box down into the hole with a short rope. The box comes to rest at the bottom, and then Hudson releases the bitter end of the rope, watching it quickly disappear into the hole. He stares down at the grave, recalling his dream with the girl standing next to him. He realizes Katie is that girl. Hank is the one who could not be saved. He looks up, scans the light-blue sky, and quietly seeks the words to begin his confession. Hank Jackson pays his thoughts a visit: "I'm with you, my friend. Honor us all."

"Mama, Deddy, everybody, I know it seems pretty silly to invite y'all to Hank's burial, but I gotta tell y'all someth'n. Now ... this ... this will be as hard to hear as it is to say. I just need ta ..." Hudson searches within himself for the strength to tell the hardest story he's ever had to share. "Hank was much more than a lost dog. In fact, he wasn't lost at all ... I was. He knew exactly where he needed to be and when he needed to be there. To tell y'all about him, I must first tell the truth about what happened in Afghanistan—about Hank Jackson.

"Hank's whole life was a struggle: his deddy was a police officer killed in the line of duty; his mama worked endless hours to provide for her children; he was surrounded by poverty; and his brothers died young. He enlisted not because he was poor, but like me he wanted to serve his country. He was not a violent man and didn't really like what he had to do over there. He loved to learn. He used to tell me how he craved education like Booker T. Washington. He knew education was the way to give his mama a better life. Man . . . he was . . . was so intelligent, funny, and had such a positive attitude about everything in life. He wanted to come home, take care of his mama, and live the life robbed from his deddy and brothers. He never got that chance to do any of these things. He never got that chance because he sacrificed his life for me to live. We were talk'n college football one second, and a grenade went fly'n by the next. I froze . . . dammit I froze. It took me a while to remember or want to remember the entire incident. Hank grabbed me, slung me around, to use . . ."—Hudson collects himself—". . . to use his body as shield to protect me. Shrapnel ripped through him, and some hit me here in the face and on my side. He died in my arms. He sacrificed his life, his dreams, without hesitation to save mine. He offered this world much more than I ever could give. I intended to tell Hank's mama what he did for me, but'r heart gave out before I got the chance—lose'n her only survive'n child was too much on'r. Hank and his mama would still be alive, warm'n this cold world with their joy, had I shielded Hank instead. Had I not froze.

"I returned home hopeless, lost in the darkest of thoughts. I was held captive by merciless reminders of just how ugly and unjust this world can be. The devil had his grip on me, and my burden refused to give me peace. The misery would not leave my head. I could not come back. I wanted to fight everyone—don't know why . . . I felt angry for hesitate'n in the moment. Most of all, I just wanted to . . ." He pauses again. He knows this part is going to be difficult and needs to take a deep breath before picking up where he left off. "Be best I just read y'all someth'n to tell y'all what I wanted. This is hard to read, but I must read it so y'all know just how special the dog we bury today was . . . is to me." He reaches into his pocket and pulls out a folded piece of paper. He slowly unfolds the letter. He's stalling, because this is going to be hard to tell his family, especially his mama, who already looks like she knows what is written on that note. She felt those words in her nightmare. Hudson lifts the paper up as to read from it, but he knows that note word for word. Hudson takes a deep breath and then begins reading the letter:

*My dear family,*

*I love y'all! I wish I would have listened to you, Mama. I wish I would have never left, but if not me, then who? Some other unfortunate souls would be carrying this burden. I know I am not the only one. I wish I was stronger, like my dear friend Hank Jackson. I wish I could have come back the same man as when I left. I am not strong enough to be that man. You are the best family a man could ever ask for, so please don't ever believe what I am about to do is because of a lack of moral support or love from y'all. I got plenty of both from everyone. It will take much more than anyone can give to help me. Only a miracle can save me. There are no miracles. Not in this mean old world. I love you all. Please forgive me! I pray God forgives me. I pray that I will see y'all in heaven.*

*Love,*

*Hudson*

When he finishes, Hudson looks up to see his mama hugging his father. Her face is buried deep in his chest while she tries to keep her eyes on Hudson. Tears flow down her face onto Grayford's shirt. Grayford wraps his arms tightly around Savannah. He pulls her in close, so she will not look up to see that he, too, is crying. Grayford, who is normally emotionally invincible, is unable to stop the tears as his son pours out his heart. None of them are that tough. Katie walks up beside Hudson, grabs his hand with both of hers, and lays her head onto his shoulder as she weeps. They have no more secrets.

Hudson turns and kisses Katie on her forehead before starting up again. "I leaned against this tree. I listened to the whippoorwill sing his sad ole song. I put that pistol to my head, and I said goodbye to this wretched life. I was hurt'n inside, Mama . . ." Hudson pauses to gather himself, and then continues, each word laced with sad appreciation.

"But then, in my darkest moment, Hank came like that stranger in the night. He was cry'n in pain and fear, bitten by that snake. At the vet's office was the first time I saw the hell he'd lived through. Scars covered his body from head to tail. He had a broken leg that never healed right. The bullet delivered by the monsters who wanted him dead remained lodged in his head. They must have thrown him out on the side of the road like trash and left him to die. He had no reason to love or trust anyone ever again after such abuse. The people that he considered family tried to end his life when he was no longer of use to them. He had no reason to love me, but he did. He never showed me anything but love. He taught me to love again. He taught me to trust again. He taught me that life with love is far better than taking death as a merciful way to end the hurt, hate, and anger. He gave his life to save Katie. He gave his life to save me. I didn't save him that night by the pond, Mama, he saved me. The devil sent death for my soul, but God sent Hank . . . my guardian angel Hank."

Hudson kneels by the grave, and then wipes the tears from his eyes. He stares down into the grave at the wooden box for a brief moment, listening to the world around him. A light breeze brushes by him. Squirrels playing in the dead leaves suddenly scamper up the surrounding trees. He briefly closes his eyes to see Hank Jackson looking back grinning as he walks over that hill again. Hudson smiles, and then stands while looking down at that wooden box.

"I love you, ole boy. I'll see you again. I'll give ya a good sctratch'n up under your jaw, just like ya like it. I'll brang a plate of Pop Walter's smoked chicken and a peanut butter bone for ya. Love you, too, Jacks. I'll brang some Natties for us to drank while we watch the Dawgs and Tide pop pads from the bleachers in the sky. Thank you for watch'n over us, my friend!"

Hudson hugs Katie, and then walks over to his truck, where he reaches in and turns on his radio. He plays Hank's favorite blues picker for him one more time. He turns up the radio as Mr. Hurt begins picking and singing "Since I've Laid My Burdens Down." Hudson reaches in the back of his truck for a few shovels. He hands them out to the men folk. As Mr. Hurt sings and plays, the family covers up Hank's wooden coffin with that red Georgia clay. Savannah walks up to her son and wraps her arms around him tighter than she ever has before. She pulls back and looks at him. She says nothing, because sometimes no words are adequate. She turns around, grabs the shovel from Ty, and pours a shovelful of dirt over Hank's coffin. She thanks Hank for saving her son. She thanks both Hanks. They all thank them. Both the man and dog will forever have a special place in all their hearts. They will forever rest in the heart of Whippoorwill Hollow.

— THE END —

Davidson Lee Price rarely left northeast Georgia early in his life, and when he did it was but for a few days. Then one day he joined the Coast Guard and left for good. Thanks to a generous helping of long watches, he spent countless hours accompanied by only his thoughts. He accumulated an abundance of ideas and stories during the more than two decades he spent in the Coast Guard. Davidson especially liked recalling his precious childhood memories spent in northeast Georgia while staring up to the stars from the fantail of a cutter before or after midwatch. Most importantly, he treasures the many good people who entered his life and fondly remembers those lost. *Whippoorwill Hollow* is his first book, inspired by a lost shipmate.